I0577022

George Augustus Sala

My Diary in America in the Midst of War

George Augustus Sala

My Diary in America in the Midst of War

ISBN/EAN: 9783337184575

Printed in Europe, USA, Canada, Australia, Japan

Cover: Foto ©Raphael Reischuk / pixelio.de

More available books at **www.hansebooks.com**

MY DIARY IN AMERICA

IN

THE MIDST OF WAR.

BY

GEORGE AUGUSTUS SALA.

IN TWO VOLUMES.

VOL. I.

LONDON :

TINSLEY BROTHERS, 18, CATHERINE ST., STRAND.

1865.

[*The Right of Translation is reserved.*]

LONDON
BRADBURY AND EVANS, PRINTERS, WHITEFRIARS.

TO

WILLIAM HOWARD RUSSELL, LL.D.,

("CRIMEA," "INDIA," "AMERICA,")

· These Volumes

ARE MOST CORDIALLY INSCRIBED.

ADVERTISEMENT.

SOME portions of the contents of these Volumes appeared in the *Daily Telegraph* newspaper, in the form of letters from the United States, in the course of the years 1863-4, and are now reprinted by permission of the proprietors. The remainder of the work is from the Notes and the Diary which I kept during a (to me) very eventful year.

G. A. S.

64, GUILFORD STREET, RUSSELL SQUARE,
January, 1865.

CONTENTS.

MY DIARY IN AMERICA IN THE MIDST OF WAR.

CHAPTER I.

JUSTIFICATORY.

To an Intelligent American.

You are aware, dear Sir, that the great majority of your countrymen are born public speakers. You are regularly educated to oratory ; you imbibe, almost with your mother's milk, a capacity for expressing yourselves coherently ; you appear in public, and speak in public, at an age when young Englishmen, if they presumed to state their opinions in the presence of their elders, would be peremptorily requested to hold their tongues ; and so easy (as a rule) is the flow of your rhetoric, and so well-balanced are your sentences, that I have often thought that in your nonage you lisp in well-formed periods—for the periods come—and point your thoughts with mental semicolons. You are always ready to rise, address an audience large or small, move resolutions or respond to "sentiments." I never yet met with an American who stammered or "tried back" in an after-dinner speech—who dug a hole in the table-cloth with his fork, or twiddled a wine-glass, or distorted in any other idiotic manner the Demosthenic principle of action. And I am free to confess that an American barrister can address a jury without thrusting his hands beneath his coat-tails, and an American clergyman proceeds to his "seventeenthly" without wiping his forehead with his pocket-handkerchief or thumping the pulpit cushion.

On the other hand, dear Sir, you must, as an intelligent, cultivated, and travelled person, be equally aware that Englishmen are the worst public speakers in the world. The delivery of our statesmen is often marred by modesty, by nervousness, by the conventional reticence of polite society, and by an innate shrinking—however exalted in rank they may be—from addressing a mixed audience in anything approaching an overbearing or dictatorial tone. It is only when men are all free and equal that they can bully one another without reserve. A hundred circumstances intervene to dam the stream of an Englishman's eloquence. In Parliament complicated forms and by-laws of etiquette cover the most polished harangues with excrescent references to the "Noble Lord," and the "Honourable Member," and the "Right Honourable Gentleman in the chair," and "this house," and "another place." The system of verbatim reporting was, you may have heard, tried many years ago in a publication called "The Mirror of Parliament;" but the experiment was a lamentable failure. When honourable members saw their speeches in print, precisely as they had spoken them, they were horrified; and they have since been content to have their orations revised and settled by those gentlemen in the gallery who submit to toil on an intellectual treadmill for three hundred pounds a-year. Out of Parliament there are quite as many obstacles to our attaining proficiency in fluent speech. *You* may talk about every subject, human or divine—from Nebuchadnezzar King of the Jews to Pepple Ex-King of Bonny. There are dozens of topics on which we *dare* not touch, at the risk of being thought irreverent or of being hissed. You, from Chicago to Cape Cod, from Nevada to Nantucket, speak very nearly the same language, and have pretty nearly the same pronunciation. *We* speak fifty different dialects—Northumbrian, Lancastrian, Cambrian, Phœnician, Erse, cockney—*que sais-je?* Some of us lisp and some of us drawl, and some of us stutter, and many of us hem and haw, and a great many of us clap on H's where there should be none, and take away H's whence they should be left. We are always speaking, and yet we speak badly. Our philological doctors disagree. We have no Academy (thank Heaven) and no Dictionary; that is to say we have a hundred, but do not accept any as a final authority. In pronunciation, Oxford is at war with Cambridge, Dublin with both, and Edinburgh with all. The forum and the bar, the pulpit and the stage, are in virulent antagonism; one paper calls a bishop's domain a "diocess," and another a "diocese;" and between Alford and Moon— the Queen's English and the Dean's English—it is difficult to choose. *You* have made up your minds that national shall be pronounced naytional, and advertisement advertyzement; that defence shall be defense, and theatre theater, and you are happy.

Dear Sir, you may be anxious to know what on earth this can have to do with the justificatory remarks prefixed to my " Diary in America in the Midst of War." I will tell you. I have a little story to relate, and this is the introduction to it. When I first set foot on board the " Arabia," bound for Boston, and with the intent of remaining eight months in the United States, I made two solemn resolves :—the first, to tell the truth so far as my lights would permit me ; the next, to hold my tongue. A dumb dog I did not intend to be ; and during the eight months, and their extension to twelve, I took a fair share in very many pleasant and edifying parleys with your countrymen and countrywomen ; but I determined never to speak in public. Of old and aforetime I knew, from meeting you in Europe, what ready speakers you were; and I was painfully aware of the oratorical deficiencies of that nation of which I was to be, in a foreign and hostile land, the humblest representative. Yes, dear Sir, you are very fond of us, but you are always looking out for the joints in our armour, and you would like to smite us under the fifth rib if you could. You *know* you would. So I said to myself, " I speak neither better nor worse than the general run of my compatriots ; I know how well the Americans can speak, and therefore I will not speak at all." With respect to the manner in which I kept my first resolve, I leave the decision to candid and impartial men on both sides the Atlantic. If the verdict be that I have Lied, I will never set my foot in America again ; still I hope to walk up Broadway once more before I am grey.

From the end, then, of December, 1863, to the middle of

September, 1864, I never once rose on my hind legs to make a speech. I had scores of opportunities, but I cautiously evaded them. Even when my letters to England had made me most unpopular, a Courteous Committee at Milwaukee — to whom I hereby render my best thanks—wrote to me, asking me to lecture throughout the Great West, and offering me a pocket full of greenbacks. I humbly declined. It was my business to hold my tongue. But, in this same month of September it came about that I was invited to a most hospitable gathering at a beautiful place called Glencove, about thirty miles up the East River. There was to be a *fête champêtre* in the grounds of a châlet, very closely resembling that which poor Albert Smith had painted as a proscenium to his show at the Egyptian Hall; and in the evening there was to be a grand banquet at the close of which the promoter of a certain railway to the Great West was to present the Engineer-in-Chief thereof, in commemoration of the successful consummation of the work, with a magnificent service of gold plate. The proceedings were to wind up with a concert and a grand display of fireworks. We ascended the East River, some fifty or sixty strong, in a tug, and had a " magnolious" day. You know, dear sir, what Americans and Anglo-Americans can do in the way of hospitality. It is emphatically with them a " big thing." We dined in a manner that would have made Lucullus envious, abased Barras, and given Cambacérès " fits." I think that if any guest had hinted a wish to have the biggest pearl at Tiffany's dissolved in vinegar by way of a *hors d'œuvre*, our kind host would have despatched an express to New York for it. Not a

word of politics was talked during nine hours. The Stars
and Stripes and the Union Jack floated amicably side by
side on the lawn; the band (Germans, of course,) gave us
"Yankee Doodle," "God save the Queen," and the waltz
from *Faust* with strict impartiality; and although the health
of the President of the United States was proposed before
that of Her Majesty, we who were Britons agreed that, as the
proposer was an Englishman, he had done the right and
courteous thing. There was, of course, a great deal of
speech-making, and very good speech-making too; but when
I found it was beginning to "burn," as they say at Blind
Man's Buff, in my immediate vicinity, I timeously withdrew.
I sloped up dark alleys, and lost myself in umbrageous
bosquets, and smoked the secret Cabana in remote summer-
houses, and thought that out of the speech-peril I had
escaped by the skin of my teeth. It was two o'clock in the
morning ere a steamer was ready to convey us back to New
York. We crowded on board, a happy and hilarious company. Not soon shall I forget the ringing cheers with which
we greeted our jolly host and the kind, handsome lady, his
wife, as the vessel cast off. I found out a very comfortable
settee, and lay at length, rubbing my hands at the thought
that another day had come, and that I had made no
speech.

But. Oh, that But! *But* there happened to be on board
a certain sea-captain, famous in the *fasti* of the Cunard
packet service, in which he holds the rank, by seniority, of
Commodore. A stout Commodore,—stricken in years, but
bearing his honourable white hairs as lightly as though

they were snow-flakes. A strict disciplinarian at sea, not executing gambadoes, or cracking jokes, or securing the odd trick on evil nights, but pre-occupied in the task of taking care of your and my life, dear Sir. On shore, however, the Commodore unbends, takes his " tod," smokes his cheroot, sings a good song, tells a good story, and is, generally, the jolliest of good fellows. No one enjoys an " outing " more than he. Now this Captain had had his eye on me for nine hours. It was not an evil eye, but a sly one. He had marked me down for a speech. He is a capital improvisatore, and, in a patter song of which one verse was devoted to peculiarities of some member of the company, he made so pointed an allusion to me that I had no alternative, when he had finished, but to rise on those so much-dreaded hind-legs, and speechify. Of course, I made an absurd exhibition of myself. I blundered out several strings of incoherent non-sequiturs, and sat down at last covered with shame as with a garment. I have no wish to report a speech which was never meant to be reported ; but I may give you, in a very few words, the gist of that which I said. I alluded to the abnormal and exceptional position which I held in the States, and the notoriety which, however personally obscure I might be, attached to the correspondent of a well-known English newspaper. I pleaded that I had arrived in the States branded and ticketed as an enemy to American insti-tutions, and that my coming was heralded by all kinds of scurrilous newspaper articles setting forth that I was a noto-rious libeller, and that my only object in visiting Yankee-land was to abuse the Yankees. I remarked that within a

very few days of my setting foot in New York I had an interview with the editor and proprietor of one of the leading
newspapers of that city, and that gentleman said to me :
" Well, sir, you've come to report us, *and I suppose you'll
cut us up.*" I made answer that I was not a reporter, but a
man of letters pretty well known for good or evil in my own
country, and that I had no more wish or intent with malice
prepense to " cut the Yankees up " than to cut up my grandmother. I urged that what literary repute I might have gained
in the United States as a writer of books I had deliberately
sacrificed to the necessity of recording and commenting upon,
day after day, the ever-changing scenes of an embittered controversy and a bloody strife. I strove to show that no Englishman whatsoever, however favourable—and enthusiastically
favourable—his opinions might be to the cause of the North,
could, at that precise moment of time, hope to succeed in
pleasing or satisfying the majority of Americans. And, finally,
I candidly confessed that I was, by constitution, by predilection,
and by habit a grumbler :—that for a long series of years I
had, from one end of Europe, been grumbling and fault-find-
ing, that I had grumbled up and down France and Germany
and Italy and Russia, and that for a long time I had earned my
living by grumbling at my own countrymen—by picking holes
in their manners, their customs, their speech and their actions ;
but that this incessant bagpipe drone of complaint was not
entirely due to a diseased liver, or discontented mind, and an
unlucky lot, but the rather to a strong, though perhaps not
very definite impression that there were a great many things
in the world and in the ways of men—(my own included)—

which needed mending; that they might be so helped
towards reparation by a man endeavouring to tell Truth and
denounce Wrong and uphold Right; and that, although I did
not by any means set myself up as a philanthropist or a
redresser of grievances, I had always striven, to the best of
my ability, to stand up *for* the Right, and to plead the cause
of the poor and oppressed person, that the strong man might
not spoil his goods, nor hale him to prison without a warrant.
All this I told my auditory, and this much more. That,
although the hospitality I had received in the United States
had been lavish and generous and splendid, I should consider myself a toady and a lickspittle if I paid for so many
dinners and so many fêtes by so many puffs and so many
panegyrics. That I had found many things at which to
grumble during my transatlantic travels, and that I had
grumbled at them in accordance with what I deemed my duty
and my birthright. That where I had blundered I should be
glad to rectify; that where I had unwittingly done injustice
I should be glad to make amends; that for the corns on which
I might have trodden I was sorry, but that Nature had provided me with hob-nail boots, and that I had not the art of
tripping about gingerly, like a Pantaloon in slippers. That
I knew that much that I had said had aroused the indignation of the American people; but that had my criticisms been
couched in any obsequious or time-serving form *I should
have earned their contempt*. And that I had too deep and
earnest a respect for a great, a noble, but a perverse and mis-
guided people, not to prefer being abused like a pickpocket
to being despised by them. This was my peroration: my

" *Hier stande ich : Ich kann nicht mehr. Gott hilfe mir :*
Amen ;" and here ended my first and last attempt at public
speaking in the United States.

The Americans among my hearers were probably, in proportion to the Britons present, eight to one. They received
my address very cordially ; but I knew them to be gentlemen,
and comfortably tired out with a day's pleasure, and disposed
to be on the best of terms with everybody and everything.
Their applause, gratifying as it was, could only be accepted as
perfunctory. With a far different feeling did I receive the con-
gratulations of sundry stalwart and swarthy men, the sailors
and stokers of the vessel. These honest fellows had formed
an outer ring while I was on my hind legs. It appeared to
them that they had a perfect right to listen to what was
going on, and I had no wish to gainsay them. I even heard
an occasional " That's so," or a " Bully for you," while I was
babbling ; but when I was " through " and had " orated "
my fill, I shall never forget how one gaunt, grimy, flannel-
shirted man after another came up to me, thrust forth a
knotted, coal-dust smirched hand—more than one forefinger
was decorated with a big signet ring, I can tell you—and
grasping mine, remarked, " Sir, I have Heard what you have
Said, and, as an American, I should like to shake Your
Hand." The which they all did most heartily. I thought once
—being vain and ambitious, as most of us are—that I had
realised the acmé of human felicity, when the Lord Mayor of
London was good enough to drink my health at a public
dinner ; but on reflection I am convinced that the " proudest
moment in my life" was when those stokers on board the

East River Steamer told me that, as Americans, they would take my hand,

This story, which to some may appear trivial, to others superfluous, and to all wearisome, is to most intents and purposes my Justification for the eight hundred pages which are to follow.

It need scarcely be pointed out, dear sir, that such a confession as I have made in the foregoing pages,—a confession that I grumbled for twelve months, because I am given to grumbling, and am saturnine and unsocial, can only be received as a plea in abatement. A more definite explanation is needed to justify strictures which I admit to have been severe, but the severity of which I am unable, even now, to modify. I should have been false to my trust had I concealed or glossed over that which I thought demanded censure ; but I should be equally false to it now, did I neglect to state the grounds from which that censure rose.

Parenthetically, on the foregoing head I may beg the question. Many persons—English as well as American—may say when they read this : " What on earth does it matter whether the man praise or censure ? Who cares one doit about what he thinks or writes about the United States ? He is obscure, he is stupid, he is ignorant. His voice has no weight, his verdict is valueless. His book will have but a small circulation, and will be soon forgotten." There is the question as I have begged it. Now, I answer. So far as the United States are concerned, the Americans *do* trouble themselves about the utterances of the obscurest, the stupidest and the most ignorant of penny-a-liners, if that penny-a-liner happens to be an Englishman, and republishes his impressions in book form. You know, dear Sir, that these volumes will be reproduced in the North, and will have thousands more readers there than they will probably have in England. You know that if the book were entirely favourable to your countrymen and your cause, your newspapers would be filled with extracts from it; and you know equally well that, as it is, the unfavourable passages will be singled out in order to afford an opportunity for abusing the author. The Americans are not indifferent to the opinion of *any* Englishman. They may vehemently declare they are, but they know better. I daresay that I am a Fool, and dull, and conceited, and a bore; in fact, I know that I am often all these. I am aware that, as a man of letters, I am not fit to hold a candle to the tourists who have gone before me :—to Basil Hall, to Marryatt, to Fanny Kemble, to the Trollopes, mother and son, to Miss Bremer, to Miss Martineau, to Edward Dicey, to Robert Chambers, to Charles Mackay, to Grattan, to the Howitts, husband and wife, to Sir Charles Lyell, and Lady Emmeline Wortley, to say nothing of such really great writers as Charles Dickens and William Howard Russell. But, miserable hack as I may be, nothing will prevent these hack writings from being as public in the States as Barnum's Museum. Notoriety and celebrity are, I need not hint, two very different things; but Americans are forced to be as familiar with the name of Old Doctor Jacob Townsend as with that of Ralph Waldo Emerson;—just as in England the names of Alfred Tennyson and Monsieur Francatelli are both household words. One belongs to the library and the other to the kitchen; but both are known.

In America you may endeavour to dismiss this book with a sneer, and call its author a "Holywell Street Scribbler," whereas, in England, a more elaborate attempt will be made to depreciate that which I have written on the ground that I am a slovenly and tedious writer, that continual egotism and irritating digressions deface my writings; that I often blunder in quotation and overload my sentences with long-sounding words—that my orthography is defective and my syntax faulty; in a word, that I write rubbish, and am a worthless fellow, anyway. I have grown accustomed to this sort of thing, and it does me good. But neither sneers nor snubs, genteel raps on the knuckles nor savage shovelsful of mud will alter the fact that the Journal in which I wrote the letters which form the nucleus of this work has a daily circulation of over one hundred thousand. Thus, giving three readers to each paper—a fair average, I apprehend—more than a quarter of a million persons read that which I had to say about America every day, on which one of my letters appeared: unless, indeed, they were so disgusted with the first one that ever afterwards they closed their eyes or skipped the page when they came to "America in the Midst of War." These letters may not have made me favourably known. I have lost by their means, indeed, a great many friends, and gained a great many enemies—but they *have made me known*— known as well as Mr. Horniman with his tea, or Mr. Miles with his sixteen shilling trousers. Horniman and Miles and I will all probably be forgotten ten years hence; but, as it is, we have gotten publicity, and there is an end of the matter.

" *C'est icy ung livre de bonne foy, lecteur*," old Montaigne says, in a preface to a book which is all about himself. And you may perceive, dear Sir, that if my book have no other merit, it possesses at least that of candour. There is another prefatory remark by Messire Michel not inappropriate to this undertaking : " *Si c'eust été pour rechercher la faveur du monde je me feusse paré de beautez empruntez: je veulx qu'on m'y voye en ma façon simple, naturelle et ordinaire, sans estude et artifice, car c'est Moy que je peinds.*" Should a healthy man be ashamed to avow that his Book is Himself, and that in whatsoever he writes that treats of individual thought or individual opinion, he must be, to a great extent, his own hero? What do they matter : the spiteful and envious sneers, the paltry accusations of egotism. *No man alive can be so vain to others in print as he is vain to himself in the recesses of his own heart;* and the conviction of this is my sole excuse for telling you a hundred times over what I have eaten and what I have drunk ; when my corns hurt me, and when I had the toothache ; what I thought of my friends, and what my friends thought of me. Had I thought it right to build my book on any other model I should not have left a happy home and an assured livelihood, and a host of kind hearts who had known me from my infancy, to knock about for twelve months and more in a strange land and a cruel climate among strangers who hated me. I should have gone to the Library of the British Museum, and in due time, with the aid of Mr. Panizzi's shelves, produced two bulky octavos as modest as Mignon and as dull as ditchwater.

This parenthesis, it must be granted, is of the lengthiest. Come we back to the point from which I started :—the need to set forth the things which prompted me to look upon America more through a lens that was *couleur d'orange* than one which was *couleur de rose.* Why did I grumble ? At what did I see cause to grumble ? At these things, mainly :—

First : It is the common and notorious assertion of Americans that their government is the best in the world; that a pure democracy, such as they have established, secures to every man, without the slightest distinction of race, rank, fortune, or creed, the enjoyment of the fullest personal and political liberty, and that republican institutions have blessed the American people with an amount of aggregate and individual happiness as is unknown to those who are subject to the venal and effete monarchical rule prevailing in Europe.

I found, *per¯contrâ,* that the government of the Northern States—States utterly free from the influences of civil war—was practically a despotism, and that despotism arose not from any military exigencies, but from the deliberate conviction (expressed at the polling booths) of a majority of the Northern States, that the Constitution was a failure, that the doctrine of State Rights, which is the very back-bone of that Constitution, was obsolete and impracticable, and that a " strong government " was the one thing needed, and that to make that government strong it was necessary to place supreme and illimitable power in the hands of one Man.

Proof: The President, without formally establishing martial law, did by a new Proclamation entirely annul and abrogate the Constitution by emancipating (on paper) the slaves of all persons who held property in the Seceding States and had taken part against the government.

Again. The President's prime minister, William H. Seward, Secretary of State, once boasted that, by merely touching a "little bell" he could have any person arrested in any part of the Union, and detained in custody wheresoever and for so long a period as he chose. That this boast was not an idle one is shown by the arbitrary arrest of hundreds of persons, not legally accused of any statutable offence, but on the mere decree of Mr. Seward, the Secretary of State, and Mr. Stanton, the Secretary of War, and their incarceration, for indefinite periods, at Fort Lafayette, in the Bay of New York ; at Fort Warren, in the Harbour of Boston ; at Fort McHenry, near Baltimore ; and at the Old Capitol Prison, at Washington, in the District of Columbia. These persons were denied bail or mainprise ; they were refused communication with their friends, their relations, and even their legal advisers ; they were fed on coarse and repulsive rations—one, a British officer who had unwittingly conveyed some Confederate correspondence from Baltimore, was confined for many weeks in Fort Lafayette before permission was granted him to receive the not very luxurious gift of a chair, and was during that period compelled to clean out his own cell and perform other loathsome offices ; and often they were turned out of prison as arbitrarily as they had been immured therein : without trial, without enquiry, and without explanation. All this was done, not under the declared pressure of martial law, but in the Sovereign States of New York and New England ; States living in the peace of the Republic, and in which the Habeas Corpus Act had never been suspended, and the ordinary course of the civil tribunals never interrupted. Again, the President, or the Secretary of War, or both, did, by a simple firman, order General Dix, the military officer commanding at New York, to arrest the proprietors of two newspapers, called the *World* and the *Journal of Commerce*, and imprison them in Fort Lafayette, for the offence of having inserted in those papers a proclamation which was subsequently found to be forged. More than this : the publication of the *World* and the *Journal of Commerce* was forcibly suppressed ; the clerks and compositors were expelled from the premises, and the offices held by an armed guard. It was notorious that the proprietors of the *World* and the *Journal of Commerce* had been in this matter the innocent dupes of an impudent swindler, and so strong was the feeling of indignation excited by their imprisonment that they were released from custody on the very night of their arrest ; but the sequestration of their property, to their great pecuniary damage, continued for some days longer ; and, when they sought for redress before the courts of justice of their State, the judges, in refusing it, explicitly stated that they did not consider it expedient to interfere with the action of the Central Government at Washington :—in other words, with the despotic power of Mr. Lincoln. Let it be noted that the author of the forged proclamation in question, one Joseph Howard, although on discovery arrested for common decency's sake, was treated with much consideration, and dismissed after a very brief detention, avowedly because he was a member of the Black Republican party, and had considerable personal influence at the White House. The lenity shown him may very forcibly be contrasted with the extreme and inhuman rigour which was experienced by two citizens of New York, named Donohue and Ferry, who were accused, during the Presidential Election, of fabricating soldiers' votes, and who, although they might have been tried and punished for that offence by the regular courts of their State, were arraigned before a military commission sitting at Baltimore, and, being convicted on evidence which even their adversaries admitted to be flimsy and unsatisfactory, were *sentenced to imprisonment for life.*

I do not conceive, dear sir, that it is germane to this argument to enumerate—if they could all be enumerated—the various acts of tyranny and oppression committed by the Government of the United States, by their civil and their military servants in the States where martial law had been proclaimed, or where their authority was disturbed or imperilled. *À la guerre comme à la guerre ;* or, if you like an older aphorism, "Amidst the clash of arms the laws are silent." I will not, therefore, in this place say one word of the atrocities wreaked on defenceless people by the Federal commanders in the States of Maryland, Western Virginia, Kentucky, Missouri, Tennessee, and Louisiana ; of the reign of Terror inaugurated by Payne at Paducah, and by Washburne at Memphis ; of the devastation of the Shenandoah Valley by Sheridan, by Custer, and by Merritt ; of the murders committed by Federal soldiers and the robberies committed by Federal officers; of the standing crops that have been burnt, the fruit trees that have been grubbed up, the cattle and horses that have been carried off; the whole cities and villages that have been destroyed; of women ravished, children maltreated, aged people turned out of doors, churches gutted, negroes stolen, and smiling farms laid waste. The consideration of matters such as these will more appropriately enter into a chapter entitled the "Horrors of War." Nor need I more than cursorily allude to the charges brought against the Federal Government of having systematically interfered with the freedom of election in the North—notably in the States of Maryland, Pennsylvania, Ohio, and Kentucky,—of having hedged round the ballot-boxes with soldiers with fixed bayonets, and caused those who cast their votes against the Government to be insulted and outraged;—of having summarily dismissed from office all clerks suspected of ill feeling towards the present order of things,—of having largely and shamefully bribed those who could serve its interests;—of having tampered with the United States mails, and opened or stolen the correspondence of persons supposed to hold opposition views, and of having exercised a general system of intimidation, corruption, and violence. Charges such as these have been openly made during the past year; but I cannot speak of my own knowledge of their truth or their falsehood. So far as I can tell, *my* letters were never opened; and the only voting I have seen has been in the States of New York and Massachusetts, where everything appeared to be conducted in a most fair and straightforward manner. I will conclude, however, that

c 2

which I have to say regarding the " despotism " which I im-
pute to have replaced the formerly free institutions of the
United States by the narrative of a case which appears to
have attracted but little attention in Europe, but which I
cannot help regarding as a pivot on which much of this controversy regarding despotism and liberty must turn. I mean
the case of Don José de Arguelles.

" Napoleon Bonaparte, first of his line, and called the Great,"
I wrote on the 18th of May, 1864, " was for a long series
of years permitted, by a complaisant and conquered continent, to act unrestrictedly according to his own will and
pleasure. He did what he liked with his own, and with that
which was not his own. He rarely hesitated to abuse the
vast power he had seized, and to show himself what is called
on this side the water a ' kinder despot.' He ravaged con-
tinents, overran whole countries, revolutionised States, demolished dynasties, and gave away crowns as though they had
been candies. He tore the Pope from his palace, and made
a French general master at the Vatican. He seized upon
British subjects, and made inoffensive travellers prisoners of
war by thousands. He burnt our merchandise wherever he
found it. He violated the territory of Baden, arrested, tried,
and executed the Duke d'Enghien. He shut up Toussaint
l'Ouverture in a damp dungeon, and allowed that brave and
intelligent black man to die of the chills and a broken heart.
He caused Hofer, the Tell of the Tyrol, to be slain. He
banished Mme. de Stael, and guillotined Georges Cadoudal. In
short, he was a terrible Bashaw. *On le laissa faire.* People
murmured; but they obeyed. They shrugged their shoulders,

but they bowed their necks to the collar. The glory of his
great achievements threw the dark and cruel and meanly per-
fidious acts he was continually committing into the shade.
Yet, as the last straw is said to break the camel's back, and
the worm will turn when trodden upon, there was one deed
done by Napoleon towards the close of his career—one barbarous, heartless crime, done in the mere spiteful wantonness
of arbitrary power—which filled all Europe with horror, with
terror, and with amazement. By his order a humble German
bookseller, named Palm, was seized and shot. Only the very
barest of suspicion of disloyalty towards the great Emperor
and King attached to him. The man was murdered in cold
blood. Campbell the poet is said to have ironically proposed
Bonaparte's health at a supper-table, as a benefactor of the
literary species, on the ground that he had shot a bookseller;
but, in sober seriousness, wherever the dismal tidings of this
judicial assassination penetrated, they were received with the
profoundest indignation and the darkest forebodings. The act
of vengeance wreaked on a private citizen was so hideous,
yet so mean and petty ; the blood-shedding was so gratuitous ;
the murder of the Leipsic bookseller was so obviously the
result of capricious, unbridled, reckless tyranny, that men
who had hitherto glorified and extolled the conquering hero
began to regard him with aversion and dismay. To the
' Austrian marriage and the Spanish ulcer' Napoleon was
wont to ascribe his own downfall ; but he might have added a
third cause to those which undoubtedly brought about his
ruin. When the plain frock and round hat of the citizen are
no longer a protection ; when the peaceful burgess is torn

from his home by armed and irresponsible myrmidons; when distinct nationality is no longer a guarantee against the aggression of a foreign despot, the whole of society becomes naturally filled with anger and alarm. Quiet communities feel as though a wild beast were prowling round them. No one can tell whose turn to be devoured may come next, and at last, obeying the sheer instinct of self-preservation, they unite against the common enemy and destroy him.

" The American people have, in their wisdom, for the past two or three years suffered the rulers whom they have set over them to do pretty much as they liked in *their* wisdom. The Constitution being in danger, they have forborne to grumble if the authorities at Washington have occasionally dispensed with the use of the Constitution altogether. It became necessary at all hazards to save the ship of the State, and so masts and rigging have been cut away, and the passengers' luggage, and sometimes the passengers themselves, thrown overboard. Mr. Lincoln has poured on, and the people of the Great Republic have endured. To murmur against unconstitutional acts has become disloyal. To talk too much about the Habeas Corpus is to incur the suspicion of Copperheadism. The Bill of Rights in America has been dishonoured and protested, and the Palladium of American liberty is of no more account than a cracked tin kettle. Still the public have been patient. They have seen Fort Lafayette and the old Capitol crammed to repletion with political prisoners. They have seen a merciless conscription over and over again enforced. They have heard the doctrine of confiscation and spoliation openly and systematically advocated. They have allowed the

most bungling and the most profligate of financiers to pawn
the national credit, to fritter away the national wealth, to
forestall the public resources, and, by the unheard-of inflation
of an equivocal paper currency, to endanger the stability of
the most energetic commercial community in the world, and
to menace private citizens with pauperism and ruin. All
these oppressive measures they have borne with cheerfulness
and submission. The exigencies of the commonwealth have
been pleaded to justify the abrogation of sound doctrines of
finance and the suspension of a wise code of laws. But there
is one thing the American people will not stand. They are
as justly jealous as we ourselves are of the right of asylum,
and they have been, until recently, as justly proud of the
inviolability of their soil as a refuge for the oppressed of
every nation. When the mistaken zeal of Commodore
Wilkes, in the affair of the ‘ Trent,’ imperilled the existence of
pacific relations between the United States and Great Britain,
the good sense of the American people led them to concur in
the action of their government in giving up the prisoners
taken from the deck of a British ship—led them to see that
a great principle was at stake, and that by refusing the ren-
dition of Mason and Slidell a most perilous and ominous precedent would be set. An intemperate sailor had outraged
the law of nations, and had been for a moment applauded by
the unthinking and backed up by the malevolent ; but in the
end better counsels prevailed, and the Americans were content to do as they would be done by.

" A case has just occurred which more nearly touches on
the right of asylum, and which more clearly brings the

sanctity of the soil of a free country into question, than even the affair of the 'Trent.' All New York is in a fever of indignation at the kidnapping, spiriting away, and ultimate deportation to Havana of Colonel Arguelles. The story, so far as it is known, is one of the strangest and one of the most scandalous that can possibly be conceived. There came recently to the Empire City a Spanish gentleman, named Don José Augustin Arguelles. He was accompanied by his wife, and the pair took up their quarters at a well-known hotel in the most crowded part of the town. Senor Arguelles was a colonel in the Spanish army, and had been Lieutenant-Governor of Colon, a district in the southern part of Cuba. He came well furnished with letters of introduction to New York. He had had, it appears, a quarrel with General Dulce, the Captain-General of Cuba, and considered himself to have been grievously wronged by that exalted functionary. According to Colonel Arguelles's own showing—and it must be understood that I by no means authoritatively indorse his statement, considering only that his story is good until another one is told—he was a victim to his opposition to the slave-trade. A cargo of negroes, ten hundred and seventy in number—by far the largest importation to the island that had been known for many years—had been 'run' on to the coast. They were captured by the troops of the Government, and the question of their disposal came within the jurisdiction of the Lieutenant-Governor of Colon. Colonel Arguelles represents that he was waited upon by M. Zulueta—the most notorious slave-trader in Cuba, and perhaps in the world, and whose name, as identical with that of a gentleman who was tried for slave-trading at the Old Bailey some twenty years since, but acquitted, may be familiar to you—and offered an enormous sum of money in hard dollars if he would consent to what is delicately termed a 'transaction,' and allow the captured Africans to be sold into Cuban bondage. The Captain-General had already, it was hinted, been 'squared.' Colonel Arguelles indignantly refused to come to terms. He saw in this perhaps not only an opportunity for performing an act of public virtue and private morality, but of bringing General Dulce to grief. He had been a member of the Spanish Cortes; he had some interest, and in very high quarters, at the Court of Spain, and it may be that he cherished the hope of supplanting his chief and rival in the honourable and lucrative office of governor of the *siempre fidelisma isla*. At all events, the arrangement with M. Zulueta fell through; whereupon—still according to Colonel Arguelles's showing—the baffled slavemonger moved General Dulce to subject him to a series of unmerited persecutions. His character blackened and his prospects endangered, Colonel Arguelles resigned both his post and his commission, in order to bring his superior officer to justice, and sailed for New York, *en route* for Europe, determined to lay his complaint before the Cortes, and, if necessary, before her Majesty Isabella Segunda herself. He was not permitted long to revel in the delights of New York society. He was in the city just a sufficient time to ventilate a few of his wrongs in an American and a French newspaper published here, when his career was suddenly brought to a close. Early one morning a hackney-coach, containing two or three deputy-

marshals of the United States, drove to the door of Maillard's
Hotel. They entered the house, pushed by waiters and
chambermaids, burst into the room occupied by the colonel
and his wife, dragged him from his bed, and hurried him
away no one knew whither. All that day his friends sought
for him in vain. The different station-houses were visited,
but the police on duty knew nothing about him. He wasn't
in the Tombs ; he was presumably not at Blackwell's Island ;
he had certainly done nothing to merit incarceration in Fort
Lafayette. At last he was discovered at an obscure jail in
Ludlow Street ; but no sooner was his presence there ascertained than he again mysteriously disappeared, and all trace
of him was lost. His wife was distracted ; his friends were
furious. The United States' marshal, Mr. Murray, was applied to for information, but declined giving any. At last it
began shrewdly to be suspected that the colonel had been
put on board the steamer 'Eagle,' just then starting for
Havana. The aid of some detectives belonging to the metropolitan police was secured by the colonel's friends ; the 'Eagle'
was pursued down the bay, and boarded *before she reached
the Narrows*. She was thoroughly overhauled, but no Colonel
Arguelles was to be found. The scent was once more lost.
His friends, however, were determined to unravel the mystery. An influential New York gentleman, whose character
was above suspicion, and whose loyalty unimpeached, started
for Washington in company with Madame Arguelles and the
correspondent of a European newspaper, and sought an interview with Mr. Secretary Seward. The Secretary of State
received the deputation in a manner in which pomposity was

mingled with sentimentality, and embarrassment with both.
First, he refused to recognise the right of the deputation to
inquire at all as to Colonel Arguelles's whereabouts; then he
made a shuffling exculpatory explanation of the colonel being
accused of complicity in the slave trade; and finally he strove
to ride out of the difficulty on the high horse of didactic
morality, by observing that 'no person who had sold human
beings into bondage could expect an asylum in the United
States.' Mr. Seward might just as well have remarked to
his hearers, 'Thou shalt not suffer a witch to live,' or recited
to them a passage from the Koran. The snubbed deputation
were, however, not disheartened. They unearthed the Spanish
minister. That diplomatist yielded to discreetly applied
pressure; and from him they learnt that Colonel José
Augustin Arguelles was arrested in New York by virtue of
a requisition made to the Government of the United States
by the Captain-General of Cuba; that his arrest was made
under the direct authority of Mr. Secretary Seward, and that
he had been put on board the 'Eagle' *after* she had passed the
Narrows, in custody of Spanish police-officers, and two of the
American deputy-marshals who had arrested him; and that
he was now on his way to Cuba, there to be delivered up to
the tender mercies of Captain-General Dulce.

"It remains to be seen whether the great and free American
people will tolerate for one moment longer this most monstrous
outrage on their personal liberties and their personal honour.
It remains to be seen whether the representatives of the people
in Congress will do their duty to their constituents, and force
or shame the Government into explanation and reparation.

It remains to be seen whether the countrymen of that brave and honest sea-captain who, when the Hungarian refugee, Martin Kossta—a man who was barely a postulant for the proud privileges of American citizenship—was kidnapped in the streets of Smyrna, laid his ship alongside the Austrian brig 'Hussar,' on board which Kossta had been conveyed, beat to quarters, ran out his guns, double-shotted them, and swore that unless the man were given up in half-an-hour he would blow the German from the water 'like the peel of an onion.' It remains to be seen whether the nation who share with Britons the glory of offering to all who are in peril from the tyranny of unjust rulers a sanctuary and a safeguard, will tamely submit to have their good name and their repute for hospitality and generosity dragged through the mire by Ministers who appear to be emulous of the commingled attributes of Torquemada, of Fouché, and of Jonathan Wild, and to unite the perfidy of a familiar of the Inquisition with the cunning activity of a Bow-Street runner. In England a Minister of State who had been guilty of such a mean and shabby thief-taker's trick as this would not be in office twenty-four hours after the exposure of his conduct in Parliament. It was as much as all the immense influence brought to bear by the great Sir Robert Peel on his party and the country could do to save Sir James Graham from ruin in the Post Office letter-opening business. We are a people who have great faith in precedents; and a precedent having been fortunately discovered of a couple of letters opened by Secretary's warrant in the reign of Queen Anne, Sir James Graham escaped condign punishment, but re-

mained indelibly covered with well-deserved popular odium.
But there is no precedent, either in England or in America, for
kidnapping people in their beds, and, without even the semblance of a form of justice, hurrying them on board steamers
and delivering them up to their enemies. Louis Napoleon,
in 1851, certainly seized MM. Cavaignac, Lamoricière, Thiers,
&c., at a somewhat untimely hour; but he had avowedly
overturned all existing government; and, even under those
exceptional circumstances, the proscribed representatives
were arrested by commissaries of police duly provided with
warrants. They were conveyed to well-ascertained places of
confinement; they were not kept *au sécret;* and they had
not been in prison four-and-twenty hours before the President,
in a public proclamation, strove to justify his conduct. The
authorities at Washington have, it is true, and most tardily,
ventured upon a semi-apology for the kidnapping of Colonel
Arguelles, as may be learnt from the following semi-official
statement telegraphed to New York : 'It is understood that
an arrangement has been entered into between our Government and that of Spain for the purpose of rendering up
slave-traders who escape from Cuba to the United States,
and from the United States to Cuba. In this connection the
arrest of Colonel José Augustin Arguelles is significant.'
'In this connection,' it might be understood that something
of the nature of a treaty of extradition has been concluded
between the United States and Spain, whose sudden and
virtuous indignation against the slave-traders, at whose doings
she has connived for so many years, cannot be too highly
commended; but, granting that it is a most excellent thing

mutually to give up thieves, and murderers, and forgers, and man-stealers, it would seem expedient, it would seem at least decent, to make the arrest publicly—to justify it by some evidence more credible than the ex-parte statement of a man vehemently suspected of being himself over head and ears in a most infamous traffic; to bring the person accused before a magistrate, and to refrain from relegating him to bondage, and perhaps to assassination, until he has had an opportunity to be heard in his own defence. It is very much to be feared that the unfortunate Colonel Arguelles will never be seen alive again. The Government may be brought to a due sense of the shameful disregard of public and private right of which it has been guilty; Marshal Murray and some of his subordinates are to be prosecuted, it is said, before the grand jury, for their share in the kidnapping; it is not impossible even that a gunboat might be sent to Havana to demand the body of the captive; but it is a matter of doleful dubiety as to what state that body would be in when surrendered. The climate of Cuba is very hot. The *vomito negro* is a disease of frightfully rapid operation. Dead men tell no tales; and José Augustin Arguelles must know a great many things of a nature to compromise some of the most respectable people in Havana.

"Whether this unlucky Spanish colonel live or die, the fact nevertheless remains, that the laws of the United States have been most disgracefully set at defiance, and the fair fame of its people most wantonly befouled, by the action of the Federal Government. It matters little whether Arguelles or Dulce, or both, have been mixed up in the slave-trade. Little good would arise from an analytical discussion on the relative morality of Spanish officials. Nor is it for one moment to be denied that the kidnappers of black men ought to be punished both in this world and the next. But how about the kidnappers of white men ? How about the deputy-marshals who pulled Colonel Arguelles out of his bed; who are said to have been heavily bribed for the swift and secret performance of their knavish task; and who have taken a trip to Havana with their victim, to be fêted, no doubt, on their arrival by the Spanish alguazils, their accomplices ? How about Marshal Murray, the discreet corregidor who set the myrmidons in motion ? And, finally, how about the Honourable William Henry Seward, Secretary of State in the Cabinet of Abraham Lincoln, who has sold his country's birthright for a mess of olla-podrida, and conceded to a Spanish viceroy that which poor brokendown Abdul Medjid refused disdainfully to concede to Francis Joseph of Austria and Nicholas of Russia. ' No,' quoth the Mahometan sultan, when he was summoned to surrender the refugee Louis Kossuth ; ' I will keep the Giaour from hurting you for a year and a day, but I will never give him up to you.' And all Christendom cried ' Bravo !' to the turbaned Turk."

We learnt subsequently that on the arrival of this most unfortunate gentleman at Havana he was taken before General Dulce, and bitterly reproached with having " caused a scandal in a foreign land." That he was then thrown into a noisome dungeon, into which descent could only be made through a trap in the roof by a ladder in the Morro Castle ;

that, after many weeks' confinement, he was tried before a court-martial, not on the slave-dealing issue, but for military insubordination, and sentenced to degradation and a long term of imprisonment—whether in chains or not, I know not. And this is the last, probably, that the world will ever hear of Don José de Arguelles.

With this monstrous case, dear sir, I close my argument as to whether the United States, in the year 1864, possesses anything approaching "the best government in the world."

Second. I was told, I was assured (I mean as one of the British public) that the American Civil War was undertaken by the North, much less for the purpose of repressing an unnatural and parricidal rebellion on the part of the South, than for the purpose of liberating four millions of blacks from a cruel and humiliating bondage. I was told that the rebellion was fomented by a few thousand arrogant and oligarchical slaveholders ; that the hearts of the people of the South were not in the war, but that it was a crusade in favour of human freedom, and that the North were only bent on the emancipation of an enslaved and oppressed race. Here is the Confession of Faith of the North, written by Mrs. Julia Ward Howe, one of the most admired poetesses of New England, professedly as a "Battle Song of the Republic." I have heard it sung to the familiar anti-slavery air of " John Brown," by a Massachusetts regiment twelve hundred strong, and the effect under those circumstances was almost inconceivably fine. You must excuse the seemingly blasphemous "vigour" of some of the expressions. Those expressions are accounted utterances of genuine and heartfelt piety in New

England, where there yet dwell descendants of Captain Hew-Agag-in-pieces-before-the-Lord, and Lieutenant Bind-their-Kings-in-chains-and-their-Nobles-with-links-of-iron, and where children are still christened with long-winded scriptural appellations, recalling "If Christ-had-not-been-born-thou-would'st-have-been-damned-Barebones." I need only remind you of the first and last stanzas of Mrs. Howe's stirring lyric :—

Mine eyes have seen the glory of the coming of the Lord ;
He is trampling out the vintage where his grapes of wrath are stored ;
He hath loosed the fateful lightnings of his terrible swift sword,
          For GOD is marching on.

     *   *   *   *   *   *   *

In the beauty of the lilies CHRIST was born across the sea ;
There's a glory in his visage that transfigures you and me ;
As He died to make men holy, let us die to make men free,
          For GOD is marching on.

There is to this song a refrain, beginning "Glory, Glory, Hallelujah !" which, from the disagreeable effect it might have on European ears, I refrain from quoting.

I was told by politicians, by newspaper editors, clergymen, by private gentlemen, by ladies, that the one great object of the war was to set the Black Man free ; that, although the martial ardour of the North had first been fired by the attack on Fort Sumter, and the legions of the Republic called to arms simply to compel the South to return to their allegiance, and although there had been at first no intention whatever to interfere with their "domestic institutions," that is to say, with slavery (an intention explicitly disavowed by Mr. Lincoln himself in his inaugural address in March, 1861), there had gradually arisen in the minds of even moderate men a firm conviction that slavery was at the bottom of this trouble, that it was the root of the evil, and that, ere ever the Union would be restored on its former basis, slavery must be demolished root and branch, and utterly stamped out. I was told that the cruelties of the Southern slaveholders had reached a point which humanity and policy could no longer tolerate. I was shown dozens of books, pamphlets, leading articles, in which cruelties and enormities, in comparison with which the horrors of " Uncle Tom's Cabin " were but as milk and water, were charged on the slave system. I was bidden to believe that the polished and kindly ladies and gentlemen with whom it had been my lot, for years, to associate in Europe were, at home, gloomy and reckless tyrants, who passed their lives in overworking and torturing their slaves. I was bidden to regard a plantation as a kind of Inferno, where at every step you met women tied up for punishment, and heard the sibillant rush of thongs through the air; where the whipping-post the cow-skin, the paddle, the gyves, the yoke, and the branding-iron were permanent institutions, where the miserable bondsmen and bondswomen went half-naked, were half-starved, and were worked from twelve to eighteen hours a-day, and where, if they succeeded in escaping from their intolerable thraldom into some Dismal Swamp, they were hunted down by savage bloodhounds, and brought back with their flesh half torn off, their limbs, then to be tied up to a beam by their thumbs, a post thrust between their legs, and their toes barely touching the ground, and flogged till the blood ran down their heels. I was told that after this scourging their bloody backs were washed down with brine. I was told that they were kept for days in the stocks or the bilboes, their faces exposed to a burning sun and to the assaults of innumerable flies. I was told that pregnant women were not exempt from the lash; that they were forced to toil in the rice swamps within a few days of their confinement, and that a favourite amusement with a facetious overseer was to compel a son to flog his own mother, and a husband his own wife. I was informed that in every plantation there was a Harem and that every planter was a Sultan, that he flung his handkerchief to any black houri he chose, and woe be to her who declined his condescending patronage. I was told that the Amuraths of the South never experienced the slightest scruples in selling their cast-off mistresses or their base-born children; and that on the auction-blocks of Charleston and New Orleans beautiful young girls, as white as you or I may be, dear sir, were, as a common occurrence, exposed for sale, and that they were as commonly bought for the vilest of purposes by the proprietors of dens of profligacy. I was told that in every town in the South there was a public calaboose or whipping-house, whither masters and mistresses who had no regular apparatus for torture on their own premises—who were too lazy to become themselves the executioners, or too sensitive to have execution done under their own eyes—were accustomed to send their slaves to be punished, and that women and young girls were, as a matter of course, dragged to these places, stripped, and lashed by the hands of men. I was bidden to believe that the long-descended and high-minded gentlemen of Virginia were habitually engaged in the loathsome and degrading calling of rearing slaves for the markets of the extreme South ; that the breeding of black human cattle was as favourite a pursuit with a landed proprietor in the Old Dominion, as breeding heifers or sheep might be with an English country gentleman, and that when this live stock was sufficiently plump and strong to labour in the rice-grounds or cotton-fields of Carolina or Tennessee, negro traders came to purchase the "likeliest young niggers," and took them away, shackled and manacled, to be sold into hopeless bondage down South. I was shown photographs of negroes whose backs had been lashed into one bleeding mass of mashed up muscle, or whose limbs were covered with the blisters raised by the paddle—who had been branded with their owner's initials on the forehead and on the cheek, whose ears had been clipped, whose nostrils slit, and whose tongues cut out. And, finally, I was told that these four millions of black people were sunk in the most abject and entire ignorance of every branch of knowledge, secular or divine—that it was a crime to teach them to read or write— and that missionaries who had attempted to preach the Word of God to them had been banished, cowhided, tarred and cottoned, ridden on rails, hanged, and shot. And I was asked whether, as an Englishman and a Christian,—whether as the countryman of Clarkson, of Wilberforce, of Granville Sharpe, of Brougham, of Macaulay, and of Buxton—I could, for very shame, deny that these were horrors and these were scandals which cried aloud for abrogation, or that a nation who had undertaken to abrogate them was engaged in a righteous and a holy war.

I heard all these things. I heard and read too what the other side had to say and write. I could not penetrate into the Southern States; but I went to Cuba, and saw, during two visits to that island (I went to Mexico in the interval) negro slavery in full operation on the plantations on the factories. I do not pretend to know much about anything, but I claim to have studied the question of slavery for very many years with intense and concentrated industry—to have read nearly all that has been written on the subject—from Blue Books to Anti-Slavery Reporters—during the last fifty years; and, in early youth, to have had much *viva voce* instruction as to the practical working of slaveholders, for I came on the mother's side from a long line of West Indian Planters who owned slaves and did not torture them. When my mother, dear sir, was brought to England sixty years ago to be educated, there came over with her three black slave-women, and these women used to sit on the stairs all day in London, shivering, and crying to be sent back to Demerara. And slavery, sixty years since, in British Guiana, was no joke.

These are the result of my studies. That I believe slavery to be an evil, and to a certain extent a curse : but that it is not a worse evil nor a worse curse than Prostitution, than Drunkenness, than Pauperism, than the tyranny of capital over labour, or than the greed for wealth. I believe that it is not half so great an evil and not half so great a curse as that Devil's own Game—War, and as that Devil's own creed which strives to preach the doctrine that there is a " God of Battles," and that Almighty God can, under any circumstances, look with aught save sorrow and abhorrence on the

spectacle of His creatures cutting one another's throats.
And I believe that although cruelty to anything that lives,
parlant or mute, is wicked and detestable, the cruelties said
to be inflicted by the Southerners on their bond servants are
in the main gross and malevolent exaggerations, and that, in
any case, it is better that a refractory negro should have a
sound thrashing than that A. B., who never saw C. D. before
in his life, and cannot possibly have the slightest grudge
against him, should fall upon him, shoot him with bullets,
rip up his bowels, stab him in the heart, or batter his brains
out, and call that Glorious War.

I believe that for thousands of years unavailing efforts have
been made to civilise the black natives of Africa, and that
those efforts—missionary enterprise and the Republic of
Liberia notwithstanding—will continue to be unavailing. I
believe that the negro in his own country is not to be
civilised. I know that when the missionaries do get hold of
him and teach him his Catechism and baptise him, his Christianity very soon deteriorates into a kind of Obeah worship
grafted on Exeter Hallism, and that he howls out his " Glory
Hallelujahrums " and .his " Bress de. Lord's " without the
slightest idea of the real meaning of his invocations :—and
that in fact the deity he invokes is only Mumbo Jumbo in a
white choker. *I believe that he is and has been ten thousand
times better off as a bond-servant in the Southern States of
America than as a free negro in the North, and ten million
times better off as a negro, at all, in America, than as a
denizen of Dahomey or Ashantee, and that if he is sometimes flogged and sometimes sold down South, his blood is*

not shed to fill a pond for a "great custom," and his skull is not scooped out to form a calabash for his sovereign to drink rum from. I believe that he is naturally inferior to the white man in mental organisation ; that his defects and his vices are not to be eradicated by education ; that he will always (in the aggregate : of course there are individual exceptions) be lazy, indolent, and slovenly, good-natured and kind-hearted, but subject to inexplicable fits of caprice, sulkiness, obstinacy, and perversity :—willing and obedient only when he fears the eye or the hand of his master ; inconceivably vain, trivial, and puerile, always as lecherous as a monkey and often as savage as a Gorilla, and finally totally unconscious of or indifferent to the moral laws—let alone such legal enactments as teach that lying and stealing are wrong. I believe that this is the negro. I believe that he will make a capital sailor in a ship where there is a good boatswain, an excellent footman or coachman in a household where the master and mistress keep a tight hand over their servants, a valuable soldier under white officers and stern drill-sergeants (in time, and if he is strictly disciplined *and smartly dressed,* after the pattern of our West India regiments), a useful body servant, an active hotel waiter, and an incomparable barber. But I believe that he must always have a " boss " or a master or guide of some sort over him, with power to punish him when he misbehaves himself; and I believe that in default of this master, guide, or " boss," he will go to the Devil, as he has gone in Hayti, as he will go in Liberia, as he would go in Jamaica were not the magistrates and the police too strong for him, and as he has been going in his own country, Africa, for I don't know how many thousand years.

They told me when I came to America that the great heart of the country was set upon the destruction of slavery. Perish the Union, perish the country, perish every white man in it; but that eminently helpless dark-coloured person must be freed from the questionable oppression he has so long endured, and so contentedly suffered. He must have entire liberty—to do what? To dig trenches for the white engineer officer; or with his mangled body to make fascines and gabions for the white man's forts; or to wander about to pilfer, and starve, and rot, as he is doing just now with great regularity and despatch in a hundred places where he has been set free. The abolition of slavery, the Radicals maintain, is not to be left, as all humane and sensible men desire it should be, to another generation, happily free from the passions and the prejudices which disfigure the existing one. Able and patriotic but temperate men are not to be encouraged to devise a scheme whereby a great national evil may be gradually and equitably, but effectually, abolished. " No, no," the Radical cry runs; "slavery must go, *hic et nunc*. No compromise! no compensation! It must go. It is punctured in the spinal marrow. It is reeling and staggering like an ox that has been stricken with a pole-axe. Never mind those who may be crushed by the toppling down of its huge bulk. It is doomed, and it must die." So the negro is to receive forthwith his gift of the white elephant—freedom. I wonder "what will he do with it." Sir Bulwer Lytton would be puzzled to answer the question. I met in Washington a lady, as loyal of course as she was accomplished, who told me that she once owned a female slave. The poor woman was about to become a mother. My informant—as it is the kindly custom of Southern ladies to do—busied herself in preparing for the advent of her bond-servant's infant. In good time she gave the slave money to purchase baby linen. "Well, Peggy," she asked one day, "what did you buy?" The slave told her. *She had bought a silk umbrella!* Such was her notion of a *layette.* Were this a solitary instance, or one that I had heard at second hand, I should be ashamed to quote it; but hundreds of witnesses could, if needful, be put into the box to prove how utterly childish and irresponsible, the vast majority of these poor people are. From the old slaves who crawl about the houses of their owners, fed for nothing and not worked, saying and doing what they please, *and sleeping with their feet so thrust into the embers on the hearth that they scorch their toe-nails off,* to the little black brats snuggling like so many guinea-pigs about the floors of Southern houses ; from these to the women who buy silk umbrellas instead of childbed linen, and who come roaring to their mistress for remedies if they have a sore finger or a soft corn —who will only take medicine when they are sick from her hand—and who, *as mothers, are so shamefully neglectful of and so wantonly cruel to their children, that the white ladies are often compelled to take the little ones away from their unnatural parents to preserve their lives*—it is the same lamentable case of an inferior and impracticable race. And in the North—the free North—the land of liberty, of intelli-

gence, of newspapers, and Methodist chapels, and common
schools; do they fare better there? I declare that, of all
the miserable and woe-begone objects I have ever beheld out
of a Russian gaol or an Italian lazar-house, the free negroes
I have seen in New York are the wretchedest and most forlorn. Take away those who are coachmen or servants in
private families, and who are clad in some kind of decent
livery by the employers; take away a proportion of mulat-
toes and "bright" coloured people (among which class the
women are often given to tawdry finery in apparel, but
seldom to personal cleanliness); take away a few, a very few
old negroes, who have made money by storekeeping, and
wear broadcloth and tall hats; and the residue are a listless,
decrepit, drowsy, cowering race, always going to the wall,
always sliding and slinking away, always ragged, always dirty
—lying and pilfering and tipsifying themselves in a feckless,
shambling kind of way—horribly overgrown children—*crétins*
whose *goîtres* are on their brains instead of in their throats.
In the back slums of New York you meet them prowling
about with baskets full of scraps and offal. When the police
rout out some dilapidated tenement at the Five Points, they
are sure to find negroes lurking and snoozling among the
rubbish. Let a streak of sunshine be cast across the pavement, and you are sure to find a negro sitting on a doorstep,
basking in the radiant warmth. The negroes at Washington
are sturdier, comelier, more intelligent fellows. But they
have been bred up not to freedom but to slavery. At
Baltimore the railway porters are athletic, active, and willing
negroes. Only the day before yesterday they were slaves.

Turn them loose in the blessed land of freedom, and see how long it will be before they hopelessly deteriorate. There is, I believe, a proviso in the laws of the State of New York, by which negroes who have acquired a certain amount of property—some fifty or sixty pounds sterling—are entitled to vote. Last year one of the candidates for the mayoralty of the Empire City was accused of having gone down to a meeting of these moneyed negroes, and promised them all manner of fine things—permission to ride in the street railway cars among the rest—if they would vote for him. The accusation was I hear unfounded, and a mere electioneering ruse; but, had it been otherwise, the candidate would have taken but little by his motion. There are certainly not three hundred coloured people who can justify such a claim to the franchise, in this city of a million of inhabitants.

But is the existence of the educated negro, of the "learned nigger," to be denied? By no means. There are President Roberts of Liberia, and Mr. Frederick Douglas, just as there were Phillis Wheatley and Toussaint L'Ouverture. There was the Hottentot Venus, and there was Mr. Lumley's "Black Swan." But how many more? and how lamentably few are the intellectual plums in this huge black pudding. That the negro, however, can sometimes say a shrewd thing is unquestionable. I have been told of an "intelligent contraband," who, escaping from Dixie into the land of Abraham, was pressed by a white patriot to enter into the military service of the North, but manifested an unaccountable reluctance to shoulder a musket. "Why don't you enlist, Ginger?" asked the white patriot. "Wal, mas'r," replied the contraband,

"Did yever see two dogs fightin' for a bone ?"   "Certainly, Ginger."   "*Wal, did yever see de bone fight?*"   "Not I." "Wal, mas'r, you'se both a fightin', and Ginger's de bone, an' he's not gwine to fight in this hyar difficulmty." The conclusion arrived at by the intelligent contraband was, I think logical.   I hope the story is not apocryphal, or the invention of some white minstrel of the Christy or Bryant race, who blacks his face and sings songs the like of which were never heard in Dixie.   You will often, also, get a drolly shrewd reply, or a cutting bit of repartee from a negro.   In "giving evasive answers" they are unapproachable.   A friend of mine had a negro butler who had embezzled from four to five hundred dollars.   When arraigned before a family council for his misdeeds, he " concluded to own up there had been a little misapprehension," *i. e.*, that he had stolen the five hundred dollars.   There is a very good story told of a negro witness who was called to speak to the character of a brother darkey, and who gave him a very bad one.   "Do you mean to say he's a thief, sir?" thundered the cross-examining counsel.   "I'se not gwine ter say he's a tief, sa," replied the witness; "buff wattersay's dis.   If I vers a chicken, an' I saw dat nigga' loafin' round, *I'd roost high*, dat's all." Equally evasive is the reply of the negro who is asked by his master whether he is for Lincoln or for Jeff Davis.   "I'se for de Lord, mas'r," he answers.   "He'll work out his salvatiums.   *Bress de Lord.*"

The coloured people have, it is well known, a considerable aptitude for mimicry.   But it is mimicry of that order which, as children, we were told used to lead to the catching of baboons. The hunter laid his trap—a tub of water—and at a distance from that a tub full of birdlime. He caught the eye of the baboon, stooped, and laid his face in the water. The imitative brute watched him ; walked to the next tub, and thrust his muzzle into the birdlime. So the baboon was caught. Negroes will imitate to the life the follies and the absurdities of the whites. They will put on the *petit-maître* airs of their employers. I saw at Washington a waiter who, in moustache, whisker, turn-down collar, and even to a lisp and a limp, was the image of Lord Dundreary dipped in a vatful of ink. There are many black clergymen, schoolmasters, and lecturers, who can talk by the hour together, and use the longest words, and all the outward forms and symbols of argumentative discourse ; but the mimicry and poll-parrotism break out at last. A friend, himself an ardent Republican, gave me recently a forcible illustration of the painful shallowness of the negro intellect, even when trained to an apparently high degree of culture. He was riding in a railway carriage, and close by him were two full negroes, one a minister of some one of the innumerable denominations that here obtain ; the other a " class-leader " in a Sunday school. Both were well-dressed, neat, fluent, and scrupulously courteous and urbane. It was a Sunday morning, and the clerical negro was reading an illustrated newspaper, say *Harper's Weekly*. The class leader took occasion to express, very respectfully, his surprise that his companion, " a minister ob de Gosple," should be perusing so mundane a publication on the Sabbath. The clergyman, in a torrent of verbosity, justified himself, mainly on the principle that to the pure all things were pure. "Oh, sa! I admit de question," the other replied; "but I tink you gyrate too much." "Pray dispossess yourself of dat conception, sa," quoth the clergyman, "it is not de gyration, but de develoff-ment, &c., &c.," and so on through mere verbiage. "There, now your argument is a little diminutive," the class leader interposed. This unlucky remark broke down with one blow the pack of rhetorical cards which the sable ecclesiastic had been building up. Somehow the word "diminutive" was not to be found in his copious vocabulary. "*Diminufive you-self, you dam black niggar*," he screamed out; "*what, you call me diminufive, you ugly cuss? I cave you dam black head in.*" And to it they went, tooth and nail, till the hard skulls "collided" and the wool flew by handfuls. You will please to observe that when coloured people quarrel they exchange the word "nigger" as a term of reproach very freely. I give this conversation precisely as it was related to me by the gentleman who overheard it.

I have heard a story of a judge who addressed a poor wretch convicted of petty larceny in this fashion. "Prisoner, Providence has endowed you with health and strength, *instead of which you go about the country stealing ducks.*" I had been fed with all these fine tales about "righteous war," "holy crusade," "regeneration of an oppressed race," and the rest of it, *instead of which*, I found the black man at the North a despised, derided, degraded, persecuted, mal-treated outcast. I found that in the month of July, 1863, the mob of New York had been burning negro orphan asylums and hanging negroes to lamp-posts for the simple offence of being negroes. *Instead of which,* I found that a negro at the North was not permitted to compete with a white man in any lucrative or honourable walk of life, and that he was not even allowed to earn his bread by the sweat of his brow. That so far from keeping the meanest corner-grocery or ribbon-and-tape shop, he could not be a bar-keeper or serve in a drapery-store ; that there were no negro carpenters, tailors, shoemakers, or bricklayer's labourer even ; that he was not allowed to drive an engine, or stoke a furnace, or act as conductor to a horse-car. That if he entered one of those cars, or an omnibus, he was liable to be turned out neck and crop on the mere complaint of a delicately sensitive white person. That he was not admissible to the white man's church, to the white man's theatre, to the white man's concert-room or lecture-hall. *Instead of which,* I found him lurking in policy-shops—the pettiest of gambling-dens—or keeping the doors of faro-banks. I found that he, all nigger as he was, was not suffered to become a nigger minstrel, or at least to commingle with the high and mighty whites who blacked their faces for the delectation of the audiences at Wood's or Christie's. *Instead of which,* I heard the negro cursed and vilified on every side as the cause of the war and the only obstacle to peace. *Instead of which,* I have heard it said five hundred times by educated and intelligent American gentlemen that if the South would only come back to the Union they might keep their slaves in *sæcula sæculorum;* that the genuine abolition party was still an insignificant minority of fanatical enthusiasts ; and that if Republicans as well as Democrats were polled on the two

questions, " Union with Slavery," or "Disunion without
Slavery," the vast majority would be for the Union and the
"Domestic Institution."

And these, dear sir, are the two prime reasons why for
twelve months I incessantly grumbled. You told me, you
told us, you told all England and all Europe, that yours was
the freest country in the world. I found it governed by a
worse than Russian despotism. My own immunity from mal-
treatment is no proof of the liberty you enjoy. Personally
you may have despised me. *Nationally you did not dare
touch one hair of my head.* The meanest of British subjects
could not be treated like Don José de Arguelles. I was as
safe at the Brevoort House as in Guilford Street, Russell
Square. Besides, I know your good nature, and the innocu-
ousness of your rage, and while I have been damned in the
columns of your newspapers in the morning I have socially
dined with your foremost editors in the evening.

You told me, you told us, you told England and Europe
that yours was a righteous war and a holy crusade to emancipate the Black Man. I have found the Black Man as I have
described him, decidedly not better, and as decidedly much
worse for your efforts in his behalf. The more cruel among
your slavedrivers—for that you have had a Legree among
you, now and then, I no more question than that we have had
a Governor Wall or a Mother Brownrigge—sometimes
whipped the Black Man to death. You have been emancipating him into the grave by the thousand and the tens of
thousands. You will emancipate him out of the land at last
altogether, and there are a good many of your countrymen,

dear sir, who will opine that such an affranchisement of ex-
tinction and extermination would be about the best thing
which could happen for the United States of America.

You may object—and I have heard this objection pettishly
adduced, time and again—that the decay of your liberties and
your inconsistency in the treatment of the Black man are no
business of ours. Why should we meddle in your concerns?
Que diable irions-nous faire dans votre galère? I am reminded " in this matter" (and to help out *your* argument, dear
sir,) of the story of Deacon Peabody and his pigs—a story
which I daresay I do not quote correctly. It run somewhat
thus : Somebody halloaed over a fence to Peabody, crying :
" Say, Deacon, the pigs are rooting up your potato patch."
To which Deacon Peabody answered, " 'Taint any consarn o'
your'n ; they're my pigs and my potato patch." Have we,
then, any right to call your attention to the fact that certain
unholy swine are grubbing up a garden in which once grew
the choicest fruits and the fairest flowers? I answer that
we have. Your great and standing complaint against us—a
complaint which is a hundred times bitterer, and is more sorely
felt than any alleged grievances about Alabamas, Floridas,
Tallahassees, Alexandras, Slidells and Masons, St. Alban's
raiders, Lake Erie pirates, and what not—is that, since the
commencement of this struggle, the governing classes of
England have denied you their sympathy. By the governing
classes I mean not only the Lords and most of the M.P.'s
and the moneyocracy, but those who govern by reason of
their capacity or their social influence. You have the
fanatics, the visionaries, the donkeys and the doctrinaires of

Great Britain on your side; you have John Bright and a part
of Manchester, and the conceited and cracked-brained scio-
lists of the *Tom Brown* school; you have Professor Goldwin
Smith and Mr. George Thompson ; but the majority of cultivated Englishmen, albeit they may abhor slavery, and depre-
cate recognition of the South, do not sympathise with the
North. You would have given your ears for such sympathy.
You would give your ears for it now. One-half of your
abuse of England is due to the fact that you consider
England the only country worth abusing. America is a
stage, and Americans are always acting to a British
audience. Why have we hissed ? Why haven't we applauded ? Why do we withhold our sympathy? For three
reasons, dear sir.

First, because we conceived that the South, if it found its
connection with the North intolerable, had quite as great a
right to secede from it as you had to secede from us in 1776,
because we wanted you to take our tea, and pay for some
two-penny half-penny stamps. I have seen the stamps
and the tea in the Museum of the Historical Society at
Boston.

Second, because we conceive that you have not been sincere in your declaration that the war was undertaken and
carried on for the liberation of the oppressed and enslaved
African ; and because we believe that the real object of the
war is to obtain domination over the South, and that you
would throw the negro overboard to-morrow if you could
restore the Union by sacrificing him.

Third, and last, because the history of the war as set

forth by your own writers and speakers has proved it to have been conducted under circumstances of rapine, spoliation, and atrocity, than which the wars of Attila or Genseric can show nothing more flagitious, and in a spirit worthier of Pagans and Cannibals than of Christian gentlemen.

As for the other things I have grumbled at they are as the shadow of the shadow of smoke. What does it matter now, if Mrs. Trollope saw a gentleman at the playhouse put his feet up on the ledge of the dress circle, or was shocked at the spectacle of a young lady in Virginia lacing her stays in the presence of a black footman? Mrs. Trollope is dead. We must all die. "You know you must," I quote Jeremy Taylor. Will it matter ten or fifteen years hence if one surly English traveller the more or the less found fault with your hotels or your spittoons, your *cuisine* or your cock-tails, your quack advertisements or your railway cars, the square-toed boots of your men, or the false back-hair of your young ladies? Has all that the travellers have said for thirty years prevented New York from numbering in the year 1864 a population of one million of souls? Will ten thousand grumblers prevent your becoming in another half century a nation seventy millions strong? There, let the grumblers be ; and the fools who declare you to be " sunk in a hopeless abyss of ruin." You are pretty deep in the mire just now ; but you will come out of it some day stronger and better in every way. Did not Dean Swift once invent a factitious proverb : " The more dirt, the less hurt"? May that be *your* case.

This is the end of my justification. The rest of the book

must speak for itself. The only merit I claim concerning it is that the things I had to say against the Americans were uttered whilst I was living amongst them—were said to their face and in their teeth, and that I waited until I came home to say that which was favourable of a people of whose many great and noble and generous qualities there cannot be a sincerer admirer than I am—among whom I spent many happy months, and where I have left many of the dearest friends I ever had in my life.

CHAPTER II.

DOCTOR MAGINN once began an article on poor Haydon, the painter, in *Fraser* with these agreeable words, " Come along, donkey, and be cudgelled ;" and he proceeded to cudgel him accordingly. That was the style in the good old days of " slashing writers." Now it is very easy to apostrophise the City of New York with a " Come along, Gotham, and be described," but it is by no means so light a task to describe it.

Consider its size. Have you read Camden ? Are you familiar with Stow ? Have you taken down one of the volumes of the great Crowle Pennant in the Print Room of the British Museum ? Have you Charles Knight's "London" on your own library shelves ? Are the names of J. T. Smith, and John Timbs and Peter Cunningham, familiar in your mouth as household words ? Do you know how many hundreds of articles about London antiquities and London life and London characters there are in that dead-and-gone periodical " Household Words" itself ? And Paris ! Are there not Mercier and Edmond Texier, and scores of feuilletonistes, satirists, and antiquarians writing, week after week, scores of sketches of Paris, grave or solemn, in scores

of papers big and little ? Pelion has been piled upon Ossa
in the way of description of the two great capitals of European civilisation ; yet it is felt on all sides that not half the
truth has been told—that in both London and Paris there
are innumerable inner recesses and penetralia which are still,
to most intents and purposes, a *terra incognita*, and that
there are as many thousand denizens of the French and
English metropolis, knowing not their right hand from their
left, as there were in Nineveh of old.

And why ? Because they are so enormous, and their
population is so prodigious. A lifetime will not suffice for
description when we have to deal with millions. We may
take one cluster of streets, a few groups of character, half-a-
dozen phases of life ; but we do, at the most, but fringe the
huge continent of brick and stone, and, when we are broken
and exhausted, are mournfully conscious of the vast outlying
districts we have failed to explore. We have been but as
topographical Newtons—as children picking up pebbles and
shells on the sea-shore while the great ocean of life lay un-
discovered around us. " Oh ! my Book, my Book ! " murmured the dying Buckle at Damascus. Poor fellow, he
knew that with all his well-filled, common-place ledgers,
with all the noble volumes he had actually put forth, he
had but written, as yet, the Preface to the History of Civilisation.

Do not believe that the mania for excess in architecture
was destroyed by the confusion of tongues. In most of us
who think that we can think there is implanted, inherent
and innate, an ambition to set about the building of Babel.

We all want to do the " big thing on Snyder"—to write the Big Book. Some of us are privileged to reach the second or third story, some even rise to the attics. To one or two in a generation is it given to wave a flag from the chimney-pots, and see the end crown the work : then they may walk to and fro in their gardens at Lausanne, like Gibbon, chuckling softly and rubbing their hands : then perchance they may regard their accomplished labour as Dom Calmet did his Dictionary of the Bible, and sigh, " I shall never live to correct the errors which are in that work;" these are the fortunate ones—the elect ; but how many are destined to faint and falter and die, or ever the foundations are dug or the scaffolding reared ?

The British public, to say nothing of my publisher, would be extremely dissatisfied were I to confine this work to a description of the aspect and a commentary on the manners of New York. Yet, give me a thousand pages and I could fill them all—aye, and with smaller type than that which Messrs. Tinsley have allotted me—with variations on this solitary theme. New York, from the Bay ; New York from the top of old Trinity church ; New York from the Central Park ; New York from Brooklyn Heights; the merchants, the bankers, the hack-drivers, the rowdies, the stock-jobbers, the hotel-keepers, the bar-tenders, the corner grocery keepers, the quacks, the photographers, the dandies, the corn-cutters, the editors, the blacklegs, the shoulder-hitters, the " hard cases," the militia colonels, the bounty-jumpers, the crimps, the dry goods drummers, the water-side sharks, the " war widows," the niggers, the miscegenators, the free-lovers, the

spiritualists, the railway-conductors, the policemen, the trot-
ting-match jockies, the pilots, the gold speculators, the belles,
the boarding-house keepers, the log-rollers, wire-pullers, pipe-
layers, engineers, financeerers, war-parsons, office-seekers,
poets, artists, Ethiopian minstrels, critics, connoisseurs, Irish
hod-carriers, German tailors, bootmakers, fiddlers, trumpeters,
and lager beer-sellers, the refugees, thieves, loafers, knaves
and fools of New York the tremendous. I want a page for
each and every one of these types of character, and five
hundred more for the five hundred additional types which
will surely suggest themselves so soon as ever I get a pen in
my hand.

I want space to describe the oyster eating at Fulton
market, and the ice-cream devouring at Taylor's. I should
properly go through the great hotels *seriatim*, and give a
separate chapter to the Astor House, the Fifth Avenue, the
St. Nicholas, the Everett, the Metropolitan, the New York,
the Prescott, the Astor Place, the Brevoort, the Hoffman, the
Clarendon, the Albemarle, the Lafarge, and even the Jones
House ; for all of these hostelries are peculiar and characteristic. Then I should take the theatres of New York—the
which, I may remark, are the prettiest and most comfortable
in the whole world—and wander from the Academy to
Wallack's, from Niblo's to the Winter Garden, or from "Four-
forty-four" to the Bowery. After that should come an
appreciative essay on the three gastronomic temples owned
by the immortal Lorenzo Delmonico—let it be recorded to
the honour of that urbane restaurateur, that so far as his
Fifth Avenue establishment was concerned, and although he

knew the subscriber to be an enemy to the United States, he gave that subscriber frank and cordial credit, and could only, by vehement entreaty, be persuaded to send in his bill at the expiration of every month. Following the triple Delmonico should come at least twenty pages devoted to the Maison Dorée, the second great restaurant of New York (some connoisseurs declare it to be the first), and a shorter article on the Casa Reilly. Then we might have something discreet to say about the divers "tigers" that are to be fought all night, and sometimes all day—by which I mean the gaming-houses—and the enlivening games of faro, euchre, poker, and old sledge. Then we might take the cars to one of the hundred ferries, and watch the huge East River steamboats bound for the Sound and the Fall River, or cross to Brooklyn, or Hoboken, or Jersey City, or Staten Island, or wander for hours by the waterside, and the crowded wharves, and mingle with the salmagundi of all nations just vomited forth at the Emigrant Depôt at Castle Garden. Or, being Sunday, we might attend Grace Church the fashionable, and gaze upon Mr. Brown, the stout and superb sexton thereof, or enter the pews of more staid and orthodox Trinity, or go and hear Doctor Chapin on Universalism, or Dr. Cheever upon blood-shed, or the Reverend Henry Ward Beecher on the Gospel according to Joe Miller. I need at least two chapters for the Central Park, one for the beautiful landscape gardening displayed there, the ornamental bridges, the magnificent carriage drives, the garden of acclimatization, the charming blending of sylvan and rocky scenery; and another chapter for the wealth and fashion and splendour of the afternoon

Corso, the elegance of the dandies, and the beauty and grace
of the fair equestrians. Then, I think I would write from
forty to fifty pages about the pretty toilettes and prettier
faces one meets with on Broadway, on a fine afternoon—say
between Union Square and Canal Street. After that a
genteel description of Fifth Avenue, right from Washington
Square to the Reservoir, should follow. After that, if you
pleased, we would take a stroll among the old clothesmen in
Chatham Street, that transatlantic Holywell Street—skim
through the Fourth Ward—see where once all the poverty
and vice of the infamous Five Points festered and seethed,
but where now are schools, mission-houses, and lodging-
houses for little newsboys; or plunge head over heels in
the humours of the Bowery—its Lager Bier Gartens and
halls for the performance of the much-loved nigger-minstrels.
A considerable section should be devoted to the underground
life of New York—to the myriad cellars, now splendid and
now squalid, which yawn beneath the feet of the wayfarer,
and which are now bullion-offices and exchange brokers, now
bars and grog shops, now oyster and now ice-cream saloons,
now German "*barbier stüben*," now stationers' shops, now
restaurants where "meals at all hours" are advertised. Stop.
I am reminded in this connection, as Mr. Abraham Lincoln
says, of a little story. There was an ordinary down town
once, where, for the sum of fifty cents, you were entitled to
sit down at a table groaning with substantial viands, and eat
as long and as much as ever you chose. A gaunt man from
Maine, a Solon Shingle kind of individual, entered this
ordinary one day, and proceeded to cram his fifty cent's

worth. He went in for the beef and he went in for the mutton, and he went in for the turkey and cranberry sass. He was death on squash. He devoured stewed tomatoes until you might have thought he was Eve's brother-in-law. He was a whale at sweet potatoes. He punished the squash, the celery, and the cold slaugh, awfully. He roamed like a bee from flower to flower—from beefsteak to huckleberry pie, from Vanilla ice-cream to pork and beans, from succotash to meringues, from Phipps's ham to Indian pudding. He ate like Gargantua, like Bernard Kavanagh the Fasting Man (when there was nobody looking), like Ben Brust in "Gideon Giles the Roper," like Dr. Johnson at Streatham, when the veal pie and plums were to his liking, and there was plenty of capillaire to pour into his chocolate, and good store of anchovy sauce wherewith to souse his plum pudding. He ate until the guests regarded him with affright, and the waiters gathered round him and scanned him with minatory looks. He finished up with a fishball or two and a couple of cobs of hot corn with plenty of fresh butter, drank a mighty draught of cold water, ordered a tooth-pick, and tendered fifty cents in payment for his inordinate feed. The "boss," or master of the establishment, folded his arms, and with knitted brow and quivering lips replied, "Don't see it, stranger; I guess it's a quarter more." "Why," expostulated the gaunt man from Maine, pointing to a printed notice on the wall, "I guess that paper says 'dinner, fifty cents.'" "Yes," rejoined the "boss," "*but when a man eats as if there was no hereafter, we charge him seventy-five cents.*" The connection in the eating-house-keeper's mind between moderation in eating and a belief in a future state, struck me, at the time the story was told me, as being exceedingly droll.

Having left the cellars I might—if you would only concede me the thousand pages I covet—mount four or five flights of stairs with you, and see what the artists of New York—a worthy, jovial, hard-working, catholic crew they are—were doing in their studios. Then we might pop in—hoping we did not intrude—on the editors. Subsequently we might pay the Bohemians a visit, take a glass of genuine English pale ale at the "House of Lords" in Houston Street, a queer comfortable hostelry very un-American in its aspect, bearing the same relation to literary-theatrical life in New York as the old "Crown" in Vinegar Yard did to the London Bohemia in the days when the Punch Club was in its glory, and the Douglases, the Howards, the Harries, the Marks, the Alberts, the Ebenezers, the Percivals, the W. M. T.'s (sometimes) of old heard the chimes at midnight. Which chimes are now very dumb indeed, and the few survivors of those triple bob majors have forgotten that they ever heard them. Perchance at the "House of Lords" we might meet a famous actor or two, a critic or so, a poet who has not yet made his fortune by dabbling in Erie or Harlem, a painter—stay, the painters mostly affect the muslin-curtain-hung bowers of the "Waverley"—and any number of newspaper men. It may not be their ordinary haunt, for I saw very little of Bohemia while I was in America. It was my business, you see, to travel in a strange country, and I had no right to go home before my time. Aha! I hear my old friends Hircius and Spungius

screech—"The vagabond confesses that he is a Bohemian."
Yes, I was born in the Armo-gasse, just off the Cour des
Miracles, in the city of Prague. I was brought up among
the Zingari, attained some proficiency in the Rommany lan-
guage, and have some slight knowledge of the affairs of
Egypt. I had a sister called Esmeralda, who was very fond
of a goat, was much beloved by a deformed wretch by the
name of Quasimodo, and was unfortunately hanged on the
Parvis of Notre Dame de Paris. My putative mamma,
Azucena, got into trouble (through some tender passages of
mine with a certain Leonora—*non di scordar di me;*
Lenny—) and was barbecued on a gridiron by the cruel
Conte de Luna, Chairman of Quarter Sessions, and member
of the Society for the Suppression of Vice. I know all the
harbours on the sea-coast of Bohemia. I can tell fortunes if
you will cross my hand with silver, and whisper a horse if
you will lend me one, and I think I could do a little tinkering
if you would confide to me your kettle. I wonder what a
Bohemian really is. Sam Johnson, I suppose, was one—the
glorious old Doctor, who kept school and slept on bulks and
in the ashes of glass houses, who kicked his heels in Chesterfield's ante-chamber and cowered in a horseman's coat behind
a screen in Mr. Cave's dining-room, eating humble-pie and
correcting the proofs of the Parliament of Lilliput ; who was
a dozen times locked up in a sponging-house, and had to
write "Rasselas" to pay for his mother's funeral, and was given
to carrying home exhausted wantons on his back, and to
entertaining in his house blind women and starved-out
apothecaries, and lived to write the "Lives of the Poets" and

the "English Dictionary." I suppose this man, whose bio-
graphy Peers and M.P.'s and Professors are now glad to
annotate and gloze over, was a Bohemian. But, I suppose,
the drunken, conceited, crack-brained, worthless scamp,
Jemmy Boswell, and the gross, fat-headed brewer, Thrale, who
gorged himself at last into a fit of apoplexy and died from
overeating, were not Bohemians. Oh dear no ! Jemmy was
the heir to a baronetcy, and Thrale was a parliament-man—
a gentleman of high social position, and the proprietor of a
brew-house in Southwark, which his widow sold to a Quaker
for a hundred-thousand pounds, vending, not only so many
boilers and vats, but " the potentiality of growing rich beyond
the dreams of avarice." And I think that were Spenser and
Shakspere alive, and were they to go into partnership as
poets, they would be held, in the opinion of the Court News-
man and the select circles, vastly inferior to Barclay and
Perkins. Bohemians ! Why, David the King was a Bohemian. Why, Napoleon the Great was one. Work hard
and scorn the world, and the dullards and the dolts will fling
Bohemian in your teeth. To the subscriber, Bohemianism at
the *mezzo cammin* of life resolves itself into having worked
twelve hours a day for many years, into having paid his
butcher and his baker and avoided that Insolvent Court
through which so many non-Bohemians have genteelly passed,
with never having been indebted to a patron for a penny, to
a minister for a place in the Custom House, or to a critic for
a kind word.

The " House of Lords " is a tavern, and therefore beyond
the pale of gentility ; but I shall ever preserve a kindly re-

membrance of the place, for there I first met Artemus Ward, the drollest of living American humorists.

Could I say anything more—if you granted me those thousand pages—about New York? Good lack! my tongue and pen should run faster than ever well-trained mare flew over the Fashion Course. Wall Street and William Street! —what might not be written about the Gold Room and the Stock Exchange, the speculators in " corners," and the jobbers who were " short" of Harlem? Maiden Lane, what opportunities for word painting do not thy stores, teeming with multifarious merchandise, afford! John Street, is there nothing to be said concerning thy steel! Pine Street, could not pages be indited concerning thy counting houses! Nassau Street, stands there not, at the corner of one of thy blocks, the office of the *New York Herald ;* and out of the *Herald* and its editor and proprietor might not many chapters be made ! Why, a whole volume or two has been written on James Gordon Bennett. Do not Fourth Avenue and Sixth Avenue invite description ! Shall nothing be said about Grand Street ! Am I to pass by the grand Pompeian clothing establishments of Broadway and Canal Streets ; the dazzling goldsmith's wares of Tiffany and Ball and Black ; the sumptuous, marble-fronted, dry goods store of E. T. Stewart ; the numberless *modistes* and *fleuristes* of the fashionable quarters in silent contempt ! A chapter for Washington Market ; a chapter for the Tombs ; a chapter for Brady the photographer ; a chapter for the Dusseldorf Gallery, another for the Cooper Institute, another for the common schools, another for the free-lovers, another for the express and railway ticket-offices, another for the "Oriental Saloons with pretty waiter girls," another for the boarding-houses; ten chapters, at least, for Shoddy—Cotton Shoddy, Gold Shoddy, Scrip Shoddy, Contract Shoddy, Political Shoddy, and Petroleum Shoddy, and still my task would be but half accomplished. I should have then left out the somnambulists, the mesmerists, and the fortune-tellers, the characteristics of Mackerelville and the curiosities of Communipaw, the sports of High Bridge, the delights of the Bloomingdale Road, and the beauties of the Greenwood Cemetery over the water; to say nothing of the Astor and Mercantile Libraries, Barnum's Museum, the City Hall, and the art collection of the Aspinwalls, the Wrights, the Lennoxes, the Barlows, the Grahams of New York and its vicinity.

But I haven't got the thousand pages. I am near the end of my tether already; and it has come to this: that of a city of a million souls I can give you no more detailed account than can be comprised in a narrative of a walk down Broadway.

Now Broadway is literally the back-bone of New York, and indeed the shape of the city proper is not unlike that of the fish called the sole. Assume Broadway to be the spine, the bridge over the Harlem river the head, the Battery and Castle Garden the tail; the ferries to Brooklyn and Jersey City the fins, the avenues running parallel to the spine the roes—but there are eight—and the streets that branch off at right angles, from Eighth as high up, I think, as Seventy-third Street, will stand for that fringe of small bones in the sole which, nicely browned, you are always tempted to eat, and which half-choke you. My Manhattan fish must be a sole *à la Normande,* for the shores of New Jersey and Long Island will represent the edges of the dish, the East and the North, the Harlem river, and the Bay, will stand for the sauce, and the numerous exquisitely beautiful islands which dot the surface of these waters may do duty for the morsels of mushroom and cockscomb which make the garniture of a *sole à la Normande* so delicious. The simile I have striven to establish may be but questionably appropriate, since a sole is the one fish quite unknown in the New York market. Aha! my luxurious brothers, you have no soles. You may order one at Delmonico's, or the Maison Dorée; but they will bring you a sorry substitute in the shape of a *filet,* a *gratin,* a *Normande,* or a *friture* of flounder.

Well, then, I will take this vertebrated column, and endeavour to trace its course through the great corpus of Manhattan :—only I must begin with the lumbar vertebræ, then touch the dorsal, and terminate with the cervical.

I came to New York, on the twenty-ninth of November, 1863, by the wrong door. I should properly have chosen, in England, one of the New York in lieu of the Boston steamers of the Cunard line. As it was, instead of crossing the Atlantic "right away" in the superb "Scotia" or the luxurious "Persia," and entering the beautiful bay of New York by the Narrows, I chose, or had chosen for me, the comfortable but rather slow-going "Arabia," a Boston boat. Eleven days would have sufficed to bring us direct to New York; but in the voyage to Boston we consumed fourteen and a-half—were half-smothered in the usual fogs about the banks of Newfoundland, and delayed the usual twelve hours at Halifax, too short a time to see anything of the place, and too long a time to be moored by the side of a coal wharf. Then, when we reached Boston, we had to pass through the ordeal of a Custom House (of which I shall have to speak more in detail anon), whose officers have, to say the very least, a great deal to learn in the way of civility. We had to wait several hours for a train from Boston to Stonington, where we left the cars to enter one of those floating palaces, the river steam-boats, and we did not arrive at Pier Some-thing-or-another, East River, New York, before seven o'clock in the morning. Here some travelling companions, Ame-ricans, total strangers to me when I went aboard the " Arabia," but eminently polite, cordial, and obliging—*as all Americans who have travelled in Europe are*—left me. I felt very much like an oyster at the bottom of a barge. The 'tween decks of the river steamer looked so very big. Another three-quarters of an hour were consumed in extri-cating my luggage from the monstrous pile of trunks and carpet-sacks which crowded the gangway; and, in spite of the admirable system of checking (the which I cannot too often praise, nor too highly recommend for adoption in England), I found that the task of getting what belongs to one very tedious and very trying to the temper. You see that I did not yet " know the ropes," *i.e.*, understand the ways of the country ; nor, indeed, had I yet learnt the ways of any country where nobody will render you any assistance, and where even you are often unable to purchase for a pecuniary consideration the services of your fellow-man. Everything is attainable on the North American continent, if you only choose to strive for it, save human bone and muscle.

The complaint of Tom Hood's Needlewoman would be out of place here. Bread is very cheap, and flesh and blood are very dear. And rightly so, perhaps ; although, by a strange inconsistency, in this very land where a man's labour is so expensive, they hold his life very cheaply, and kill him with much more alacrity than we starve him.

I got my traps at last, and selecting from a yelling crowd of hack drivers on the wharf (they were fortunately not permitted to come on board) one particular person whose face I thought looked honest, I entered his two-horse vehicle, saw my affairs chained and grated on behind, and desired to be driven to the hotel to which I had been recommended, and to the proprietor of which I had a card of introduction :— the Brevoort House, in Fifth Avenue. In this I showed, once more, my ignorance of the "ropes." I ought, in the first place, to have secured my hack driver, given him my brass luggage checks, got into his carriage, and waited tranquilly there until he had removed my trunks from chaos. Next, I should have made a bargain with him ere I engaged him. The result of my neglecting to do so was, that the rascal, when I arrived at my journey's end, had the face to charge me five dollars, or one pound sterling (say fifteen shillings in actual bullion, gold being then at between forty and fifty premium), for a five miles' drive. I use the term rascal advisedly. I am sure that all unprejudiced Americans will agree with me, that, on the whole surface of the habitable globe, there does not exist a more villanous and unconscionable crew of extortioners than the hack drivers of New York. I mean those at large, and those who casually ply for hire. If you go to a decent livery stable, they will let you a capital carriage and pair, with a civil and intelligent driver, charge you but moderately, and give you "tick" besides. I had a friend who always took six months' credit for his coach-hire. If you engage one while you are staying at an hotel, they will put your carriage hire in the bill, and not charge you more than a moderate commission for doing so. But these are among the "ropes" of which you do not learn the use until you are just ready to leave the country. A year in the States, abating two and a half months I spent in the West Indies and Mexico, cost me just a thousand pounds, which, with gold ultimately at a hundred and fifty premium, represented about two thousand five hundred per annum; and the major part of this time I was alone; yet I have very little doubt, that, were I to return to the States, and to stay there a similar period, even with gold at a more inflated rate, I should not spend more than five hundred pounds.

Young Traveller, I beseech you to bear these things in mind, if you would save money in the States. Lay in a copious stock of boots, gloves, overclothing and underclothing, before you start; don't smoke cigars, or, if you must, bring them with you; drink lager beer (if you can) instead of claret or champagne; live at a boarding-house (also if you can) instead of an hotel; patronise the horse-cars, to the exclusion of hackney-coaches; never ask anybody to dinner; never play euchre at Saratoga, poker at Baltimore, roulette at Washington, or faro anywhere; avoid junketings to Catskill or to Long Branch ; lead a virtuous life ; and when down town, dine at Bangs ; and you will be, if not happy, at least economical in New York.

The hack driver discovering that, in my inexperience, I was quite willing to allow him to take an inch, was not slow in availing himself of the opportunity to seize an ell. I was entitled to the entire interior of his vehicle—had I consented to receive any travelling companions the law would only allow him to charge me fifty cents for my ride—but he doubtless thought that he might as well make a good thing out of me, and accordingly favoured me in the course of our journey with no less than three fellow-insides. I daresay that the rogue openly plied for fares as he drove me along. I did not demur, having been such a very few hours in America. I thought it might be, as the Spaniards allege, when subjecting you to any particularly outrageous measure of extortion, "*un costumbre del país.*" My first companion was a very tall officer in the army, with a red flannel shirt peeping from above the collar of his uniform, and who looked as though he were in the habit of going to bed but very rarely—and then of retiring to rest in his clothes. There was a good deal of whiskey in his hair, and of compound alcohol in his breath. He was perfectly affable, but very drunk, and his conversation was mainly made up of incoherent inquiries to the subscriber as to what was the general opinion of the "boys" as to the personal character of "Cheesewright," coupled with the slightly irrelevant information that he had lately given Cheesewright h——. As I had not the honour of Captain Cheesewright's acquaintance—I may as well call him Captain for courtesy's sake—I was naturally unable to enlighten the officer in the red shirt on a topic in which he appeared to take so much interest. The remainder of the time I passed in this gentleman's company he occupied first in withdrawing from the toe of his left boot a roll of dollar bills, which he had seemingly stowed away there for safety when the whiskey began to get into his hair, and next in endeavouring to adjust round his neck a paper collar. He left me at the Astor House, where I presume he was satisfactorily "fixed up" by the dexterous barbers of that establishment, and with the aid of hair brushes, combs, *pommade hongroise*, bay-rum, and a cocktail or two, was enabled to make quite a genteel appearance at the Astor House *table d'hôte*; but he took care to repeat to me, as he left the carriage, that the h—— he had given Cheesewright was of the very liveliest and completest description.

During the twelve months I passed in America, I suppose that I met and conversed with at least five hundred officers in the army of the United States. With many, and of all ranks, from generals to second-lieutenants, I had the honour to be on terms of considerable intimacy. From several members of the staff of General Dix I received a great deal of kindness and courtesy; and to General Dix himself I had the honour to be presented. The gallant officer in command of the Department of the East did not threaten to send me to Fort Lafayette, as he is said to have threatened poor Mr. Manhattan,* but, on the contrary, was exceedingly polite, and

---

* This person's name was Joseph Scoville, familiarly called "Joe." He had been private secretary to Mr. John C. Calhoun, and was at the time of

only regretted that the friend who introduced me to him had come too late to enable the General to lend him his yacht for an excursion up the East River. From a number of officers of every grade and every arm of the service, I received in Virginia nothing but cordiality, hospitality, and attention. The very fact, indeed, of being an Englishman was at the head-quarters of the Army of the Potomac a passport to every kind of urbanity and civility. Is it, then, gross ingratitude for the favours I confess to have received to set down that the first officer I met in New York was "tight," and looked as though he had not been to bed for a week? I hope not. I should be ashamed to say *ab uno disce omnes*. The plain truth of the matter is that the American officer is, like every-thing else in the Northern States, a "little mixed." Side by side with the scholar and the gentleman, the young man of family and fortune, the graduate of Harvard, the millionaire, perchance, you will find some worthless "cuss," some incor-rigible "hard-case," who in the armies of England and France would be forthwith cashiered; but who in the legions of the

his death "Reader" to the Common Council of New York, the members of which august body passed resolutions of regret and condolence with his widow on the occasion of his demise. I never met "Manhattan," and although I could not, of course, but hear a great deal about him, I see no reason, in his case, to depart from the maxim " *de mortuis*." He has been described to me by many cultivated Americans as a man of rare but mis-directed abilities. He wrote a novel, entitled in the United States *Vigor*, and in England *Marion*, in which there is a kind of apotheosis of Mr. James Gordon Bennett, and in which, floating in the midst of a *cloaca* of obscenity, there are some very curious revelations of the life of New York thirty years since. The New York press were very much enraged at "Manhattan's" letters to the *Morning Herald* and *Standard* having been in any way deemed expositions of the thought or feeling of Americans on political topics. He was, I believe, by birth a South Carolinian, and in politics a Secessionist.

North is permitted to retain his commission and his shoulder straps, either because he has some miserable political influence, or because officers of a higher moral status than he are hard to get, and his superiors do not care about going further and faring worse. Since the time of which I write, a great many of the hardest "cases" in the Union Army have been weeded out, and scarcely a month has elapsed without some especially disreputable "cusses" being turned out of their regiments by sentence of court-martial; but enough remain to render that "mixed" element of which I speak a very visible and repulsive presence.

This was my first travelling companion. I am photographing simply from the life, without ornament and without surplusage. My next was a clean-shaven gentleman, with a very high shirt collar, blue spectacles, an elaborately plaited frill, a broad-brimmed hat, and a long bottle-green surtout with brass buttons. He might have been a wealthy merchant or banker, or a gentleman of independent means. I bade him good morning, but he did not apparently hear my remark, and I did not care to "argufy" with him. Perhaps he took me for a "confidence man." He had with him a market-basket, containing, as I live, a red cabbage, a quantity of oyster-plant, several eggs, and about a pound and a half of raw beefsteak. Why not? Why should not elderly gentlemen go to market at eight o'clock in the morning if they so choose? At all events, the sight was novel and strange to me, and I put it down as another *costumbre del país*. I have since been given to understand that the custom of gentlemen going to market, although still obtaining in some of the cities, particularly in Philadelphia, is not nearly so prevalent as it was a quarter of a century since, and that in New York at least it is, with frugality, simplicity, early hours, and other old-fashioned practices, fast dying out.

The old gentleman with his marketing alighted a considerable way "up town," and my third and last fellow-passenger was a lady, who rode a considerable distance with the subscriber. She was young; not pretty, but passably good-looking; and very neatly and becomingly dressed. In particular I remember that she had a velvet bonnet, an ermine tippet, and a warm merino dress. Few as the hours of my stay in the States had been, I had already become aware, from my first railway journey, and from my first voyage in a steamboat, that the stories so frequently told of the cross-questioning and generally inquisitive characteristics of the people, were mere exaggerations, and that they are, on the contrary, extremely taciturn, and averse from colloquy with strangers.*

---

* The first question I put to a stranger on board the steamer from Honington subjected me to a reply which I considered to be so much deliberate rudeness. A knot of individuals were smoking at a table in the fore-part of the vessel, and the atmosphere, from tobacco and kerosene lamps, being rather hot and choky, I asked one of them if there were any means of reaching the upper deck. I did not know that on this upper deck no passenger was allowed. The person whom (civilly enough) I addressed, " guessed I might get there by climbing up the guys." That night I asked no more questions. I have sometimes fancied that the churlishness and bearishness I so frequently encountered were due to the fact of an Englishman carrying his country about with him in his countenance and on his tongue, but this I am led to believe now is not the case. The Americans are quite as surly to their own compatriots as to foreigners—*unless they are introduced to them.* For example, it is all but impossible to obtain a civil answer from the *employés* on a railway ; yet, on the occasion of my second journey from Boston to New York, having with me a young gentleman

But the young lady in the ermine tippet and velvet dress was, to my surprise, extremely communicative. She asked me where I came from, and when I told her that I was an Englishman just arrived, informed me that she had been twice to Canada, and that she had " royal blood in her veins."

from Harvard University, he was good enough to introduce me to the mail agent of the train, with whom, of course, I shook hands. This functionary inducted us into his private van, found a seat for us on the mail bags, allowed us to smoke, accepted a nip from a private brandy-flask, entertained us with political and social discourse, and was in all respects a model of obliging politeness. I was somewhat tickled also, many months later, when at a depôt at New York, and having a lady with me, I had asked at least a dozen times, and quite unavailingly, which was the shore-line train to Boston, being ultimately hailed by a gaunt gentleman in a yellow "duster," who was smoking, and reading the *Evening Post*, with his body on one chair and his feet on the top of the back of another, and who accosted me (we had wandered very far up the platform) in these remarkable words, " *My Christian friend, you're goin' a darned sight out of your way.*" I dare say this gentleman was in the employ of the railway company ; still we took his intimation as an extreme act of condescension. On the other hand, every American friend has scores of stories to tell you of the loquacity of eccentrics they have met in railway cars. Here are two or three culled at random. An esteemed Bostonian told me that once, happening to take out his watch (which was a repeater) in a car, a bony finger (the nail in half mourning) was pointed over his shoulder until it touched the dial, and a nasal voice asked, " *What do yer g'in for sich?*"—meaning how much he had paid for his watch. So, too, an Englishman in our legation at Washington told me that, going to Grover's Theatre one night, and happening to have a very handsome fur coat on (it was mid winter), the box-keeper proceeded to stroke him down, as though he had been a cat, exclaiming, " By ——!" (details unfit for publication), " *that's fine!*" Then there is the story, familiar perhaps to English ears, of the man with the wooden leg, who, being asked by a fellow-traveller how he had lost that limb, promised to tell him, only on condition that he should ask him no more questions, and the pledge having been given, proceeded to say that *it was bit off*. Finally, there is the anecdote of the gentleman who, anticipating the flood of questions with which he was about to be overwhelmed, forestalled his interrogators by making a clean breast of it in this wise : " My name's Colonel Zeph. B. Tompkins. I was born to hum, and raised down ter Martha's Vineyard. I'm forty-seven year old, and I kyant help it. I'm go'in ter New York, *and, if I like it, by —— I'll buy it!*"

I have not the least idea of what she meant by this ; but I know she told me so. Finally she said that she would be very pleased if I would call upon her. I could not do less than tender her my card. She remarked that she had no cards of her own about her, but that she resided at number something or another East Such-and-Such a Street. She was perfectly calm, self-possessed, and well-behaved, and she left me in a maze of utter bewilderment. Was this, I asked myself, another *costumbre del país?* The first American friend to whom I related this anecdote laughed, shook his head, and opined that the lady in ermine was a "hooker"—that is to say, an improper person. I don't believe she was. I believe this country to be so eccentric and so abnormal, that this and a hundred similar adventures might happen to a stranger during the first week of his stay ; only, and *per contrá*, it is quite feasible that he might remain five-and-twenty years in America without experiencing so queer a rencontre. Whoever and whatever the lady was I never found out. I forgot the number in the street she gave me, but I ascertained that the street itself was a perfectly respectable one. I tell the story as it occurred, with a full foreknowledge that many unthinking persons will laugh at me for having told it ; but of this I am certain, that, all man of the world as I vainly imagined myself to be, I was as completely perplexed and nonplussed by the lady in ermine as Peter Simple was by the obliging damsel he met at the Common Hard at Portsmouth. It is a luxury in the midst of a life full of very hard and cruel realisms to find that for once, if only for five minutes, you have been as innocent as a sucking-dove.

You know how difficult it is at your first rapid passage through a great city to gain even the feeblest idea of the aspect of the place. Some travellers have a rapider grasp of purview than others, and the education given by Robert Houdin's father to the aspiring conjuror would not be a bad preparation for a rapid tourist. M. Guizot's impressions of a rapid drive through the English metropolis on a wet day, in the memoirs of his mission to the Court of St. James's, is about the best sample extant of a clear, comprehensive, and accurate survey of a heterogeneous mass of externals, and London is perhaps the most difficult city in the world thus to describe *à la main*. St. Paul's is a stand-point from which to judge only a very small portion of the city, and when M. Guizot first came to London the new Houses of Parliament were not built. Milan is easier: the exquisite cathedral incompasses you and overshadows you everywhere. St. Petersburg is easier: almost everything worth seeing in the city of the Czar is visible from the Admiralty Square. Constantinople is easier still: you have but to stick to the view from the Golden Horn. Brussels is easiest perhaps of all: you are at once impressed with the Hotel de Ville, the Maison du Roy, the house of the Brasseurs, and the street at whose corner stands the Mannekin—" men may come and men may go, but I go on for ever "—and these are Brussels.

There is not much to be made out of New York, from the first *coup d'œil* at eight-thirty on a rainy morning. There are no public buildings of importance. There are few open spaces. One street succeeds another street, and one street is painfully like another street. Broadway, immeasurably long

as it seems to be, is not wide : at early morning its population is not picturesque ; and from the window of a hackney-
coach you can scarcely realise the altitude of its edifices.
Thus, and from the fact of the basements of the hotels being
mostly occupied by shops, I was not aware that I had passed
the St. Nicholas, the Metropolitan, the Lafarge, and the
Prescott. The Fifth Avenue, which, from its enormous size,
packing-case look, and comparatively isolated situation, can
hardly be mistaken anywhere, we did not pass. I don't
think the driver, although he had a fare so very ignorant of
" the ropes," took me more than a mile and-a-half out of my
way in order to set down the young lady in ermine. When
I was left alone I thrust my head out of the window, and, at
the risk of getting splashed up to the eyes with mud, tried to
see as much as ever I could ; but the result was not satisfactory. No grand temples, no imposing public offices, met
my view. I was not in the region of the great banking-
houses. I was being borne through a huge wilderness of
houses, houses, houses—all alike, all tall, all many-windowed,
all flat and uncorniced, and unporticoed :—all of the packing-
case style of architecture, in fact. Still, wet and cheerless
as the morning was, there abode not about the square flat
houses that desparate hue of dinginess engrained on London
by centuries of long leases and burning of coal-fires. A
London house seems to have been built, in the first instance,
to last for ever, and the fire-insurance plate of the Sun or the
Phœnix let into the brickwork has the venerable appearance
of a Roman medal. Then, addicted as we are supposed to be
to Quakerlike plainness in the exterior of our habitations,

there is probably no people on earth so fond as are the
English of sticking all over their houses trashy ornaments in
compo :—friezes without architraves, columns without cor-
nices, caryatides that do not support anything, vases that hold
nothing, masks and bas-reliefs that do not mean anything.
Regent Street is a kind of stucco-pie, full of this architectural mince-meat. The general effect is *nil;* but the
details are wonderful in their petty copiousness. This certainly has the advantage of giving to each house a distinctive
appearance of individuality; redeems to some extent the
grimness caused by the coal-smoke, and makes London,
albeit all but colourless, the least monotonous city in the
world. Which is a paradox, but is nevertheless true. In
Paris and the great continental cities the eye grows weary,
almost to despair, by the continuous succession of blank
stone walls, with here and there a grim *porte cochère,* the
desert being only relieved at the expiration of half-an-hour's
fatigue by some magnificent public edifice ; but in London,
grubby and dingy as every building is—from St. Paul's to a
pickle-shop—scarcely any two buildings are exactly like each
other. There is a difference in the pattern of a window-blind,
in the height of a door-step, in the colour and graining of the
door, in the model of the knocker or the area-railing, in the
fashion of the name plate, in the shape of the bell-handle.
Englishmen's houses are identical, and yet not alike ; just as
English John and Thomas are twins, and yet differ in a
hundred different characteristics. I am speaking of middle-
aged London. In the new metropolis which is starting up
around us there would seem to be a tendency towards the

uniform and stereotyped style of architecture ; and for that
reason I can scarcely imagine anything more dismal to a
lover of diversity in out-door life than the interminable series
of terraces, gardens, and groves—as grand as Gog and Magog,
but as like one another as two peas or two Southdowns—
which occupy the site of once cheerful and smiling market-
gardens at Bayswater and Old Brompton—I beg pardon :
Tyburnia and South Kensington :—I beg pardon again :—
Westbournia and Albertopolis.

The New York houses I have animadverted upon as somewhat monotonous are, let me hasten to admit, in the lower
part of the city, say from the Battery as far as the City
Hall Park. Above this point, and for many miles upwards, a
new Broadway extends, in whose edifices the wildest exuber-
ance of architectural whim is visible. But in old New York
—if any part of a city in which no tenement to which
Europeans would seriously accord the stamp of antiquity can
be termed old—the packing-case order naturally prevails. The
Dutch houses of New Amsterdam were mostly of timber, and
were in process of time burnt down. The first English colo-
nists were New Englanders : innovating, impatient, not over-
burdened with taste, and indeed contemning as useless, if not
denouncing as ungodly that which we admire as æsthetical.
Sir Christopher Wren is said to have planned the city of
Charleston, and the influence of the great architect may have
had as much to do with giving an aristocratic *cachet* to the
State of South Carolina as had the fact of its Constitution
being drawn up by John Locke.* But no Sir Christopher had

* This Constitution must have been, by all accounts, a wonderful docu-

anything to do with the building of New York. The place grew up anyhow, and you know of what kind is the colonial "anyhow." Four walls are run up, and covered with a roof, and pierced with so many doors and windows, and fit for occupation either as a store or a dwelling-house. The very name of " store " has a colonial sound, and conveys a rough- and-ready, impromptu, higgledy-piggledy mode of stowing away merchandise. When plate-glass windows are put into a store, and chandeliers, gilding, carpets, and easy-chairs are plenteous inside, and gentlemanly assistants—adepts in the arts of " dressing " a window, and " shaving " the ladies—are engaged, the store should, according to European notions, become a shop; but the Americans have chosen to retain the appellative of early colonial days.* There are receptacles for

---

ment. I never had time to disinter it from the shelves where it lies dor- mant, although I have little doubt that it is to be found, either in the Astor Library or among the treasures, "rare and peculiar," of the Bibliotheca Barloviana—the last of which is perhaps the richest collection of books on American subjects in the whole world. There was a triple order of aristocracy in John Locke's scheme: Palatines, Caciques, and Landgraves—Heliogabalus and Jack the Painter!—and vestiges of this wonderful oligarchy were extant, I am told, within the memory of men still living. A South Caro- linian gentleman I knew was acquainted with a family of "Palatine Smiths." It is almost needless to say that the great English philosopher's plan would not work.

* A charming volume might be written on those same colonial days, and, for aught I know, some New Yorker may have already done for the Empire city that which the New Englanders have done so charmingly for Boston and other Down East cities. But I never met with such a book. *Knicker- bocker's History* is confined to an account of the Dutch dominion in New Amsterdam, and breaks off at the cession of the island of Manhattan to Charles the Second's Duke of York. I should like to know something about the old Bowling Green, where are now the offices of the Cunard Steam Packet Company, but in the centre of which once stood a statue of George the Third. There is a legend that the statue, unpedestaled, headless, and otherwise mutilated, was within the present generation to be seen in a

goods to be sold by retail in Broadway, the most magnificent perhaps that can be found on the surface of the habitable globe; but they will continue to be "stores" to the end of time, unless our cousins consent to a compromise and call them *magasins*. They can't call them *dépôts*, that is the name they have conferred on their railway termini. They are precluded even from dubbing them "establishments," for when Shoddy sets up its carriage, Shoddy calls that carriage an "establishment." In America, therefore, kindly Mr. Paddy Green's standing reference to the status of Herr Von Joel might imply that the Herr would always be retained about Evans's as a groom or a coachman.

A compromise! Why not? America should be the land of compromises. If I err not, a certain Andrew Jackson, in his message to the Congress of the United States, in the year 1836, uttered something approaching the following words :— *" The peace of the country depends on the maintenance in good faith of those Compromises of the Constitution upon which the Union was founded."* Had those wise words been

builder's yard "down town:"—none so poor as to do it reverence. Poor old George! it seemed to be his lot to lose his head on both sides the Atlantic. Other antiquaries have it that the statue is still piously preserved in a good old Tory family somewhere on the Hudson River—a family who keep their Thanksgiving Day on the 4th of June, and hold the belief that the Lion and the Unicorn are destined to resume their sway in the state of New York. Such a family must have been that of the De Lanceys, of whom a story is related that one of its scions, a certain Colonel De Lancey, a Tory of the '76, being on his death-bed, and being told by the attendant clergyman that it was his duty to forgive all his enemies, including a family by the name of Livingston, who were great Republicans, and had gotten possession of a large part of the De Lancey estates, replied, that "he forgave them all; *but that if he met a Livingston in Heaven he would kick him!"*

remembered, instead of watchwords of frenzy and malignity,
and hatred, at any time within the last four years, what rivers
of blood might have been forbidden to flow!

But what need have I to harp on the bloodshed question
while I am merely staring out of a hackney-coach window at
the packing-case houses " down town" on a wet morning
Now, a caveat as to their packing-case appearance. They
are very plain—Puritanical, almost, in their bare simplicity of
outline ; but they are relieved from ugliness by the gay and
festive appearance given to them by the innumerable signs
and the colossal announcements stuck all over their fronts,
and mostly in gilt letters, setting forth the names and occupations of the store-keepers. For the design and nature of
the signs see the subscriber's paper on Schenectady ; but
there they are on a provincial and modified scale : in New
York they absolutely astound the beholder with their huge-
ness and their variety. When you have seen a succession of
broad-brimmed hats painted a bright scarlet, and each about
eight feet high ; of brightly Dutch-metalled opera-glasses,
about six feet long ; of umbrellas which seem intended to
realise a thermometrical quotation and accommodate ninety-
two in the shade ; of watches and clocks the circumference
of whose dials passes conception, and gloved hands the
dimensions of whose digits baffles belief—when you have
gotten all the premonitory symptoms of amaurosis by staring
at all these preternatural effigies, you may lead gently up to
ophthalmia by blinking at the big gilt letters, setting forth
avocations quite unknown in Europe—" Express Agencies,"
" Colonies formed to all parts of the Continent "—(by which

are meant caravans of emigrants purposing to the West, to
Nevada, or Arizona, or haply to the Great Salt Lake and the
city of the Mormons)—" Railway Ticket Offices," whose
wealth of nomenclature would have overjoyed that Hansom-
cabman who offered to drive the old gentleman out of his
mind for eighteen-pence : for the first time in your life you
feel yourself brought in almost actual contact with places that
in Europe seemed as shadowly far distant as the country of .
Khoordusch or the realms of Prester John.   Through tickets
to Milwaukee, St. Paul's, and Prairie du Chien.   " No change
of cars between Salamanca, Toledo, Chicago, Cincinnati, St.
Louis, Memphis "—the great Wall of China, if you choose.
" Steam to Havana, to Nassau, to New Orleans, to Hayti, to
Santo Domingo, to Aspinwall, to Chagus, to Panama."   " All
the way to San Francisco for two hundred and fifty dollars."
" Tickets to Halifax, Boston, Portland, St. John's, New Brunswick, Liverpool, London, Paris, Bremen, Hamburg, and the
World's End."   Huzza!   Three cheers !   That, if you please,
is the enthusiasm of the subscriber.   As a rule, I am heavy
and dull, and difficult to move.   I cried once when I went to
see Miss Bateman at the Adelphi ; but I am convinced now
that it was a cold in the head which made me weep, and not
compassion for the woes of the Jewish maiden.   But I never
could pass a railway or a steamboat ticket-office on Broadway without feeling inclined to fling my hat into the air, cast
all my responsibilities to the winds, rush into the office, buy
a through ticket for anywhere or everywhere, hurry back to
the hotel, pack up a valise, and scamper to the One Hundred
and Twenty-Eighth Street dépôt, or to Pier Five Hundred

and Eleven, North River, and there take rail or boat for the
regions of the Immeasurable Unexplored. I know that I
shall be off to Owhyee or Antannarivo some day : I know it ;
I feel it ; I read in imagination the strictures of the critics
carping at me because, while in Madagascar, I have discoursed
on the Rue St. Honoré, or have found the Sandwich Islands
very like Sydenham.

These big signs, these bigger proclamations in gilt letters,
covering almost every available inch of the house fronts,
cannot fail to bring to your mind one vivid impression—that
you are a spectator of a "comic scene" on the grandest
scale in a pantomime at the Theatre Royal, Brobdignag.
This image I know to be, to a certain extent, a plagiarism.
Mr. Charles Dickens, in his description of Boston, has put on
record something very like it. But Mr. Dickens' pantomimic
idea had only reference to one phase of the "comic business"
—say the scene where the "Post-office and Cornchandler's"
is next door to the "Ladies' School." Everything Bostonian
appeared to him so bright and shining, and unreal, that he
expected at every moment to see Clown and Pantaloon come
round the corner, or Columbine, in the guise of a smart
housemaid, issue from a doorway to indulge in a *pas de deux*
with Harlequin. New York was, to the subscriber, much
more practically pantomimic. In early life I had a great
deal to do with those strange entertainments. I have
assisted to paint many acres of comic scenes. I have executed many hundred alphabets of announcements, satirico-
political or puffico-commercial, on "flaps" through which
Clown or Harlequin jumped, and which subsequently changed

to something else. As it is, I can scarcely pass a " Little Dust-
pan," or an " Original Wellington Boot," in my own country,
without cogitating as to whether something " practicable "
might not be made of it. In New York I was incessantly
pursued by such thoughts. Surely those hats, those dial
plates, those gloves, those umbrellas, were not constructed
merely to advertise the wares of 'cute tradesmen. But my
pantomimic meditations were purely mechanical. I never
expected to meet Clown in the guise of a profligate practical
joker, or Pantaloon in the semblance of a gouty and naughty
old gentleman, or Columbine as a brief-skirted light o' love,
or Harlequin as a limber-limbed acrobat. The *dramatis
personæ* of pantomime belong to old and traditional countries.
Here is an etching by Callot of the Carnival of Venice two
hundred and odd years ago. Squaquarra, Cucurucu, Cucubu,
Zerbino, Francatrippa flourished in 1634, just as Clown and
Harlequin, and Pantaloon and Columbine flourish in Europe
now. But the Americans do not appreciate these diverting
vagabonds. *Mendici, mimi, balatrones*—they would be out
of place in the U. S. This is a serious country—a land of
strenuous effort and hard work. The mendicant must be
sent to the almshouse on Blackwell's Island ; the mimo must
hire an " agent in advance," and " run " his show through
the States. If Clown is caught stealing sausages, he goes to
Sing Sing ; Columbine marries at sixteen, without asking
Signor Gerontes' consent. Harlequin, instead of dancing
about in parti-coloured tights and spangles, goes down town
every morning by the Fourth Avenue cars, and is all day in
Wall Street, " operating " in Harlem, or securing his " corners "

on Fort Wayne; while Pantaloon is far likelier to die of dyspepsia at thirty-five, than to live to be eighty and have the gout. Yes; Broadway, with its big signs and placards, looks like a pantomime; *but it is a pantomime behind the green baize curtain.* In lieu of the glittering and tumbling pantomimists, you have a concourse of busy silent scene-painters and carpenters and machinists, toiling with a grim persistency. The scene-painters and carpenters very often hail from Germany or from Ireland. The "full-blooded Yankee" likes to be stage-manager, prompter, or treasurer, and to do the "bossing."

Early in the morning as it was when I first rode down Broadway the shops were all open, swept and garnished; a duly umbrella'd crowd jostled each other along the footway; and our carriage had often to come to a momentary halt owing to a block of drays or waggons, of light carts, or private carriages even, together with swarms of Broadway "stages" or omnibuses—somewhat narrow 'busses, so it seemed to me, hung very high, and with doors swinging wide open, and all thronged with grave gentlemen demurely going down town on "business." Everybody in New York has business to do of some kind or another.

My driver, for some occult reason of his own—probably because at certain points the main thoroughfare was, ere nine o'clock in the morning, inconveniently crowded—branched off from time to time from Broadway, and pursued the tenour of his way through back streets. There, for the second time in my life—the first I had seen were in Boston yesterday afternoon—I met those monstrous Noah's

Arks upon wheels, the horse-cars. They are like Noah's Arks, and nothing else; and, since the war, have no more than the railway ones been exempt from a visitation of "creeping things." The only American flea I ever met with was in a street car. He was as big as a theatrical flea —you know, stuffy dress-circle of the Theatre Royal, Barbican, or as the *Pulex literarius* which was wont to haunt the old Reading Room of the British Museum. Locomotion *on* a street railway and *in* a street car is not unpleasant. You glide along very smoothly and very swiftly; the jingling of the horses' bells is soothing to the ear; you know that although the poor animals are drawing a caravan containing from thirty to forty passengers, the rail makes their task comparatively lightsome, and they are not half so cruelly worked as the omnibus horses on Broadway; and if you can only procure a seat, or are not compelled to give the one you have to a lady, you may be sufficiently comfortable for a twenty minutes' drive. But in an independent wheeled vehicle the first sensation of passing over a street railway is anything but delightful. The passage of the wheels over the trams produces a grinding, rasping, jolting sensation, that penetrates to your very marrow. If you have a tooth given to aching, or a corn given to shooting, I will back the street tram—if you be unaccustomed to it—to stir up the latent demons. All the Avenues save one running parallel to Broadway have a double line of rails laid throughout their entire length. Most of the side streets are similarly cut up. Broadway and Fifth Avenue, the chief thoroughfares, are alone exempt from this most levelling tram system.

It is an immense convenience to persons of moderate means, for you can go from one end of New York to the other for five cents. Consider the difference between that Lilliputian tariff and the five dollar fares of the hacks! There is a great deal to be said on both sides of the question of American locomotion; but it appears to me, in any case, certain that New York could no more get on without street railways than we in London could get on with them.

I should not, perhaps, have omitted to state, that what few remains of antiquity New York might have possessed thirty years since, were all but entirely swept away by the Great Fire of 1836. In the lower part of the city I have often vainly looked for edifices, not alone of the Carlovingian or Jacobian era (and such there surely must have been in a city which, for all its youth, can still date back two hundred and fifty years), but even of the old red-brick pigtail structures of the three first Georges. The fire of '36, however, accounts for all. This awful conflagration destroyed nearly seven hundred of the principal houses and stores, and occasioned a loss of twenty-five millions of dollars. Instead of wasting their time, however, in idle despondency, the whole population of this surprising city were immediately on the alert to repair the mischief that had been done. Plans of rebuilding, on an improved scale, were immediately brought forward: and innumerable ingenious modes of borrowing money started. The rows of packing-cases were run up in no time; and ere the embers of the conflagration were cold, New York began to smile, and to liquor up amidst its ashes. A great many people were

ruined : but a great many more dated the commencement of
their fortune from the Great Fire. It began on a cold December night, and burnt down the greater part of Wall
Street, Hanover Street, the Merchants' Exchange, Earl
Street, Beaver Street, South Street, and many more familiar
thoroughfares. The fire was at last arrested at the Reformed
Dutch Church, in Exchange Place. Gunpowder was used
for the purpose of isolating the burning blocks, but not
effectually until the fire had raged for sixteen hours. One
may well imagine that the great alarm caused by this fire
led to the development of the admirably organised and
efficiently directed Volunteer Fire Service of New York—a
service whose scheme and details every nation in the civi-
lized world would do well to copy. But it does not appear
to have taught the Manhattanites common prudence or
caution. The number of fires in New York every year is
absolutely astounding; and the yearly average of Fourth of
July conflagrations is scandalous. I suppose the people like
fires. It gives the roughs a chance of running "wid der
masheen," and of telling recalcitrant "Moses" to "git out o'
them hose." I never knew a people so wantonly careless
about fire. Their stoves, their gas, their lucifer-matches,
their cigar-tips, their bonfires, their torchlight processions,
their Chinese lanterns, are all so many provocative elements
towards keeping them in a perpetual blaze. They may
argue, perhaps, that there is no use in keeping a Fire Department in such wonderful working order if there are no
fires to call the steam fire-engines, the hydrants, and the
hose-carriages into practice. But this system of providing

the means, in order that the end may be attained, strikes me as being very like fitting Hobb's detector locks and patent catch-bolts on a stable door, in order that it may be most carefully locked after the steed has been stolen. But it is idle to reason with "our folks" on this—or, indeed, on most other matters. If you take them to task, they accuse you of being an enemy to democratic institutions.

How many of these things I actually saw and meditated upon from the carriage window before, as an American traveller, I was twenty-four hours old, I leave to the discernment and discrimination of the reader. But I did see and think about a great many of them. There was plenty of time, for it seemed as though I should never get to my journey's end. At last the man landed me on the steep white marble steps of the Brevoort House, a handsome mansion, but not over-huge, at the corner of Eighth Street, or Clinton Place, and Fifth Avenue ; the most comfortable hotel on the American continent, and in many respects the best restaurant in the world. I will endeavour to justify this high eulogium by-and-by.

The porters, it must be admitted, were not very eager to set about discharging my luggage from the coach, for it is a matter of much uncertainty when you arrive at the Brevoort whether you will be able to gain admission to its upper chambers. In the first place, it is an hotel, and not a caravanserai, and the accommodation is limited. I don't think the number of bedrooms exceeds one hundred. In the next place, Mr. Albert Clark, the proprietor (from whom, in the course of a twelvemonth's acquaintance, I experienced nothing but civility, kindness, and attention), is somewhat particular about the status of the guests who wish to sleep as well as dine at his house. A traveller staying at the Brevoort is known, not by the number of his room alone, but by his name. He has an individuality; he is recognised; and at the big caravanserais he is merely one or two numerals, as the case may be, in a column of statistics. I knew an old lady in Liverpool once, who kept an alehouse, not for profit, for she had plenty of money, but in order to enjoy the conversation of a select few. For all bar there was her little front parlour, and, but for a beer-engine in one corner, and a row of bottles and glasses on a shelf, you might have imagined the room to be a boudoir. A stranger, say, would enter, and call for a "gill o' ale" in a tone which, somehow, displeased the old lady. "Yill!" she would thunder, "Thee gits na' yill heer! *Thee's nit classical. I'se nowt but classical fouk here.* Git oot wi' thee!" If you were classical the gill of ale was brought to you by one of her two pretty daughters, and the old lady did not much care whether you paid for it or not. Indeed there was one specially ragged and unclean person a frequenter of the little ale-house in Button Street, who went, if I remember right, by the name of "Lily-white Muffins," who was incurably drunken and dissipated, but who was a famous Latin and Greek scholar, had been a fellow of a college at Oxford, and whose conversation was still charming. "Lily-white Muffins," the old lady would cry, "thee's gude for nowt; but thee's classical. Sally, gi' t' auld deevil a gill o' yill." And many a gill of Welsh ale did that deboshed scholar consume at the old lady's expense. You must be,

you see, classical after a fashion to be welcome at the Brevoort.
Mr. Clark doesn't like rowdies ; he abhors loafers ; he has set
his face against " hard cases ;" he would prefer not to have
anything to do with Shoddy. Suddenly enriched diggers
from California, or petroleocrats from Oil City, may be vastly
profitable company, but Mr. Clark would rather they went to
the Fifth Avenue, or the St. Nicholas. He has a prejudice
against patrons whose sufferings from whiskey in the hair are
chronic, who require cocktails earlier than 6 a.m., who are
given to sticking their feet up on the chairs, or to expecto-
rating without reference to the contiguity of a spittoon. He
deprecates political discussions at his bar, or " difficulties " in
his vestibules. The consequence is, that his establishment is
mainly frequented by the wealthy, cultivated, and quiet
Bostonians—members of the codfish aristocracy, if you will,
but still codfish very delicately crimped and garnished with
the finest oyster sauce—by army and navy officers of high
rank and by their families ; by travelled American gentlemen,
who have learnt in Europe to know what real comfort is ;
and by the best class of English tourists. The guardsmen
who used to come down from Canada, and the linesmen who
come down now ; the British and foreign diplomatists from
Washington, and a few wealthy English merchants settled in
New York, but who happen to be bachelors and prefer the
luxury of a well-ordered hotel to cheerless and comfortless
furnished lodgings, with, perhaps, a wandering nobleman or
two, or an occasional Cunard captain, are all to be found at
the Brevoort. The only hotel which for comfort and privacy
can compete with this excellent house is a smaller establish-

ment called the Clarendon, near the Academy of Music; but
there is a drawback to the Clarendon in the fact that you are
obliged to take your meals at a *table d'hôte* in lieu of a restaurant *à la carte*. I deliberately praise the Brevoort, chiefly
because its celebrity among Americans places it beyond
puffing. What good would puffery do to Swan and Edgar,
or Howell and James, or Mr. Benson the watchmaker, or
Mr. Poole the tailor? They are well enough known as it is.
Next, because I wish to save any intending tourists to
America the annoyances, and often the positive agony in-
separable from a stay in one of the colossal caravanserais.
Away from New York it is Hobson's choice—the caravanserai
or nothing; but *in* New York, if you prefer quiet, peace,
comfort and civility, to noise, confusion, rudeness and misery,
go to the Brevoort or the Clarendon—but *I* prefer the first—
and not to one of the thundering barracks, where guests by
the five hundred are fed like so many wild beasts. The
ordinary run of English travellers in the States have been
fed with stories more or less apocryphal about the splendour
and luxury of the St. Nicholas and the Fifth Avenue, and
proceed thither as a matter of course. They find a great
amount of external show and magnificence ; but if they are
travelling alone they are most shabbily lodged, they cannot
get anything fit to eat or drink—for there never was such a
setting forth of Dead Sea apples as an American bill of fare,
and unless their tastes are as coarse as a collier's mainsail,
they are profoundly miserable. How many times have I
been asked to dinner by English friends just arrived in the
States, and who have put up, for the reason that they thought

it was the "thing," at one of the gigantic barracks, and have
undergone the purgatory of an ill-dressed, worse-served
dinner, washed down by villanous wines at monstrous prices,
and put on the table by a set of uncouth, unkempt, untutored
savages, who were a disgrace to the name of waiters. And
how often have I endeavoured slily to seduce my hosts away
from the Barmecide gorgeousness of the barracks to the sober
but satisfying delights of the Brevoort.

Let us be just, however. There is one large hotel—one of
the largest indeed—in New York, and conducted on the
American (or gregarious *table d'hôte*) system where a
stranger may really be comfortable. This is the New York
Hotel in Broadway, close to Eighth Street. The *cuisine* here
is excellent, and the *chef*, M. Louis, a real *cordon bleu*, whose
simulated *pâté de foie gras* (in particular) runs the genuine
Strasburg article very hard. If a traveller does not choose to
stay in the hotel itself he may obtain very comfortable sleep-
ing-rooms and private parlours at a *succursal* to the New
York, (the St. Julien House hard by, which is wholly let out
in bachelor chambers,) taking his meals at the N.Y. The proprietor of this hotel, Mr. Hiram Cranston—a very prominent
member of the great Democratic party, is in every sense of
the word a Gentleman, and enjoys the esteem, not only of
those with whom he is intimately connected, but even of
his political opponents. I had letters to Mr. Cranston
from several persons of weight and position in Europe, both
English and American, and had I chosen to live in his hotel
could have passed an exceedingly pleasant life ; but I was
deterred from making it my abode, in the outset, by one serious

consideration. *Noscitur a sociis* is a maxim which obtains
very strongly in the States. A man is known not only by
the company he keeps, but by the hotel he frequents. Thus,
the Astor House is an Administration and commercial hotel ;
the St. Nicholas is a Californian house ; the Fifth Avenue is
Shoddy ; the Metropolitan financial and moderately democratic; the Everett, ditto; the Prescott, Western; the Brevoort, anti-slavery, but aristocratic ; the Clarendon, aristocratic,
and without any politics at all. The New York labours
under the misfortune of being incurably Copperhead, and at
least nine-tenths Secesh. Mr. Cranston is as loyal a man as
any in New York, but he sympathises. The great Cuban and
Mexican dons go to the New York ; the great Southerners
who have escaped Lafayette by the skin of their teeth are
sheltered there. Mr. Cranston has not been molested, for every
one knows him to be an honest man who wishes every kind of
good to *la chose publique ;* but, as I have hinted, he does not
pander to the prevailing tyrant nor shut his doors to the oppressed party. The arrival of every stranger in New York and
the particular hotel he has selected are facts duly chronicled in
the evening papers. Wishing to steer a middle course, and *not*
wishing to be irremediably branded as a malevolent Copperhead, I did not go to the New York, and for some period even
kept aloof from Hiram Cranston, and from a social circle which
I had subsequently occasion to discover was the most genial
and the least prejudiced in the whole States. As it turned
out I might have saved a great deal of money by going in the
first instance to the N.Y., and paying my two and a half
dollars a day for board—two and a half *in gold*, be it under-

stood, which means from five to six in greenbacks. It did
not matter in the long run whether I stayed at a Copperhead
house or a Black Republican one. I was not the less to the
New York press a " bloated miscreant," a " malignant
buffoon," a " fat cockney," a " lying scoundrel," a " debased
libeller," and a " hired emissary of the British oligarchy."

Although on this wet morning I had no more claim than
I usually have to be " classical," and although I don't fancy
that newspaper reporters, as a rule, are given to patronising
the Brevoort, Mr. Albert Clark, fortified by the card of introduction I had brought with me from a friend in Páris, was
kind enough to take me in ; and within another hour I had
bathed, dressed, breakfasted off kippered salmon, mixed tea,
and dry toast, which would have done honour to the " Tavis-
tock " in Covent Garden, or to the " Old Ship " at Brighton
—(most cosy of British hostelries, I salute ye both !)—breakfasted, too, in a coffee-room, which, for handsome appoint-
ments and perfect neatness, might vie with any similar
apartment in a Pall Mall club, and was ready (the rain
having ceased) for a pedestrian excursion down Broadway.
What else my Diary tells me should be said about New York
hotels, New York streets, and New York society, will be found
in another chapter.

CHAPTER III.

A CHRISTMAS IN CANADA, TO WHICH ARE ADDED THE
MISERIES OF ROUSE'S POINT, AND AN ACCOUNT OF THE
TYRANNY OF MYERS.

YES ; there is something in " the flag." There is magic in
a coloured rag, after all. I no longer question the brilliance
of the stars, the iridescence of the stripes, which, in a kind of
patriotic *delirium tremens*, the American sees perpetually
dancing before their eyes. Look at the sun till you wink,
and then try to read a book or a newspaper, and each page
will be blurred in a glorious prism. Our curious cousins are,
as is well known, in the habit of continually contemplating
their Bird of Freedom, whose home is in the rising, not the
setting, sun. The eagle may look at the blazing orb with
impunity ; but the human biped, surveying the eagle, is apt to
grow dazed with much staring at the sun-wrapt bird. Hence
he beholds the flag in everything ; in the blackguard ribaldry
of the "New York Gorilla," the sentimental bloodthirstiness
of the "New York Black Joke," and the equable and consistent mendacity of the "New York Ananias' Journal"—with
which is incorporated "Sapphira's Miscellany"—joint editors,
Hon. T. Mendez Pinto, Major Longbow, and Baron Munchausen. When our curious cousins' children come home for

the Christmas holidays, the first thing they do is to climb on the shoulder of the black servant, and nail up " the flag " outside their papa's hall door. " The flag," in miniature, appears on joints of meat, and on the cupola crusts of apple-pies. In Boston they made " the flag " up into roller-blinds for the windows of their trim and cosy-looking houses. When the news of the first overt act of secession, the firing on Fort Sumter, arrived at New York, I am told that the horses in the street cars all carried "the flag " in their cars, and that the Wall-street brokers wore " the flag " in their button-holes. In a Penitentiary School at Deer Island, Boston, passing through one of the class-rooms, I saw that the teacher had chalked on a black board, for the little criminals to learn by heart, a piece of poetry beginning, " Our Flag——" I stayed to read no more. This is, all over, American. We give our felons and paupers beef and pudding on Christmas Day. Our cousins make the Fourth of July their saturnalia, and on . that day their prisoners and captives are regaled with a banquet of bunkum, in which the *pièce de résistance* is " the flag." Of course it appears on all the *cornets* of sweetmeats, and on the covers of all the candies which by hecatombs are sold at this season of the year. Somewhere " down town " in New York I have heard there is an ingenious bar-keeper—a real " professor "—who, for fifteen cents, and by the aid of dexterous manipulation, in parabolic curves, from one glass to another, of brandy, lemon-peel, syrup, sugar, and crushed ice, will contrive to give you a configuration of the American flag in the form of a " drink." This patriotic beverage, this glori-fied cocktail, this eye-opener *in excelcis*, has not yet come within my purview. When I meet with the stars and stripes at the bar I will report concerning them.

There is a pleasant little sketch in oil, by the most accom-- plished of American landscape-painters, now in the gallery of a gentleman at New York. This sketch exhibits the form and hues of the Union flag in—what think you?—in a glowing sunset! An electric telegraph post forms the staff. The suffused sky is ruled in parallel lines of crimson, and a sufficient number of stars have obligingly risen to complete the blazonry. The conceit is original, if not felicitous. It runs hard the "poor Indian," whose untutored mind sees Omnipotence in thunder, and hears it in the wind. It can only be rivalled by that ghastly fancy of Gustave Doré in his pictured legend of the Wandering Jew, shadowing out the procession to Calvary in the clouds and in the sunshine, in the waves of the ocean, and the tangled branches of forest trees, and the flames of the furnace. I have little doubt of the Americans being sincere in their devotion to "the flag." They really think it a grand and noble and beautiful ori- flamme. They would die for it. They *have* died for it, and continue to die for it every day. They are rushing into national bankruptcy, and a probable despotism, and a pos- sible reign of terror, for the sake of "the flag." "Breathes there a man with soul so dead, who never to himself hath said"—I refer you for the remainder to Sir Walter Scott. Only, for my part, being short-sighted, I cannot discern the very slender line of demarcation between ardent patriotism and bragging bunkum. Being blind and stupid, I cannot quite make out where the *Love* of country ends, and the *Boast*—

the selfish, arrogant, conceited Boast of country—begins. So, as a little child, when they set me lessons in the Old Testament, used I to be puzzled to determine whether the fierce Jewish kings, who filled chapters with burning supplications for *their* enemies to be smitten, for *their* oppressors to be cast out and put to confusion, were in reality praying to a merciful Creator, or fostering and pampering their own wicked lusts for dominion and for vengeance.

You see that, many lines ago, I acknowledged the potency of what I may term "American flaggism ;" only one is apt to grow tired of this interminable laudation of the star-spangled banner. And at Christmas-time especially is there apt to come over an Englishman the feeling that he too has a flag, and that there is something in it. I began to pine, on Tuesday last, for *my* flag. Appreciating and admiring to the very fullest extent the patriotism of the Americans, I still claimed a right to keep a small stock of "flaggism" for my own private consumption. The meteor flag of England, Campbell stirringly told us, will continue terrifically to burn for many a long day. I had the heartburn with it on the 22nd of December. Congress having adjourned over the Christmas holidays, it appeared to me that I had a right, in the interest of my flag, also to adjourn for a few days. An English friend who had just come from St. John's, New Brunswick, to join me at New York, was of the same opinion. "There is nothing doing here," he represented ; " there will be nothing doing at Washington for a fortnight. Suppose we went somewhere and ate our Christmas dinner—even if it were at an inn—and drank the Queen's health and thanked Heaven

for all things, upon British ground and under the cheery
shadow of the Union Jack ?" I adopted at once this
patriotic and convivial suggestion. I knew my friend to be a
man of great gravity of countenance, wary and experienced in
Transatlantic travel—knowing " all the ropes " of locomotion,
as our curious cousins say, and competent to "put me
through " and "post me up " on all topics. He faithfully
promised that I should be back in New York, after seeing
both the Canadas, Niagara, Buffalo, and Pittsburg, by the
1st of January, 1864, in time to make the indispensable
visits of New Year's Day. He promised, and I believed
him. "I am yours," I said; and we paid our bills at the
Brevoort House, posted our letters to go by the "Asia" on
Wednesday from Boston, and blithely proceeded to buy an
"Appleton's Guide."

The price of " Appleton's Railway and Steam and Naviga-
tion Guide," is twenty-five cents, as against our sixpenny
" Bradshaw." In bulk it is about equal to the famous English
" vadetecum." It is printed in bolder type, illustrated with
many maps, divisional and sectional, and is decidedly more
lucid in arrangement than ours. It purports to be published
" under the supervision of the railway companies." It contains
some ingeniously-engraved dials, called " Time and Distance
Indicators," from which, if you are clever, you may find out
that you are a long way from where you want to go, and that
your watch and the clock at the hotel are at variance. Its
fly-leaves are of course full of advertisements. It comprises
an almanac and calendar, some useful hints to travellers,
some exulting statistics of the population, commerce, and

inexhaustible internal resources of the United States, and several pages of more or less humorous anecdotes and jokes. Printed on stout paper and neatly sewn, the book, as a work of polite literature, written in the choicest American English, is perhaps cheap at a quarter of a dollar. I say to you, never-theless, young Brittish man, purposing to travel in North America, beware of "Appleton." Don't lay out the most insignificant "yellow-belly" — the smallest change for a "greenback"—on it. For purposes of consultation it is not worth a cent. "Bradshaw" is harder to understand than the Zendavesta ; but, once understood, "Bradshaw" is full of veracious statements. It is a sore tribulation ; but it is a "c'rect card." "Wal, Tu," really means something, even if a lifelong education be necessary to comprehend the "Wal" and the "Tu." But "Appleton" is a roguish mockery, a merry delusion, a jocose snare. It is a "Yankee notion," and the result is deception. As a railway guide-book "Appleton" is utterly and recklessly untrustworthy.

The proof of the pudding shall be in the eating. Take the following as an example of Appletonian accuracy. We were bound for Montreal, in Canada. We reached the railway dépôt in Thirtieth Street, New York, shortly after seven o'clock on the morning of Wednesday the 23rd of December. The train was to start at 7.25 A.M. We purchased, at the rate of 11 dollars 75 cents apiece, two lengthy green tickets, divided by perforated lines into compartments, and with coupons attached. These tickets were to stand us in stead to the city of Montreal. According to "Appleton," we were to reach Poughkeepsie—once famous as the abode of Andrew

Jackson Davis, a "seer" now said to be "played out," or eclipsed by modern spiritualists, and so fallen, poor seer, into the "sere and yellow" himself—at 9.42; at 11.50 we were to be at Albany; at 12.15 at Troy; at 1.20 at Eaglebridge. By three in the afternoon Rutland was to be reached; by 5.35, Burlington. Then we were to arrive at Rouse's Point, close to the Canadian frontier, at 8.34; at St. John's by 9.30; and at Montreal by 10.30 P.M., all in the instant Wednesday. To accomplish a journey of four hundred and one miles, a period of fifteen hours was thus needed. In England we should have made the distance in nine hours; but let that pass. "*Crede* 'Appleton,'" I thought, and was satisfied. We were to be carried during our journey over the Hudson River Railway; over the Rutland and Burlington; over the Vermont Central; and over the Montreal and Champlain— all belonging to different companies; but these lines, we were assured, never failed to "make connections," and we were entreated to believe that we ran no risk of "laying over." To "make connections" means, in the parlance of our curious cousins, to catch a train departing from a junction immediately subsequent to the time you arrive there by another train. It is the equivalent of the French "*correspondance.*" If, through your own dulness, or implicit belief in "Appleton," or the *laches* of the engine-driver, you "miss a connection," you are obliged to "lay over"—that is, to wait a number of hours, sometimes an entire day or night—till the desired train arrives, and the ravelled sleeve of "connection" can be knitted up. The Americans are much given to boasting of their adroitness in so dovetailing their railway journeys into one harmonious trunk. I have not yet entered an American cemetery; but I should not be in the least surprised to read, engraven on a tombstone, an inscription setting forth that a certain citizen was an attached husband, and a tender father, and a faithful friend—that he travelled constantly in dry goods, and that he never "missed a connection" till he became a widower, nor "lay over" till he died.

Now mark, if you please, the sequel. The trip to Albany and Troy, by the Hudson River Railway, was an extremely pleasant one. We had the morning newspapers, and intelligent youths passed to and fro in the cars offering for sale "fig and gum drops," the delicious American eating-apples, and neatly pirated editions of works of English standard literature. There was a smoking car, moreover, and everything was cheerful and hopeful. The intense cold was compensated by the brightness of the sun and the exquisite beauty of the wintry landscape. The banks of the Hudson River very much resemble, and are very nearly as picturesque as, those of the Rhine. The villas that nestle in its bosky thickets, or are reflected in its calm blue depths, are charming. We passed Manhattan, Yonkers, Sing Sing, Rhinebeck, Coxsackie, and Stuyvesant. We saw the Catskills and the Hudson Highlands, and I lost myself in placid day-dreams of Rip Van Winkle and Woolfert's Roost; of Washington Irving at Sunnyside, and N. P. Willis at Idlewild; of the Emperor Frederick Barbarossa, and the Devil and Tom Walker; for the Rhine lost itself to me in the Hudson, and the Hudson in the Rhine, and at any moment I should have been prepared to arrive at Rolandseck or Andernach, to survey the Siebengebirge looming blue in the far-off, to see the dark heights of Ehrenbreitstein towering cloudwards, or to hear the echoes of the Lorelei. A very rough-and-ready breakfast of ham and eggs, despatched with a blunt knife and a two-pronged fork at Poughkeepsie, dispelled this illusion; but my trip along the Hudson River will, come what may, be marked in my diary with the whitest of stones.

Tribulation began at Troy. There is a great, howling, slovenly station there. We changed carriages, and then we learnt, not from any official—for there are few officials on American railways, and the few are surly; not from asking questions from fellow-passengers, for out of ten questions you may ask, to nine you will probably receive no answer—but from inadvertent eavesdropping, that the statement in *Appleton* respecting our arrival at 10·30 p.m. at Montreal was a facete hoax. We might get to Essex Junction; we might reach St. Alban's; we might possibly even be taken so far as Rouse's Point, which is distant only fourty-four miles from Montreal; but there we should certainly have to "lay over" for the night. It turned out that in the *December* number of *Appleton* the *summer-time tables* of the New York and Montreal line had been printed. The work when examined was found to swarm with similar impudent misstatements, and steamers were declared to be plying on rivers which, at this season of the year, every man knows to be securely locked up with ice. I wonder what would become of Messrs. Adams's business if they were to print in the December number of *Bradshaw* the August time-tables of the London and North-Western Railway.

After this all became gloomy despondency and irritable doubt and uncertainty. I began to despise my companion for having brought me on a wild-turkey and plum-pudding chase. I had hopes, if we reached Montreal by Wednesday night, or at least Thursday morning, of some friendly country-man, to whom I had letters of introduction, asking us to dinner on the festive Friday. But I now despaired of being able to present those letters as I had contemplated. Decency forbade the attempt to strike up an acquaintance within a few hours of Christmas dinner time. You must not follow up your turkey too closely ; *est modus in rebus,* even in the matter of eleemosynary mince-pies. On his part, I daresay my friend began to hold me in abhorrence, because I had discovered the futility of *Appleton,* and his own fallibility as to making connections. We spoke little, but glowered at each other moodily. I conjecture that he determined to cut me out of his will ; but I made up *my* mind not to cut him out of my next letter.

The slightest sparkle of gratulation from a " flag " point of view came across me when I found Troy in commotion at the news that Mr. J. C. Heenan had been defeated in pugilistic encounter by Mr. Thomas King. For once in my life I approved of prizefighting. For full five minutes I wore Mr. King's colours in my bosom—figuratively, of course. Observe that, eight days before, the news-boys had been crying about the streets of New York an "extra" of a sporting newspaper, containing a bogus telegram of King having been "whipped" by Heenan. Troy was much cast down at the intelligence received by the Asia. Several inhabitants of the "wooden-

horse city" who joined us spoke in bitterly mournful terms
of the "Benniker Boy's" having been "whipped." I wonder
whether the *New York Knuckleduster* will make the fact of
one rough having got the better of another rough a *casus
belli* against England. I perceive that the account of the
piratical seizure of the Chesapeake had been accompanied by
a sensation line, "Base Complicity of the Blue-noses"—implying that the desperate act had been gotten up by the inhabitants of Halifax. *Pari passu*, I am prepared to hear that
Tom King is notoriously Secesh, and that his backers were
all Copperheads. By the way, *his* head must have been
made of something harder than copper to stand Mr. Heenan's
blows.

You shall be spared an enumeration of the icebound hovels
we passed; of the ice terraces we ran along; of the forests
we dived through; of the times we changed from one stifling
set of cars to the other; of the crowds of men with fur caps,
and women with close-fitting padded and quilted hoods in
lieu of bonnets, against whom we were jostled. The oftener
we changed trains the worse the accommodation seemed to
become. How the lamps smoked! how the stove generated
maleficent gases! how the men spat! how the babies
squalled! how those two negresses in Watteau hats jab-
bered! and how that fat old darkey in the corner by the stove,
with his feet, of course, jammed against its almost red-hot
sides, snored! These were, with a single exception, the first
coloured people I had seen in an American railway train.

There was no refreshment-car attached, no smoking-car,
and, though we crawled along at a snail-like rate, no halt for

lunch or dinner. We were journeying through Vermont, the
"Green Mountain State;" but the rime of frost on the
dungeon-like windows prevented me from admiring the snow-
capped hills, the forests of evergreens, the tidy towns, and
village churches built of marble, of this really picturesque
State. By this time you are beginning to perceive that
things were not appearing *couleur de rose* to the subscriber.
It was enough for him to know that it was very cold,
and that *Appleton* was a deceiver. Forty-five minutes after
the hour marked in the time-table we made Essex Junction,
left our seats, and waited one hour and a half for another
train to take us to St. Alban's. There was a kind of refreshment-room here, and some really good oyster soup. Such a
thing as a glass of sherry, or beer, or a *petit verre* was not
procurable. We were in the State of Vermont, and there
the Maine liquor law ostensibly obtains. Because Neil Dow
was virtuous, there are cakes, but no ale. At half-past ten
at night—the time *Appleton, passim*, of our being due at
Montreal—we started from Essex Junction, and at half-past
eleven we reached St. Alban's. This city of about seven
thousand inhabitants is said to be "quite a place." It has
a very large railway engine and carriage factory; and boasts
—literally boasts—of two first-class hotels. We chose that
which was declared to be "excelled by none," the Tremont
House. There were about twelve passengers, lady and
gentlemen, purposing for the Tremont, and but one hackney
coach available to convey them thither. Nine of our number,
however, were packed, somehow, into the lumbering, high-
springed vehicle, which has a bench in the midst of its

interior, where the passengers' legs should be, but where other passengers crouch on their hams, somewhat after the manner of the chaplain in the coach-and-six of the Lord Lieutenant, who went to the popinjay match in "Old Mortality." As the roof of this ark was likewise crowded, I declined making one of the party; and, laden with bags, umbrellas, and buffalo robes—the last of which a man accumulates unconsciously in wintry travel in these latitudes, just as a tourist on the continent of Europe who has started for a short trip, and eked it out to a long one, accumulates shirts —I walked through the almost blinding moonlight, and over the slippery frozen road, to the Tremont. I will give the Vermonters every credit for their moon. It is magnificent.

My friend had accepted the last place on the stool of repentance in the hackney coach. I found him very cold and very rueful. He had ridden half a mile in the dark, had had all his corns crushed and most of his ribs compressed, and was, as a culmination of woe, uneasily apprehensive that he had been sitting on a baby. "I know something gave a feeble wail," he said, "and then all was silent." I tried to reassure him, suggesting that, haply, babies in this country were checked as luggage; and in America no luggage duly checked can ever come to grief. It is never lost, never injured. The corners are a little rounded off in a long journey, that is all. The landlord of the Tremont Hotel, St. Alban's, Vermont, for a little man with a bald head and clad in a suit of homespun, was decidedly the most solemn and imposing personage I ever beheld. It was easy to gather, from his port and mien, that he considered St. Alban's to be

the only real, genuine, and important city in creation; the
Tremont House, St. Alban's, the only establishment deserving
the name of an hotel in the universe; and himself, subject to
the constitution of the United States, the sole A 1, copper-
bottomed, teak-built, water-tight-compartmented, lifebelt-pro-
vided, experienced-surgeon-carrying, supreme, unequalled,
and enlightened Vermonter, Green Mountaineer, and Hotel-
keeper, to be found between the two ends of a rainbow or
the apex of the Empyrean and the basement floor of the
unfathomable limbo down below Nathaniel. Struggling to
the bar as well as bags and buffalo robes would allow me, I
mildly informed his Tremendousness that I required supper
and beds for two. He loftily waved me off with a pen;
appeared for some moments absorbed in pure mental abstraction; then pensively consulted several ledgers; then, in
a tone of calm authority, demanded to know if we were
"going north." I replied that we were going to Canada, and
that, as the train was to leave St. Alban's for Rouse's Point
at six o'clock on Thursday morning, we wished to be called
at five. "You will be called at a quarter of five," responded
his Tremendousness. This is a key to the entire system of
treating travellers in the United States. You are seldom
allowed to have a will of your own. It is not what you want
to do, but what the landlord, or the waiter, or the scullion
wants, that is to govern you. You are to breakfast, dine,
tea, sup, rise and go to bed precisely as it may happen to
suit, not your convenience, but theirs. A timid traveller does
as he is told, and is miserable. A fretful traveller loses his
temper, and takes nothing by *that* motion. A cool and reso-

lute traveller just lets the people around him know that, subject to the laws of reason and decorum, "*and* the constitution of the United States," he intends to do, not what they want, but what he chooses to do himself. Then, with a curious alacrity, the despots "cave in," and, although they may "guess you *air* ugly" (*i.e.*, angry), you are positively allowed to do what you like with your own.

Touching supper. After we had entered our names in the "Hotel Register," which is here kept at every house where travellers lodge, from the six-storied hotel to the meanest roadside inn—not happily to subserve, as in Europe, political or police purposes, but to gratify the harmless curiosity of village gossips and bar loungers—we asked for something to eat and drink. We were informed in a tone of gravity, and almost of reprobation, that "Supper was in course of preparation," and that in due time we should be "notified" of its being ready. We certainly did not expect soup, or fish, or made dishes; but after the high praise we had heard bestowed on the Tremont, we were led to indulge in hopes of a hot and plentiful meal. It grew however to be so very near midnight before supper was announced, that my companion, who was fatigued and in delicate health, gave up all hopes of obtaining refreshment, and went to bed. The subscriber being cast in coarser mould (he is, in fact, "death on victuals," as is observed of one having a hearty appetite), he waited. The doors of a "dining hall," which had hitherto been rigorously locked, were at last flung open, and I was suffered to enter a whitewashed apartment, containing a long table laid out for "supper." The "style" of the whole thing was perfect. There was a "*Je ne sais quoi*" about it. Nothing at New York, or Boston, or Philadelphia could have surpassed that whitewashed hall, so far as "style" was concerned. It equalled Mivart's. It threw the Louvre into limbo. The landlord looked in for a moment to assure himself that all the requirements of "style" had been fulfilled, and then composedly withdrew. I saw him afterwards pacing up and down a wretched little vestibule containing a stove and a spittoon—the former diminutive, the latter monstrous. His head was thrown back, his pen was behind his ear. His entire aspect breathed a calm and almost melancholy consequentiality. If any doubt or perplexity could have entered that bald and placid head, it must have been on the question as to whether he made Mother Nature or Mother Nature him.

The presence of style at the Tremont House, however perfect it might have been, failed perhaps to compensate for the absence of suppers. There was, permeating through the ill-ventilated place, a powerfully meaty smell in this refectory, recalling the odour of an engine factory next door to a cookshop. For a long time there was nothing else. At last one attendant Hebe appeared with cheese and crackers—stylish to look at, but undeniably mouldy. This Hebe was Irish; she was a stout but uncombed young person. Soon afterwards another waitress entered. This nymph was tall and gaunt and American. She bore a huge pitcher of iced water—a most wholesome beverage, but somewhat cold comfort for Christmas. I should have preferred egg-hot. I thought when I saw the Vermontese nymph's apron and bib, and her hair

screwed off her temples in butterfly bows with a high comb
behind, that I beheld the versatile Mrs. Barney Williams in
her admired impersonification of the " Yankee gal." For the
nonce I elected to be " Pesky Ike," and expected every
moment to be addressed as " Keemo kimo," and asked
whether I would have " my high, my low," or " my right fol
iddle diddle " for supper. The female Vermonter was a
Phillis, but not neat-handed. In a nasal mezzo-contralto, to
which the grossest caricature of the American dialect I ever
heard on our stage was perfectly tame, she asked me if I
would have "steack or tryaipe." A taste for tripe is among the
few human vices to which I am not addicted; and my brief
experience of American beef had not led me to look upon
steak as a very dainty viand. I asked, failing offal, if I could
have anything else. " No," curtly replied Mrs. Barney Williams, "yeou kyant; ain't that eneough ?" I bowed, and said
I would take steak. She brought me, on a cold plate, a
curled-up flap of something hard and greasy and cartilaginous,
which looked unpleasantly like a piece of an Ethiop's ear,
fried. I asked if I could have anything to drink with my
supper—some beer, some cider, or some wine. " This is not
A bar," said Mrs. Barney Williams, severely ; " guess there's
water and tea, and that's all." Upon which I made some
rather uncomplimentary allusions to Mr. Neil Dow and the
Maine Liquor Law. This brought in the landlord, who, with
sedate affability, whispered that he could " fix " me anything
I wanted " quietly." I declined, however, to be supplied sur-
reptitiously, and as a favour, with that to which I conceived
that, as a peaceable *bonâ fide* traveller, I had a right; and as

I couldn't get on with the fried Ethiop's ear after the first
mouthful, I retired from the " hall " sulky and supperless.   I
did not care to bandy words with the Phillis who was not
neat-handed.   She did not like me evidently, and I recipro-
cated the sentiment.   But, for anything I know to the contrary, she might be the sheriff's daughter or the mayor's
sister-in-law, and accustomed to go out on Sundays with a
" magnolious " parasol and a " spanglorious " crinoline.   An
American " help " is no menial.   She is spoken of, not satiri-
cally, but in simple good faith, as " the young lady " who
" picks up " the house and " fixes " the dinner-table.   Before
she agrees to enter a family she cross-examines her mistress
as to whether the house is provided with Hecker's flour, and
Beebe's range, brass pails, oil-cloth on the stairs, and hot and
cold water laid on.   Then she states the domestic " platform "
on which she is prepared to act.   " Monday I bakes ; and nobody speaks to me.   Tuesday I washes ; I'se to be let alone.
Wednesday I irons ; you'd best let me be that day.   Thursday I picks up the house ; I'se awful ugly that day in temper,
but affectionate.   Friday I bakes again.   Saturday my beau
comes.   And Sunday I has to myself."   The " help," I repeat,
is a young lady.   She devours with avidity the romances, all
about love and murder, in the *New York Ledger.*   She at-
tends lectures, and may, some day, deliver lectures herself, or
become a member of a Woman's Rights' Convention ; and it
is because she is a Young Lady, and the persons who require
her assistance do not choose to run the risk of being driven
raving mad by her perversity and her impertinence, that so
many married couples in the United States never venture on

housekeeping for themselves, but live from year's end to year's end in uproarious and comfortless hotels.

I read a story once in a western paper about a terrible young lady at Cincinnati, a Sunday-school teacher, who, having been calumniated by Mr. Mack Barnitz, a Methodist class-leader, went to a saddler's store and purchased a trenchant cowhide to castigate him withal. " Guess you'd better not whip children with that cowhide," hinted the dealer who sold her the horrible *flagellum.* " 'Tis for big ones," responded the terrible young lady, whereupon she proceeded to complete her marketing by the purchase of a quarter of a pound of cayenne pepper. Next Sunday morning she went to church, sat in the same pew with Mr. Mack Barnitz, uprose suddenly at the end of a hymn, apostrophised Mack as a liar and a villain, cowhided him within an inch of his life, and then " washed his face all over " with the cayenne pepper. The elders and the deacons wrestled with her, and them also did she pepper. She would have peppered the parson had his reverence been imprudent enough to approach her while she was " ugly." I reflected seriously upon this story as I retired from the presence of the Vermont Phillis, and, observing that there was a pepper castor among the " fixings " of the supper-table, I trembled.

I was too hungry to go to bed, so I wandered about moodily till one in the morning, and from one stove-reeking apartment to another. Fortunately, I had a cigar-case with me. I know the Americans to be a nation of commendably early risers, and I attribute much of their material prosperity to this habit ; but I don't know when they go to

bed.   There always seems, in an American house, to be somebody up.   At the Tremont House, St. Alban's, the watchers
were numerous.   Two of my fellow-passengers per train,
who had been reading newspapers all day, had settled themselves comfortably down with their feet resting on the ledge
of the stove, apparently with the purpose of reading newspapers all night.   In the middle room there was a recruiting
officer in a Tyrolese hat and tarnished shoulder-straps.   He
was hard at work at a round table covered with papers, and
occasionally received deputations of One, who approached,
muttered, spat, hawked, and withdrew.   The recruiting placard, of which he had seemingly just corrected the proof, lay
before him.   I timidly approached and read it.   I was quite
welcome to its perusal, and indeed I fancy the officer would
have willingly enlisted me, or any other two-legged, two-
armed man on the spot.   Vermont is not behind New York
in the fervency of its recruiting rhetoric.   The appeal I read
was quite equal to the " Follow the drum," " March, march,
New York and Rhode Island," and " Go where glory waits
thee," broadsides of the Atlantic cities.   The " Green Mountain Boys," as the Vermonters are pleased to call themselves,
were incited to emulate the " glory of Allen and of Warner."
They were informed that a few " smart young men," veterans
or otherwise, were needed for an artillery corps, just to " finish
up " the rebellion, which was already trampled under foot.
Their duties were to be light—their reward prodigious.   " You
have no picket duty," the placard went on to state ; " you
have no forced marches.   While others plod their weary way
on foot, you ride."   I thought upon our own recruiting baits

for " smart young men " during the Crimean war and the
Indian mutiny; the chromo-lithographic allurements held
out; the irresistible inducements of " coffee and hot rolls on
the line of march ;" and, surmising that the world was, as
nearly as possible, the same world all the world over, I went
hungry, but pacified, to bed. There were no chamber candles
at the Tremont House. There was no gas in the sleeping
apartments; but, on application to the lofty little landlord, I
was supplied with a species of cruet filled with Kerosene oil,
and garnished with a cotton wick. It smelt hideously on
being extinguished, and filled the room with a fatty smoke
which nearly choked me. I fortunately went to sleep, and
woke up alive ; still, in case of asphyxia or any other casualty,
there was medical aid close at hand. I was in room seven-
teen, and in room fourteen " Mrs. Doctress Laoese Smith "
had hung out her sign. " Mrs. Doctress Laoese Smith "
was to be consulted at all hours. She cured everything; she
promised all things, including secrecy. For all that ended in
" is," for all that ended in " ism," and for all that ended in
" ia," she was infallible. Closely-printed handbills, headed
" See what a woman can do !" were freely stuck upon the
walls of the Tremont. Testimonials, signed " Cynthia Pike,"
" Betsey Vose," with many others, proclaimed her pills to be
" purely vegetable." I slept and dreamt that Mrs. Doctress
Smith was attending me for chronic elephantiasis, and that
Cynthia Pike had inveigled me, by promises of unlimited
greenbacks and Drake's Plantation-Bitters, to enlist in the
Green Mountain Boys.

In the raw morning we rose, swallowed some scalding

coffee, were charged a dollar and a half apiece for the accommodation we had *not* enjoyed, and were jolted in the Tremont coach to the station. Soon after six a train started for Rouse's Point. They had forgotten to kindle the fuel in the stove, and the cold was almost unbearable; but we were consoled by the thought that at Rouse's Point we should "make connections," and be landed by breakfast time, say, by half-past nine, at Montreal. Please to observe that we had already been twenty-three hours on the road, and that fifteen hours was to have been, according to *Appleton*, the duration of our journey. A very intelligent young mechanical engineer, an American, who sat over against us in the cars, told us that the "machine shop" at St. Alban's was a very extensive and highly important one. Let me notice for the benefit of comparative philologists, that what we call a "shop"—a place where articles are sold by retail—our curious cousins call a "store," and that what we designate a factory—a place where articles are *made* by wholesale—they term a "shop." Their nomenclature may perhaps be justified by some old English precedent with us nearly obsolete. In English builders' yards and manufactories, the by-laws governing the workpeople are called, I think, "shop-rules."

The intelligent engineer first dashed our hopes in respect to breakfasting at Montreal by telling us that "he didn't think it likely," and that we might deem ourselves fortunate if we arrived by noon. He then entered into general conversation, informed us that he was going to Toronto, that there were a good many Liverpool "chaps" and London "chaps" working in the St. Alban's "shop," and that on the whole he approved of the "old country." I happened to mention my supper misadventure of the previous night, whereat a saturnine grin stole over his countenance, and he remarked that, liquor laws notwithstanding, he would back Vermont for a show of drunken men against any other State in the Union. "You get the stuff on the sly," he said. I had heard of the so-called show of the "striped pig" as one illicit method of obtaining alcohol in Maine; but in Vermont it would seem that when you have the "office" given you, and enter the "right place," you ask "how the baby is?" The keeper of the drug, or fruit, or grocery store, whichever it may be, winks, and says, "Bully." You go downstairs into a cellar or a back yard, and find, in a remote corner, a cupboard full of whisky, brandy, or rum bottles. You fill for yourself, drink, replace the bottle, and on going out present the proprietor of the "baby" with ten or fifteen cents, wherewith to purchase, I presume, a coral for the infant. The health of "the baby" in Vermont is asked after with much solicitude.

Now it may have struck you that in grumbling because I could not obtain anything stronger than tea to wash down a meal after a long and fatiguing journey I was unjust and unreasonable. In Rome you must live with the Romans. Being in Vermont I was perhaps bound to do, without complaining, as the Vermonters did. If the legislature of that State, or of Maine, or elsewhere, discovering that hotels and railway refreshment-room keepers could not vend beer, wine, or spirits without their customers getting mad drunk and shooting or stabbing one another, and that a licensed tavern was a chronic cause of *delirium tremens*, robbery, and

profligacy among the community—if, in this embarrassing
conjuncture, they determined in their wisdom utterly to
abolish and prohibit the liquor traffic within their boundaries,
I, as a foreigner, could have apparently no possible right to
protest.   Being a stranger in the land, I am certainly under
a tacit obligation to conform to that land's manners, customs,
and enactments.   But I conceive it to be hard, if not cruel—
to be absurd, if not preposterous—to deny a traveller who
does not wish to get drunk, but only to take a little fermented something at his meals for his stomach's sake—a
glass of wine or a mug of beer; when, at the same time, it
is patent and notorious that the people who *do* want to get
drunk can so intoxicate themselves on the sly at any hour
of the day or night, and that the Liquor Law in Maine, Vermont, and elsewhere, is a sham and a lie.   I don't think it
tells much in favour of the morality or the honour of a
commonwealth when its citizens chuckle over a consistent,
although clandestine, violation of its laws.   I think an honest
man would rather go thirsty than become an accomplice
in a cynical fraud and imposture.   Perhaps it is better
to drink cold water than to rush to the exhibition of
the "striped pig," or dive into the cellar where the "baby"
is on view.   I am informed there are grocers in the
State of Vermont who will sell you convivial catsup
and Worcestershire sauce, one bottle of which is warranted
to produce inebriety.   Druggists dispense artful medicines
which make their takers "tight."   Half the "bitters" and
"cordials" advertised are only alcohol in disguise; and
decoctions of quassia and gentian are mingled with a fiery

kind of rum, called, from the labyrinthine gait to which its
consumption leads, "tangle-leg." Hypocrisy, however, surpasses itself in the vendition of tin cubes, neatly painted and
lettered to represent Bibles and Testaments, but which are in
reality case-bottles of whisky. I need scarcely say that, in
carrying on the liquor traffic " on the sly," the vilest poison
is sold at extortionate rates, and that the rich people who can
afford to keep a " baby" for themselves import wines and
liquors of the best quality, and get drunk behind their own
window-shutters with great alacrity and contentment. The
whole of which facts I commend to the notice of Mr. Wilfred
Lawson and the beatified sages of the United Kingdom
Alliance.

We were very glad, at half-past seven in the blue-grey
morning, to reach Rouse's Point. We were within a mile
and a half of the British frontier, and a two hours' ride would
bring us to Montreal. Judge of our amazement, our fury,
our agony, and our despair, when, on arriving at the point,
we were coolly informed that the train for Montreal had just
left, and that it would be half-past seven in the evening,
exactly twelve hours thence, before another train took its
departure. This was too much. Somebody, I think, swore.
I know *I* did. There were at least twenty of us—men,
women, and children—shut out on the slippery ice on a bitter
morning, with no other prospect than that of " laying over."

Some of our companions had seemingly already experienced
the tender mercies of Rouse's Point. An infuriated gentleman with a large beard, a scalskin cap, ditto gloves, and
cunningly-embroidered moccasins, who had charge of one of

the prettiest young widows and one of the prettiest young
widow's sisters I ever travelled with, said he would be some-
thinged if he stood this, and that he would "have it out of
Myers." Suddenly there arose a cry for Myers. Rumour
took up Myers's name, and bore it on the wintry breeze.
People who had never seen him, nor five minutes before
ever heard of him, cried, "Onward to Myers!" More experienced voyagers mentioned him with grim disparagement
as "old Myers." I felt my fingers crisp, my cheek tingle,
my teeth grow firm-set—I felt that I must see Myers or
die.

Myers was simply the traffic manager of the Montreal and
Champlain Railway. We found him, after ten minutes'
sliding and stumbling about the rambling dépôt, in a vast
timber counting-house, the principal ornaments of which
were any number of mendacious time-bills, a high stool like
that which gaol-warders sit upon to see that the prisoners do
not talk, and a gigantic stove—which last I can compare to
nothing but the Foul Fiend himself, for it was nearly red-hot,
and had *two pipes* branching from its lateral walls like
horns. In front of this demoniacal machine stood Myers,
warming his spine. He evidently knew what was coming.
He had had to do with infuriated travellers, probably, five
hundred times before. He was ready for anything. When
Mr. Artemus Ward, journeying over the plains to California,
was seized and plundered by predatory Indians, the Sachem
who stripped him made him a speech, and said he hoped to
meet him in the Happy Hunting-Grounds. "If he du," adds
Mr. Ward, in his account of the transaction, "there will be

a Fite." But Myers was ready for any number of "fites." He was in fighting trim. He wore a very close-fitting vest or jerkin or polka jacket of knitted woollen stuff, so that you had no chance of laying hold of the skirts of his garment, and his spiky grey hair was cut close to his head, so that you could grasp no lovelocks of his, and procure no purchase if, with tentative thumbs, you strove to gouge him. He was a little man who wore spectacles, and was probably sixty years of age; but he was emphatically All There—lithe, agile, vivacious, defiant—full of resource, fertile of expedient, and as hard as nails.

A chorus of complaints, of maledictions, of indignant requests to know what our detention meant, greeted Myers on our entrance. He was not dismayed. From the front of the stove he leapt with cat-like agility to the top of the high stool, laid the foot of one leg across the thigh of the other, looked through his bright spectacles at me, and shaking his forefinger, said, "You've asked me one question. Let me ask you another. Why wasn't the Vermont Central Operator at his post?" As, up to this moment, I had been wholly unaware of the existence of the Vermont central operator, I was naturally unable to answer this question, and Myers consequently had me on the hip. In answer to subsequent inquiries, he replied that he could do nothing. We must "lay over" till half-past seven at night. There was, to be sure, a freight or luggage train which left Rouse's Point for Montreal at half-past two in the afternoon; but he had no power to permit us to go by this, which, as a rule, did not carry passengers. If the Vermont central operator had been at

his post, all this—*pace* Myers—would not have happened.
It was the duty of that remiss official to have telegraphed
the previous night that we had arrived at St. Alban's several
hours overdue. Then—according to Myers—the Montreal
and Champlain people would not have started their train
from Rouse's Point until ours had arrived to "make connections." As it was, they had heard nothing of us, and caring
nothing for us, I suppose, had let us "slide."

To Myers's surprise, however, we declined to enter into
his serene scheme of "laying over" quietly. We determined
to telegraph the Grand Trunk Railway at Montreal for a
special train, or at least for permission to have a passenger-
car attached to the freight-train of half-past two. Myers
allowed us to communicate with the Montreal authorities,
but he did not hold out the faintest hopes of our wishes being
acquiesced in. He didn't think it could be done, he said.
We might telegraph. I must admit that Rouse's Point was .
very liberal in the matter of telegrams. We might have
flashed epic poems or five-act tragedies along the wires all
day long had we possessed a taste that way.

As it was absolutely necessary for some time to elapse
before an answer could be received to our message—which
we couched in an urgent and almost impassioned style—we
asked Myers where we could obtain some breakfast. He
grinned, like a grey-haired little gnome. "I mustn't tell you,"
quoth he. "I live in a glass house. I mustn't recommend any
hotel." Being pressed, however, he informed us that there
were two superior hotels in the place—the Massachusetts
House and the Webster House. We threw up a greenback

for choice, and it fluttered down with Mr. Lincoln's portrait uppermost, the which we agreed to denote Massachusetts— for Mr. Lincoln is very unlike Webster, especially that Webster whose Christian name was Daniel. The inevitable hackney-coach was in waiting to jolt us off to the usual over-heated tenement, with its gigantic spittoons in every corner, its naked dining-hall and its breakfast of beefsteaks, pork-steaks, eggs, salt butter, and scalding tea. At the Massachu-setts House, however, there was a bar, where all kinds of liquids were retailed at the rate of ten cents a glass. In explanation of this cheering fact, we were informed that we were no longer in Vermont, but in the more cosmopolitan State of New York, a corner of which, at two days' and nearly four hundred miles' distance, pokes its nose into Canada.

Not readily shall I forget the philosophical equanimity with which two of our belated companions bore this, to me, scandalous and intolerable delay. While the handsome traveller in the sealskin cap, who had charge of the pretty widow and her sister, was raging up and down like a lion at feeding time who fails to discern the keeper's wheelbarrow with the shinbones of beef coming round the corner,—while the pretty widow herself was pouting, and her prettier sister whimpering with vexation,—while one hot-headed French Canadian, losing all patience, rushed off to hire a waggon and team and drive to St. John's, twenty miles distant, and a more cautious Statesman availed himself of a train to Ogdens-burg, whence he could cross to Prescott, on the Canadian side, and so by a circuitous route reach Montreal some time between Christmas and New Year's Day,—the two philosophers never murmured, never desponded. They calmly alighted from the coach at the Massachusetts House, carrying between them a valise. This they opened, and produced what seemed to be a carboy of chemicals, but was in reality a bottle containing some two quarts of whisky. They were hardy, horny, Scottish men. It was just eight in the morning. They ordered tumblers, hot water, and sugar. They sat down calmly, with the whisky bottle between them, as though about to listen to the lecture of some good book, and, brewing themselves two steaming tumblers of toddy, were speedily rapt in the contemplation and absorption thereof, and allowed Myers, and Rouse's Point, and a vain and giddy world, to go by.

It was now noon, and the toddy-tumblers of the philosophers had been replenished more than once ere a courteous reply arrived to our message. Myers was brought to confusion, and humbled in an exemplary manner. A passenger-car was attached to the freight-train, which conveyed us as far as St. Lambert, at the foot of that wonderful Victoria Bridge which spans the St. Lawrence at Montreal, and there the officials of the Grand Trunk Railway had kindly provided an engine to take us across the bridge. Otherwise, there being no footway, and the half-frozen river being practicable neither for sleighs nor for canoes, we should have been forced to remain many more weary hours at St. Lambert. As it was, when at half-past seven on the evening of the 24th of December we were landed at the Grand Trunk Dépôt, in Bonaventure Street, Montreal, we found that it had taken us just thirty-six hours to accomplish a railway journey of four hundred and one miles.

It was a mercy, at all events, that I was not compelled to spend the joyous season of Christmas at Rouse's Point. It was no fault of Myers that I did not. I have since come to look upon this malevolent freight-agent as a kind of subdued fiend, and when I meet my dear travelling companion, and we have a talk about old times, he often interposes in our roadway gossip such an exclamation as, "Oh! that Myers." Few beings of earthly mould could have endured the mean temperature of his counting-house as Myers did. It was insufferably hot. In one corner he had a vast pile of logs. He might have been a grand inquisitor bent upon burning all us martyrs to railway mismanagement, alive. Failing a Ridley or a Latimer, this Torquemada of Rouse's Point, whenever he was greeted with a fresh complaint, turned round to his stove, stooped down, presented, like Washington Irving's Stout Gentleman, the disc of his nethers to the spectator, and crammed many logs into that fiery furnace. He was always stoking his stove.

I hope there is a law of libel in the United States of America. I should like the Vermont Central and the Montreal and Champlain Railway Companies to bring an action against me for declaring that our detention at St. Alban's and at Rouse's Point was utterly scandalous and unwarrantable. There was no snow then upon the rails. There was no mishap to either car or locomotion. Our journey was protracted to thrice its publicly advertised duration, either in sheer wantonness and recklessness, or—as has

been since shrewdly hinted to me by numerous Americans—
to serve the ends of the hotel-keepers of St. Alban's and
Rouse's Point. Does anybody get a commission, I wonder,
on the profits accruing from belated travellers? Are any
letters of advice ever despatched containing such items as
"Credit you 2 dolls. 25c. for two Britishers chawed up in this
location?"

I would entreat you to observe that, in penning a narrative
which to the cursory reader may appear only a grotesque
catalogue of petty details and ordinary misadventures, I have
had a sufficiently serious end in view. This four hundred miles'
journey to the Canadian frontier afforded me my first opportunity of looking behind the scenes in the United States—of
rubbing the gilt off the gingerbread—of contrasting the sober
polished dignity of Boston and the glittering splendour of
New York with the shiftless, slovenly squalor which too often
marks the interior of the country—and of remarking how
the railway system of America, which has been bragged about
and bolstered up to impose on the European market to an
almost incredible extent, breaks down in effect under the
slightest pressure, and shows itself deplorably deficient in
comfort, punctuality, cleanliness, and discipline. And pray
bear in mind that my strictures have applied as yet not to
the vast wildernesses and but yesterday trackless prairies of
the West, but to the well-settled, thickly-populated, and
highly-pious states of Vermont and New York. Indeed, I
have heard that they manage things much better in Illinois.

However, we were timeously rescued from the grip of
Myers, and the chances of passing our holidays on the frozen

bosom of Lake Champlain, with the alternative of a trip to the equally congealed region of Lake Memphremagog. Memphremagog! ye hyperborean powers, what a name for a place in which to sing Christmas carols! Myers, whose attributes were Protean in their mutation, turned up as a ticket-clerk before we started by the goods train. They told me afterwards that he was likewise a custom-house officer and a carrier. Perhaps he is an amateur photographer and a minister of the New Connection to boot, and delivers lectures in the evening on the American Constitution and the Origin of Species. He tried hard, in his capacity of ticket-clerk, to "financeer" us out of an additional forty cents, maintaining that our tickets were only good to St. Lambert, a village on the hither side of the St. Lawrence; but, as we had bought and paid for our tickets to Montreal direct, we declined to enter into his views, and he "financeered" in vain. Irritated by long-drawn-out woes, my companion began to say very strong things about chicanery and fraud. I was in better mood, however, now that we were really off, and bestowed on Myers a parting and fervent benediction. I hope it did him good. I can see him now, spiky and spectacled, standing on the platform, and chattering his wicked old teeth at me.

The British frontier is about a mile and a half north of Rouse's Point. The Canadians declare that the Point ought to belong to her Britannic Majesty, and not to Uncle Sam, and that when we agreed to accept as our boundary the 45th parallel of latitude, we were led to believe, from maps designedly falsified, that Rouse's Point was north of that parallel, and within our territory. The place, however, seems to have been all along a kind of debateable land. The Americans, some few years since, seemed equally puzzled with ourselves to determine to whom it belonged, and abandoned the construction of a half-finished citadel, which went afterwards by the name of Fort Blunder. They have made up their minds now in right earnest as to their property in the Point, and a tremendous fortress is being rapidly completed, commanding the mouth of the St. John's River and Lake Champlain. Fort Blunder has become Fort Fact.

It was at a place called Stott's, I think, that two tiny indices told me that we had entered upon another country. A comfortable-looking custom-house officer, with an ample waistcoat and bushy whiskers, entered the car and asked if we had anything liable to duty in our luggage. Of course we had not anything; and on retiring the comfortable custom-house officer—he was an Irishman by the way—absolutely wished us "Merry Christmas." I was almost petrified with astonishment. Was the world coming to an end? What could an American official mean by being civil to anybody? A large Canadian swathed in furs, who sat near me—they run to an enormous size, these Canadians, and in their winter garb would be fearsome were they not jolly—informed me that we were in the dominions of "our good Queen." I have translated the Canadian. He said *notre bonne Reine*, and naturally, for he was a Frenchman. Then, scratching away the frost from the pane, I saw by the road-side a horizontal bar of wood between two perpendiculars, very much like a gallows. It was not that emblem of civilisation, but a sign-post, and thereon were painted in the two tongues the words, "Railway crossing—*Traverse du chemin de fer*." From this I was enabled to realise the conception that we were now in the land of half-and-half— of about perhaps the most curious and bizarre medley of Franco-Anglicism, or Anglo-Gallicism, of conflicting speech, creed, manners, and customs, with which I was ever permitted to make acquaintance.

I was very glad to find myself under the sway "*de notre bonne Reine;*" but I should have dearly liked to see the Royal Arms up at the little post-office at the next station we came to—Grand Ligne. So many thousand miles away, and fresh from a somewhat surfeiting banquet of democracy in the Great Republic, a man is apt to feel so loyal that he would be glad even to accept service of a writ, for the sake of its beginning "Victoria by the grace of God." The lion and the unicorn made no sign at Lacolle, nor at the considerable French town of St. John's, nor at Lacadie, nor at Brosseaux; but we never halted to take in a fresh cargo of passengers without becoming aware that the big, burly, bearded, bass-voiced fellows who came tumbling into the cars, laughing and joking, and the black-eyed, ruddy-cheeked, white-teethed, lissome lassies who accompanied them, had little community of race with the spare, sad, taciturn people whom we had just left south of the 45th parallel.

Canada has often been declared by the wise men south of that parallel to be "knocking at the door of the Union." With all humility, I may venture to express the opinion that, if Canada ever resorts to that method of verberation, it will be after the fashion adopted by Mr. Clown in the pantomime. You have seen him knock at the door of a respectable house-keeper, and then cunningly lay himself down athwart the threshold—his parti-coloured stomach prone to the step. Out comes the respectable householder in answer to the summons, and down of course he tumbles over the perfidiously prostrate pantomimist. If Canada knocks for admission, America would do well not to listen. For the rest, the assertion that the British provinces are anxious to join the American Union is about as baseless and as absurd as the counter-allegation I have as often heard, that the State of Maine is anxious for junction with the British Crown. Sugar and salt, ice and fire, black and white, Alpha and Omega, are not so easily married. Precisely as the most rampant English Radical is ten times more a Tory than the most advanced American Conservative, so is the least ardent Republican in the United States five hundred times more democratic than the wildest disciple of Mr. Bright.

We had one Canadian in our midst, who was quite up-roarious in his loyalty, sang in broken English snatches of "God save the Queen," and endeavoured to "rile" his American neighbour by offering to buy a hat full of green-backs from him at the rate of twenty cents to the dollar. The Yankee, however, was placable, and took it all very good-naturedly, offering, in return, to buy as much gold as "ever he heard of" from him at par. And so we went on through the snow till darkness closed up round us, and merged the great pine forests into one sable curtain, and the lamps in the cars were lit, and only the increased rattle and roar and the shrieking of the engine told us that we were passing through the colossal tube of the Victoria Bridge. Then, suddenly, a "half-and-half" French conductor put his head 'in at the car door, and exclaimed, " Dis is Point St. Charles ; but, by gar, I'm go on to Bonaventure Street right away." I asked him if we should be long ere we reached our destination. He answered cheerily, " Five minute ; we go dere as fast as beans." Of the rapidity in progression of the aforesaid esculent I have no exact know-ledge. There was some hidden reference, perchance, in the conductor's simile to the beanstalk immortalised by Jack, but it was certainly odd to hear a Frenchman talk of "going as fast as beans."

" I'm Murphy !" " I'm O'Kelly !" " Ask for Kinahan, yer honour." " Good luck to ye, take Shaughnessey's sleigh !" " Captain, shure it's Macgillicuddy that always drives ye." These were the cries that greeted us as we emerged shivering from the dépôt in Bonaventure Street, Montreal. At once we were encompassed by the wild Irish. They all wanted to drive us anywhere. But to be called " Captain," and " Yer honour !" to find civil and humorous Irishmen ! surely the world was coming to an end again. It had been my fortune during the past four weeks to gaze upon Irish humanity under two very widely varying aspects. I shall never forget my Sunday's journey from Dublin to Cork, and through the soft and smiling south—the country made beautiful and joyous by Heaven—the delicious expanse of wood, and water, and green knoll, and purple mountain, all marred and disfigured by the groups of ruined, windowless, doorless, roofless cottages,—the long lines of unhinged gates and hacked-down fences—the results of evictions, the monuments of man's cruelty and oppression. I shall never forget the forlorn and rickety shandrydans, and their inconceivable ragged and unkempt drivers that conveyed us from one station to another, and the tattered rabble that hung about the place of embarkation. I shall never forget that the last view I had of Ireland was on the jetty at Queenstown, and in the shape of a horde of lamentable ragamuffins of both sexes and all ages, holding out their dismal dirty hands for alms—alms that were flung them as one would fling nuts into a cageful of baboons. When I landed in America I found another Irishman—the Irishman with a pocketful of greenbacks—the Irishman who had waxed fat and kicked—the Irishman who ate meat three times a day, and had a vote, and hated the Saxon, and let him know it—the rampant, ferocious Irish-American. But in Murphy, whose sleigh we engaged to take us to the St. Lawrence Hall Hotel, Montreal, was a third and entirely different specimen of the Celt. He was very independent, but exceedingly jovial. He would have his rights, but he was infinitely obliging ; he wouldn't be tyrannised over, but he didn't want to tyrannise over us ; he was a merry, hard-working, civil, prosperous fellow ;—and I am given to understand that there are a great many thousands of Murphies in her Majesty's British North American provinces.

Murphy had two fat horses in his sleigh, and he rattled us at a tremendous rate through the streets of Montreal, which a severe frost had made as hard as steel, and as slippery as

glass. If from time to time, ceding to the excitement of
the moment, he threw up his arms, kicked up his legs, and
uttered a sound somewhat akin to Mr. Walt Whitman's
"barbaric yaup," is Murphy to be blamed? I think not. A
Russian ischvostchik would have done the same under
similar circumstances. Pardon this allusion to the ischvostchik; but there are sleighs in Russia as well as in Canada,
even as there is a river in Marathon and a river in Monmouth, and both are very much alike. There are few things
on earth so exhilarating as a sleigh-ride in good company,
and with plenty of buffalo robes; but only imagine the
enhancement of your ecstasy when you know that a remu-
nerative fare awaits you at the end of your journey!

Murphy disdained to make any overcharge. He asked but
75 cents for that which his cousins, those irreclaimable
savages and extortioners, the hackney-coachmen of New
York, would have demanded three or four dollars for. And,
in addition, he had cheerfully carried our luggage from the
car and loaded his sleigh with it—a condescension of which
no New York jarvey would have been guilty. Still, Murphy
very speedily gave us to learn that he was not to be trifled
with, and that he had a practical acquaintance with the
fluctuations of American currency. In the innocence of my
heart I offered him, having no silver, a dollar's—well, I won't
say "worth"—but a dollar's representative value of ten- and
five- cent notes. "The divil a bit of me takes *that*, yer
honour," quoth Murphy. "*Shure, I could snaze it away.*"
Nor would he look at an entire legal-tender dollar greenback
from Mr. Chase's own mint. Nor would he regard with

favour a certain two-dollar bill of the bank of St. Alban's, as yellow as a canary bird and as ragged as Sylvester Daggerwood's pocket-handkerchief, which I have been striving, but unavailingly, to sell at a ruinous discount any time this last six months, and which I am willing to dispose of to any collector for twopence sterling. Would you like to invest in the issue of the Ox Bank of Pyquag? Murphy would have nothing but silver, and so we asked the clerk in the office of the St. Lawrence Hall to pay him.

The entire silver coinage of the United States seems to have found its way into Canada. The decimal monetary system has been legalised in our possessions—though the shopkeepers are given to pricing their wares in shillings and pence—and a few dollars and cents bearing her Majesty's effigy are current; but the immense bulk of the circulating silver medium bears the cognisance of the stars and stripes. In gold, English sovereigns divide the palm with the American eagle and double-eagle—the last of which is perhaps the most beautiful and splendid coin ever moneyed in any mint. I wonder whether melancholy thoughts ever come over Americans travelling in Canada, when in an alien land they see passed from hand to hand the gold and silver pieces which should be in their own. I am afraid they indulge in no such sad reflections. The Americans have discovered an alcoholic principle in pulp, and have got drunk with paper. Paper, they say, is better than silver, better than gold; and so the woolly-headed idol wears paper collars, and the name of Wall-street should be changed to that of the Rue Quincampoix.

In Montreal we spent a thoroughly English and jovial Christmas. It would be indecorous, however, in me to mingle public matters with a from-day-to-day record of the enjoyment of private hospitality. I may discreetly hint, in any case, that from the civil and military authorities in Montreal, and from several members of the Executive Council, Provincial Parliament, we received a great deal more kindness and courtesy than one of us, at least, deserved. And I may add that her Majesty's Scots Fusilier Guards and her Majesty's Grenadier Guards were both quartered at Montreal, and that they were both very much alike—especially the Grenadiers —in their readiness to show attention to their wandering countrymen.

"Appleton's Illustrated Handbook of American Travel" informs its readers that the population of Montreal is nearly seventy-five thousand, and is steadily increasing. The inhabitants of Montreal maintain very stoutly that they number over one hundred thousand, and that they are going on fairly for a hundred and ten. At any rate, it is the most populous city of British North America, and it is most picturesquely situated at the foot of the Royal Mountain—"Le Mont Réal" —from which it takes its name. The city stands on a large island, at the confluence of the Ottawa and St. Lawrence Railways, and in fertility and cultivation is considered the garden of Canada East. The solid limestone quays along the banks of the St. Lawrence are unsurpassed by those of any other city in America, and, uniting with the locks and cut stone wharves of the Lachine Canal, they present for several miles a display of continuous masonry which has no parallel.

There are no hideous levees here, as on the Mississippi and the Ohio; but a broad and noble terrace separates Montreal from the river throughout the whole extent of the city.

The suburbs are full of handsome limestone mansions— solid as well as tasteful structures, the abode of wealthy English and French merchants. The two nations are pretty equally balanced in numbers—the French, perhaps, preponderating. The Roman Catholic—allowing for Irish as well as French worshippers—is, of course, the dominant religion. Among the Protestant sects the Episcopalians and the Scottish Presbyterians seem to have the sway. There is a very remarkable Roman Catholic Cathedral in the Place d'Armes, whose twin Gothic towers, seen from afar off, bear no inconsiderable resemblance to that other Notre Dame on the banks of the Seine. Of other Catholic churches, of convents and nunneries, there is an almost endless succession. The Established Church of Scotland has two very beautiful fanes —one, St. Andrew's, looking like Salisbury Cathedral in miniature. The Church of England has a noble cathedral, Christchurch. The Wesleyans and Independents have respectively chapels in—please to observe the salmagundi of languages—Griffintown and the Rue Montcalm, Gosford-street and the Rue Radégonde. By a parity of disparity an exclusively French village in the environs, where you may read on the sign-boards the ensigns of "forgeron," and "cafétier," and "maréchal ferrant," is called Mile-end. The oddest *mélange* I remember was in the case of a worthy Frenchman on the road to the Royal Mountain, who sold tea and sugar, and called his store "La Grocerie Royale." The terminology of "grocerie" suggesting a compromise between "épicier," on the one part, and "grocer" on the other, was, to say the least, ingenious.

When I state that the Bank of Montreal is one of the finest examples of Corinthian architecture to be found on the American continent; that the Rue Notre Dame is full of gay and handsome shops, very like those of the Rue St. Honoré at Paris; that the Bonsecours Market is an imposing edifice in the Doric style, which cost two hundred and eighty thousand dollars; that the Court-house, or Palais de Justice, and the Post-office, are both vast and noble structures, and that the city is full of cottages, and schools, and hospitals, the *blasé* and the indifferent among my readers may perhaps begin to yawn, and to say that they have heard all this sort of thing before. I respectfully submit that, to all intents and purposes, they have heard this sort of thing but very seldom. I am bold enough to think that about nine-tenths even of my educated countrymen have about as definite an idea of Montreal, of Toronto, and of Quebec, as they have of Owyhee or of Antananarivo. Is it impertinent in me to assume that many in England are as ignorant as I was the day before yesterday? It seems to me that, abating a few merchants, a few engineers, and a few military men, it has hitherto been nobody's business in England to know what the Canadas are like. It is not the "thing" to go to Canada. One can "do" Niagara without penetrating into the British provinces. English artists don't make sketching excursions thither. The Alpine Club ignore it. Why does not some one start a Cataract Club? We let these magnificent provinces, with their inexhaustible productiveness—for asperity of climate is no sterility—their noble cities, their hardy and loyal population, go by. We pass them in silence and neglect. We listen approvingly while some college pedant as bigoted as a Dominican, but without his acumen, as conceited as a Benedictine, but without his learning, prates of the expediency of abandoning our colonies. If we meanly and tamely surrendered these, the brightest jewels in the Queen's crown, can we tell into whose hands they would fall—what hatred and ill-will might spring up among those now steady and affectionate in their attachment to our rule, but from whom we had withdrawn our countenance and protection ? But Canada has been voted a " bore " and to be " only a colonial " would apply, it would seem, to a province as well as to a bishop. I have not the slightest desire to talk guide-book, or even to institute odious comparisons, by dwelling on the strength and solidity, the cleanliness and comeliness, the regard for Authority, the cheery but self-respecting and respect-exacting tone which prevails in society; the hearty, pleasant, obliging manners of the people one sees at every moment in this far-off city of a hundred thousand souls, with its cathedrals, its palaces, its schools, its convents, its hospitals, its wharves, its warehouses, its marvellous Tubular Bridge, its constantly-growing commerce, its hourly-increasing prosperity, its population of vivacious and chivalrous Frenchmen, who, somehow, do *not* hate their English and Scottish fellow-subjects, but live in peace and amity with them, and who are assuredly not in love with the Yankees. But it really does make a travelling Englishman " kinder mad," as they would say south of the forty-fifth parallel, when he has just quitted a city which, in industry, in energy, and in public spirit is certainly second to none on the European continent; and which, in the cleanliness of its streets, the beauty of its public buildings, and the tone of its society surpasses many of them—to know that a majority of his country are under the impression that the Canadian towns are mere assemblages of log-huts, inhabited by half-savage backwoodsmen in blanket coats and mocassins ; and that a few mischievous or demented persons are advocating the policy of giving up the Canadas altogether. Happily there is a gentleman in Pall Mall who has been to Canada—who has seen Quebec, and Toronto, and Montreal. The name of that gentleman—the first in our realm—is Albert Edward, Prince of Wales; and he knows what Canada is like, and of what great things it is capable.

CHAPTER IV.

How many rivers we crossed on the night of the 22nd December, 1863, on our road along the "shore line" from Boston, in the commonwealth of Massachusetts—pray mark the word "commonwealth :" in all public documents, advertisements, and the like, the descendants of the Pilgrim Fathers never fail to keep before the eyes of the citizens an assertion of State rights, internal sovereignty, supremacy, independence, and so forth—I cannot now rightly determine. My guide-books were packed, and my maps snugly rolled up, preparatory for that trip into Canada, where, upon British soil, I spent Christmas-day. Nor, I am afraid, had I been told the names of all the rivers, would the information prove of much avail to me at this moment. I have a bad memory for figures. No less a personage than a United States judge interrogated me lately respecting the tonnage of the port of Liverpool. I broke down shamefully. I was out of my reckoning, I fancy, about eighty thousand tons. But consolation was my portion when my questioner confidentially hinted that he, too, had no head for statistics ; and that, happening once in England to be asked at a dinner party, by a distinguished *savant*, what was the death ratio in his native State, he answered boldly and at hazard, "one in forty-seven," being entirely ignorant as to whether it were actually one in a million or one in two.

There were many rivers, I am certain, across which our train was ferried, and in all those rivers there was ice. Did we cross the Penobscot? I think so; but, at all events, you will be enabled to correct me by the aid of a gazetteer. When the train is slidden on to the deck of a ferry steamer the dreadful jarring and jolting of American railway locomotion temporarily cease. You feel no more the land-sickness —quite as agonising sometimes as that of the sea—the wheel-nausea leaves you; you glide along softly, smoothly, quietly. Last night, however, the water passage was of no dulcet kind. I could hear the ice spitefully backbiting us and digging into our ribs as we sped along; I could hear it cracking and groaning, "like noises in a swound." Railway traffic, when there is water in the way, is fast becoming beset with tribulation. Yesterday's night train from New York to Boston was half a dozen hours late. The ice was here, the ice was there, the ice was all around. We were more fortunate, and made the dépôt in Twenty-seventh Street, New York, by half-past six in the morning, having left Boston at half-past eight the previous night. We had accomplished a journey of two hundred and thirty miles, or thereabouts, in ten hours. No very great pace, perhaps, but tolerable. If you have hitherto thought that the most go-a-head people in creation run railway trains that can equal our Brighton or Didcot expresses in speed, you are mistaken. The average rate in the United States is twenty miles an hour; but I have little doubt that the first American who reads this will declare me to be a base calumniator, and that there are lightning expresses out west that run one hundred miles in sixty minutes, habitually.

It did not so much matter, perhaps, what time we—for I had an American friend travelling with me—arrived in Twenty-seventh Street. We were occupants of a very comfortable double-berthed state-room in a sleeping-car. At the moderate outlay of one dollar a head we were privileged to undress and to go to bed. The conductor of the train was probably of Sancho Panza's opinion as to the inestimable virtues of sleep. He let us sleep. Having paid our dollar, we were, he held, clearly entitled to slumber as long as ever we pleased. The citizens who had reposed in the remaining berths arose as it suited their convenience, drew on their boots and went on their way. It was no business of theirs to wake us up. No officials came to disturb us. We might have snored as long as the Seven Sleepers of Ephesus, or until the train, sleeping cars and all, went back to Boston, had I not haply chanced to wake up, and to find that I was very hungry, and that broad daylight had set in. Then remembering that this was the 22nd of December, and that the just-elapsed 21st was the shortest of the whole year, I scrambled out of my berth apprehending that, at the least, high noon had struck. It was, however, but eight o'clock. Then we shook ourselves, shivered, and went after our luggage.

This is a country in which a man has to look after himself. This is a land in which, save from negroes, you cannot, even by paying for it, obtain solicitous and obsequious attendance.

Ten to one the subordinate—if you met a subordinate—whom you attempted to fee, would fling the paper douceur at your head, with a curse.   It may do a lazy man, and one who has been accustomed to be waited upon, good to have to wait upon himself.   It is salutary, but exceedingly disagreeable. It gives you a proper idea of man's dignity, independence, and the rest of it.   There was no one in Eden to black Adam's boots; Eve had to hem her own apron.   It is a grand thing to find yourself among patriots, who will see you in the hottest corner of Tophet before they will render you a common act of civility.   It makes you long to be, not yourself, but one of your British ancestors who went naked, daubed themselves all over with blue paint, rowed about in coracles, and burnt human sacrifices in wicker-work shrines under the mistletoe bough.   Those were the real times of freedom and independence.   When M. de Montalembert wants a fresh bath of liberty he should come to Twenty-seventh Street, New York, and try to get his luggage on a cold morning.

Did I happen to mention to you at the Cunard Wharf at Boston, when I first landed from the America, the Irish gentleman, doubtless a descendant of many kings, who was supposed to officiate as a porter in the Custom House, and whom I respectfully begged to assist me in adjusting the straps of a portmanteau which was slightly reluctant to close in consequence of the entire and originally neatly-packed contents having been turned topsy-turvy by the examining officer—did I tell you that this ornament to the Green Isle, whom I had intended presenting with fifty cents for his trouble, bade me " do it myself," accompanying the advice

with a pointed reference to my eyes and limbs? I saved my
fifty cents, but I took my first plunge in the bath of liberty.
The baggage superintendent at the Twenty-seventh Street
dépôt was likewise from Erin the Green. I have no doubt
that his remote progenitors are favourably mentioned in the
Annals of the Four Masters. Our luggage consisted of two
heavy portmanteaus. We had booked them at Boston, and
received the ordinary brass counter-checks. These checks
we gave up, and the portmanteaus were placed at our disposal. But how were we to carry them away, considering
that we were heavily laden, in addition, with umbrellas, rugs,
bags, and writing-cases? At this central railway dépôt there
was not one omnibus and not one hackney carriage to be
seen. There were half-a-dozen hulking Irishmen hanging
about, but not one of them would lift a little finger to help
us carry the two trunks into the street, where we might have
hailed a passing vehicle. Half-frozen, then, and baggageless,
we had to walk a couple of hundred yards, and wait for a
horse-railway car—these cars do not take luggage—which
conveyed us to the Brevoort House, a most comfortable hotel,
conducted, not on the American but on the European principle. We had previously asked the Irish superintendent, as
we were not Samsons enough to carry the load away ourselves, to permit them to be rebooked and left till called for,
giving us fresh checks. This he savagely refused to do. On
our arrival at the Brevoort we sent one of the civil and well-
disciplined servants of the house to the station with a description of the luggage written on a card, and instructions to
bring them back in a coach. The superintendent sent his

curses by return by way of compliment, and refused to give
them up. I wanted a warm bath and my breakfast, but I was
compelled to take another carriage, at the expense of a dollar
and a half, and proceed to the terminus again to demand the
portmanteaus. The superintendent told me that if he chose
he would make me wait there till two o'clock in the afternoon. To this proposition I demurred, and ventured to
inform him that if he did not surrender them instanter I
would jump over the counter and seize them by main force.
I beg to state that I am not by nature bellicose, and that if I
had been at the battle of Solferino I should probably have
turned much greener than Mr. Kinglake accused the Emperor
Napoleon of turning. The superintendent was the bigger and
the heavier man, but I thought it best to assume a courage I
seldom asserted, trusting to the driver of the carriage, who
was an American, tremendously tall and bony, who stood by,
enjoying the whole scene with much quiet gusto, to see fair
if anything like a " difficulty " arose. To my surprise the
superintendent gave in, and sulkily pushed the portmanteaus
across the counter. There was no fight in him, of which I
was unfeignedly glad. " Well out of it," I gratefully murmured, as the driver, with civil alacrity, proceeded to load the
roof of the carriage. The superintendent and I exchanged a
few words before departing. I told him that I would complain to the Company, and he told me in return that I might
go to Halifax. Then I remembered how very absurd was the
threat of appealing to authority in a city where authority,
unless it has a drawn sword or a loaded blunderbuss in its
grip, is derided and contemned. With joy I reflected that

Providence had gifted me, when provoked, with a highly
abusive Tongue. I am happy to hope that I strewed every
flower of eloquence I could cull from my garden of invective
on the head of decidedly the most insolent savage with whom
I ever yet made acquaintance. I never saw a man so infuriated. He soon exhausted his stock of execrations, and at
last absolutely danced with rage. He recovered coherence,
however, as we drove away, and yelled after me, that " such a
murtherin' black-hearted villain as I oughtn't to live." There
was something in that, O baggage superintendent ! How many
of us are fit to live, and how long ? And again I reflected,
when calmness came over me, that this was but Nemesis
after all. Perhaps I am connected by marriage with the
family of some tithe proctor, who in days gone by distrained on
the potatoes and the pigs of the finest peasantry in the world.
If we hadn't tried to foist Wood's halfpence on the Irish
people, that superintendent might have given up the port-.
manteaus earlier. Woe for Vinegar Hill, and the Boyne
water, and the pitch-cappings and half-hangings, and the
raids of the Orange yeomanry, for these, quite as much as the
flowers of eloquence, have made me, in the eyes of the baggage
superintendent, a " black-hearted and murtherin' villain."

" That cuss," observed the driver, when we reached the
hotel, " was deliberate ugly. Directly they've left off car-
ryin' a hod they turn ugly—those Irish do. They put me in
mind of what the judge said to a witness t'other day. They've
as much brass in their face as would make a wash-pail, and
as much sass as would fill it." Happily my driver was not an
Irishman. As balm to a wounded spirit commend me, how-

ever, to a first-class hotel breakfast in the United States.
After striped bass, broiled, fried oysters, stewed oysters, stuffed
clams, scrambled eggs, Massachusetts sausages, buckwheat
cakes, Graham bread, and milk toast, with perhaps some
Havana oranges or Catawba grapes as a wind up—stay, I
have left out the tender loin steak with fried potatoes, and
the hominy boiled and fried, and the pig's feet breaded—it
is hard, indeed, to be in an uncharitable mood with any of
your species. And harder still was it this morning to feel
morose or " deliberate ugly " in view of the beautiful wintry
weather, and Broadway crowded with gay dresses and pretty
faces. Ah ! those charming wearers of fur mantles and Paris
bonnets—bevies of minx and sable-backed ducks who flutter
through the great promenade of New York from Union Square
down as far as Canal Street. The little children are home
from school, too, just now, and Young America, in knicker-
bockers, in braided caftans, in Algerian burnouses, in scarlet
gipsy cloaks, in hats and caps of every form and feathers of
every hue, in cloth gaiters and Hessian boots, and frilled pantalettes,—the darlings in long fair ringlets and frizzled ringlets,
in muffs and boas, and capes and tippets—Young America is
amazing in Broadway ; laughing, racing, jumping, romping,
rushing hither and thither, dragging its parents and guardians
whithersoever it listeth, and generally productive of solace
and delight to the beholder. The Americans notoriously and
habitually spoil their children. They give them whatever
they ask for ; candies, toys, books, dolls, fine clothes, and little
Union flags to wave about in their games. In very few
American families out of New England—where, to be sure,

some of the vigour of the Puritanic manners yet obtains—
is there anything like discipline or subordination to be found
among the younger branches. The corridors of every hotel
are full of pretty, fair-haired, noisy, delightful children. They
crow and scream, and playfully essay to kick in the panels of
your door. Then out may come a nurse, and more rarely a
parent, who scolds them soundly and threatens " switching,"
at which the children laugh, for they know that the threat
has no fundamental basis. The American ladies are very
angry with Mr. Anthony Trollope for having stated, in an
otherwise admirably candid and observant book, that the
children in the States are fed upon pickles. Whether such
condiments form an integral portion of their diet I do not
know ; but I trust I shall not be blamed for hinting that a
few of the most uproarious juveniles in the Union might be
the better for a little " switching." Such merry but indomitable young dare-devils I never saw. But, plead the American .
mammas, it is useless as well as mischievous to correct them.
If punished never so slightly, they fall into hysterics, or have
the sulks.

However, this being Christmas time, the children have a
prescriptive and indefeasible right to be as noisy as ever they
please. Who shall gainsay them so late in December ? Not
I, for one, who have been wandering up and down Broadway
trying to conjure up, from the throng of laughing lineaments
around, something to remind me of one dear little face
thousands of miles away—a face that by this time, I trust, is
beginning to beam very sunnily over the Christmas goodies.
Happy faces are beaming, too, here in abundance ; there is

Christmas, thank God, all the world over. And if you feel strange or lonely, what can you do better than look up in the night at this wonderfully clear American sky, and watch the twinkling stars ? And when you have made out the old familiar friends, and recognise Charles's Wain, driving for ever and ever, with equal pace, through the great highway— the same Wain you saw in your Cockney Camberwell—you know and are thankful that the same kind Father is there to protect those dear to you at home, and to watch over you, a wanderer.

With a sky Italian in its dark blue tint, with the sun shining, with the streets crowded, with the shops teeming with toys and confectionery and holiday presents, and with cart-loads of evergreens to deck churches and houses lumbering by, there are but two little drawbacks to your pleasurable enjoyment of the season. The first is in being told that at New York, for some reason or other difficult of explanation, Christmas Day is not held as so bright, glorious, and convivial a festival as the 1st of January. On Christmas Day, I believe, all good folks go to church, and there are family dinners ; but New Year's Day is the real time for jollification, for paying visits, and drinking hot punch and making presents. The second drawback is in the constantly recurring remembrance that the country is at war. The gay and impulsive people of New York have run away with the delusion that all signs and symptoms of the existence of civil strife have been banished from their sumptuous streets ; but a stranger, a foreigner, cannot be half an hour in Broadway without becoming disagreeably aware of the fact that at nearly every hundred yards a great, insatiate monster is fuming for men to come and be killed. The natives have grown accustomed to the banners flaunting across the roadway, with inscriptions calling for " Thirty thousand more volunteers," or vaunting the enormous bounties promised to recruits by the committee of supervisors. Their ears are dulled to the monotonous croak of the horse-leech's three daughters, crying out, " Give, give." They fail to see the slatternly soldiers lounging on the steps of the recruiting offices, or the busy agents and brokers hunting up recruits in bars and groggeries, in front streets and back streets, on wharves and on ferry-boats, wherever they can lure, wherever they can catch them. The foreigner cannot help seeing this. It is not strange, perhaps, that the sight should jar on him. It is no business of his, of course. It is impertinent in him to object to war, even in the abstract, or to remind his neighbours that Christmas is a time for friendliness and forgiveness, and that the shepherds in the dawn, who saw the first Christmas Day, sang their carol when all the world was hushed and tranquil, and universal peace reigned over sea and land.

CHAPTER V.

NEW YEAR'S DAY is, in New York, about the most unfavourable day in the year for making up a mail to Europe. It is, at least, unpropitious when it falls on a Friday, and the steam-ship of the Inman line leaves Pier Forty-four, North River, on the ensuing Saturday, as it will to-day at noon. You should make up your mail, it may be argued, on Thursday; but how are you to do that if you only left Niagara on Wednesday night and the New York Central and Hudson River lines wouldn't keep their time? Besides, there is that "latest intelligence," so anxiously expected, so tardy in arrival. Ere you close your letter, an "extra" of the *New York Plugugly and Staten Island Shoulder-hitter* may announce that Charleston has fallen, that the miserable inhabitants have grown weary of spending their Christmas by Gilmore's Greek fire, and that the "flag" waves over Sumter; that Richmond has arisen in its might, torn Jeff Davis, as the ungrateful Hollanders tore their Grand Pensionary, to pieces, and rushed into the Union again, on the amalgamated platform of peace between North and South and war to the bitter end with Great Britain. Such things are quite possible, albeit not very probable, in this astound-

ing country. I once declared after a month's residence in
America, that I should not be in the least surprised at
meeting a citizen with eight heads and a tail walking down
West Twenty-first Street, Fifth Avenue. And were I to see
that sight, I should be quite prepared to find the New York
press asserting that to be born with a tail was a good and
holy thing, and that, to preserve the Union and punish the
piracies of England and the perfidy of France, it was
essential forthwith to nominate the eight-headed citizen as
President of the United States. Do you think I am writing
in jest ? I am writing in the mournfullest earnest. I verily
believe that were a deserter from one of our English regiments of foot in Canada to turn up at Washington, forswear
his nationality, develop rare military capacity, march on to
Richmond, and crush out the rebellion, there would be found
in New York journals of vast power and influence regretting
that the fact of the heroic reprobate not being an American
born was a bar to his promotion as chief of a magnificent
republic. They would elect Genghis Khan or Attila, King of
the Huns, over the heads of a Washington, a Jefferson, an
Adams, a Webster, or a Clay, did those statesmen live, or
could these degenerate days produce peers for the departed
worthies—they would nominate Sylla instead of Cincinnatus,
if he would only undertake to " whip " the South with
scorpions. They would cry out for Barabbas if he would
" rush " the Confeds into the Gulf of Mexico.

But this is New Year's day, and there is no question of
nominating Presidents. For the next twelve hours the
republic may slide or not as it pleases. Lollipops to-day

reign supreme over Greek fire. Visiting cards have precedents over the newsboy's extras. The most powerful and the
most profligate of the New York papers contained this
morning not one word of abuse against England. Its
editorials were absolutely good-tempered—one leader being
devoted to puffing a Mr. Bonner, the proprietor of a cheap
periodical, full of sensation romances, somewhat resembling
our *London Journal*, and another containing half a column
of facetious advice to Mr. Horace Greely to get a new suit
of clothes. The amenities of the New York Press are rare,
but charming.

I have already hinted that Christmas, as we understand it
—the Great Day—the day for turkey, plum-pudding, and
mince-pies, forfeits, hunt the slipper, holly, and mistletoe—
was not kept to any great extent in the Northern States.
Boston of late years has observed something approaching our
notion of Christmas; but I have been assured, and on very
serious and trustworthy authority, that the convivial celebration in Massachusetts of the great Christian festival was
quite a modern innovation, and was mainly due to the popu-
larity of Mr. Charles Dickens's Christmas books. I was loth
to believe this; for, with admirably quaint humour, the
Americans often divert themselves by relating to a foreigner
all kinds of droll fictions about their national manners and
customs—simply *pour rire*—and screeching afterwards with
rage when they find the foreigner has fallen into the funny
trap, and set down in a book all the fibs that have been told
him. The person who talked to me about Christmas at
Boston was, however, no joker of jokes; he was a gentleman

M 2

of weight and gravity. He told me that he remembered thirty years since that it was held by the stricter Bostonians as almost sinful to be jolly on a Christmas Day. On Thanksgiving Day there was as much feasting and revelry as you chose; but on the twenty-fifth of December the stern ideas of the Pilgrim Fathers still obtained. Their descendants were of the opinion of the pietists in "Hudibras," who would have nothing to do with fat pig, goose, custard, or plumporridge at Christmas—holding those cates to be at least prelatical, and almost papistical. Righteous and reverend folks were those Pilgrim Fathers. They came out in the "Mayflower," and then, so wicked libellers say, sent the sanctified bark to Congo, and she brought back an assorted cargo of niggers.

Suddenly came the "Christmas Carol," to be followed by a bright race of "Chimes," and "Crickets on the Hearth," and "Haunted Men," and Christmas became fashionable in Boston. To keep Christmas was to be one of the *literati*; but this is a case, perhaps, in which the gift-horse should not be too narrowly looked in the mouth. It is, at all events, curious to find the clever people of New England condescending to learn a lesson in humanity from a writer whom, reading and admiring more than any other living author, they still denounce as a detractor of their institutions and an enemy of their country.

New York has not chosen to follow the Bostonian lead. The Empire City takes little account of Christmas Day, and devotes all its energies to the celebration of the First of January. This, perchance, befits a people who are perpetually boasting of being young and new, and above old-fashioned usages and antiquated prejudices. They worship the rising sun. They turn their backs on yesterday, and live only for the present hour. Boston, on the other hand, as obstinately refuses to have anything festive to do with the new year, and looks upon the New Yorkers as little better than Pagans for their January junketings. There are a good many subjects on which the inhabitants of the great American cities are diametrically opposed to each other; but there is one on which they are unanimously agreed—their infinite superiority to the rest of the civilised world.

New Year's Day is ushered in by no ringing of bells and no firing of cannon; the "flag" even is not displayed from steeples or from windows in more than usually multitudinous folds. I am given, however, to understand that there is a considerable consumption of early morning stimulants. As a rule, indeed, our cousins begin to drink with the dawn. No sooner has Aurora rubbed her eyes with her rosy fingers, than she proceeds to open the bar. Chanticleer crows, flaps his wings, and immediately indulges in a cocktail. I am on friendly terms with a gentleman who began New Year's Day at seven a. m., by quaffing egg-nogg at an hotel bar with "one of the first bankers in Cincinnati." The banker introduced him to the bar-keeper, who, shaking hands, promised to look after him during his stay in the city. Just imagine Robarts, Curtis, and Co. looking in at the bar of the Blue Boar for a pint of purl, and Barclay, Bevan, and Tritton dropping in "promiscuous" with Prescott, Grote, Cave, and Co., before eight o'clock for a quartern and three outs.

The Americans, I cannot repeat too frequently, are an eminently hospitable and generous people. A stingy American is a monster. You hear of no gripe-fists, no pinch-pennies. They make their money quickly, and they spend it quickly. They have no time to be miserly, for a short life and a merry one is at least the New York motto. When a broker finds Wall Street frown upon him, or a merchant is on the eve of bankruptcy, he proceeds to Delmonico's, and has a capital dinner, with plenty of Cliquot champagne. In prosperity he might condescend to Mumm, or dry Verzenay; but when his estate promises to pay something under five cents in the dollar, nothing less than the Veuve Veuve's best brand will suit him. He not only dances over a volcano—he liquors up while he is in it. A "smart" American may "do" you; but you are welcome to any amount of terrapin soup and canvas-back duck at his expense. Captain Kidd, the buccaneer, will scuttle your ship, and strip you as bare as a robin; but he will treat you to a roaring supper at Taylor's before he forces you to walk the plank. In their pleasures the American people are, I think, the most dismal people upon earth. In their business transactions they are the most jovial. They propound conundrums in their counting-houses; they light big cigars over their ledgers, and vary posting-up with sups of Bourbon whisky.

On New Year's Day the hospitable character of the people finds full vent. If you possess five hundred friends and meet them, you will have very great difficulty in escaping the drinking of five hundred drams. If you wish to keep sober, you must remain at home; but to lie snug on New Year's

Day, if you be of the male sex, is an atrocious and unpardonable social offence. You are bound, under penalty of excom-
munication and ostracism from polite society, to pay your
New Year's visits. Therefore, to avoid the five hundred
friends and their five hundred drams at five hundred bars—
where each of your friends generally finds five other friends
of his, so that the number of drinks ultimately reaches two
thousand five hundred—the most prudent course you can
pursue is to make your calls in a hackney-coach.

The close carriage, however, does not by any means offer a
guarantee for your reaching your hotel again with a clear
head. At every house you stop you are invited to eat and
expected to drink. What the Mayor is doing at the City
Hall, thousands of citizens are doing at their own houses.
Arrayed in your Sunday best if you like, but not in evening
dress, you ring at a door; a black servant with a very large
silver waiter in his larger white-gloved hands responds to the
call, grins in a familiar manner, takes your card or not, precisely as the rush of visitors may make encroachments on his
time, and allows you ingress to the drawing-room. Then you
find the lady of the house—any number of ladies of the
house—in full dress, gloved, laced, and blazing in diamonds.
You bow, sit, wish and are wished a happy new year, utter
the first nonsense that comes into your head, seek the gentleman of the house—any number of gentlemen of the house
—slide into a banqueting parlour, and find yourself lunching
and hobnobbing for the fifth, the tenth, or the twentieth time,
just as the case may be, or your visiting list may be extended
or contracted. You will discover that most of the ladies you

visit have a dozen pretty sisters, and the gentlemen, upon
an average, rejoice in twenty-five cousins. Then there is a
floating population of uncles and aunts, and nephews and
nieces, and any number of small children, who don't count.
You are not required to stay long on these visits; you must
make room for the fresh arrivals. You are not expected
to talk about Shakspeare and the musical glasses. A fixed
grin of seasonable joyousness is, perhaps, the best mould into
which you can cast your countenance. It occasionally happens that when a gentleman with a lengthy visiting list
reaches home at sundown, he is unable to do anything but
grin—save, perhaps, stumble. He has had enough; he has
had too much—of visiting, I mean. At some houses, where
there may have been but one lady, he has seen two. His
mind is a radiant chaos of oysters pickled, oysters stewed,
and oysters fried—of pheasants and ducks and quails—of
chicken and lobster salad—of every wine the vintages of
France and Germany and Portugal can produce—of a little
rare old Cognac, and peculiar Bourbon perhaps. He is happy,
but speechless.

This kind of thing goes on all day and nearly all night
long. How the ladies can endure the fatigue I cannot understand; but they do endure, and seem to delight in, it. *They*
don't drink Moselle; *they* know not Bourbon; *they* have not
the consolation of Cabanas and Imperials. They sit and
smile and shake hands, martyrs to the cause of hospitality.
Visits are paid as late as ten o'clock at night, and then there
are suppers, and dancing parties, and concerts, and other
festivities.

This is New Year's Day in New York. It is the closest
of holidays. The theatres are open, and crowded by the
million; but all the shops are hermetically sealed, and the
Upper Ten Thousand stay at home, light up their houses
from garret to basement, and feast their friends. The additional consumption of gas must be enormous. In the streets
you don't meet any ladies—only gentlemen, trotting from
house to house paying visits. The exercise is exhilarating;
the refection perilous. But you must go through with it, or
be ostracised.

The compositors and pressmen won't work on New Year's
Day; and on the morning of the 2nd of January there are
no newspapers. Everybody, it is to be presumed, has been
paying visits. Everybody has been jolly. A few may wake
up with headaches. New Year's Day in New York is not
the less one of the cheerfullest and most humanising celebrations extant among a noble but perverse people, who have
repudiated the greater part of the traditional observances to
which Europeans pin a reverent and affectionate faith. I
wish—abating the plethoric eating and drinking—that it
were always New Year's Day in New York, and in the whole
of this magnificent empire of Democracy turned crazy. It
does me good to see a people habitually melancholy, reserved, or in their most humorous temper grimly saturnine,
become for once in a way as merry as grigs and as jolly as
sandboys. If they would only laugh a little more, and chew
the cud of politics and pigtail a little less, these worthy
cousins of ours; if they would only banter each other somewhat, instead of interchanging eternal assertions of being a

chosen, perfect, and peculiar people, like the Jews of old—they would not, in all probability, be quite so angry with foreigners, who cannot help smiling at their grotesque characteristics—exactly as those foreigners have been in the habit of smiling at what they deemed absurd at home—but who are glad to admit their manifest power and to recognise their many generous and sterling qualities.

CHAPTER VI.

NIAGARA! Fearful word; ominous and overwhelming always to the literary mind. I have looked upon it for months as a monstrous bill, for ever coming due, and which I have over and over again renewed, but for which I can procure now, even at the most exorbitant rate of interest, no more days of grace. "It has got to be done," as our cousins say. The watery Sphynx has, for the last time, thundered forth her tremendous conundrum, and I must answer it or be devoured. Of course I *shall* be devoured—demolished, and annihilated. I shall go over the Falls of Incapacity, be smashed to pieces at the base of the Table Rock of Stupidity, be carried down to the Rapids of Censure, to turn up, after many days, mangled and dismembered in the Whirlpool of Criticism. How can I ever hold up my head again in print after attempting Niagara? Had I not better walk the back streets—as Beau Brummell advised his friend with the ill-made coat to do—until the thing has blown over? Had I not better start at once for San Francisco, and avail myself of those free passes to the Great Salt Lake City—"pass the bearer and one wife"—with which a friend was recently good enough to present me? Had I not better stuff my ears with cotton, put on blinkers, or take up my quarters in the deepest dungeon beneath the castle moat, or in any other place where darkness, and silence, and solitude are to be found? I shudder to picture myself walking about, surrounded by a hostile population pointing the finger of derision, and sneering, "There goes the man who tried to describe Niagara—the impudent cuss!" He who fired the Temple of Ephesus earned the execration of posterity; but how would it have been had his lucifer matches been damp, and his enterprise turned out a fizzle? Orsini, with his murderous grenades, managed to kill a score of innocent people, and was righteously guillotined. His deed excited horror; but suppose he had only singed off his whiskers when he was drying that fulminating mercury in the frying-pan? People would have laughed at him. Guy Fawkes has become a puppet, a grotesque monster, a scoff, like Gog and Magog; but why? Merely because he failed. Had he really succeeded in blowing up the Houses of Lords and Commons he would have left a dark but an imposing memory.

I had some thoughts, when I was staying at the Clifton House in August, 1864, of appending as a foot-note to one of my letters home the remark: "There are some waterfalls hereabouts, which are said to be pretty." Or this: "For a description of the Falls of Niagara the reader is referred to the works of Mr. Charles Dickens, Dr. Charles Mackay, Mr. Nicholas Woods, Mr. N. P. Willis, Baron Humboldt, Sir Charles Lyell, Professor Agassiz, and ten thousand more or less accomplished tourists, *savans*, and sketch-writers." But to do that would have been impertinent. It would have been taking a liberty with the British public, and the British public does not like liberties. You may swindle, you may deceive, you may hoodwink, you may even bully the British public, but beware of indecorous familiarities. Barnum has never been forgiven for telling the world how easily he had humbugged it. So I staved off Niagara as long as I could; tried to lay the ghost in the Red Sea; put it off with specious excuses; kept on saying, "To-morrow, to-morrow;" but *hodie mihi.* My to-day has come. "Rosin up, thar'," cried the captain of the Mississippi steam-boat; "stand on the safety-valves; give her goss, and let her rip. *I mean to pass that boat, or bust!*" He passed her, and "bust" into the bargain. An equal fate may be mine; but I must rosin up and give my pen "goss," at the risk of its "ripping." Understand, to begin with, that I abandon any attempt at fine writing, at picturesque narrative, or at striving to emulate that which has been done, and done admirably, by a hundred famous men of letters. This is no case of *nolo episcopari,* but of a poor varlet who knows that he is not competent for the place of sexton, yet is bound by fate to become a candidate for the office. It will be my aim not to indulge in any "high falutin" description of a scene too grand, too awful, and too wonderful to be described with anything like the remotest approach to the majesty it displays and the reverent astonishment it commands; not to rack my brains or a Roget's Thesaurus to find sesquipedalian words and far-fetched similes, but to set down in my own language the impression made by an unusual spectacle on a

coarse and common mind.   I wish to note the scene as I saw
it, with its every-day and perchance vulgar environments.
A Cockney's view of Niagara may be repulsive, but it need
not be wholly uninstructive.   There are some minds which,
although deficiently cultivated, are intuitively imbued with
poetic insight, and with an appreciation of the Art Idea.
Such a mind had Thomson, who, while yet a raw young
Scotchman, summed up, in one line, all that the most erudite
connoisseurs in art could have written on the masterpiece of
ancient sculpture : "So stands the statue that enchants the
world."   There is nothing more to be said.   So it stands, to
this day, in Florence, actually, completely, and any further
criticism upon it is supererogation.   And yet, although I
would not give two cents to hear what Mr. Ruskin thought
about that wondrous embodiment of abstract beauty, I
would give many dollars for a detailed criticism on the Venus
de' Medici by the Reverend Mr. Spurgeon.

Niagara was the first famous waterfall I had as yet seen ;
for Terni and Lodore had not been among the European
lions I had visited, and it was not until many months afterwards that I was permitted to see the exquisitely beautiful
falls of Montmorency, near Quebec, and the wonderful
cascade of Regla, in Mexico.   My first trip to Niagara was
made in the last week of December, 1863, and I had endeavoured to saturate myself with an idea of what the place
was like by gazing on the Niagara pictures of the admirable American artists, Church and Gignoux.   I had been,
with an esteemed English friend, making a rapid Christmas
tour through Canada.   We had come from Montreal down to

Toronto, a distance of between three and four hundred miles, and were thus nearing the river which serves as a boundary-line between the British provinces and the United States.

We halted on a raw, murky winter's evening at Hamilton, distant about forty miles from Niagara : and just one word is necessary to explain the manner in which we were travelling. Through the courteous kindness of the authorities of the Grand Trunk Railway of Canada—to whose managing director, Mr. Brydges, and to whose accountant-general, Mr. Hickson, I owe my warmest acknowledgments—there had been placed at our disposal one of the most elegant and commodious saloon-carriages it was possible to conceive. In another place I have referred more in detail to the construction of these locomotive palaces ; but for my present purpose it will be sufficient to observe that our car was the one which was built for and occupied by the Prince of Wales on his journey through Canada, and which is now used by the directors of the Grand Trunk on their periodical business trips. With commendable modesty, the directors have obliterated from their car all superfluous gilding and unnecessary symbols of splendour ; but no amount of quakerisation could render the car uncomfortable ; and, with a lounging and drawing and smoking room, two sleeping apartments, a kitchen and pantry, plenty of books, an amply supplied commissariat, and a civil French-Canadian servant, all running on one set of wheels, it may easily be imagined that we had a "good time" of it. We halted then at Hamilton to look up her Majesty's Rifle Brigade, much renowned in those parts for their urbane hospitality to

pilgrims.   There we recuperated.   We dined royally at
mess, our hosts insisted on seeing us to the dépôt ; and
later in the evening there must have been, I think, a
kind of harmonic meeting in our car.   External evidence
would seem to prove that we enjoyed ourselves very much,
for I remember seeing my esteemed friend—a gentleman
habitually of great gravity of countenance and solidity of
conversation, and whose head is as white as the snows on the
summit of Popocatapetl—endeavouring to perform an intri-
cate trick, which consists in picking up, with your teeth, a
silver sixpence from the floor, a black bottle remaining
meanwhile erect on your head.   Whether he would have
succeeded in this feat is uncertain.   I only know that while,
his cranium surmounted by the black bottle, he was
crouching on his haunches after the manner of an Iroquois
Sachem at the council fire, the shrill yell of a whistle was
heard ; our friends had to bundle out as best they could ;
and the train to which our car was hitched went clattering
off.   I am afraid the black bottle was broken.

It was just the grey of the winter's day when our
French-Canadian valet entered my state-room.   "No boots
to-day," I said, "I will wear moccasins."   "It vas not de
boots," he made answer ; "you are dere."   "Where?"   I
asked, sleepily and querulously.   "At Niagara, sare."   I
sprang from my cot, and made a toilette so swift that the
circus-rider who becomes in the space of five minutes a
belted knight, a kilted Highlander, a buy-a-broom girl,
General Washington, and William in "Black-eyed Susan,"
all the while careering madly on one bare-backed steed,

might have envied my celerity. I was at Niagara. Where
were the Falls? About a mile and a half distant. How
could I reach them? There were hack carriages in plenty
at the Great Western Railway depôt—for the G. W. had
kindly permitted the G. T. car to run over their line—at the
foot of the Suspension Bridge.

I was enabled to secure a little ramshackle "one-horse
shay" of a curricle, with a horse not much bigger than an
Exmoor pony, and such a very tall and stout Irishman for a
driver, that I expected every moment, with my superabun-
dant weight, that the springs would break, and the entire
concern go to irremediable "pi." The Irish driver was jocu-
lar and loquacious, but appeared somewhat disgusted with
the world in general, and Niagara in particular. To every
remark he made he added the observation that it was "a
divil of a place." I asked if there were any tourists here
just now. "Begorra, there's nobody," he replied. I asked
which was the best hotel. "Begorra, there's none," he responded; "they're all shut up. It's a divil of a place." I
was somewhat disconsolate at the receipt of this information,
so I asked him if he knew where we could get some breakfast. "Divil a bit of breakfast is there for love or money.
It's a divil of a place;" but he added, with a glance of that
sly humour for which his countrymen are unrivalled, "the
Falls are in illigant condition, *and you may see them all the
year round for nothing.*"

He was driving me along the brink of a steep and abrupt
precipice—a mere ledge of road, like the commencement of
the Cornice. at Genoa. On the near side arose, not moun-

tains, but rows of naked larch and stunted pollard. Beyond them were the ice-bound fields, with here and there clumps of the black funereal pine, standing like mutes at the door of one who had died in mid-winter. The snow was all around, in lumps and nuggets—in festoons, as though old Father Christmas had hung his trees with bundles of store-candles—in great sheets, deep and compact, with the thin layer of last night's frosty glaze upon them. The sky looked thick and soft—a very blanket-covering of snow that was to fall soon and envelop us. The stark saplings came up rigid and spiky through the ghastly mantle, like the beard from the cheek of a dead man. There was an evil wind blowing about a few leaves, so brown and withered that they must have belonged to the autumn before last. The declivity of the precipice looked horrible, and hundreds of feet down, so it seemed, rushed along a black, swollen, and sullen river.

"Stop till I give him the bhutt," cried the Irish driver. The little horse had become recalcitrant. He was sick, perhaps, of seeing Niagara for nothing, and planting his stumpy little legs very wide apart, refused to budge any more. The driver reversed his whip, shortened it, and with the "bhutt," or butt-end thereof, proceeded to belabour the dorsal vertebræ of the unhappy little animal till I threatened to alight and not pay him. The very word "bhutt" had, however, apparently operated as an incentive on the Niagara-Exmoor pony, and he started afresh. The road made a slight curve. "Begorra, there they are!" cried the driver, pointing with his whip. I strained my eyes, looked down, and saw, so close upon me that I thought I could have leaped into their midst, but they were at least a mile distant—the Falls of Niagara.

How it was that the ramshackle shay, the little horse, and the big driver utterly vanished from my view and remembrance, I shall probably never be able to realise. I suppose I must have got out of the chaise somehow, and given the man a dollar; but how it all came about I have not the dimmest recollection. I found myself standing on the very edge of the precipice, straining with a dull stare of absorption at the two Falls—the American and the Horseshoe—which were within my view. I saw over against me the Niagara river running between steep and precipitous banks, very much resembling those of Clifton Heights in England; and over the bank opposite to me there was rushing with almost mathematical exactitude an enormous stream of water. At the base a great cloud of foam and spray arose. This was the American Fall. Then the bank stretched away, and I could see some large and small houses, and an island thickly wooded, at whose head was a lighthouse-looking tower, approached by a causeway. This was Goat Island and Terrapin Tower. Then the lower bed of the river became a *cul de sac*, a blind alley, its finial being curved in a great wall of rock, and over this was precipitated from the upper bed a much more enormous stream of water, its edges raggeder than those of the American Fall, with much more foam at the bottom, and casting up not a cloud, but a column of spray—a column like a water-spout—like Lot's wife—like the Pillar that went before the Israelites by day and night

—and rising many scores of feet above the level of the cataract.   This was the great Fall, the Canadian Fall, the Horseshoe Fall.   This forms the half-circle from Goat Island to the
Canadian side of the river.   Three parts of it belong incontest-
ably to Great Britain, and it can only be seen to advantage
from the British side; but our cousins are very angry that it
should be called the Canadian Fall, and claim more than
half of it as their own.   Indeed, when they go abroad,
Americans are accustomed to speak of the Falls of Niagara
as being exclusively one of the glories of their magnificent
country, and as much part and parcel of the United States
as Plymouth Rock or Bunker Hill.   The width of the
Horseshoe Fall is said to be 144 rods, and its perpendicular
height 158 feet.   It derived its name of Horseshoe from its
shape, of which some traces are still visible; but it must
have altered its shape considerably, as large masses of rock
in its neighbourhood fall every year.   Sir Charles Lyell is of
opinion that 1500 millions of cubic feet of water pass over the
Falls every minute.   " I should think," remarks one *savant*,
" that the river would exhaust itself."   Yes, when Lake Erie
and all the upper lakes, with their vast tributaries, give out,
Niagara will be no more.

These then were the famous Falls I had come so far to
see ;—144 rods wide, 158 feet high, 1500 millions of cubic
feet of water tumbling over a wall of rock every minute, a
column of spray 200—some say 300—feet in altitude.   Well,
I confess that as I stood staring, there came over me a sensation of bitter disappointment.   And was this all ?   You
who have seen the field of Waterloo, who have seen the

Pyramids, who have seen St. Peter's, bear with me. Was this all? There was a great deal of water, a great deal of foam, a great deal of spray, and a thundering noise. This *was* all, abating the snow where I stood and the black river beneath. These were the Falls of Niagara. *They looked comparatively small, and the water looked dingy.* Where was the grand effect—the light and shade? There was, it is true, a considerable amount of effervescence ; but the foaminess of the Falls, together with the tinge of tawny yellow in the troubled waters, only reminded me of so much unattainable soda and sherry, and made me feel thirstier than ever.

I found a wretched little place open, half tavern and half Indian curiosity shop, but on the roof it had a belvedere. I was permitted to ascend to this, and a civil negro serving-man volunteered to accompany me. There was a good view from the belvedere, and I remained staring at the Falls for another half-hour, the negro remaining silent by my side. I asked him, almost mechanically, whether the water was continually rushing over at that rate. I had spoken like a Fool, and he answered me according to my folly. "I 'spect, massa," he said, "they goes on for ebber and ebber." Remarks, as absurd and incongruous as mine, have become historical among the *ana* of Niagara. A Swiss watchmaker observed that he was very glad "de beautiful ting was going." He looked upon it as some kind of clockwork arrangement, which would run down and be wound up again. Everybody knows the story of the 'cute Yankee who called it "an almighty water privilege." It *is* one, and would turn all the mill-wheels in the world. "Here creation's done its d—dest," remarked another; and, quoth a fifth, " I guess this hyar suckles the ocean-sea considerable."

I went back to the railway dépôt, and found my friend dressed, rosy, and clean shaven. I told him gloomily that I had seen the Falls. "Bother the Falls," he remarked, blithely. "Let's go out and forage for some breakfast." He was an old hand at Niagara, and was principally concerned at the knowledge that, the season for tourists being at an end, the Clifton, the Cataract, and the International, the principal hotels at Niagara, were all closed. We crossed the Suspension Bridge, however, on a voyage of discovery, and, after much hunting about, found on the American side a third-rate house open, where, for a dollar, we obtained an indifferent meal. Then we started to do the lions. Everything looked dreary and dingy white, save the Shillibeer pines, and the negroes, who were of an ashen liver hue. The roads were very slippery; but fortunately we wore cloth moccasins, or pedestrianism would have been impossible. Beyond negroes, a few hack-drivers, and the keepers of half-a-dozen shanties for the sale of Indian curiosities and ice-creams—ice-creams on the twenty-third of December!— there did not seem to be any inhabitants at Niagara. There is a little straggling village on the British and on the American side, but both have a most woe-begone and poverty-stricken appearance. The shut-up hotels looked inexpressibly gaunt and spectral. There were no guides or hotel touters about, which was a blessing.

Being on the American side, we crossed a smaller suspension bridge to Goat Island. We wandered around its half-snowed-up lanes, and then, so slippery was the ice, crawled on our hands and knees along a stone causeway to Terrapin Tower, and from its summit looked upon the Falls. Then we went to see the Rapids by the Cataract House, which appeared to me a mass of intolerable suds, and put me in mind of nothing half so much as a gigantic washing-day. There was no colour, no light and shade: nothing but water and foam, water and spray, water and noise. And everything dingy. We were lowered down an inclined plane in a species of horse box on the American side, and there found a ferry-boat to convey us across the Niagara river to Canada. From the river there was a much better view of both Falls. They looked considerably taller, but they were still dingy. The boatman was a most savage-looking person; cursed us when we paid him in paper instead of silver, and I thought when we landed that he would have dismissed us with a clout of his oar, as Charon does in Gustave Doré's picture of the souls crossing the Styx in the "Inferno." Then we scrambled over stones, rimy with ice, and slipped down glassy declivities, *à la Montagne Russe*, and creeping close to the base of the fall, right under the lee of Table Rock, peeped at the masses of frozen spray and great blocks and boulders of ice piled one atop of another—a cold eruption of the Glacial Period.

We thus wandered about, talking very little, until early in the afternoon, when my friend suggested lunch. We had ascended to the river bank on the Canada side by this time, and in the highway, close to Table Rock, found, to our great joy, that Mr. Sol Davis's well-known establishment was open.

Mr. Sol Davis sells Indian curiosities, and Lowther Arcade and Ramsgate Bazaar nicknacks of every description ; and a very stiff price does Mr. Sol Davis charge for those objects of vertù.   Mr. Sol Davis likewise sells cigars and stereoscopic slides of the Falls ; and Mr. Sol Davis has, to sum up his wealth of accommodation for tourists, a bar in the rear of his premises where exciseable articles are retailed.   Mrs. Sol Davis is a very comely and affable matron, with a sharp eye to business ; and Miss Sol Davis is very beautiful, but haughty.

Mr. Sol Davis, junior, the fourth in this worthy quartette, is a character.   Said he to me, when he became better acquainted with me :

" What might be your business, now ? "

Wishing to keep within the limits of the truth, and at the same time not to be too communicative, I replied that paperstaining was my business.

" Ah ! paper staining.   Do pretty well at it ? " continued Mr. Sol Davis, junior.

I said that I did do pretty well, considering.

" Ah ! " pursued my interlocutor, " you should go in for felt hats.   My brother-in-law went out to San Francisco a year and seven months ago, and he's made a hundred and fifty thousand dollars, all out of felt hats.   Think of that ! "

I did think that, in case the paper-staining business came to grief, I would follow the friendly advice of Mr. Sol Davis, junior, and go in for felt hats.

We lunched at Mr. Sol Davis's, in a very cosy little back parlour, and an admirable roast fowl and a capital bottle of

Médoc we had. Then my friend took a nap, and then, feeling somewhat relieved, with a fragrant " planter " from Mr. Sol Davis's private box between my lips, I strolled out to have another view of the Falls. It was now about three o'clock in the afternoon. I stood on the brink of Table Rock and gazed once more on the great, dreary, colourless expanse of water, foam, and spray. And this was Niagara, and there was nothing more.

Nothing ? With a burst like the sound of a trumpet, the sudden Sun came out. God bless him ! there he was ; and there, too, in the midst of the foaming waters, was set the Everlasting Bow. The rainbow shone out upon the cataract ; the sky turned blue ; the bright clarionet had served to call all nature to arms ; the very birds that had been flapping dully over the spray throughout the morning began to sing ; and, looking around me, I saw that the whole scene had become glorified. There was light and colour everywhere. The river ran a stream of liquid gold. The dark hills glowed. The boulders of ice sparkled like gems. The snow was all bathed in iris tints—crimson, and yellow, and blue, and green, and orange, and violet. The white houses and belvedere started up against the azure like the mosques and minarets of Stamboul, and, soaring high behind the Bow, was the great pillar of spray, glancing and flashing like an obelisk of diamonds. And it was then I began, as many men have begun, perchance, to wonder at and to love Niagara.

CHAPTER VII.

As I stood gazing on the sun and the rainbow, and the glittering spray and the sparkling snow, and as the constant roar of the cataract had become to me, through its even monotony of sonorous continuity, quite soft and subdued, the very oddest, the very absurdest, the most incongruous thing it is possible to conceive, happened. I am almost ashamed to set it down here. I feel that Niagara should be held as holy ground, and the mean and the grotesque rigidly excluded from its precincts. Shall I blot that which I have penned? Shall I at once and for ever resign the chance of being able to say anything noble or spirit-stirring concerning the Falls of Niagara? Shall I calmly write myself down for life a Bœotian? By dint of strenuous labour, tedious recapitulation, and dexterous plagiarism, I might have got out of these Falls in the way of fine writing, something which, although intrinsically base metal, might have passed current until the electro wore off and the dross was palpable. But the thing must be done. I stand committed to vulgarity. I have made the waters of Niagara muddy, and it is too late to talk of their crystal purity.

It was too bad. I thought I had worked myself up to the

proper state of rapture. The sun had worked marvels in me. I was absorbed. I was wonder-struck. I was delighted. Here was the grand sight—the Show of Shows—the spectacle that, from the most unimpressionable, extorts the exclamation of wonder. I remember once travelling from Verona to beyond Padua with an English commercial traveller who, unlike the majority of his jovial and communicative class, remained for fifty miles obstinately taciturn. I tried every device to engage him in conversation, but failed in all. He was hopelessly mum. By-and-bye we left Padua, and were rattling over that long causeway which bridges the lagoons. All at once there started up on the horizon the domes and spires of a great city. My dumb companion and I had both thrust our heads out of the carriage-window, when he gave a kind of shriek, and exclaimed, "By Jove, there's Venice!" And who can refrain from such an interjection when he first sees the sun shining upon Niagara? I was invoking Phœbus Apollo—I was crying "Evoe!" or "Mehercle!" or "Stunning!"—when an abominably ludicrous thing happened.

It was in this wise. Mr. Sol Davis is a thrifty man, and keeps live stock. From the rear of his premises there came gravely and consequentially waddling towards me a certain domestic bird. This bird, it may be, flattered himself that his plumage was white; but, contrasted with the virgin snow over which he sacrilegiously waddled, he had a dirty, tawny hue. And the varlet thought, no doubt, that he had red legs. Red! These, and his splay web feet, were of a dingy cinnabar tint, like unto the worn-out jacket of an untidy militiaman. His bill was unbearable. He was the ugliest biped I ever set eyes upon ; and yet I dare say Mr. Sol Davis thought him in the plumpest of condition, and intended to send him presently into the States, with a view to the Christmas market. There, the truth must out. He was a Goose, and this beast of a bird waddled to the brink of Table Rock, and stood beside me, gazing out upon Niagara.

It would be a mean and paltry thing, I knew, for a strong man to kick a goose—or rather a gander—over a precipice. It would have been a cruel and dishonest thing to steal Mr. Sol Davis's property, or wring its neck. Yet something must be done, I felt. Why didn't he fly away ? Why didn't he waddle back ? No ; there he remained, ruminating, and occasionally gobbling, to himself. Perhaps he was indulging in aspirations that the sage and onion crop had failed, and that he would not be roasted until next Thanksgiving Day. I told him savagely to get out of that. He turned his bill and his eye upwards to me, stood on one leg, and hissed slightly, as though to say, " Have I not as much right here as you, brother ? What do you think of the Falls, any way ? As for me, I am blasé. I am a Goose. Men may come and men may go, but I and the Falls go on for ever. More rain drops from the heavens, and sinks into the mountains, and gushes from the source, and feeds the lakes, and flushes the river, and rushes from Erie to Ontario, and tumbles over these rocks, and is shattered into spray and becomes vapour, and in time gathers again in clouds, and falls once more in rain. More goslings chip from the shell, more mother-geese drive off with strong wing and angry hiss the barn-door cat, more geese are baked and roasted, or are set before fires, or caged in coops and crammed that their livers may swell, and the fatty degeneration be made into pies. I am a Goose, and have gone on for thousands of years. And you, brother ? I was in Noah's Ark. I saved the Roman Capitol. I once laid golden eggs. The clodhopper thought he had killed me, but here I am again. How old is the world, and for how many thousands of years has this cataract been roaring, and I, or my brothers, who are me, hissing and gobbling on the edge of the precipice ? " I declined to answer the implied questions he propounded. I left the abominable thing in deepest dudgeon ; and for my part I don't see anything cruel in the process of preparing *pâtés de foie gras*, or plucking geese alive.

"The goose had hung high "—I use a Yankee locution—when I had first seen the rainbow. Now it was hanging low indeed. To thicken my gloom the sun went in, and all became, as before, dingy, colourless, and shadowless. Slowly and sadly I walked along the precipice road towards the Suspension Bridge, when I came on some one standing, as I had stood, on the verge of a crag, and gazing on the Falls.

He had his dog with him—a patient little black fellow with ragged ears—a poverty-stricken mongrel cur. Mange had marked that dog for her own. He looked as though he had been bred a turnspit, but, that branch of business declining through the introduction of bottle-jacks, had attempted the water-spaniel line of business. Poor little beast ! He shivered and looked lamentably uncomfortable in his sporting character, but was quite meek and resigned. His master was somewhat under the middle size, but was a brawny,

thickset fellow. The facial angles of his countenance would
not have been amiss on a medal representing one of the
Twelve Cæsars, for his nose was purely aquiline, his cheek-
bones high, his lips firmly set, and his chin broad and massive;
but there his classicality stopped. His forehead was low;
his eye, though black and lustrous, small and sunken ; and
his head, so far as I could discern for the fur cap he wore,
thatched with long, coarse, matted black hair—raven black if
you please, but the sable of a raven who has fed on anything
but succulent garbage. He was very dirty, very ragged, and
very greasy. Wrapped round him was a blanket coat,
patched here and there with scraps of leather ; his loins were
girt with a wampum belt, but the beads were broken and
lustreless. There was some shabby embroidery, too, on the
canvas pouch he carried at his side. His legs were swathed
in bandages of coarse linen, with criss-cross ligaments, such
as Italian brigands wear, and such as you may note in the
statues of the Gauls of old. On his feet he wore moccasins,
and these offered a curious contrast to the poverty of the rest
of his attire, for they were of new black cloth, glowing with
parti-coloured *passementerie*, and, in their embroidery, quite
a marvel of bead-work. On one arm rested a long duck-
gun with bright barrel, and his shot-belt and powder-flask
hung on his hip opposite the pouch. He had been out birding—
seeking, perchance, the ptarmigan or the capercailzie, or more
probably in quest of smaller and prettier quarries, such as
that exquisite little blue bird of Canada which forms a centre-
piece to the feather fans made by his race, and which are
sold at an enormous advance on their wholesale price by the

curiosity-dealers with whom both sides of the Niagara river abound.

There he stood, silent and motionless, contemplating the raging waters. He was plainly a poor devil, and the clothes he had on would not have fetched two dollars and a half. His gun was the most valuable part of his accoutrements, and the stock of that weapon, even, was worn and notched. He had been out probably for many weary hours, and would not gather more than fifty cents by his day's work. He was, in Yankee estimation, a worn out "cuss," shattered, unclean, and oleaginous—a creature to be "run-out" or stamped down as though he were a 'possum or a skunk. And even here, on British soil, he was looked upon as a kind of bore and encumbrance, not, it is true, to be absolutely maltreated or violently expelled, but so prevailed upon to "move on," and generally wiped out, as early as the proprieties of civilisation would permit of that process. This was clearly no place for him. White hunters could be found to catch the blue bird as well as he, and white women in crinoline could make the fans as deftly as the blanketed squaws of his feeble and scattered race. Niagara was wanted for tourists and excursionists, for hotel-keepers and guide-book sellers. He was an anomaly and an anachronism here. It was time for him to clear out. Do we not read in the works of the Yankee bard—

> " Here the wild Indian once did take delight,
> Hunted the buffaler, fished, fit, and bled ;
> Now the inhabitants are mostly white,
> And nary red."

Yes, this was a Red Man. He was the first North Ameri-

can Indian, in his own land, I had seen. I am not about to
get up any spasmodic enthusiasm concerning the Noble
Savage. He is, I am aware, at a painful discount just at
present, and I confess that his nobility is, in the main,
nonsense, and he himself a nuisance. I have seen a good
deal of him in Canada since my first meeting with the bird-
man with the duck-gun at Niagara. I have seen him five
million strong—whole-blooded and half-blooded in Mexico,
and I am bound to admit that according to our ideas of
civilisation—and they need not be quite infallible ideas, after
all—he is, at the best, but a poor creature. I have nothing
favourable to say about the war paint, or the war path, or
the war dance. The calumet of peace has, I know, been
smoked to the last ashes. I give up the Noble Savage
morally. I confess him to be a shiftless and degraded vagrant, who does not wash himself—who is not at all scrupulous
about taking things which do not belong to him—who will .
get blind or mad drunk on rum or whiskey whenever he has a
chance—who is not a much better shot than a white man,
and who has only one special aptitude—that for playing at
cards, at which he will cheat you. But, fallen and debased
as he is, not much more picturesque than an English gipsy,
and quite as dishonest, nothing can rob him of a certain
dignity of mien, a composure of carriage, and an imperturba-
bility of countenance, which the descendant of a hundred
European kings might envy. Nothing moves him, nothing
excites his surprise, nothing excites him to merriment. A
friend told me, that travelling once in Nova Scotia he came
on an Indian village, where a chief was being installed in

office. He was invited to take part in the festivities, and was regaled at a grand banquet composed of one dish. What do you think it was ? Conger eel, cut into pieces about four inches long, Indian corn and molasses; yet the manner in which the chief ladled out this horrible mess *from a tin slop-pail* was, according to my friend, the most dignified and imposing performance he had ever witnessed since, in days gone by, he had seen a Royal personage presiding at a public dinner. On the other hand, when Lord Aylmer was Governor-General of Canada, he had occasion to receive a deputation of Indians from some remote part of the province. His lordship was a very merry nobleman, and something exceedingly ludicrous in the costume of one of the Sachems happening to strike him, he could not repress a smile. The deputation took no verbal notice of that which they doubtless held to be an insult, but immediately and silently withdrew, nor could they, by any offers of firearms, blankets, beads, or firewater, be induced to return.

And so this Red Man stood grave and immobile, surveying the Falls. His dress was a mean and bastard compromise between the past and the present; but in port and visage he was the same Indian who, with unquivering lip and unfalter-ing eye, looks upon the dying Wolfe in Benjamin West's picture. There he stood, statuesque and dumb, heeding me not, heeding nothing, seemingly, but his own thoughts. Of what may he have been thinking? Perhaps in this wise : " All this was once mine. The river and the Falls, the bank and the brake, all belonged to the Red Man. In their bark canoes my fathers shot the rapids more skilfully than the helmsmen of that black boat which puffs smoke from a pipe on its deck, and makes a noise like the whip-poor-will in pain. All this belonged to me, and now I am a vagrant and an outcast, and the white man chaffers with me for the birds I have slain." Poor copper-hued child of the wilderness! Perhaps he was listening for the flutter of a wing, and keeping a sharp look-out for the blue-bird of Canada. I went on my way, and saw him no more.

But he, and the gander, and the roar of the Falls haunted me for many winter nights. Have you not experienced, landing from a long sea voyage, the rocking, and tumbling, and oscillating motion of the ship which has brought you to your bourne, long after you are free from that thraldom? You are on dry land, on carpeted floors, on smooth turnpike roads, on paved streets—and yet you seem to be rolling and pitching as in the days when you strove to get your sea legs. So is it with Niagara. Shut your eyes tightly as you will, press down your fingers on the orbs ; but in the eyes of your soul you will see the Falls still, plain and distinct as on the table of a camera obscura. Stop your ears, stop them with cotton, stop them with wax, but in the ears of your mind you will hear the dull, constant roar of the cataract. And I seem to see and to hear it now as I write.

CHAPTER VIII.

THE burning American summer came, and with my travelling companion, whose head was not as white as the snows on the summit of Popocatapetl, I had been to Saratoga, and had seen its lions till we had grown somewhat sick of them. It was then we waited for a train at Schenectady, and, taking the New York Central, hied once more towards the Suspension Bridge and the Falls. It was six o'clock in the morning ere our eighteen hours' jolting and shaking came to an end. The State of New York, to those who are compelled to traverse it in a railway car, seems about the longest State that mortal ever waded through. You think you have given it the go-by, and are deep in the heart of Maine or Vermont, when, lo! the State of New York has you on the hip again. It must be longer than Upper Wimpole Street, which Sydney Smith on his death-bed considered the closest definition of a thing without end ; and the New York Central resembles, in one sense, the London, Chatham, and Dover, for it is everywhere. This is the famous railroad which Mr. Dean Richmond " runs " as a political " masheen ;" and out of the N.Y.C.R.R. have come many notable log-rollers, pipe-layers, and financeerers generally.

We were well out of the cars—for who is not well out of
an American railway car, or can suppress a feeling of gratitude when he is quit of that penitential van ? We had been
unable to procure berths in the sleeping car, and had done
our eighteen hours cooped up on those wretched little stools
of repentance the which, for the purpose I presume of adding
insult to injury, are often covered with crimson velvet and
decorated with carving and gilding. What was the name of
the cardinal whom Louis the Eleventh put in a cage so narrow, and so artfully constructed, that the miserable captive
could neither sit, nor stand, nor lie at ease ? Balue, was it
not ? Ah, but King Louis should have seen a passenger car
on the New York Central, or any other Yankee railroad.
That would have given him hints—even as Southey's Fiend
gathered hints for improving the prisons of Tophet by
inspecting a solitary cell in Coldbath Fields—and would have
enabled him to give Balue additional " fits."

What an exquisitely beautiful morning it was! Racked
and contused as we were by the merciless rail, how happy and
cheery we felt at the knowledge that we had come to our
journey's end, and for a whole week were about to enjoy
Niagara. I could not be angry with anybody. I could not
grumble at anything. I remembered, with a smile, a kind
and hospitable friend—the kindest and most hospitable,
indeed, of all Washington bankers, and in this every English
traveller will bear me out—with whom I used to dine, and
who would banter me with " Is the salt to your liking, sir?"
" Do you find anything amiss in the bread, sir ? " " Have
the forks too many prongs, sir ? " And at Niagara I felt

inclined to make a clean breast of it, and confess that I was incurably given to quarrelling with my bread and butter. It was *such* a morning! All nature seemed to have just come home from the wash; and in the whole domain of domestic art is there anything more brightly beautiful than a basket full of clean linen? How fresh it smells! What a radiant sheen it has! Without soil, without crease, how pure and innocent it is! And there, I declare, is the laundress's little bill neatly pinned to the corner of a napkin. Never mind the little bill. It will keep. *Mañana,* as the Dons say. We will treat the little bill to-morrow. To-day we will give to the joys of clean clothes.

We had had a fierce drought at Saratoga, and had left the country for miles and miles burnt up, with fierce fires raging in the underbush. But the spray of the Falls seemed to have fulfilled all the purposes of irrigation at Niagara, and the trees were green and sparkling with dew. There was just enough dust in the roads to make them look clean and powdery. There were just sufficient tiny clouds in the sky to stand forth like jewels—festoons of pearl, garlands of amethyst, tassels of opal, sprays of sapphire, on the blue vestment of the morning. Razor-sharp and diamond-distinct was every roof, every leaf, every twig, for, it seemed, miles and miles; you saw everything. The atmosphere was without prejudice. It had nothing to hide, and was proud of what it had to show. The birds were twittering by hundreds, and, now and then, bursting into a delicious concert. The spontaneity of these little feathered Bedlamites reminded me of a remark of a young mother who, when I asked her why her baby, without any previous excitement, crowed so loudly, replied quite seriously that she supposed it was because he was so glad he was born. I suppose it is because they are so glad they are born that these birds sing so. Mr. Babbage, of course, would object to them. It is certain they do kick up a deuce of a clatter, and that the blackbird by himself makes quite noise enough to require a whole Act of Parliament. That blackbird!—who is brown, by the way—I knew the rogue well enough, though the last time I had heard him was many thousand miles away and many years ago. He and five hundred fellow-madcaps used to come down from the tall old trees on to the lawn of a house in Bucks where I lived. They would come very early in the morning, often when I had been working all night, and cry " Open the shutters! open the shutters! Let the sun in and have your breakfast!" And then at sunset, when I sat down to dinner, they would gather again on the lawn, and sing, " Come along, Tom, the piper's son, arn't you very glad your day's work's done?" And here was the blackbird again, as bold as brass, and in as beautiful voice as ever. Our luggage had somehow been mislaid, notwithstanding the system of checking in use all over the States; but, in view of the beauty of the morning, I bore up under that *contretemps* quite blithely. It came to hand, however, at last. What mattered it if the bottom of a bonnet-box had been kicked out, and if a wonderful travel-ling arrangement of fancy woods known as a Saratoga trunk had been jolted into a misshapen mass of loose planks ? Was not this a summer's morning, and were not we at Niagara ?

They charge you, I think, a dollar in greenbacks, or fifty

cents in silver, for the privilege of passing the Suspension
Bridge in a carriage—a stiff toll, semingly; but what of that ?
Think of the marvel of a suspension bridge crossing the
Niagara River. This wondrous bridge is just two miles
below the Falls, is eight hundred feet long, and soars at an
altitude of two hundred and thirty feet above one of the
maddest streams in the globe. It is owned by a joint-stock
company, and is said to have cost half a million of dollars,
when dollars were dollars indeed. The first wires were flown
across by means of a kite, and the first transit from shore to
shore was made over these wires by the engineer and his wife,
in a basket. The bridge is double, or two-storied, and over
the carriage and foot road there is a railway, along which pass
the cars of the Great Western of Canada to connect with the
New York Central. Our driver, this time, was neither an
Irishman nor a negro, but a full-blooded Yankee, gaunt and
grim, and taciturn as the free enlightened Northerner, wheresoever you find him, generally is. He made no response to
my comments on the fineness of the morning, and seemed to
take it rather in dudgeon that I directed him to proceed to
the Clifton House, which is on the Canada side, in preference
to the International or the Cataract House, which are on the
hallowed territory of the United States. Perhaps he took me
for a Secesh who had been skulking through New York in
disguise, and was now about to take refuge on British soil
There were many such this summer time. The notable
Niagara peace negotiations were making one half of the North
wonder, and the other, and larger half, laugh. The Confederate Commissioners—Messrs. Holcombe and Thompson—

were at the Clifton ; another Southern agent, Mr. Clay, was
at St. Catherine's Springs, a few miles distant from Niagara ;
Mr. George N. Sanders was also " on hand ; " and the notorious Mr. W. Cornell Jewett, who had just dubbed himself
" Colonel," was dodging about from one side to the other of
the Falls, fetching and carrying messages between the emissaries of the South and Mr. Horace Greeley, who, with Major
Hay, the President's private secretary, were in mysterious
sederunt on the American shore. The only break in our
driver's taciturnity was when we had about half reached the
middle of the bridge, when he turned towards us and gravely
asked whether I thought Mr. Lincoln's " To whom it may
concern" missive was " bogus," or a " real live thing ? " Had
he not been a Yankee he would have concerned himself, I
should imagine, but very little about the truth or veracity of
that laconic intimation.

But I had little time or inclination to answer him, for in
the middle of the bridge you can see the Horseshoe Fall quite
distinctly. It was now, in the morning beams, one golden
mirage of glory, and the column of spray against the deep-
blue sky was indescribably lovely. I bade the driver, when
we had crossed the bridge, drive as near to the brink of the
precipice as he safely could ; and then I leant forward, and
revelled in the change of hues which had taken place since
I was here last. Nature had broken prison, and was solacing
herself for her long captivity by a hundred erratic freaks. It
was just late enough in the summer for the foliage, when the
sun shone longest and strongest, to assume the first phases of
those magnificently varied tints—now dazzlingly chromatic,

now mellow—which make the American woods during the fall take the guise of that wondrously variegated featherwork tapestry which the old Aztecs used to work such marvels in, and the secret of which is not yet lost among the modern Mexicans. An untravelled European, looking for the first time on a representation of autumnal scenery—say by such an artist as Bierstadt, or Hart, or Kensett, or those two great masters of aërial perspective, Church and Gignoux, whom I have already named, might be apt to think the brilliance of colour exaggerated, the suddenness of contrast forced and unnatural. I have seen at Niagara—on the thickly-wooded hill of Vermont—in the Valley of the St. Charles in Canada —on the banks of Lake George and Lake Champlain—but especially on the shores of the Hudson river, trees and shrubs that were in colour as scarlet as a soldier's coat, as yellow as an orange, as crimson as blood, as purple as a king's mantle, as blue, aye, as *blue* as a turquoise. The hues are literally as bright as those of the plumage of tropical birds; but the contrast of colour, bold as it is, very seldom becomes inharmonious. The exquisitely pure atmosphere seems to tone down and refine everything. It is a new revelation in local colour; but a revelation which all who run may read.

The change in the whole aspect of the place since I had been here last was in every way astounding. A ban had been taken off, an interdict raised, an indulgence granted, a jubilee proclaimed. I had left Niagara a solitude; now, even at six in the morning, it was crowded. Carriages full of tourists passed us coming and going. Pedestrians thronged the road. Artists were sketching; and beggars—yes, posi-

tively, beggars—were tendering the hand for charity. To the
great honour of the United States and Canada, a professional
mendicant, from Cape Cod to Quebec, is an extremely rare
personage to be met with. But Niagara is a privileged place,
an idle place, a sight-seeing place ; and the beggars are as
much at home there as in an Italian piazza or a Spanish
portal. Moreover, Niagara in summer swarms with brides
and bridegrooms. Next to the White Mountains it is the
chosen spot where happy couples like to pass their honey-
moon ; and who can refuse a begger ten cents during the
first blissful fortnight when he thinks that he has won everything in the world worth having ?

Where on earth had all these people come from ? In
December there had been comparatively nobody at Niagara.
The Irish hack-driver, the Sol Davis family, the Indian with
his dog and his duck gun, and the goose—or rather the gander
—that had been my companion on the brink of Table Rock—
name these and ourselves, and the whole sum of the winter
population seemed to be attained. Now humanity was rife.
I absolutely saw a little blackguard boy turning "cartwheels"
in front of the Clifton House. I was stricken almost dumb
at the sight, for in the States little boys have something
better to do than turn cartwheels. They can drive two-
wheeled carts, and earn a dollar a day at that. How oddly
these old acquaintances start up ! You go to a circus, say at
Copenhagen, or at Constantinople, and hearing a Tom Fool jest
in your own tongue, discover that the clown is an Englishman. I was staggered once, alighting from the diligence
which had brought me over Mount Cenis to St. Jean de

Maurienne, to hear a "Clean your boots, sir?" and to see kneeling on a fragment of rock, with the blue hills of Savoy behind him, an ex-member of the Shoeblack Brigade. He had had, perhaps, a difference on theological subjects with Lord Shaftesbury, and had sought refuge from polemics in foreign parts.

The commerce of Niagara must be intrinsically of little value; a large paper mill is turned by the Grand Rapids, but otherwise the Falls, though they toil continually, do not spin. Yet everybody seems to have something to sell; I mean everybody in the suburbs and round about the Falls, for in the shops of the two villages proper there is nothing doing. Two such wretched hamlets as those on the Canadian and the American side I have not seen out of the south of Ireland; but leave their shambling streets for the open, and you will find the road dotted with innumerable huts and booths full of things to be sold, and people eager to sell them. What connection the paltry little Anglo-French chimney ornaments you meet with in Houndsditch or the Lowther Arcade can have with the grandest cataract in the world I do not know : yet here they all are—sham porcelain, ormolu brooches, bracelets of Scotch pebble, earthenware poodles, baskets of shells, and William Tell's cottage in plaster of Paris, all retailed at most exorbitant prices. You carry them away as relics of Niagara, though you know very well that most of them came from the Faubourg St. Antoine. The Indian curiosities are more a speciality of the place, but many of the fans, moccasins, cigar cases, and tobacco-pouches sold are no more Indian than was our Yankee driver. Prodigious sums are charged for them, and it riled me, so to speak, to find at the head of the bridge leading to Goat Island one of these "museums" of curiosities kept by a great hulking, bearded Yankee, who was turning in the dollars as though he were dry goods selling in Bleecker-street, New York, and entering in a huge waste book the sales effected by two pretty, slender, Yankee girls, his assistants. There he was at the back of the "museum," in a railed-off counting-house, and very much did he resemble a huge spider in his web. A counting-house and a set of books at Niagara! Fancy "taking stock" of Nature, and posting up the Infinitely Beautiful! But this is the way with the Yankees. There never was such a mistake as to call them an industrious people. Shrewd, ingenious, active, energetic, enterprising they are, if you will; *but they won't do a stroke of work if they can help it.* They like "bossing." They prefer to "run the machine"—to stand on the bridge speaking-trumpet in hand, instead of slaving in the stoke-hole. For them the counting-house, where they can post up the profits at leisure: to others the actual handiwork. If there is any hard work to be done they hire an Irishman, a German, or a negro to do it ; and I dare say that hack-driver chafed at the task of taking the reins, and looked forward to the day when he should "run"* a livery-stable of his own, as a preparatory

* "To run" is a term which is so purely a modern American locution, that I cannot let it pass without brief comment. It means, to start, organise, and conduct a given undertaking. You may "run" anything—a railroad, a bank, a school, a newspaper, a quack medicine, a spiritualist lecture, a gas-works, a giant, a dwarf, a locomotive engine, a galantee-show, or an administration. "*I* run this government," said Mr. Abraham Lincoln to a friend who was remonstrating with him on some ministerial escapade,

step to being nominated Minister to Russia or Secretary of the Treasury. "Excelsior" has in the States often a very queer signification; and I shall never forget a conversation I once had on this head with a remarkably shrewd, clear-sighted New Englander. We were speaking of the Dignity of Labour. "*The Dignity of Labour be darned!*" coolly remarked my interlocutor; "*there ain't no dignity at all about it. It's much more dignified to make a hundred thousand dollars a year out of a royalty on a patent. If there ain't no other way than to earn your bread by the sweat of your brow, why you've got to do it; but I never knew a man yet that wasn't glad to get rid of his labour and to hire folks to do it, or that didn't look back upon the days he had to labour as a cussed bad time. I've often heard a rich man say that he was proud of having been a journeyman bricklayer, but I never heard one say that he'd like to be a journeyman bricklayer again. If labour was such a dreadful dignified thing, why should we be all in such an almighty hurry to become foremen and masters? Say.*" And, indeed, I think that on both sides the Atlantic a great deal of cant has been talked about the " dignity of

---

"and I alone am responsible for its shortcomings." Finally, you may "run" a religion. I was talking to a clerical gentleman, on board a steamer, of the little foothold which the sect known as Universalists, and of whom Dr. Chapin is so eloquent an exponent at New York, seems to have obtained in Boston. "Yes, sir," replied the clerical gentleman; "I guess Universalism's pretty well played out in the State of Massachusetts. A friend of mine he run a chapel in that connection for six months down to Boston, but she never paid working expenses. Well, sir, he concluded to clear out; and now he's got a good old Congregationalist concern running on the same premises, and paying her way handsomely." Item—you also "run" a candidate for Congress or the Presidency.

labour." We know that it is the lot of many of us, and we are told on the highest authority that it is meant, not as a blessing, but as a punishment; but to assert that about the grandest and noblest thing in the world is to work sixteen hours a day for fifteen shillings a week is often a convenient delusion, fostered by people who are not compelled to labour for the consolation of those who are.

Niagara in summer, it need scarcely be said, abounds with photographers, and you may have your *carte de visite* taken with the actual Falls—Horseshoe or American—as a background. The drawback to this is that the light is behind you, and that you generally appear in the photograph as black as a sweep. Then there are the bird-stuffing shops and the ice-cream saloons, by scores; and on the U. S. side almost every way-side cottager has Pie to sell, and candy too. Bars are plentiful, but are kept hidden. There are organ-grinders too, and you may hear the valse from *Faust* contending with the steady music of the Falls. I am glad to say that the Falls have the best of it. Finally, there is one great plague and nuisance on both sides of the river, in the shape of a legion of guides and hotel-touters who are neither submissive nor good-natured like their European brethren, but twenty times more importunate, and withal dictatorial and occasionally insolent. I don't know how the penal laws stand hereabout with regard to throwing an hotel-touter over the Falls of Niagara. In the opinion of Mr. Artemus Ward it might be "arson in the third degree;" but I can scarcely fancy the authorities would be very hard on an outraged tourist if he sent an impudent guide down the Grand Rapids.

They bore your life out. They want you to see or to buy everything—to put on a waterproof dress and go *under* the Falls, to ascend the Belvedere and look *over* the Falls, to see where the hermit was drowned and where the Caroline was burnt; to drive out to the Observatory and Brock's Monument, and the Burning Springs ; to go here and there, and to pay everywhere. A lively French Canadian, gossiping to me about Niagara, remarked, " It is a horror. It is a Barnum Museum with a *vente à l'encan*. It is full of brigands who ask you to buy. I am asked to buy the skull of le Général Brock. I am asked to buy the sword of Monsieur de Salaberry. He not kill there. I am ask to buy, what you call, a racoon ; and, horror of horror, one miserable, he say, 'Sare, you buy one piece of the pantaloon of Mr. Sam Patch, who jump over the Fall, and break his neck.'"

There is one thing you do not see at Niagara—literature. With some difficulty, at a few of the museums, you may obtain an indifferent guide-book, and the Hamilton and U. S. newspapers are cried about by newsboys when the mail trains come in ; but, beyond skimming through the telegrams, nobody reads at Niagara. You may lounge, you may loafe, you may saunter, you may moon, you may potter, you may eat lotuses, you may smoke, you may enjoy your *kef*, you may flirt, you may dance, you may drink; but you must not, or rather you cannot, study. There is a great open book before you, a book whose pages are infinite, whose lore is untold, and whose teaching Eternal.

CHAPTER IX.

Do you remember that wonderful night-picture in the "Sartor Resartus," when the sage of Weissnichtwo ascends to his garret watch-tower, and takes a survey of the city? Asmodeus, when he lifted the house-tops off, and showed the student what Madrid was doing—all her gaieties and all her wickedness—has a keen insight; but the High-Dutch pedant imagined by Thomas Carlyle transcends even the lame devil in sweep and vigour of observation. He leaves nothing out. He sees it all. The night camera is of the lucidest. The courtiers at the Residenz bowing and scraping in the wax-lit saloons; the dowagers squabbling over their whist and their "æsthetic tea;" the equerries whispering soft nothings to the maids of honour behind the heavy crimson window-curtains; the professor in his studio, moistening his seventeenth pipe of tobacco with his sixteenth mug of bock-beer, as he collates the Pandects of Justinian with the Belfast Town and Country Almanack; the sceptic proving to an admiring conclave in yellow beards and blue spectacles that the idea of a Cosmic Creator is a delusion, and that the Bible is a mythus—poor sceptic, he will be obliged to believe to-morrow morning in the existence of his washerwoman, when she comes battering at his door for her little account; Gretchen in her attic, unloosing her bodice, or plucking the leaves from the flower-stalk with a "loves me, loves me not;" the nurse that is asleep, and the sick man that lies awake, staring at the wall-paper; the baby that is dying, and the baby that is being born; the beaten schoolboy forgetting his stripes in balmy slumber, with his peg-top under his pillow; the thieves in the night-cellar counting their booty; the landlord piling up his empty beer mugs, and reckoning up the entries on his slate; the tired-out dog, creeping under the lee of a barn, to dream of a paradise of bones with fat and gristle lying thick upon them; the students reeling home, chanting the *Gaudeamus igitur* more or less out of tune and rhythm; the beggar emptying his wallet, and un-winding the bandages from his apocryphal sores; the peasants slowly trooping, trudging townwards beside their lumbering waggons, laden with the milk and eggs and poultry which are to feed the great human hive to-morrow; the sentinel pacing up and down in front of the barracks, his bright bayonet gleaming in the moon-light; and the three men in the gaol dungeon who are to be hanged to-morrow, pressing their hot heads against the bars, staring out at the darkness —the forerunner of the greater blackness which is to come— and sucking in their last mouthfuls of air and life; these are among the things which Herr Teufelsdrökh might have seen or figured to himself from his eyrie. Some of them I think he has really set down in inimitable Carlylian prose; but I have lost the hang of the phrases. It is so long since I read

the " Sartor Resartus," and the only copy I possess is so many
thousand miles away.

I would that some Herr Teufelsdrökh, or some philosopher
with his breadth of thought and sharpness of purview, would
mount with me this night to the cupola which dominates the
Clifton House, and tell me what is going on on either side of
the Falls of Niagara.   For I feel that my pen is but a cripple,
hobbling painfully over the paper as I strive to give shape
and coherence to the thoughts that stir me.   What should
there be, it may be asked, to describe beyond the usual peace
and cheerfulness and tranquillity which reign here ?   Niagara
is the quietest of places.   Beyond the continual roar of the
waters, which, from its continuity, is at last suggestive of
perfect stillness, there is scarcely a sound to be heard.   A
few miles up the country, and the brightest and noisiest birds
abound ; but here I miss the feathered songsters.   Save at
sunrise and just before sunset, and for a very short time, they
seem to shun the Falls.   Perhaps the roar frightens them.
Perhaps the spray.   And yet I think that an eagle, flapping
majestically over the great expanse of tumbling foam between
Terrapin Tower and the Horseshoe, would be a grand and
terrible sight.   The noise of wheels is seldom heard at Niagara
by night.   After sundown so much as a buggy will seldom
venture out, for there are no public gas-lamps, and the roads,
running along the very edges of the precipices, are destitute
either of parapets or of palings.   A false step, a startled
horse, a drunken driver, and over you go, a hundred and fifty
feet, to worse than Tarpeian destruction.   And, again, that
steady, persistent coronach, which the cataract is always

chanting, is sufficient, thank goodness ! to drown the abominable screech of the railway whistle, and that unearthly stertorous outcry peculiar to American locomotives. Trains may rattle over the Suspension Bridge, but you hear them not. The cataract absorbs all.

Like Eutychus in his third loft, I have drowsed to sleep while the Falls were preaching their eternal sermon ; but happily there is a railing to my high-up verandah, and I do not fall, to be taken up dead. I look out and find the night very dark, starless, and moonless. I cannot even see the Falls, although I never cease to hear them. Only far away, where I know the opposite river bank to be, and then again farther to the horizon, there are sparsely dotted here and there some little pins'-points of yellow light. Those I know must be in houses. I sit up very late in my loft. By twos or threes the little pins'-points disappear ; and at last the only light left is the glowing crimson of my cigar tip. Then I shut out the smell of Niagara—for it has a smell, a bracing, hardy, almost salt-water odour—and its bodily presence, for the wind drives the spray over to the Clifton House, and covers your garments with tiny pellicles of moisture, that sparkle like diamond-dust; but the sound I cannot shut out, nor would I if I could. Then I turn into my room, where the bright lamp is—the glass globe trembles from the omnipresent concussion caused by the Falls—and go to work.

I want some one to tell me what is going on over there where the lights were, and below and around me where all is dark—who the people are, and of what they are thinking, this most momentous night. Failing the guiding counsel of

the philosopher, I am driven to the vaguest guesswork. I
dine every day at a *table-d'hôte* with two hundred people. I
am not on speaking terms with more than six of their
number, and of these three are old Washington and Montreal
acquaintances. I keep myself to myself, and can but guess.
In addition to the usual colony of English tourists and officers
—who are just like English officers and tourists all over the
world, and who would admire the Falls a great deal more if
the pale ale at the Clifton House were not sour instead of
bitter, and if there were any soda-water to be obtained—
there is a fair sprinkling of burly, big-bearded, woollen-
bloused and broad-chested Canadians, with their wives and
families, honestly doing the lazy, and luxuriating in the brief
but bounteous summer. But these are not the people who
puzzle me. What are this crowd of others doing? of what
are they thinking? on what errand are they bound? All
day long they wander to and fro like phantoms. I conjecture
them to be Americans, for they smoke much, and are gaunt
and sallow, and affect the bar, and swallow many cocktails,
and, between meals, are much given to sitting in the piazzas
with their legs stretched out, and their feet against the pillars,
at an altitude considerably above the level of their heads.
But I feel assured that they are not Yankees. You never
hear them brag. They seldom speak, within my hearing at
least, of dollars; they are full of a very grave and quiet
courtesy; they seem rather subdued than otherwise; and
their womankind, although they have often handsome gold
watches and chains, positively come down to breakfast and
dinner in the plainest dresses of cotton and woollen stuff.

We have had one or two bevies of Yankee belles dropping
down upon us during the week; but the "trim little damsels,"
with their bright eyes, their coral lips, their blooming cheeks,
their false tresses, their "illusion waists," their flowers,
feathers, diamonds, and laces, their vivacious prattle, and
delightful, coquettish, winsome ways, have grown frightened
at the staid and almost lugubrious gravity of the Clifton
table-d'hôte. We have no dancing here at night, no pianoforte tickling, no flirtations in the corridors. This is not
what the bright halcyon birds of Yankeeland bargained for,
or are accustomed to endure. Alarmed and disgusted, they
have usually cut their sojourn much shorter than they originally intended, or have tripped across to the American side,
and settled down in the livelier International or the Cataract
House.

Why are those gaunt and sallow men so solemn, so sorrowful almost, in mien? Again I take refuge in guessing.
These are Confederates; the exiles of the Distracted States.
They are not just now in a humour to be jocose. They see
nothing to make merry about. Their wives and daughters
would rather not dance, and they wear cotton and homespun
dresses because their mothers and sisters down in Dixie are
in rags, and they think it indecent, not to say heartless, to be
flaunting in silks and *point d' Alençon* while those who are
dearest to them are clad like beggar-women. I saw a very
pretty Southern lady once in New York, every one of whose
ten finger-tips peeped through the tops of her gloves. She
had mended these gloves, she said apologetically, a great
many times; but somehow the holes would burst out again.

I wonder whether her stockings—I am sure she had pretty feet—were in the same distressing state. But she did not intend to have any new gloves yet awhile, she said. She would wait. They were in direr straits at Richmond. Meanwhile, she was working very hard to get some little comforts together for the Confederate prisoners at Elmira.

They come and go noiselessly, these Confederate persons, and foregather in corners, where they hold stealthy counsel, and they have generally newspapers in their hands. These they do not read in the expansively loafing manner common to the Yankees, who are accustomed to spread them out on their knees like napkins, or hold them out at arm's length, going right through them, from Mr. Fessenden's appeal for his two hundred millions, to the editorials; from the bogus telegrams of a Copperhead conspiracy in Missouri, to the paragraph, " strange, if true," relating that Mrs. Londerback, of Hickory township, Illinois, has, at the age of seventy-eight years, been safely delivered of twins—see the " World," of the 3rd of August, 1864. The Confederates fold their papers small, as if they wished to bring only one particular portion of a column under view. They con the particular portion over and over again, and pass it from one to another, nodding and winking in an occult manner. If haply they adjourn to drink, they liquor up stealthily, and do not clink their glasses. They pay in specie. Then they glide away on their own occult business, and are seen no more until dinner-time. These are clearly not the persons to drink champagne at six dollars fifty a bottle, to put on waterproof dresses and stumble down Biddle's stairs into the Cave of the Winds

under the American Falls, to make pleasure parties to the
Whirlpool, or court capricious beauty amidst the whir of the
Grand Rapids, or ramble about Goat Island to the bathing-
place where the Hermit was drowned, or buy peggalls, and
wampum mocassins, and bird-and-feather fans, at the Old
Curiosity Shop. Those *agrémens* are to be found on the
American side. It is as much as the exiles' lives are worth
to cross the ferry or the suspension bridge. They are marked
and proscribed men. Delators are here—correspondents of
the New York republican papers, chafing in their daily
columns of rigmarole that rebels should be allowed to plot
with impunity on British soil. Spies are here in plenty.
Judas is biting his nails with rage to think that he cannot
earn thirty dollars in greenbacks by betraying these de-
nounced ones, who lounge very quietly in the piazzas of the
Clifton House, or saunter to the very limit of the acclivities
of the Niagara river, looking over at what was once their own
country—gazing at the frail white tenements and darkling
forests of pine and larch. There is America. There is the
State of New York. How the Yankees would rejoice to lay
hold of them! How the telegraph would flash the news of
their arrest from one end of the North to the other! How
swiftly would quarters be found for them in Lafayette, or
Warren, or the Old Capitol! But the Confederates are
prudent men, and give the territory of the Union a wide
berth. We English are a patient people; but I don't think
we should stand an Arguelles kidnapping expedition into
Canada.

Philosopher, tell me what thoughts are agitating the

Southern mind this night, when the papers have brought us the Petersburg news in full, and the best and worst for either side is known. In the room beneath me there may be silently brooding or tossing restless on his bed a man who was once rich and prosperous and powerful, with horses and camels by thousands, and a "very great household" in slaves, so that there was no man like him in the South. Then the evil days came, and he cast in his lot with his native State, and signed some Secession Ordinance, and was forced to fly. Of his vast possessions there remains to him now only an old negro, his bond-servant—although he is in a land where slavery has legally no existence—and who helped his master to escape when his life was in danger, and remained behind to see if he could save any remnants of his property. But the Sabeans have smitten everything, root and branch; servants, cattle, sheep, and camels have been burned up, and put to the edge of the sword; and the old negro stands before his master now like the messenger before the just man of the land of Uz—"I only am escaped to tell thee." How does he bear the news, this ruined Southerner? Is he elated? Does he foresee an end to his troubles? "Glorious Confederate victory!—total rout of the Federals!—disaster to the Union arms!—wholesale slaughter of Yankees!"—it is thus the sympathising Canadian journals strive to raise his hopes and feed his pride. The end may be coming. The abortive assault on Petersburg may be the end of the summer campaign; in that grim conference on board the steamer on Sunday morning there may indeed have been hinted the word "retreat," and Abraham Lincoln may have acquiesced in the suggestion. What though this were the last act of the bloody drama? What though the baffled and exhausted legions of the Potomac slowly melted away from before Richmond and Petersburg, and left the beleaguered cities to their own devices? What though the "wayward sisters" were at length permitted to depart in peace? It would be a glorious consummation to the struggle which the South has carried on for four years, with such astonishing endurance and with such indomitable valour. He, the exile, the outcast, the wanderer without a country, without a home, without a name almost—for to European Governments he is still but a "so-called" Confederate—might once more become a magnate in the South, with a voice in her councils and a position in her society. But can the past ever return? Can the grave give up its dead? He had three sons. The bones of one lie mouldering in Slaughter Pen. One fell at Gettysburg, with a bullet through his heart. The third and youngest pines, emaciated and fever-stricken, in a Federal prison, and his house—the house in which his forefathers lived two hundred years ago—it was first plundered by Sheridan, and then burnt down by Hunter. And may not the hope of victory, of peace, of independence, prove delusive? How many times has the cup of success been at the Southern lips? how many times rudely dashed away? He is a man of shrewdness and experience. He knows what Grant is—cold, patient, obstinate, looking over defeat as a giant looks over a puddle; always gazing at the mountain height in the distance; never faltering in his determination to reach it at last. What if this should prove another

Vicksburg? He knows the calibre of Abraham Lincoln. He neither overvalues nor undervalues him. He accounts him a vulgar, cunning man, avaricious of power, bent on domination, callous to popular censure, determined to hang on to office even by the skin of his teeth. He knows that the farmers of the Great West, who have made mighty fortunes out of this war, are heart and soul with Abraham Lincoln. His continuance in office means more war, more contracts for flour at ten dollars a barrel, for oats at a dollar a bushel, for pork at forty dollars a cask. He knows, moreover, how much fanaticism, strength, solidity, momentum, there yet remain in the North; how lightly, as yet, her material resources have been drawn upon; how able she is, if she have the will, to carry on this war, and furnish fresh supplies of men and of money too for years to come. He knows that, to acknowledge the independence of the South would be to the North as bitter a humiliation as to an honourable man to receive a slap on the face or a tweak of the nose.

Again, close by him may be a lady, tenderly nurtured, lapped in luxury from her cradle upwards; she, too, has read the news. She may have read them with a fierce though silent joy, with a proud upheaving of the heart to think that the cunningly-devised plot has collapsed, and that the horse and his rider, the captains and the men of war, have been engulfed by the earthquake themselves had devised. Or, perchance, she has listened to the tale with a dull apathy. She is scarcely glad to hear that her countrymen have gotten the better of their foes. It is too late. She is tired out. Her hair has turned grey. Her heart is dead. Peace, independence, cannot bring back her dead children, her ruined home, her household gods, the little relics of the old country handed down from generation to generation, the birds and flowers she loved so well. It is futile, perhaps, to mourn over a broken piano, over the portrait of a little child hacked to pieces by Federal sabres, a rose-bush rooted up, a grape-vine charred to ashes. But it is human nature so to grieve, for these little paltry things make up what human beings call home. That home is black and desolate now. The old slave gardener who, when she was low-spirited, used to pat her on the shoulder and say, " Never mind, missus, our children are getting on so nicely "—he meant *her* children, that most darkened darkey ; —the sable " Aunty " who would boast that she " brought her up," and her mother up too ; her friends and neighbours ; the pastor she sat under ; the family doctor ; the village store-keepers even—they have all gone down the troubled stream into the ocean of blood and desolation. What does it matter to her if Lee or if Grant get the upper hand ? She is a widow, and alone, and tired out.

And across the river. Philosopher, what is being dwelt on there ? Those little pins'-points of yellow light were from lamps in rooms. Of what were the watchers thinking ? They knew the tidings ere we did. How did they brook the news of the great bankruptcy of their hopes ? In one Northern paper, and on the very page which contained the narrative of the appalling disaster to the Federal arms, I read an account of how ex-Governor Ramsey, senator from Minnesota, had just returned from the front ; how sapping

and mining were the order of the day; how he had had an
interview with General Grant, who had expressed himself as
"entirely confident of complete success," and wished the
public only "to possess their souls with patience" until his
plan was matured. But telegrams travel faster than the
travelling of ex-governors and senators from Minnesota.
The public have waited, the plan has been matured, the
event has culminated, and with what result? What bitter
disappointment, black despondency, raging sense of shame
and humiliation, there must be beyond the river where those
lights were twinkling! Psha! not at all. There has been
dancing to-night at the Cataract, and dancing at the International. The American side of Niagara was never so full,
so brilliant, or so gay. The walks and drives are crowded.
The sound of music and revelry is incessant—the consumption of champagne and ice-creams tremendous. The market
for flirtation is thronged. Nobody seems to care a rush
about the war, the thousands who died the most horrible of
deaths in the explosion, the bombardment, and the assault.
The young and the heedless don't care ten cents about
Petersburg; while the older and more earnest shrug their
shoulders and say, Well; it's only a check. The North has
been foiled, but not beaten. We can afford a dozen such
disasters, while a single one like that at Petersburg would
utterly overwhelm the South. We are thirty millions to
their seven. We don't mean to cave in. Grant, or somebody else, must keep on "pegging away," and try again and
again until he succeeds. "What! a republic of thirty
millions, rich, intelligent, energetic, and intrepid, to be van-

quished by three hundred thousand slaveholders—and this
in the middle of the nineteenth century! As well might a
pop-gun dismount and silence an eleven-inch Dahlgren or
Parrott. No, the contest can have but one result. No
terms—no truce—no parley ; but down with the accursed
rebellion." These words are the "Tribune's," not mine ; but
they aptly express the sentiments of the most fanatical, and
therefore the most earnest, Northerners.

Between the adverse factions surges the eternal voice of
Niagara, as though murmuring "Peace ! peace !" But men
grow accustomed to its voice, and callous to it, and at length
heed it not at all.

CHAPTER X.

THE WORMS.

IT is the last straw that breaks the camel's back. I had been kneeling, metaphorically speaking, in the court-yard of a caravanserai at Smyrna any time during six months, meekly bowing the hump to the remorselessly accumulated load. I had borne it all ; raw silk, figs, dates, flax, hemp, myrrh, ambergris, opium, rhubarb, and magnesia—insult, obloquy, reproach, misrepresentation. I had endured quietly. I knew that I was a Camel, and that it was my lot to be a carrier and not to grumble. I cherished the hope of rising anon, and, hearing the tinkling caravan bells, and, after plodding for many a weary rood through hot sand finding myself at Mecca—I mean at home. I could have borne more burdens even, had they been adjusted with tolerable decency to this patient back. The oppressor's wrong, the proud man's contumely, the insolence of office, the ferocity of hack-drivers, the sulkiness of railway conductors, the assaults of rowdies, the boys who sell " fig and gum drops " in the cars, the infernal hotel gong, the hardness of the times, gloves at three dollars twenty-five cents a pair, champagne at seven dollars a bottle, cigars at sixty cents apiece, the young lady next door who was perpetually hammering at the valse from *Faust*, and always breaking down over the first bar, anything, in fine, you please to mention—anything but this. But there is a limit to human sufferance. There is a point beyond which it is perilous to pile up the agony of mortal man. I didn't bargain for *this*. I never contracted to undergo the whole seven plagues of Egypt concentrated into one hideous and abominable nuisance. You will naturally wish to know what the terrible infliction I denounce is like. Stay but a moment and you shall hear.

I was taking my walks abroad in Fifth Avenue, one summer's morn, meaning harm to no man, and with my heart full of sweet and placid feelings towards the United States. I loved *pro tem.* the Loyal League, admired the Cabinet, and adhered to the Monroe doctrine. Suddenly I saw, advancing towards me with fierce and rapid strides, an Old Lady. Now I am not afraid of ladies. In youth I was wont to be alarmed at them all, the young and the old; but I can bear a great deal of Woman by this time. She has ceased to appal the subscriber; she wouldn't have anything to do with him when he yearned for sympathy; but now, when she has nothing to give, or he, the rather, nothing to accept, she is kind. This was, nevertheless, a very fearsome old lady to look upon. She was tall and wore no crinoline, and was crowned with a coal-scuttle bonnet. She had spectacles, also, and a very hard hickory-looking face beneath them. " This is an old lady from New England," I mused. " I see it all. She is from the State of Massachusetts. Residence East Hallelouia, profession widow, religious proclivities Heterodox Congregational. This is the old lady who is a

great hand at broiling shad, preserving cranberries, scrubbing
floors, and making apple pasties and berry pies. Her father
was a Deacon; her uncle a Select Man; she has two sons,
Zeke and Ike, whom she switches frightfully, and her grandmother, one of the ' hunky girls' of the '76, broke her china
teapot after the last family Souchong had been thrown into
Boston Harbour and took never another cup of the refresh-
ing beverage until the evacuation of New York by the
Britishers." I drew aside to allow this respectable but formidable female to pass; but to pass me was apparently not
her aim. She meant mischief. Her eyes were inflamed with
ire. Her lips moved as though in wrath. She held in one
woollen-gloved hand a monstrous gingham umbrella; and
with it she made as though to strike me down. She
brandished this weapon of offence, this gingham Excalibur,
above her head. She swung it to the right and the left. She
brought it down, in the " St. George " with a force and precision which, had I been stricken, must have cloven me from
the nave to the chaps.

She delivered the carte and the tierce and the reason
demonstrative. She was clearly cunning of fence; and I
thought I would see her blessed ere I fought with her. Her
umbrella was, at last, within an inch of my nose. The hair
of my flesh stood up. This old lady had evidently sworn to
have my blood. Conscience makes cowards of us all. But
who was she? A Woman's Rights Convention delegate? a
Black Republican? a manufacturer of chewing tobacco? a
spiritualist medium? or an abolitionist lecturer? I had
made up my mind for the worst, and was preparing either to

fly or to cast myself at the feet of the vengeful old lady, and
sue for mercy. "Transatlantic female," I was on the point
of saying, "spare me. I am very sorry for it. I cave in. I
am not young, nor tender, but I am an Orphan, and peni-
tent. Spare me, for the sake of your Banner in the Sky, of
the Lone Star which shines above the statue of the Father
of his Country in Union Square—of that great American
eagle who, with untarnished wings, is flapping out the blear
and bloodshot eye of Treason and Rebellion all over this
vast continent—from the dusty turnpikes of Todd's Tavern
to the swampy shores of Bayou Sara. Spare me for the
sake of our common blood, our common language, our
common creed; for the sweet sake of Shakspeare, who was
our common Grandmother—of Spenser, who was our mutual
Cousin-german, only ninety-nine times removed—of Milton,
who, it is well known, came of a reputable family, down to
Salem, Mass., and was educated at Harvard, and who was
the common Uncle of us all. Spare me for the sake of
Civilisation, Humanity, and the Brotherhood and Sisterhood
of Nations." I was rehearsing this little speech, the tropes
and flourishes in which are, I am free to confess, culled from
the vocabulary of Orator Pop, when the old lady rushed by
me, still wildly waving her umbrella, but with singular cle-
mency, forbearing to knock my head off. And, looking back,
I beheld her still urging on her career down Fifth Avenue,
towards Tenth Street, brandishing her gingham all the way.
Was she mad? Was she in a spiritual ecstasy, and speeding
from a Revival? No, a hasty remark she made as she
passed me at once explained the mystery of her proceed-

ings. In a tone of dolorous agony she cried, " Oh, them worms !"

Yes, those Worms. They are the Seven Plagues of Egypt to which I adverted anon. They are the bane, the scourge, the nuisance, which, in the merry month of June, make a man's life a torment to him. The side walks of the streets of New York, faithful to their Dutch origin, are bordered with trees, principally limes and elms. In joyous June, when they are in full leaf, and their verdure has not been burnt up by the white heat of the summer sun, they are refreshingly umbrageous and look very pretty. But these trees are, one and all, infested by a horrible little reptile, known commonly as the "measuring worm," the "canker worm," or the "pace-maggot," but which, according to scientific authorities, has quite as much right to be called the "geometer," the "arpenteur," or the "hindrometer." It is of a dusky olive in hue, with a tawny head and a pea-green tail. It is about as long as a bit of string, and as big as a piece of chalk—stay, the length of the middle joint of your little finger affords an apter standard of measurement. I don't know whether it has any eyes; but, when touched, a hideous green matter exudes from it. This worm swings by an almost imperceptible cord or filament from the branches of the highest trees, as of the lowliest shrubs. As you walk along the street, myriads of these worms are hanging motionless in the air. Suddenly they bob against your nose, they slide down your shirt collar, they enter your eye and sit on your lid. Open your mouth, and a worm slides down your throat. They light on your hands and your feet. A lady

comes home from walking with her parasol tasseled, and the
hem of her dress fringed, by these beastly worms. When
they have munched their fill of the young leaves of the trees,
they spin out of their own depraved bodies a slack rope of
gluten ; and down this aerial bridge they slide till they are
within a distance of five feet from the earth. There they
ruminate, till, gorged with vegetable dirt, these green leeches
tumble down on the pavement, where they wriggle and
wallow, and, after a time, I trust, die. The flagstones are so
speckled with surfeited worms, that, on the finest and most
cloudless afternoon, you may fancy it is just beginning
to rain. As I have said, they specially affect to perform
their Blondin and Leotard performances on a level with the
faces of human beings walking erect, and the only way to
prevent their choking or blinding you is to arm yourself with
a stick or an umbrella, and slash them away as you travel.
The old lady I had met was evidently, and of old, aware of
the worms, and of the means to combat them. Hence her
violent and apparently hostile demonstrations with the
umbrella.

These detestable reptiles are no mere petty nuisance. They
are destroying the finest trees in the streets of New York.
You might take them to be pipe-layers, or log-rollers, or
lobbyers, or members of a municipal " ring," so speedily and
so completely do they devour every green thing. Like every
other social nuisance, the worms have their friends, and one
enthusiastic student of natural history writes to the papers to
claim for them " a certain amount of brains or at least of
instinct." He watched, it seems, a flock of birds light upon a

tree full of worms. The reptiles, knowing full well what the intent of these early birds must be, hastily skedaddled down their air-ladders, whence, like the showman's kangaroo who took refuge down his own throat, they doubtless, if worms can cachinnate, derisively guffawed at their baffled pursuers. The birds flew away, and then the worms went back to gobble up more leaves. The strangest circumstance about these diminutive "cusses" is that their appearance in New York is a comparative novelty. Ten years ago they were unknown, and they are rarely seen in the streets of the New England towns, which are bordered by the most beautiful trees. Are they emigrants, I wonder? Did they land at Castle Garden? And how is it that they got clear off the Battery without being crimped by the bounty-jumpers—without being hocussed and kidnapped and sent to serve in the army of the Potomac, or on board the Mississippi flotilla? Are there any emigrant worms at Rikers Island, who try to desert when they get sober, and find that they have been swindled, and, in a mad attempt to swim ashore, are shot by the sentries? There used to be Hessian flies—are there any Irish worms? The householders of New York are reduced almost to despair by these intolerable little pests. Persons of philosophical temperament shrug their shoulders, and remark that the worms are, after all, not so bad as the Draft, or the Arguelles case, or the Morrill Tariff. And, again, it has been remarked that, by a grotesque coincidence, the worms and the barrel-organs come out together. You seldom see these "Alfred Le Measurers" before the end of May, you rarely hear an organ before the beginning of June. By this time the first are squirming, and the last are grinding all day long. To make the matter worse, these most disgusting libels on the caterpillar tribe are but in a chrysalis state. They turn out to be, in the long run, not reptiles, but insects. In a month or so they will cast their slough of dusky olive, and blunder about the world and the gas-burners as the large, uncouth moths which, from the loose, white, flowery pollen with which their wings are covered, are known as " millers."

I hope, if these few remarks find any American readers, that my mild denunciation of the New York worms will not be made use of as another count in that tremendous indictment invariably brought against any traveller who presumes to complain of anything he has seen, heard, or felt in the United States. It is not, I trust, disloyal to object to the measuring worm. It cannot be a violation of the sanctity of private life to abuse the pace-maggot. It will scarcely be urged as a flagrant example of ingratitude for hospitality received that I have been somewhat hard on the hindro-meter. My brothers, let us be just. Confound your worms ! and should these volumes reach you about the first of June, 1865, I am confident that all New Yorkers will echo my anathema. Allow me also to remark that the beautiful summer nights of New York are made hideous by the disturbance created by an intolerable little ruffian called a "tree-toad," a denizen likewise of the street arboretum. I never saw a tree-toad ; but I have been told that he is a cross between a lizard, a cricket, and that genuine article who is said to wear a jewel in his head and doesn't. He begins

about nine o'clock in the evening, and comes to an end about
four o'clock in the morning, when the flies relieve guard and
drive you mad with their buzzing. I can scarcely give an
imitation of his frightful chant ; but remembering the precedent set by one Aristophanes in his celebrated " Froggee "
chorus, I may note down the song of the tree-toad somewhat in this wise—"Chick, chick, cluck, cluck, yuk, yuk, cleck,
cleck, chuck, scheuckh !" and so on, for seven mortal hours.
An American friend who found language in everything—in
the snortings of locomotives, the puffings of steam tugs, the
jangling of bells, and the rumbling of wheels—used to declare
that he understood the speech of these night-pests, and that
it ran thus:—" World six thousand years old, and only a
tree-toad.   Education, civilization, and refinement; and only
a tree-toad.   Nothing created without a Purpose, and Only a
Tree-Toad."

Then the flies : I have something to say about them elsewhere. Then the mosquitoes : I have written a chapter
about them. And the moths ! Really I must protest against
the moth—our old enemy the measuring-worm in another
form. He ate me up, so far as my wardrobe was concerned,
bodily in three months. I happen to be very much afraid of
a Certain Person who is good enough, among other things, to
look after my wearing apparel. Who is not so afraid if he
will only have the courage to avow it ? One of the modestest
and kindest gentlemen I ever knew, a valiant captain in the
British Guards, said to me once, " I have been through the
Crimean war, and I think I could go through another Alma
and another Inkermann well enough ; but there is one thing

I cannot face—the eye of my servant when I have been on a journey without him, and when, unpacking my portmanteau, he remarks, in a tone of quiet reproach, '*I don't know what you've done with your shirts, sir.*'" The Certain Person despatched me to the United States with an ample supply of body-linen. That was in winter. When spring came the Certain Person grew anxious, and I received one morning in Mexico a threatening letter, stating that *I must be getting on wretchedly*—the italics are not mine—that the Person was coming out to New York forthwith, and that I had better be at the Cunard Dock at Jersey City on the 7th of May to await the arrival of the "Persia." The "Persia" arrived, and with it the Person ; but nearly the first words of welcome I was favoured with when, arriving at the hotel, my wardrobe was inspected, were these, " *Where are your socks ?* " My socks ! *Où sont les neiges d'autan !* I had scattered them all about the North American continent. Go ask the chambermaid at Willard's. Ask the stout squaw who makes beds at the St. Lawrence Hall, Montreal. Ask the French Canadienne who officiates as *fille de chambre* at Russell's Hotel, Quebec. Ask Antonio, who waits (in his shirt) at "El Globo" Calle del Obispo, San Cristobal de la Habana. Ask of Popocatapetl and Istlacihuatl. Ask the Peak of Orizaba. Ask the barracoutas of the Spanish Main, and the sharks in the Gulf of Mexico. Ask the bedroom stewards of the Cunard and West India Mail Companies' lines. My socks ! How was I to know what I had done with my socks? The question put by the Certain Person overwhelmed me; but I remembered that I too had put a question—a leading question, a searching question, so soon as I had set foot on the " Persia's " deck. Satiated with greenbacks and spondoulicks my soul thirsted for specie, and I said, "*Dearest, have you any gold ?*" "I must give," the Certain Person quavered, "a sovereign to William and a sovereign to Mrs. Nelson " (all Cunarders will at once recognise the best steward and stewardess afloat. "Reckless extravagance," I returned, sternly; "give them half a sovereign apiece, and be good enough to hand me the balance."

There was a residue of socks in my wardrobe, but the moths had eaten them up. They devoured, during the summer, seven pairs of pantaloons, a coat or two, and a seal-skin cap. Am I exaggerating ? Had not Mr. Charles Dickens a raven once which ate up a whole flight of stairs ? I knew a starling who swallowed the best part of an eight-day clock, but poisoned himself with the brass dial-plate and died. When the Certain Person returned to Europe I had a fresh stock of socks, and my other garments were plentifully sprinkled with camphor, cedar chips, and tobacco leaves, to preserve them from the moths. *Eheu!* my clothes have come home all holes, like a cullender or a cane-bottomed chair. The camphor, cedar chips, and tobacco proved not of the slightest use. I am reminded, "in this connection," of a story of a Dutch ambassador in Rio Janeiro, who, going home on leave of absence, stowed his diplomatic uniform away in a chest of cedar wood, and went away chuckling and rubbing his hands to think that he had given the moths the go-by. He came back, and on the eve of a court ball caused the cedar-wood chest to be opened. *Nothing was left but some gauzy fluff and the gilt buttons of his uniform.* They lay there in mathematical precision : so many for the sides, the sleeves, the pockets, the coat tails, the waist and knees of the small-clothes, but the moths had swallowed all the broadcloth and all the kerseymere. I had a tremendous fur rug—a noble rug, the spoil of many silver foxes—a rug I had possessed for years, and travelled thousands of miles with. It was duly kept in the dry pickle of cedar, camphor, and tobacco, from May to September. "Insects, spare that rug," I frequently murmured ; " in youth it sheltered me ; in wintry weather it has saved me many a twinge of rheumatism." I took this rug with me when I returned to England. It had been worth probably five-and-twenty pounds ; but, as it turned out, I had much better have sold it to a Jew in Chatham Street, New York, for two dollars twenty-five cents. We had a charming pair of passengers on board the "Persia :" a pretty, poetical, young Yankee lady, and a blooming English Major of Engineers. They were both terribly sea-sick, and could only be kept alive by sitting on deck over against the warm funnel and under the lee of the starboard paddle-box. They supported nature principally on salad and on champagne cocktails, which were concocted for them every day at 2 p.m. by a young philanthropist in the Life Guards. I never knew such a neat hand as Captain De Boots at mixing salads and " fixing " champagne cocktails. Sappho and the Sapper were accidental acquaintances, but they struck up one of those delightful salt-water flirtations which only last ten days, and mean nothing, and are nothing, but which, nevertheless, make life very cheery and pleasant. Cupidon-Cunard is the jolliest of little gods. It was quite touching to see them nestling in the shadow of the paddle-box, billing and cooing, sharing salad and cocktails, and occasionally, when the "Persia" pitched, turning green. My heart yearned towards them. I saw that they sometimes shivered, and that their provision of ruggedness was meagre. I went below and fetched my tremendous rug. I brought it on deck, and wrapped them up from head to foot—the prettiest Babes of the Ocean—the nicest bale of dry goods I had ever seen, and left them "warm and comfortable," as the poor Duke of Norfolk said when he advised the clodhoppers to sup on a tea-spoonful of curry powder. But, horror! as I enveloped them I found that my rug was ruined. The moths had been at it. It had gone hopelessly to the bad. It was perforated with myriads of holes. The skin showed innumerable bald places. It was full of ringworm; the fur could be plucked off in handfulls. My rug is not worth five shillings, and my private belief is . *that the American moths like cedar, camphor, and tobacco,* and hold them in the light of condiments such as Chutneep and Worcestershire sauce, to make their meal more toothsome.

But no more about the moths; only I say this, don't run away with the notion that allusion to a petty nuisance means hatred to the United States. I don't think the Cingalese would massacre Sir Emerson Tennent, if he went back, for describing the countless reptile and insect plagues of Ceylon —the leeches that used to hang about his horse's hoofs in crimson tassels—the white ants that drove a neat tunnel right through a set of the British Essayists and the Waverley

Novels. The Americans can't help their moths, nor their flies, nor their worms, nor their mosquitoes; and I am glad to remark, in conclusion, that from two most noxious inflictions American houses are singularly free. You scarcely ever meet with a bug or a flea. The traveller who put up at the inn at Stoney Stratford would have had no excuse for his *non sequitur* in the States. I have been in scores of American hotels, and lived in furnished lodgings, but fleas or bugs, or "chintzes," as Mr. Trollope declared American euphuists were wont to call them, never assailed me. When I went to Cuba and Mexico I was half bitten to death.

CHAPTER XI.

SCHENECTADY.

MR. ALFRED TENNYSON waited for the train at Coventry. He hung with grooms and porters o'er the bridge. He watched the three tall spires, and shaped the city's ancient legend into an immortal rhyme. I had to wait for a train an hour and forty minutes at Schenectady, in the State of New York, in August, '64, but how can the humblest of prose writers hope to make anything worthy of record out of that railway leisure which the Laureate turned to such glorious account? There is a bridge at Schenectady, constructed apparently from lucifer matches and half-inch deals tied together with twopenny twine, and very dirty and ruinous, as most public works in the States seem to be ; but there was little to be got by hanging o'er it. Schenectady being—with all respect I say it—but a one-horse kind of a place, there were no grooms about ; and as for the porters they were, failing the arrival of any travellers at Givens's Hotel, tranquilly liquoring up and talking politics in the underground bars of the city. I suppose Schenectady *is* a city ; but, at any rate, it is but an act of politeness to call it one.

There were no tall spires to watch. Schenectady is not

barren of ecclesiastical edifices, but the majority are barn-like. The Basilica—I don't know what persuasion it is dedicated to—is of wood, and whitewashed. The foundations are pine logs, and it could be moved down town or into the next county, I apprehend, within half-a-dozen hours. The only steeple I saw was a wooden one, which appeared to have begun architectural life as a beanstalk, then to have made up its mind—by breaking out in niches—to try the pigeon-cote line of business, then to have striven hard to be a factory chimney, failing which it had gone into the church, and whitewashed itself. As regards any ancient legends belonging to Schenectady, they must have faded out with its aboriginal inhabitants. Here, within two or three genera-tions, perchance, there were wigwams. The Sachem said, "let us dig the hatchet and go forth and cut up that nation;" the young brave speared trout and hunted moose, the medi-cine-man worked his charms, the squaws wove baskets and embroidered moccasins, the calumet was lit, and the war paint daubed on. It may have been so, but I am perfectly ignorant as to the period when Schenectady was "organised," and the last Indian tribe was elbowed forth into the wilder-ness, perplexed by the inventions and distracted by the questions of that irrepressible Yankee, who is always "want-ing to know," and always "fixing up" new devices.* Legends

* Our own "Patent Journal" can show from week to week a suggestive record of English ingenuity, but I question whether any such hebdomadal catalogue would equal the following, taken from one number of a New England paper:—In one week, and to citizens of New England alone, there were issued from Washington patents for "improvements in sewing-machines, for attaching buckles and straps for thread tension and thread delivery, for bullet ladles, for quartz crushers, for recovery of the acid used

there may have been in the old time of "stone canoes,"
"happy hunting-grounds," and "enchanted elks;" but they
have given place, now, to placards and wall-stencillings
relating to Sozodont, to the Night Blooming Cereus, the
Bloom of a Thousand Flowers, Kimball's Ambrosia, Van
Buskirk's Stomach Bitters, and other quackeries. Nothing
is left of the Cherokees, but disgusting mural advertisements
of "Cherokee Medicines;" and the "Mohawk Bank of
Schenectady," a pert, spruce, brown stone building, with a
plate-glass window occupying nine-tenths of its façade, is all
that remains to remind you of the savage Redskins, who
once owned the soil, and who would have experienced infinite
delight, I should imagine, in bursting into the bank, burning
the bird's-eye maple fixings, scalping the president, disem-
bowelling the directors, and sticking themselves all over
with the greenbacks in the till. For they *will* stick. The
Prussian soldiers say, that if you fling a loaf of pumpernickel
against a wall, the nasty pasty dough will stick there; and
so, if you press a ten or a twenty-five cent note on the back
of your hand, and breathe upon it, it will, after a while,
adhere as firmly as a postage stamp; so much glue, as well
as grease, has it picked up in its travels.

There was a very large refreshment-room at the Schenec-

in refining petroleum, for splitting leather, for whitening wool, for spring
clasps, for steam traps, for tackle for fore and aft sails, for a balanced
elevator, for friction clutches and pulleys, for lubricating the braces of
spinning-frames, for shaping the heels of boots and shoes, for the manu-
facture of watch-keys, for sausage-fillers and stove-pipe elbows, for cupboard latches, for dog-chains, for butt-hinges, for photographic frames, for
ice-cream moulds, for artificial eyes, for crinoline skirts, and for cess-
pools."

tady Station, where "warm meals at all hours" were advertised. I looked over the tariff, and found that "boiled
dinner" cost forty cents. What is a boiled dinner? Soup,
fish, turkey and oysters, vegetables, and suet dumplings, or
merely corned beef and hominy? Had I been hungry, or
had the weather been cooler, or had there been fewer flies
about, I would have ventured upon some boiled dinner; but
with the white furnace heat, and the maddening swarms of
insects, dinner, either boiled, baked, broiled, stewed, or fried,
was a thing not to be dreamt of. You home-staying people,
you can't know anything of active entomology until you
spend a summer in the United States. The island of Cuba
is pretty fertile in things that flap with wings, and crawl
with an unchristian number of legs; but the heat in Havana
is a quiet, drowsy heat, and during the daytime, at least,
the insects sleep, and don't trouble you. I shall never forget
finding a scorpion, which is about the size of, and looks very
like, a young lobster unboiled, snugly nestled, and sleeping
the sleep of the just, in a suit of white linen just come
home from the tailor's at Havana. There is another little
insect, too, which, if you are incautious enough to cross the
room bare-footed, is given to burrowing a hole in the ball of
your great toe, building a nest there, laying half a million of
eggs or so, and then slily vamosing; but he is the quietest
little creature alive. You notice not his coming or going,
and you are without signs of his presence for the best part of
a week, when your toe begins to swell, your blood is poisoned,
and unless you pay Don José Sangrado y Sganarella, chief
medico to the Captain-General, many ounces of gold for

blood-letting, cathartic lemonade, and mint tea—the only medicinal treatment I ever heard of in the Fidelisma Isla—you will have spotted fever, blue convulsions, tetanus, and die. Yet, on the whole, I think I prefer the insect plagues of the West Indies to those of the States. The Mexican mosquito, for instance, is a gentleman. His trumpet buzz has the purest Castilian accent, and he only comes at night and takes you *in cuerpo*. The Northern mosquito is a mean little " cuss," who stings in the noonday as well as the night. He seems, like a certain proportion of the people among whom he dwells, to experience a continual need for imbibing stimulants, and there is no end to the blood cocktails he takes at your expense. At Saratoga my travelling companion was continually startling me with discoveries of strange insects on the walls or on the furniture. There was a dreadful though diminutive monster, half beetle and half grasshopper, with a hump on its back like a Lilliputian buffalo. There was a frightful winged worm, not much bigger than a " small white," but a persistent nuisance. After all, the flies are perhaps the worst. I don't think they care for sugar. I have endeavoured to ward off their attacks by suspending pieces of paper, endued with honey and molasses, to the ceiling of the room ; but they seemed to disdain everything of the " catch-'em-alive-o " order, and preferred pork—that is to say, to settle on human flesh. Lie down on a couch, and simulate sleep, and in two minutes you will have select parties of flies congregated on your forehead, your eyeballs, your chin, and the bridge of your nose. I was never acquainted with flies so thoroughly domesticated and fond of the society of man. As I write this I have a fly on each finger, and one comfortably perched on my pen, close to the point, cooling his many feet in the black sea of thought, and deriving moral benefit, I trust, from that which I am writing. Burn him! can he read *that*, I wonder. I have striven to drown him again and again by sudden dips into the inkstand; but he is artful, and only moves further up the barrel of the pen. Beware of shaking off these inflictions too violently. These insects are ferocious, although so small, and even fly at you. They are not stupid, only deceitful. They lie *perdu* during the night, to avoid the bats and spiders; but so soon as the sun rises they are upon you. In this respect, and as provocatives to early rising, they are infinitely superior to alarums and to the crowing of many cocks.

The citizen who kept the refreshment-room at Schenectady and who had presumably passed many years of flyblown existence, was wise in his generation, and covered the whole of his line of counters, as well as his bottles, glasses, and ice-pails, with coarse yellow gauze; but I could see what cakes there were beneath this napery. I know well enough, by this time, the fare you find invariably in American refreshment-rooms. For a set meal, ham—ugh! such salt, fatless, mahogany-looking ham—and eggs; the latter always fresh and good. Then beefsteak, the toughest and most flavourless that any one not accustomed to chew hippopotamus hide can imagine. In winter oyster soup, and at all times coffee, which is generally roasted rye, pure and simple, and villanous black tea, with delicious milk. For eggs and milk our cousins are without rivals. Now and then you get a chicken, broiled to a most rich and appetising brown tint ; but as no refreshment-room knife was ever known to cut, and as the forks, which are of the rudest iron, have usually but two prongs,* an attempt to get a mouthful off the fowl—there are just five on an ordinary one—ends as a rule by its ricocheting into the bosom of your next neighbour, precisely as Mr. Edward Everett is said to have sent the hot roast goose flying into the lap of the lady in crimson satin at the Boston dinner-table. "Madam, I will trouble you for that goose," the orator and philosopher, in no wise discomposed, is reported to have said. I make the reservation, for the story has been told a hundred times of a hundred different people, and in all probability dates from the Temple of Hercules and the Book of the Sixty. For a banquet such as this, and which is called "supper," you are now charged seventy-five cents. If you eschew "supper," and seek perpendicular refreshment at the counter, you have first of all the bars where, in the non-liquor-law States, you may obtain poisonous whisky, brandy even viler, mawkish lager beer, excellent Philadelphia and Albany ale, a wretched effervescing decoction known as sar-

---

* Bear with me for a moment if with the prongs of a fork I pick up a little morsel of philology. Our cousins are frequently given to boasting that they speak and write the English language much better than we English do. Be this as it may, it must be confessed that, in New England especially, a great many good old English words long since obsolete with us still linger. In the "Reveries of a Bachelor," by "Ik. Marvel," the writer, one of the most natural and charming of American essayists, speaks of slippery morsels of ham off the sides of his *fork tines*. I was much puzzled to discover what the tines of a fork might be until I remembered an old English term of venery, "a stag of ten tynes." So the word tine or "tyne" is thus still used to express the prongs or branches of a fork.

saparilla—not unlike the *coco* the men with the turrets behind them sell in the Champs Elysées—and in New England cider as good as any to be procured in Devonshire. For eatables, these. Ice-creams. You have ice-creams everywhere, and at all seasons. I should not be surprised to learn that the convicts in the penitentiary were regaled with ice-creams on Independence Day, or that the cows in winter gave ice-creams instead of milk. In the filthiest, most tumbledown village you will find a "city saloon," where ice-cream is sold. The other day a regiment of "Confeds"—who are this year called "Johnnies :" they were "Rebs" in 1861, and "Greybacks" in 1862—marauding in Maryland, found the country all eaten up before them by their moss-trooping predecessors. To their great joy, the vanguard fell in with the proprietor of a travelling ice-cream saloon—a saloon on wheels—and his stock-in-trade was incontinently gobbled up by the hungry raiders—the first instance in the history of civilised war, perhaps, of a regiment of dragoons being fed on ice-creams. I trust that they had at least the decency to pay the eaten-out proprietor in Confederate notes.

Next to ice-creams, you are sure to find slabs of very greasy pound-cake. There was wont to be a confectioner on Holborn Hill who sold the largest Bath buns for a penny, and the largest slice of pound-cake for three-halfpence, that human eyes had hitherto gazed upon. The pound-cake was in hue a most gorgeous yellow ; but the confectioner put too much saffron both into the cake and in his buns. They pleased the eye, but they nauseated the stomach. I wonder, did that confectioner subsequently emigrate to the. United

R 2

States ? The pound-cake at the railway stations is almost as yellow as the Holborn article ; but it is greasier. Our cousins like rich food, although it by no means makes them plump and shiny, as it did Master Wackford Squeers. They are inordinately fond of pound-cake, and consume vast quantities of it at dessert. The celebrated Barnum—*I have been to church with Barnum* since my arrival on this continent— once told me an anecdote bearing on this fondness. A gentleman went to a charity dinner—a kind of banquet not very much patronised here. The American Dives " donate " without dining. " What'll ye have, sir ?" asked the negro waiter towards the last stage of the banquet. " What is there ?" " Like some ham, sir ? " " HAM ! " ejaculated the gentleman, with infinite scorn and wrath ; " d'ye think I paid five dollars to have ham ? *Bring me some pound-cake and plenty of butter with it.*" Then there are " crackers," or square butter-biscuits, good with cheese, but somewhat dry to the mouth ; sandwiches of which the less said the better ; candies, or lollipops, of every conceivable colour and shape, generally made of maple sugar, and very sickly ; and gingerbread, the which is soft, treacly, and hasn't any ginger in it. But I have kept the *bonne bouche* for the last. The *bonne bouche !* say rather the evil mouthful : the viand which is fraught with headache, heartburn, anxiety, dread, plethora, swimming in the head, fullness after meals, noises in the ears, motes or webs before the eyes, tumbling, pains in the joints, and all other symptoms of derangement of the digestive organs so eloquently enumerated in the advertisements of Drake's Plantation Bitters. That maleficent thing, that handmaid to dyspepsia, and all other its attendant woes, is PIE. I can see the Pie, in innumerable equilateral triangles, gleaming with a ghastly sheen beneath the yellow gauze. There it is ; pumpkin pie, blackberry pie, whortleberry pie, huckleberry pie— pie of all kinds, but always of the same grinning, splay shape, and with a foundation and border of flabby, indigestible crust. Talk not to me of an inflated currency, of Scranton coals at fourteen dollars a ton, and tea at twenty-five cents an ounce ; of the scarcity of nickel or copper cents,* of measuring-worms and Fourth of July fireworks, of municipal jobs and railway

* The difficulty of obtaining small change, or "pennies," as the Americans call their metallic cents, is, nevertheless, a great nuisance, and is increasing every day. It does not tell much in favour of a decimal currency. There are many small articles—newspapers, penholders, children's toys, and sweetmeats, for instance—which do not cost so much as the lowest denomination of fractional currency—five cents ; and the small tradesman, either by accident or design, is almost always out of change. "Making change" is quite an art, and persons who can "make change" in a store or restaurant are advertised for every day in the newspapers. "I'll owe you three cents," is the common remark of a shopkeeper to whom you have handed, say a twenty-five cent note in payment for an article worth twenty-two. "Thank you," I said recently to a gentleman who had served me the same trick before, and repudiated the little debt when I mentioned it ; "instead of that, I'll owe *you* two cents." Whereupon I gave him two ten-cent notes, and walked away with my purchase. At Niagara a youthful assistant in a shop, from whom I had bought a packet of envelopes, proffered me a couple of two-cent United States postage-stamps—as though anybody had any local correspondence on the American side at Niagara. I declined this arrangement ; whereupon we did a "trade." I took one of my fractionals back, and he withdrew half-a-dozen envelopes from my packet. The secret of this scarcity of "pennies" is that, being metallic, the people hoard them. The corner-grocery man who can't make change has not improbably a couple of barrels full of nickel cents down in his cellar, and is waiting for them to be at an increased premium to sell. The news-boys, when they are short of cents, issue little bits of green or white pasteboard to their customers, with "one cent," and so forth inscribed thereupon. It is due to a very interesting and honest class of boys to state that they are most scrupulous in the redemption of these certificates of indebtedness.

monopolies ; the real social curse of the Atlantic States is
Pie. In the West it is pronounced "poy," and the backwoodsmen are fond of it; but a man who lives in a log-hut and is
felling trees or toiling in the prairies all day long can eat Pie
with impunity. It is in the North and in the East, in cities
and townships and manufacturing districts, where dense popu-
lations congregate, and where the occupations of men, women,
and children are sedentary, that an unholy appetite for Pie
works untold woes. There the Pie fiend reigns supreme ;
there he sits heavy on the diaphragms and on the souls of
his votaries. The sallow faces, the shrunken forms, the
sunken eyes, the morose looks, the tetchy temperament of the
Northerners are attributable not half so much to iced water,
candies, tough beefsteaks, tight lacing, and tobacco-chewing,
as to unbridled indulgence in Pie. New England can count
the greatest number of votaries to this most deleterious
fetish ; but Pie-worship is prevalent all over the North. In
the State of Massachusetts, for instance, you have pork and
beans every Sunday, but you have Pie morning, noon, and
night every day, and all the year round. I daresay you have
often observed what gross feeders the professed teetotallers
are, and how unwholesome they look for all their abstinence
from fermented liquors. Set this down in England to a ghoul-
like craving for heavy meat teas, greasy muffins, Sally Lunns,
and hot suppers, and in the United States to an overweening
addictedness to Pie. Pie is nowhere spoken against in Scrip-
ture, as Jonathan Wild's ordinary observed with reference to
punch. Thus you will find American ministers of the gospel
gorging pie till the *odium theologicum* rises in their throats,

and they must curse their brethren or choke. Full of pride
and Pie, they wax bloated, and kick at their apostolic mission.
Plethoric with Pie, they bellow forth denunciations from their
pulpits, and roar for blood. There is nothing open and above
board in Pie. It can be eaten stealthily and in secret. A
slice off a cut pie is never missed. I have heard of young
ladies who took Pie to bed with them. I told you many
months ago how angry the Americans were with Mr.
Anthony Trollope for saying that the little children in
the States are fed on pickles. He erred, but in degree.
There will sometimes intervene a short period when there
are no fresh berries to be had, and when the preserved ones
have "gin out." Then the juveniles are raised on pickles.
At other times their pabulum is Pie. The "Confessions of a
Pie-Eater" have just been published. They are heart-
rending. Through an unconquerable hunger for Pie, the
wretched man who is their subject often incurred in infancy
the penal visitation of hickory, and brought the hairs of an
aged grandmother with sorrow to the grave. He wasted in
gormandising Pie those precious hours which should have
been devoted to study; and in the end, not only failed to
graduate at West Point, but even to marry a niece of the
late Daniel Webster. Pie darkened his mind, stupefied his
faculties, paralysed his energy. Pie forced him to abandon
a lucrative and honourable career for an unsuccessful whaling
voyage from Cape Cod. Pie drove him into exile. Deadened
to all the finer moral feelings by this ungovernable lust for
Pie, he obtained, under false and fraudulent pretences, a
through ticket for California by the Vanderbilt line; but,

detected in "smouching-a-tom-cod" from the altar of the
Chinese temple in San Francisco, he was disgracefully expelled the Golden State. It was for purloining Pie—a
digger's noontide lunch—that he was subsequently ridden on
a rail out of the territory of Arizona. Beggared, broken in
health, he deserted his wife and family, drew cheques upon
wild-cat banks, and voted on the Bell and Everett ticket—
all in consequence of Pie. At length, after a course of
"shinning round the free lunches" in quest of eleemosynary
Pie, and wolfing the hideous meal with Dead Rabbits, Plug-
uglies, and other unscrupulous politicians, in the Fourth
Ward, he was arrested in Philadelphia—being then located
on Pine, two blocks from Cedar—for passing bogus notes on
the Hide and Leather Bank, and was sent to States Prison
for ten years. All owing to Pie. I tell the tale as it was told
to me. It may read very like a burlesque; but there is a
substratum of sad truth in it. The late illustrious Abernethy
had a presentiment of the ravages which Pie was making in
the American constitution, when he rebuked his dyspeptic
patient from beyond the sea with the gorging propensities
of his countrymen. Mexico is said to owe her ruin to the
game of *Monté;* and if Columbia does not abate her fearful
craving for Pie, the very direst future may be augured
for her.

I did not partake of Pie at Schenectady. I thought I
would take a walk about the city, instead. There was not
much to be seen in Schenectady. There is a terrible sameness about American towns—a sameness which very soon
wearies, next appals, and finally disheartens you from tra-

velling backwards and forwards in the States at all. Where
is the use, you ask, of halting at Utica or at Syracuse ?
Cæsar and Pompey are very much alike ; so in the States
are Cato and Dionysius. When you have seen Utica you
have seen Syracuse, and Rochester is like both. Albany is
like Troy, and Troy like Albany. The great cities, the
metropolises, New York, Boston, Philadelphia, Baltimore,
Chicago, New Orleans, have something approaching a distinctive *cachet* and separate individuality ; although, with
the exception of the last-named place, the side streets,
branching from the main thoroughfares, are distressingly
alike ; but the smaller towns seem to have been cast in a
mould, so much do they resemble one another. The only
thoroughly original city I have yet seen north of Mason and
Dixon's line is. Washington, and that is uninhabitable. I
suppose the native Americans, on the principle of the shepherd who declared that he knew every sheep in his flock,
and that no two had faces alike, are able to discriminate
between their towns, and that to them Springfield has a
different type from Hartford, Brooklyn from Jersey City,
Newark from Wilmington. That difference of type is to me
invisible. In our England, can you point out two towns that
are like one another ? Well, an American might declare that
Manchester is like Oldham, and Oldham like Preston ; that
Bradford is like Leeds, and Birmingham like Sheffield ; but
then they are not to the manner born, and it is the shepherd
and sheep story over again.

But the melancholy and consistent monotony of American
towns—which monotony even Americans, in their candid

moments, will confess—is at once to be traced to a cause
which does not exist in Europe. Everything is new. Not
necessarily so. The character of the people makes them
impatient of and contemptuous to the past. They despise
its lessons. They will not hear of gradual development.
They have chosen to be civilised at once. The Americans
are continually declaring that they are a new and young
people; but there were houses in Boston in Cromwell's
time; there were Dutch burghers in New York and Albany
in Charles the Second's time. Philadelphia and Baltimore
are no cities of yesterday. Yet in any one of these places a
house which is over a hundred years old is a rarity and a
curiosity. Boston has some to show, chiefly in the neighbourhood of Faneuil Hall, and in the Bay State there are many
mossy old manses such as poor Nathaniel Hawthorne painted.
But in New York you may travel five miles without seeing
five houses that are even fifty years old. Either their older
houses, being constructed mainly of wood, and so naturally
inflammable, have been burnt up, or the sons have become
disgusted with the mansions where their fathers made their
fortunes, and have torn them down. No one speaks of
" pulling down " a house in America. That process is much
too tedious and methodical; the term " tearing down "
accords better with the hasty and impulsive genius of the
Western Thammuz. So their houses are new, and their
furniture is new, and their manners are new, and their servants are new hirelings from the old world.

Schenectady! There are throughout the North five
hundred Schenectadys feeding like one. A broad, dusty

main thoroughfare, bordered with trees and irregularly
paved. No three houses of the same size together; but the
same types of many-windowed factory, tumble-down shanty,
shingle villa whitewashed, and packing-case-looking shop of
dun brick, repeated over and over again *ad nauseam*. To
the whitewashed shingle villas green venetians. No knockers
to the doors; but the bell-pulls and name-plates electro-
silvered. At some gates a ragged, dirty negress, dully babbling with an Irish help—not ragged she, but dirtier. High
steps or "stoops" to the private houses, and towards evening
the entire family sitting, standing, or lounging thereupon :
the father, spectacles on nose, reading the local newspaper,
in which there is nothing to read save advertisements, eight
lines of telegraphic despatches, mostly apocryphal, and sixteen lines of editorial, setting forth that the local's contemporary—if it have one—is a liar and scoundrel, and that
its brother-in-law suffered two years in the penitentiary for
stealing a horse; the young ladies, in grand evening toilette,
staring other young ladies who may happen to pass out of
countenance; mamma, grandmamma, and two or three
maiden aunts or acidulated cousins, knitting socks for the
Sanitary Commission; and the younger branches of the
family yelling over contested candy, beating upon drums, or
—if any of them are girls, and above six years old—fanning
themselves and twirling their skirts in imitation of their
elders. I dare say, were you rude enough to peep through
the window at the table laid out for supper, you would find
there was Pie. To this add the jangling of half-a-dozen
pianofortes, and the familiar strains of the waltz from *Faust*.

In front of the stores, on what should be the kerbstone, but is in general only the boundary-line of the gutter, there are at intervals posts and joists extending to the first floors of the houses, and intended to support awnings in hot weather. It is only, however, the more liberal-minded among the storekeepers who supply such awnings for the benefit of the wayfarer. The bare beams and uprights have a shabby and comfortless look, but are eminently characteristic of all American streets, giving to them a mingled resemblance to the New Cut (Blackfriars end), London, the external boulevards of Paris, and the suburbs of Moscow. The American streets have—I may have made the observation before—a curiously Russian look; and this opinion is shared, I know, by that very keen observer and my good friend, Mr. Bayard Taylor, sometime United States Secretary of Legation at St. Petersburg. This may be owing partially to so many of the houses being built of wood, and next to the multiplicity of signs. Signboards are generally most prevalent among communities who cannot read, and this is why the colonnades of the Gostinnoi Dvors in Russian towns are so profusely embellished with pictorial emblems of the articles sold within. The unlettered *moujik* knows at once, from the hat, or the boot, or the tobacco-pipe painted on the door-jamb, where to find the commodity of which he is in quest. But every American can read and write too; whence, then, so many signs? First, I imagine, from old last-century English habits—only look at the signs clustering in Canaletto's picture of Northumberland House—and the absence of any municipal restrictions, in times more modern, for-

bidding the disfigurement of the public way by unwieldy
representations of handicrafts; and, lastly, from the enormous
and continuous German immigration. The German, you
know, can no more get on without his sign than without his
tobacco and lager beer. At all events, in all the American
towns I have seen, everybody hangs out his sign. The doctor
has his: white letters on a black plate, nailed to the wall of his
place of business. His consulting-room is called an "office."
I don't think he sees patients at his own residence; it might
shock his wife's nerves. The lawyer puts forth a very big
sign-board indeed. "Jabez C. So-and-so, Attorney, Notary
Public, and Counsellor-at-Law." Another practitioner's sign
informs the public that he is a "justice of the peace," and
agent to boot of an insurance company. Fancy Mr. Henry
or Mr. Knox doing a little business for the West Diddlesex
or the Anglo-Bengalee in their spare time!

But these are only the written signs. Their name is
legion. Everybody writes, or prints, or paints up what he
has to sell, in order that there may be no mistake. " Nails,
spikes, screws," cries the ironmonger. "Corn and feed,"
cries the cornchandler. " Flour, pork, and fish," says another
dealer. Odd trades commingle. The butcher, who calls his
store a " meat market," sells fruit and vegetables as well as
joints. The grocer transacts business in whisky and rum,
and in all likelihood has a private bar in his backyard, or
down in his cellar. The druggist dispenses " solace tobacco"
and " Excelsior chewing gum, highly flavoured." You may
buy bonnets at the bookseller's, and sweetmeats at the dry
goods store. Were Mother Hubbard to come a-marketing to

Schenectady for that Dog who was always wanting something, and doing something else preposterous and incongruous when she came home, the Dame would be puzzled, I think, to find all her tradespeople as she wanted them. Then come the signs which have form and substance, which are carved, and gilt, and painted. *Their* name, too, is legion. Wooden watches, five feet in diameter, and their hands always at a quarter to twelve—or a quarter *of* twelve in Yankee parlance ; monstrous jack-boots with scarlet tops ; bonnets that might suit a maid of honour to the Queen of Brobdingnag ; hats of all colours, such as the Giant Bolivorag might wear ; padlocks and keys of preternatural size ; boluses and syringes, eye-glasses and telescopes, all of abnormal proportions. Our old friend Sir William Wallace, or Rob Roy, or Looney M'Twolter, or Saunders M'Gillicuddy, you know; the snuff-shop Highlander stands in front of the tobacconist's, his open mull in one hand, the thumb of the other poised in air, nose-ward, with that perpetual pinch of sneeshing which he is never to snuff up. The Scotchman is a relic of the old provincial times ; a closer local colouring is visible at the rival tobacconist's, who has a life-sized figure of the lovely Pocahontas, tall feathers in her head, a bow and arrow in her hand, her exquisite features very copper-coloured indeed, and war-painted in the liveliest manner. These big, uncouth, and grotesque effigies and objects were irresistibly suggestive to me of the property-room of a London theatre during the run of a pantomime.

An Irish carman, driving a dray, with palings to its edges, like a Smithfield pen on wheels; one of the two

dandies of Schenectady in a trotting waggon so bright and
shiny with varnish, and whose big wheels revolve so rapidly
as to remind you of a cock-pheasant getting up—whir ! there
is a blaze of splendour, and then the astonishing vision is
gone ; a knot of young town hobbledehoys, or "gawks," in
felt hats and grey suits, chewing, swearing, and indulging in
horseplay at the street corner ; two young ladies, one apparently nineteen, the other twenty, coming home from
school, with their satchels full of books and their japanned tin
lunch-boxes swinging to straps—they go to school to a master,
and he ferules them till they are fourteen or fifteen ; the
never-failing, weasel-faced, ferret-eyed newsboy vending his
quires ; many more hotels than you would imagine there
were guests for, all dirty, all full, all with piazzas in front, in
which are seated men in their shirt-sleeves, loafing, reading
newspapers, and spitting, and with their feet perched on the
rails before them—a pair of soles, in fact, looking out of every
other window ; the "City Bakery," where I observe they sell
wax dolls ; the "Photographic Hall," to judge from the frame in
front of which every inhabitant of Schenectady had had his
or her portait taken half a dozen times; the "Daguerrian
Rooms," a rival establishment, with a life-size photograph of
the negro boy who carries about the operator's show-boards—
young Sambo grinning hugely, as though in delight at being
photographed for nothing ; a wounded soldier, on crutches ;
an idiot, more than half "tight," who hangs about the bars
and the railway-station ; some flaming woodcuts, announcing
the approaching advent of a Hippotheatron—in plainer English, a horse-riding circus—with that admired equestrian and

favourite, Miss Carrie Smithers; any number of white
stencilled laudations of "Sozodont" and "Plantation Bitters,"
"Brandreth" and "Herrick's" Pills, and "Old Doctor Raga-
bosh, the world-celebrated female's physician;" ice-cream
saloons—in winter devoted to the sale of oysters. This is
what I saw in an hour and forty minutes. This is Schenectady, and any other American town you like to mention.
Qu'en pensez-vous ?

A word or two more. Milliners' shops are far more numerous than they would be in a town of the same extent in
Europe; and both the newspapers and the coloured plates of
the fashions are brought down to the very latest dates. Our
cousins *must* know how the world wags, how stocks rule, and
how sleeves are worn—or die. I cannot see any public
buildings. The railway station is a scandalous shed, the
bridge is in a disgraceful state, and this is the case pretty
nearly all over the Union. Liberal almost to lavishness in
their private transactions, the Americans are in their corporate and municipal capacity most laughably stingy. With
the exception of the whited sepulchres in Washington, and
the Girard Asylum in Philadelphia, there is not a public
building in any American city which can cope with those in
second-rate Mexican towns; whereas *private* edifices of great
magnificence abound throughout the North. Our cousins
"don't see" the fun of building for the public weal or for
posterity. That the Central Park at New York should ever
have been laid out and the ornamental bridges built is a
marvel which I should like Mr. Calvert Vaux to explain.
Habitually our cousins wont spend a cent to beautify their

cities ; or, if any money *is* voted or raised for such a purpose, some ingenious lobbyer steals it *in medio*, and the scheme is dwarfed and dwindles down to the meanest proportions.

I went into a stationer's shop at Schenectady to buy a note-book. The stationer, for a wonder, was civil and talkative. " Is that Queen Victoria you've got at your buttonhole ?" he asks. I told him that it was a Spanish quarterdoubloon, bearing the effigy of Charles the Fourth. " Ah !" he continued, "it does one's eyes good to see a bit of gold in these times ; but I should like a look at Queen Victoria's face anyhow." Being bound for Canada, I happened to have some English gold in my pocket ; so I took out a sovereign and showed it him. It was an Australian one. He looked at it intensely. "Sydney Mint," he mused aloud. " Ah ! Queen Victoria reaches a long way." He gave me back my piece, and I was departing, when he called me back. " You need not mention it," he said in a half-whisper, " but I'm a countryman of that great man yonder. Yes, sir." I looked up, and saw framed and glazed a portrait of Robert Burns. In his " Yes, sir," there was the drollest possible fusion of the Yankee and the Scottish twang. Why did not he wish his nationality to be mentioned ? Had he taken out his papers, and was he a leading politician in Schenectady, of the anti-Britisher stripe ? I can call to mind no more mournfully anomalous position, under present circumstances, than that of a Briton who has become an American citizen, but whose heart is not with the North. No compromise, no neutrality, is permitted him. If he be true to his adopted country he must vilify and denounce his native land. Affec-

tion for England is treason to the Union. If I were that
Scotch stationer at Schenectady, I would turn all my greenbacks into gold—never mind the loss on the exchange—and
go back to the land of Burns.

As I trudge towards the station, I hear a locomotive in the
distance, screaming and bell-ringing,—I see a railway train
puffing and sporting along the open street, with the children
playing almost underneath the wheels:—another characteristic
of American towns. I pass a mean little wooden building,
which might be the office of a wharfinger in a small way, or
a steamboat ticket-collector, or a coal agent. But a tattered
American banner hangs over the portal. There are the usual
posters up, " Now, gentlemen, if you wish to join a heavy
artillery regiment, fall in." " Boys, attention. Highest
bounties given." This is an enrolment office and recruiting
rendezvous. Ensign Plume is within, sitting at a table,
twisting his goatee, and chewing for want of thought ; and
Sergeant Kite has just taken two promising-looking " boys "
into an adjoining grog-shop to drink. Even in this slow-
going little Schenectady we are not destitute of signs of that
America which is in the Midst of War.

CHAPTER XII.

THE reading world of England must by this time have become acquainted with the strange and marvellous adventures of Mr. Guy Livingstone's boots, for who does not read Mr. Guy Livingstone's books? This deservedly popular author's account, in "Border and Bastille," of the perils and the absolute misfortunes he encountered . through the purchase in London of a pair of military jack-boots, has been widely read and much admired in the United States. It is clear that Mr. Livingstone's boots, and those boots alone, brought him to grief. But for those confounded nether encasements, he would never have attempted to force the Federal lines, and never have been lodged in the Old Capitol prison. Bombastes Furioso defied to mortal combat whoever should dare to displace his boots; but it was through putting his boots on, and not by taking them off, that the clever English novelist, who is best known by the title of his best work, fell into the hands of the Northern Philistines, and was by them cast into the doleful durance of that Old Capitol—once a Senate House, and once a boarding-house—which has, since the new era of freedom, and the new order of things, been converted into a state prison.

It is a curious fact that my remembrances of the Army of the Potomac, as I saw it in winter-quarters, between Brandy Station and Culpepper Court House, will ever and inseparably be associated with a pair of Boots. When I left England for America, all my friends who had crossed the Atlantic said to me, " Take whatever boots you may require with you. Boots in America are very dear, and very bad." I followed this advice to the best of my ability ; but still, to a certain extent, I found that I had reckoned without my host and my Hoby. I had never contemplated a visit to an army in the field. Active campaigning I knew to be not my forte ; nor was I, when I departed, expected to send home circumstantial narratives of the pomp, pride, or circumstance of glorious war, or descriptions of the general camp, pioneers and all. If ever I seek the bubble reputation, it will not be at the cannon's mouth. Circumstances however, proved propitious for a visit to the army commanded by General Meade. I was bound to start on a Monday morning for Brandy Station ; and on the previous Saturday—the very Saturday of my presentation to President Lincoln at the White House—a friend who was inspecting my modest campaigning equipment, cried out, " Good gracious ! you don't mean to say that you intend to venture down to the Army of the Potomac without boots?" I mildly pleaded that I had several pair of double-soled elastic-sided or lace-ups with me. " Those things are all very well in their way," he said decisively, " but they're not boots." I was reminded of Brummel holding the lappel of his friend's garment between his finger and thumb, and

putting the query, " Do you call this thing a coat ?" My
boots were clearly not boots in the Potomac sense of the
term. They were pumps, patent-leathers, papouches, if you
will, but not boots. The real boots had to be bought. The
soil of Virginia, powdery and friable in the best of weather,
is converted in winter-time into a clayey, clinging mud, of
astonishing depth and dreadful consistency. To cope with
that mud, nothing but " army boots" are of the slightest
use. I went and bought me a pair. The maker, a German,
to whom I was introduced, and with whom I of course shook
hands, let me have the goods I needed as a great favour for
fifteen dollars—say two guineas. I do not say that these
boots were expensive. There was an immense quantity of
leather about them. That leather had apparently once
formed part of the hide of a rhinoceros. They reached more
than half-way up the thigh. They were square-toed, and
the toes were at least six inches across. The soles were of
amazing thickness and hardness. I never saw such a pair of
boots in my life. They threw the much vaunted artificial
integuments of Furioso far into the shade. They were more
prodigious than the boots of a life-guardsman. The Postillon
de Longjumeau might have expired with envy at beholding
them. No Brighton riding-master ever boasted of such a
noble pair of boots. They were large enough to have belonged to the husband of the old woman who lived in a shoe.
They were seven-league boots. They were incomparable.
I had them " paid" all over, first, with linseed oil, to render them supple, and next I caused them to be thoroughly
coated with waterproof dubbing, to make them impervious to

moisture. Thus caulked, seamed, and "paid," they smelt abominably. I dared not, however, put them outside my room door at Willard's, lest some guest of dishonest proclivities, maddened by the beauty of form and the majesty of proportion they presented, should nocturnally annex them. So I had to keep the boots in my bed-room, and was all but smothered by their smell. There was much conversation that night in Washington about my boots. Into one family where I was on familiar terms I was asked to bring the boots, in order that they might be inspected and criticised. I came home rather late, and the last acquaintance I passed on Willard's staircase, going to bed, called out, "Going to the front to-morrow, hay ? Heard all about those boots."

"Going to the front" is no such easy matter for an English newspaper correspondent at Washington. For any person connected with an English daily journal, independently conducted, it is all but impossible. Over and over again has the War Minister, Mr. Stanton, positively refused to grant any "facilities" to the representatives of the press who have penetrated so far as Washington, and have been desirous of visiting the head-quarters of the army. The few American reporters who are suffered to remain in camp are subjected to innumerable galling and degrading restrictions. Should they dare to comment on the probable plan of the next campaign, or should they presume to write anything which by any person in authority is held offensive, or even distasteful, they are liable to be summarily expelled the camp, and may consider themselves fortunate if they escape being arrested, sent under a guard to Washington, and immured in the vermin-infested cells of the Old Capitol. So humiliating, indeed, are many of these "press laws" for the camp, that some of the more respectable of the New York papers decline to expose their correspondents to such petty tyranny. The "New York Herald" reporters, however, give all the required pledges, and bow to all the decrees which may be promulgated; and the consequence is that the "New York Herald" is better supplied with war news than any other paper in New York.

But my lines, as it turned out, had fallen in pleasant places. The Secretary of War, had I asked him, would probably have met my suit with an unqualified refusal. I did not ask him for permission to visit the front at all. I was fortunate enough to know a gentleman who had extensive commercial transactions with the Government, and who, in pursuit of his business, had frequently occasion to go to head-quarters. On the present occasion he proposed to combine business with pleasure. He told me that he intended to go down to Brandy Station on Sunday morning, and have a "good time" of it. He was to take his wife and sister, who, on their part, and with a view to Amazonianism, were to take their side-saddles and riding-habits. Something in the way of ball-dresses was also to be included in the luggage; for on the Monday night a grand ball, given by the officers of the Third Corps, was to come off at General Carr's head-quarters. Nothing could be more delightful. My friend's partner was going, and he was to take his niece. Passes for all of us were to be procured from the Provost-Marshal-General's office, and a special train was to be provided at 10.45 on Monday morning to convey us, by way of Alexandria, to Brandy Station. Without a pass you are not permitted to stir a mile southward from Washington. A pass is required even to cross the Long Bridge over the Potomac; and the magic document, without which you are at best but a prisoner at large, is very difficult to obtain, and very reluctantly granted to persons unconnected with the military service of the Government. Civilians, unless they happen to be sutlers, or philanthropic gentlemen connected with the Sanitary and Christian Commissions, are kept carefully at bay. A few officers belonging to her Majesty's brigade of Guards in Canada have from time to time been allowed to stay a short time on the Potomac, or, rather, on the Rapidan, and great kindness and hospitality have been shown them by the officers in command—more especially by those high in position; but there is reason to believe that these amenities have been anything but pleasant to the authorities at the Washington War Department, and the visits of British officers to the Federal camp have long since ceased.

I was laid up with a very bad cold on Sunday, and could not leave by the train above designated. It was therefore necessary to procure another pass for me, and I went down with my friend's partner, and his niece, on the Monday morning. The line from Alexandria, on the thither side of the Potomac, is now exclusively devoted to warlike uses. Indeed, on the cars and locomotives the words "United States Military Railroads" are now painted in the biggest of black letters. The thousand years of peace in America are evidently over, and we are but in the fourth of the thousand years of war. The dépôt to which we drove was to all intents and purposes a camp, and swarmed with armed soldiers. When we took our trunks to the luggage-van, to have them registered for "Brandy," we found a blue-gaberdined soldier on either side of the door. Each carried a musket, and formed an impassable barrier against interlopers by the very simple process of sticking the point of his bayonet into the side of the van. We had no tickets to take for Brandy Station. The pass was all-sufficient. It entitled us to a free transit over the U.S.M.R.R., and bade all "guards, conductors, and patrols" to allow us to circulate without let or hindrance. The pass I had obtained came from the Chief-Quartermaster of the Army of the Potomac; and this Chief-Quartermaster—Brigadier-General Rufus Ingalls—was my very kind and hospitable host during the time I remained in camp.

Hundreds of officers and soldiers were going down by this train, together with some twenty or thirty ladies who had accepted invitations for the Third Corps ball. Cars not being very plentiful, the rear of the train was made up by any number of ballast-trucks—mere rows of rough-hewn planks on wheels—all of which were literally heaped with troops. I suppose we took down at least six hundred soldiers with us ; some were bound to relieve the picket guards on the line, but a sufficient force accompanied us to the end of our journey, to act as an escort. The railway communication from the Federal capital to the camp is all but safe, but not quite so. Four or five thousand Union soldiers are posted in

strong detachments along the whole length of the line.
Standing on the open platform outside our car, I noticed that
we could scarcely travel a mile without seeing either tents or
shanties occupied by soldiers smoking, reading newspapers,
eating candy, or playing cards—four species of amusements
to which the American warrior is passionately devoted—their
arms piled within convenient reach. Further on would be
scattered pickets, now of dragoons, now of Zouaves, now of
United States infantry—splendid in the one case, ragged in
the other, and dirty in all—skylarking, or playing leapfrog, or
indulging in mock boxing-matches on the very track itself.
Apart from professional pugilism, which, in its very worst phase
of rowdyism, still feebly flourishes in the great Atlantic cities,
the Americans seem to have the very vaguest notion of the
" noble art;" but you seldom meet a group of soldiers off
duty without witnessing some uncouth horseplay which, by
a very great stretch of the imagination, might be called
sparring. Now and then we came on the camps of entire
brigades; and although this dispersion of force must necessarily weaken to some extent the strength of the Army of
the Potomac proper, these outlying detachments can, *so long
as the railway is safe,* be easily and speedily called in. It
is still essential to guard every mile of it. Although this
section of the State of Virginia is ostensibly loyal, is reputed
to be in the possession of the Federal Government, and is
occupied by an immense number of troops, the guerilla bands
have not yet been rooted out. A solitude has been made,
which has been called peace; but from time to time hairy
men, in slouched hats, armed to the teeth, and mounted

on rawboned horses, put in a sudden appearance on the
scene of desolation, and make the solitude horribly lively.
There is nothing that grows upon the earth, or that is to be
found in the houses builded upon it, left to plunder; but
there are Union soldiers to kill, and travellers to rob, and
mischief of some sort to be done to the Union cause. Only
the other day Mostby and three hundred of his guerillas were
on the Rappahannock, ten miles on this side the Union
lines. The guerillas slide cleverly between the pickets,
creep into the few woods that are not yet cut down, and
make sudden dashes upon unprotected parts of this railway.
It is some time since an entire train has been captured, but
guerilla inroads in the immediate vicinity of the line are by
no means infrequent. The worst of the matter is that Alexandria itself, the once smiling city, actually within sight of
the Capitol and the White House, is not entirely free from
this pest. Almost every house in Alexandria is full of Union
soldiers; and the Stars and Stripes wave proudly from that
hotel where Colonel Ellsworth lost his life in his rash attempt
to tear down the Secession banner. Alexandria has been
bayoneted ground down, and dragooned into outward loyalty;
but Alexandria—or what is left of its original population—
is admitted, even by strong Union men, to be at heart
as incurably Secesh as Baltimore. What little aid and
comfort the Alexandrians have to spare is always at the
service of Secesh emissaries and Secesh guerillas. There
are a few farms left in the neighbourhood of Alexandria to
which you may ride out. The farmer has taken the oath of
allegiance to the Government. So have his sons. His wife

sings Union songs—while Union men are near—to the
infant on her knee ; the daughter, who brings you a glass of
water or a pitcher of cider, comes out with a Union ribbon in
her hair, and a miniature Union flag in her bosom. Loyalty
seems here to reign triumphant. The very dog that lazily
wags his tail in welcome, seems "sound on the goose," or
creditably imbued with Union sentiments. But wait a little ;
"bide a wee." Let nightfall come ; let the Union patrols
ride away ; from ingle nook or cider-press, from cock-loft or
muck-heap, are produced the terrible boots, the slouched hat,
the leathern belt, the revolver and the sabre of the Virginian
moss-trooper. The whole family becomes Secesh. The
mother fills her good man's whisky-flask. The baby crows
for State rights. The dog barks treason. The young lady
who wore the Union flag in her bosom begins to hum the
" Bonnie Blue Flag." The gaunt Rosinante is led forth,
saddled and bridled, and " it's hey for the bonnets of bonnie
Dundee," the "Lords of Convention" at Washington assem-
bled notwithstanding. These guerillas cannot do much
actual harm, for the Federalists have left them but little
harm to do ; but they keep the country in a perpetual fit of
irritation and alarm. I have often wondered why the
Americans, who, since the commencement of this war, have
shown themselves only too glad to avail themselves of hints
in military organisation and equipment, not indeed from us,
but from the military nations of continental Europe—who
have dressed up the hobbledehoys of Brooklyn in the snowy
turbans and scarlet breeches of Zouaves, and the "bhoys" of
the Bowery in the tunics and plumed hats of Bersaglieri—

should have overlooked the existence of one notable foreign force whose constitution and discipline they might advantageously follow. Why don't they get up a flying corps of Cossacks? Never mind whether they be of the Don or of the Ukraine, of Massachusetts or of Maine, of the Catskills or of the Alleghanies; but let such a corps be organised by all means. Give them the baggy galligaskins, the boots of untanned leather, the monstrous kalpacks of the Astracan, the high-peaked saddles and the interminable lances of the heroes who have lately been distinguishing themselves in restoring the reign of "order" at Warsaw. Mount them on shaggy little ponies; and, if need be, furnish them with stout, tapering-thonged whips. Seriously, the Cossack corps might do good service to the Union cause. It is idle to talk about civilization and humanity in the complexion this contest has come to. Those agreeable but impracticable figments have long since been thrown overboard. " War to the bitter end" is the Federal *mot d'ordre*. This go-ahead and uncompromising generation need not feel squeamish about fitting out a few brigades of free lances with a roving licence to rob, ravage, and kill. The engaging manners and customs which obtain on the Volga and the Don might be appropriately transplanted to the Rappahannock and the Rapidan. I look upon this as a really valuable suggestion. I venture to offer it gratuitously to the Federal Government, and I hope it may be taken as an earnest of my desire to atone for any evil I may inadvertently have spoken of the institutions of a great, a free, and a glorious land.

The view of Washington and of the Potomac river from

the Long Bridge is extremely beautiful. From one window of our car I could see gleaming in the clear azure the dome of the Capitol; from another window I had pointed out to me those Arlington Heights where, embosomed in luxuriant foliage, is a handsome white house, very like the mansion of an English country gentleman, now the residence of I know not what Washington official, but of old time the seat of a Virginian squire, an officer in the regular army, a superintendent of the Military Academy at West Point, a descendant of the famous "Light Horse Harry" of the War of Independence. "Light Horse Harry's" kinsman is far away now, beyond the Rapidan. I have seen his tents through a spyglass from a mountain top in Virginia. His name is greeted with almost adoration by his own men, with admiration in Europe, and with respect even by his enemies. And the name he will leave will be famous in story, I think—more famous than Beauregard's, as famous as Stonewall Jackson's —it is that of ROBERT LEE.

At the town or city of Alexandria we halted half an hour. Before the war there was a slave auction mart here; but that shame and scandal, I am happy to state, has been swept away. Alexandria once formed part of the District of Columbia, but was "retroceded" to the State of Virginia in 1846. The population before the war was nine thousand, most of them native Virginians, of course. Now the population may be larger; that is to say, there may be ten thousand troops in and about the town, and hordes of runaway negroes or "contrabands," contractors, clerks, sutlers, camp followers, and loose women; but I question whether the native Vir-

ginian element is at this moment a thousand strong. Union
and freedom have proved too strong for the aborigines. They
have gradually and cautiously, but securely, skedaddled. A
few once influential persons have taken the oath of allegiance
to the Government; but, discovering to their dismay that
treachery to their own side has not inspired the other side
with confidence, and being barely safe from insult and mal-
treatment from the Federal soldiers, they live in absolute
retirement, until opportunity serves for them also to skedaddle
in peace.

There was a very civil sentinel at the door of our car,
armed to the teeth it is true, but still studiously polite to
one who travelled with a brigadier-general's pass. My
friend's partner had provided a very generous commissariat,
with a view to our refection during our sixty miles' journey.
We had two baskets of anchovy and beef sandwiches, a
huge and delicious plum-cake, wrapped in a fair linen cloth,
some Stilton cheese and some of the capital biscuits called
"crackers," and a mighty demijohn of cold milk punch—
from the very same brewing, I almost thought as I sipped it,
as that glorious and memorable compound which Mr. Bob
Sawyer made, and Mr. Pickwick and Mr. Ben Allen drank,
when they journeyed in the postchaise from Bristol to
Birmingham. As we had breakfasted very early, we availed
ourselves of the halt at Alexandria to ascertain at least the
component parts of our culinary rolling stock. The demijohn was done ample justice to—although, as in the well-
known Pickwick case, several pulls were necessary to
determine whether it was really milk punch or something

else. Then we asked the civil sentinel if he would have
something to eat and drink. He replied that "he seldom
took lunch, but that he didn't mind having a bite." There
was a general officer in the car with us; but we knew that
no breach of military decorum was committed by an American
soldier eating and drinking in the presence of his superior
officer. So the civil sentinel took his bite and his sup, and
he then insisted on my accepting a cigar, the which I was
glad to smoke, although it was a very nasty one, outside the
car. The sentinel was a common soldier, very slovenly, and
not at all clean in his person and attire; but he wore a handsome watch and chain, and a carbuncle ring on his finger.
There are numbers of young men of education and of wealth
serving as private soldiers in the American army—serving
from pure patriotism and devotion to that which they deem
a righteous cause—fighting and dying with perfect patience
and willingness, and mixed up and confounded all the while
with the lowest of the low and the vilest of the vile.

A glorious sun was shining down upon Alexandria. The
sky was without a cloud. The weather was literally as warm
as June, and yet we were in the latter days of January, and
I had left New York a few days since one mass of ice, snow,
skating, and sleigh-riding. I had a quarter of an hour's
ramble about the town, for the railroad, as usual, open and
unfenced, runs through the principal street, and the children
play about, and are with sad frequency crushed under the
wheels of the locomotive. I could see few good houses, but
any number of "frame" or wooden stores, military dépôts for
forage, grain, and meat, tents and guard-houses, lager-beer

saloons, hucksters' stalls for the sale of ginger-bread and candy, and miserable shanties, crawling in and out of which were three-parts naked negro children. The darkies sat grinning and hunting in their rags for greybacks, (quite in the Genoese manner,) on doorsteps and on stumps. Old negro men, with white wool on their heads and white beards, were jabbering incomprehensible jargon, broken by the short jerking laugh, almost approaching a hysterical sob, peculiar to the race, to old negro women with montrous poke bonnets, provided with voluminous flaps or curtains, of a stuff like bedticking, to keep the napes of their necks from the sun. And the negro girls, slatternly, impudent-looking wenches, were standing at every corner, with their arms akimbo, leering and fleering and chuckling *con amore*. The negroes and the Northern soldiers have it all their own way in Alexandria.

We had plenty of newspapers with us, and I was immersed in the emotional interest of a congressional debate—I think it was upon the expulsion of Senator Davis—when one of my fellow-travellers touched me upon the arm, and told me that we were passing the old battle-field of Bull Run. We were, indeed, in the centre of the cockpit of Virginia. The ground has been the scene of two bloody battles, and, as far as the eye can reach on every side, almost inch by inch the soil has been hotly contested by Federals and Confederates. Spots were pointed out to us where desperate charges had been made, and where the slain, falling in heaps, had been buried by hundreds. But those spots were not greener than the rest. The red rain had not made the harvest grow. There was nothing growing here indeed, save a few dwarf larch-trees, some common dock and cress by the brook-side, and in the ravines some stunted jungly underwood. In the distance loomed, pale purple, with high lights of gold and cream colour, the Bull Run mountains—a spur of the Blue Ridge where the original of Colonel Quagg, the blacksmith who hated Dissenting ministers so, even to beating them when they passed his smithy, is said to have dwelt. I can find nothing else to describe in the landscape. There was nothing to remind you of the great stampede. The scene was simply a waste ; houses, farms, wayside taverns, had disappeared bodily. Whole plantations of trees had been hewn down ; and in many instances their very stumps grubbed up. The traces of turnpike roads had quite disappeared. There were no hedges, no fences, no gates, no signposts. There was no-thing—absolutely nothing but the abomination of desolation. The earth had become a desert. It had once been smiling and fertile, bringing forth its fruits in due season. For miles around there had been, three years ago, plantations, thickets, pleasure-gardens, and orchards ; temples dedicated to the worship of a beneficent Creator ; schools and wayside cot-tages ; gentlemen's seats, barns, and stables ; haystacks and wheatricks. This was part of the ancient and flourishing State of Virginia—the Old Dominion—the home of Wash-ington. I was to see more of it ere long. The country side has echoed to the huntsman's horn, as the old Lord Fairfax rode to hounds from his ancestral mansion. All this, to use a locution germane to the new order of things, is "played out." The Federals have simply acted the part of a swarm of locusts, and devoured the land. They have rioted on the fatness thereof, and they have left nothing for those who are to come afterwards.

This was the first time in my life that I had ever been in the absolute and visible presence of war. Of famous battle-fields I have seen, I suppose, my share. The famous battle-fields are apt to pall upon one. It is difficult at this time of day to get up any excitement of the spasmodic kind about the field of Waterloo. The scene is no longer awful, and it is scarcely picturesque. You go there in a four-horse coach, for an outside place on which you pay five francs. You stop on the road to drink beer. You are aware that the relics of the battle-field you must needs purchase for your friends or relatives at home are egregious impostures. The sugar-loaf monticule and the Belgian lion, with his tail between his legs, pawing a skittle-ball, do not impress you much. You go away with the impression that Waterloo is somehow a sham, a show gotten up by some Belgian Barnum. You don't want to go there again. I have seen Blenheim, and have had Oudenarde pointed out to me. I couldn't see any-thing in them. Even on the more recent battle-fields of Magenta and Solferino there is but little to awaken curiosity. You are told that from the window of that wine-shop General L'Espinasse was shot. Was he indeed? There is nothing to tell of anybody having been killed there, and you enter the wine-shop and order an omelette. The shotholes have all been neatly mended, the shattered bricks re-pointed, the blood wiped up, the every-day aspect of the place restored. I dare say that, but for the monument over the well at

Cawnpore, you would find nothing there to remind you of "the great company of Christian people" whom the Nana caused to be murdered. All battle-fields leave much to the imagination—all, I should think, except Bull Run—and yet I saw no skeleton, no grisly finger pointing from the earth, no half-buried cannon, no rusted sabres, no dinted shakoes, no shreds of clothing scattered about. What marked this place as a shambles, as an Aceldama, as a Potter's Field, as a Valley of the Shadow of Death, was its entire nakedness and desolation, and the knowledge than Man, not Nature, had made the waste. There was a complete solitude, and this part of Virginia is stated to be perfectly loyal, and quite at peace.

When we had passed the little bridge over the Rappahan-nock, however, and the tents of one of the corps of the main body came in sight, there were other signs and indices of war apparent. About thirty miles below Alexandria the Confe-derates made more than a year since a determined raid on the railroad, capturing many trains of cars, and tearing up the rails and sleepers along the line for miles towards Cul-pepper. Hundreds of lengths of rails we saw lying bent into strangely acute angles, rusted and wholly unserviceable, by the side of the track. The Confederates had made use of a cunning device to unfit these rails for service. Their practice was to heap up a huge bonfire of chairs and sleepers, and to lay the rails lengthways on the apex of the blazing pile. Thus becoming red-hot in the centre, the two extremities would droop, and, on cooling, the rails would be hopelessly bent out of all railway shape ! A cunning trick, I take it, quite fiendish in its ingenuity. When the Federals got possession of this part of the railroad again—I say this part, for a branch of it goes right down south, to Richmond—they found it cheaper and more expeditious to lay down new rails on the track than to attempt to bend the old ones into shape again. So there, by the roadside, they have let them lie. It has been thought worth nobody's while to remove them, to buy them for old stores, or even to steal them. There is more profitable plunder, perhaps, in a contract for new iron than in the mere pilfering of these old ties. So there they lie, and oxidise tranquilly. There, too, by hundreds, are the iron wheels and axles of the cars, bright red with rust, twisted and shattered, just as the Confederates wrenched them off and flung them away. Of the cars themselves a few, but not many, remnants remain. The wood has been greedily appropriated for fuel, either by the soldiers encamped, or by the half-starved negroes wandering about.

Another sign of war, and to me of the ghastliest, was in the enormous number of dead horses lying about. But that dead men were wanting, you might have thought that a battle had taken place the day before yesterday. The Americans can scarcely be accused of wilful cruelty to dumb animals, but they are certainly as reckless of brute as of human life, and are no more merciful to their beasts than they are to themselves. The condition of some of the omnibus horses you see in Broadway is absolutely shocking. The drivers don't beat them much ; but when the poor things fall down, and die of exhaustion, their end seems to be taken very much as a matter of course. The locution I have so often had occasion to quote rises to the lips of the youthful American spectator as he surveys some unhappy old Dobbin, prone to the pavement and at his last gasp, "Guess he's played out!" That is his epitaph. Never mind how hard he has worked, how old a servant he has been. He can do no more. There is nothing left in him. He is "played out." Away with him!

There are knackers, I suppose, in New York; but the brethren of Cow Cross are decidedly absent from the seat of war in Virginia. We look upon a dead horse as being worth something. His hide and hoofs and mane are marketable, and will produce shillings and pence. He can be turned into fiddle-bows, sofa cushions, women's petticoats, glue, sausages, and bristles. But to the Army of the Potomac he is not worth a cent. The soldiers' rations are abundant, and they would disdain to eat his flesh. So there they let his body lie; and there the dead horses are by scores, in every stage of decomposition, the ribs and the jawbones prominent through the ragged red hides, the legs lying along inert, the necks preternaturally elongated, the dim glazed eyes sometimes pitifully turned up to heaven. A sorry end! They have died of sore back, of consumption, of glanders, but oftener of sheer weariness and inanition. All is one, however, to a select company of crows gathered around each equine corse. The crows of the Army of the Potomac are the fattest, the sleekest, and the most clerical I ever beheld. Their eyes are somewhat dull with overgorging, but their plumage is beautifully shiny. They have the true unctuous, self-satisfied, rather imperious and intolerant ecclesiastical

look—the look that sends poachers to gaol, and condemns
nut-gathering little boys to discipline of birch. These bene-
ficed crows, these pluralist crows—for their supply of horse-
livings is plentiful—have grown so tame, that they are not to
be pelted away from their quarry by stones or frightened
from it by shouts. They gorge and gorge until you almost
fancy they are shoddy contractors. . Then, when their meal
was over, or rather when half an hour's surcease from gorging
appeared to their instinct necessary to ward off a corvine
apoplexy, they would arise in lazy droves, and with lazily
flapping wings wheel slowly over some fresh carcase, until the
instinct of voracity warned them that it was time to descend
and have another gorge. Those worthy crows! They were
so very human in their devotion to the good things of this
world. Yet, in one or two of the most unflinching feeders,
did I think I could discern something like a palled and
satiated look, as though they were thinking, " *Toujours
cheval*" was growing to be somewhat of a bore. Horse is
toothsome, we will admit, and there is plenty of it ; but, after
all, the bill of fare is not refined. One wants a change. One
pines for something more *recherché*. Ah for a battle, with
plenty of killed ! and then Oho for the fat Federal and the
lean but gamy Confederate !

About three o'clock in the afternoon the train drew up at
Brandy Station. The line in the possession of the Federals
extends as far as Culpepper ; but as we were bound for the
head-quarters of General Meade, commanding the Army of
the Potomac, Brandy was our most convenient halting-place.
General Meade, as it happened, at the time of my visit, was

sick, and at Philadelphia with his family ; and General Sedg-
wick was in command of the army.

I don't know whether there was any alcohol in store at
Brandy Station, but there was certainly a prodigious quantity
of beef. An army, a sage authority has laid down, marches
upon its belly ; and I have to compliment the Army of the
Potomac upon at least the solidity of that stomach on which,
tortoise-like, it progresses. Beef, in thousands of casks and
barrels, was heaped up all around Brandy Station ; then
came pork and flour, tea, sugar, coffee, beans, hardbread—or
biscuit—in apparently inexhaustible quantities. And yet I
was informed that I did not see before me the actual consumption of a single day.

Brandy Station is, architecturally, a nonentity. There is
an attempt at a platform, a shed for the locomotives, and a
shanty for an office of the Provost Marshal's department,
and that is all. You must not expect ticket offices, or
waiting rooms, or refreshment counters on the U.S.M.R.R.

We were expected at Brandy Station, and immediately on
our arrival were made much of. Some white handkerchiefs
had been waved to us as we neared the platform, and these
belonged to the two English ladies who, brave in their riding-
habits and their bright side-saddles, had for many hours been
setting the mud of Virginia at defiance. There were plenty
of young officers on the staff who were delighted to officiate
as cavaliers to the English Amazons. But as I did not ride,
and my friend and his partner were as bad horsemen as I,
General Ingalls' private equipage, a light spring-waggon,
drawn by a team of four spirited black horses, had been

thoughtfully provided to convey us to head-quarters. Walking, although the weather was extremely fine over head,
was entirely out of the question. The mud took care of
that. I should like you to have seen that mud. Take all
the sewage that is to be collected at the low-level outlet, add
the top dressing of all the guano islands of Peru; supple-
ment with all the sweepings of Cheapside and Holborn
Valley after a three days' rain, then amalgamate with about
the stiffest clay that a foxhunter would *not* care about
crossing, plant thickly with the "snags" or stumps of recently
cut-down trees, and scatter pools of water about at frequent
but irregular intervals, and the result might give you a faint
notion of the mud in the middle of which the army of the
Potomac were living when I saw them. That mud seemed
to me at once explanatory of much of the dilatoriness and
over-caution attributed to General M'Clellan. How could
any general, without a hundred thousand pairs of seven-
league boots, thrice bigger than my cherished ones, move any
army through such mud ? The soil was just practicable for
horses, and, under great press of leverage and good driving
for ambulances; but for the passage of field artillery, to say
nothing of heavy guns, it was simply impossible.

The common roads or turnpikes in the neighbourhood
have wholly disappeared. Roads and turnpikes and tolls—
Mr. Bradfield will be happy to hear—are alike "played out."
Only, when there is absolutely no bottom to the mud, and
the danger arises of a whole troop of cavalry being swallowed
up in the Malebolgian morass, there has been constructed a
fifty or sixty yards' length of what is termed a "corduroy

road." This is not to be confounded with the pleasant and
innocuous "plank road" of Canada. A "corduroy road"
means simply a thickly-serried row of rough-hewn logs, laid
like railway-sleepers in the mud ; only there are no rails ;
only when the wheels of your vehicle jolt over the corduroy
at right angles to the logs, every bone in your anatomy
seems to be in danger of dislocation. Your heart seems to
be forced into your liver, and that into your lungs, *e tutta la
baracca* into your mouth. If bumping, bruising, shaking,
and general discomfort amount in the aggregate to what is
termed punishment, I think the knottiest of our problems as
to convict discipline might be very easily solved. There is
some nice marshy waste land in the Isle of Dogs. Let it be
well stirred up and a corduroy road laid down, and then send
a couple of hundred convicts jolting over it in waggons without springs. How the rogues would roar ! And how their
agony would be enhanced if from their waggons they caught
sight of the swiftly, easily gliding trains on the Blackwall
Railway. This punishment would not cost so much as the
crank, and it would be, if my experience in Virginia goes for
anything, far more efficacious. How I wished as I bumped
along in the General's light spring-waggon—which, for all its
engaging name and its four black horses, was to be a most
penitential waggon—that I could change places, were it only
for half an hour, with a British felon, set to the hardest of
so-called hard labour, under the beneficent auspices of the
Earl of Carnarvon.

But of higher things I sing than light spring-waggons.
We were at the camp, and at General Meade's head-quarters.

We were in actual presence of the renowned Army of the Potomac, numbering: well, how many men? Two hundred thousand? A hundred and fifty? A hundred thousand, even? Not so. The effective force of the Potomac army, when I saw it, did not exceed seventy thousand men; and of these at least sixteen thousand were away on furlough, scattered throughout the length and breadth of the Union.

Out of the remaining, say, fifty-four thousand men, how many do you think were visible? To an utter civilian, an irreclaimable *pékin* and confirmed Cockney, who would carry, if he could, Stoke Newington to Nova Zembla, and Camden Town to Cathay, with him, there could be few things so disappointing as the first aspect of the head-quarters of a great army in fighting trim. I had seen, of course, in common with innumerable English chroniclers of small-beer tours, the camps of Boulogne and Chalons. In my own country, the petty martial camp-meetings of Chobham and Colchester and Shorncliff, and the permanent hovel camp at Aldershot, had been familiar to me. I expected to find a camp made up of huts or tents neatly ranged in parallel rows, with a solidly-constructed guardhouse, an officers' mess-room, a club perhaps, and a sufficiently handsome pile of buildings as the head-quarters of the general commanding. Then there would be numerous canteens if in England, and soldiers' cafés and dancing-rooms if in France, hospitals and kitchens, sutlers' stores, cavalry stables, pacing sentries, fatigue parties, with here and there a battalion parading. This was my idea of a camp. If expectant imagination could go further, it would have endeavoured to realise visions of vivandières

in snowy aprons, neatly-plaited skirts, and pantaloons co-
quettishly cut over the boot—of groups of staff officers, in
brilliant uniforms, blazing with gold embroidery—of trum-
pets and drums and fifes perpetually braying and tooting
and rub-a-dubbing—of soldiers off duty, lounging on the
sward or playing bowls or cricket. This was my idea of a
camp; but the predominant item of expectation was to find
vastness—a huge number of men, a huge number of horses,
the whole flanked by frowning batteries of artillery.

I must confess that my first half-hour's acquaintance with
an army on active service was sadly destructive of the fond
illusions I had formed. In the first place, there seemed,
comparatively, but very few habitations; in the next, there
appeared to be but few people about, and of those few the
majority were negroes. Where were the fifty-four thousand
men ? Where was the Army of the Potomac ? Well, tech-
nically as well as metaphorically speaking, they were " all
there"—present in the spirit and the flesh—ready to march,
to fight, to dance, and to drink — when anything to drink
could be got. The only drawback to me was that, although
topographically and telegraphically on the spot, they were
to the naked eye invisible. I suppose it is the same with
every army in the field. The Chief, the Quartermaster, the
Adjutant-General, know well enough what the strength of
the army is, and can map out to a quarter of a mile
where it lies; but to the casual and ignorant spectator all
this is mystery. The vastness of the area over which the
armed host is spread, confounds him. He is unable to realise
the fact of thousands being present when scattered around

him ; he only sees a few groups of white tents widely se-
parated. And as it is in a camp, so, I apprehend, it is in
a battle. When the great Duke of Wellington was asked by
a lady at a ball to describe Waterloo, he pointed to the
brilliant pageant which was running its course before them,
and asked her if she thought she could describe all that
was going on in that ball-room. If it be ever my lot to be
present at a battle—although of wars and its alarms I have
had enough by this time—I shall have but little to say, I
fancy, about the manœuvres of great bodies of men, desperate
charges, skilful flank movements, and so forth. Such graphic
narratives are best written at home, years after the event, with
the general's despatches and a good map before one. If ever
I were called upon to send home an account of a sanguinary
engagement between two great armies, it would most probably—if the account were candid and conscientious—be
confined to mentioning that, standing somewhere under a
tree, I could make out, through a race-glass, that something like an Irish row appeared to be going on in a field
a long way off; and that riding away, rather in a hurry,
I met many carts full of men that were wounded, and were
crying out, for God's sake, for water ; and that I saw many
ditches full of men that could cry no more, for the reason
that they were dead.

I had to make the most of the Army of the Potomac in
detail, and absorb it *poco a poco* in my mind, until, accu-
mulating there, it came at last to an aggregate which
astonished me. After all, a camp is a wonderful conglome-
ration. Order, discipline, prompt obedience, unflinching de-

termination, unvarying punctuality, method, patience, frugality, valour—what men call *virtue*, in a word—are all
there, and are all brought to bear on one object, and are
all designed to serve one end : *that of ripping up the entrails of our brother, who never did us any harm.*

General Meade, I have said, was away sick, and the simple
tent—as simple as that of a European subaltern—he ordi-
narily occupied, was closed. Hard by, on the knoll where
his head-quarters were situated, floated from a staff a blue
silk banner, with "Chief Quartermaster" broidered in golden
letters upon it. Close to this were the modest pavilions of
General Ingalls, the Chief Quartermaster in question, and
the officers of his staff.

The private soldiers of the Army of the Potomac, although
settled down in winter quarters, which, according to the
arrangements, they were not to vacate until the spring was
far advanced, were not to any extent hutted. For the most
part, they were quartered in the old bell-tent of classical,
conical form, so familiar to us in engravings of battle-pieces
from the old masters. In these bell-tents the men sleep, as
in Europe, eight or ten under one canvas roof, with their
heads to the pole in the centre, and their bodies radiating
outwardly like so many spokes of a wheel. There is also in
use in this army that remarkably ingenious contrivance,
borrowed from the French, and called by them *la tente
d'abri*. This little portable wigwam can be shared comfortably between two men on the march, is easily taken to
pieces, and is put up in a moment. It is an admirable protection against rough weather, but in the Federal army has

been found occasionally to lead to results oddly subversive of discipline. The warriors carrying the component parts of the " shelter-tent " on the tops of their knapsacks, have been frequently given on the line of march to quiet skedaddling. With three or four days' rations about them, and carrying, like the snail, their own houses over their heads, they have been enabled to camp out in the woods for the best part of a week, and in the most gay and festive manner. Then, the little picnic having lost the charm of novelty, they have regained the main body of the army as weary-footed stragglers. This skedaddling, through a spirit not of pusillanimity, but of pure truant *gaminerie*, has with much difficulty been put a stop to. In what manner? the reader may ask. A great many gallant officers at home, much better versed in military matters than I am, and accustomed to the old code of European military discipline—flogging, the black-hole, stoppages, and punishment drill—might ask the same question. There is no flogging in the American army, although its ranks contain numbers of ruffians from both sides the Atlantic whose shoulders would be much benefited, and whose predatory proclivities might perhaps be diminished, by the application of the cat-o'-nine-tails. But flogging is, it is admitted, an impossibility. The army, apart from its scum, is undeniably a patriot army. Thousands of young men of education and respectability are serving in the ranks, not precisely shoulder to shoulder—for the birds of a feather will flock together—but regiment to regiment, with hordes of the greatest blackguards in the world, a mere set of cottage-sacking, rick-burning, chicken-stealing, grand-piano-smashing banditti. It would be a mercy to flog these miscreants, to whom Colonel Kirke's Tangier "lambs" and Claverhouse's Scottish Guardsmen were babes of grace; *but the thing cannot be done.* The army, as a whole, is too noble to be beaten. There is, in the outlying military commands, a good deal of quiet hanging and shooting of marauders. Bardolph is caught stealing a pix, and meets a deserved doom by means of a penny cord, and Ancient Pistol comes to a much more respectable end than ever he expected, by being led out some fine morning to the music of muffled drums, and shot to death by a file of musketeers. But what Grant or Butler or Banks need not hesitate about doing, Meade must be chary of attempting. The Army of the Potomac is too near Washington, and too near the hydra-headed, Argus-eyed, Dionysius-eared, multi-tongued New York press, for any high-handed meed of justice to be dealt out uncommented upon and undenounced. Rarely some incorrigible deserter goes to his death from the muskets of a platoon, and sitting on his own coffin in an ambulance; but for any but the most unpardonable military offences, the punishment of death—in the Potomac Army, at least—is not inflicted. Corporal punishment is, ostensibly, not in use; but bodily inflictions of a sufficiently painful and degrading character are commonly employed. Some of these, although grotesque in aspect, are revolting in the ingenuity of the torture they cause. Did I tell you, that every morning at Washington there was a gaol delivery of the soldiers arrested by the pickets on the preceding evening for drunkenness or disorderly conduct? An officer from the Provost Marshal's department examines the

culprits as they are brought from the black-hole ; and, whenever his high and mighty caprice prompts him to issue the
necessary order, the half-sobered reveller is dragged into an
adjoining room, and subjected to the discipline of a rough
shower-bath.   This ducking of drunkards may sound very
funny ; but violent *douches* of cold water have been known,
ere now, to kill people.   That which would not be tolerated
in a gaol or a mad-house is done every day under the nose of
Abraham Lincoln and his merry men ; and what need I say
more ?   Was there not a Governor of Barataria once called
Sancho Panza ?

The Washington shower-bath is one of the most notable of
the eccentric penal inflictions which the Americans had sub-
stituted for corporal punishment, as it is understood in the
British army.   The opponents of the lash may commend it
as more humane than flogging ; but the practice does not
appear to me as any the less arbitrary and cruel.   Down at
the Potomac they are even more accomplished in the " art of
ingeniously tormenting."   There is resorted to the punishment called " tying up."   It is a summer torture, not a winter
one, and is productive of most misery when the thermometer
is, say, eighty-two in the shade.   You take your culprit and
strip him to the middle or not, according to the gravity of
his offence ; but in all cases you are very careful to leave him
bare-headed.   Next, you stretch his arms and legs out at
opposite angles to the utmost limits of muscular tension, and
you tie his extremities to any projections that may come
handy, the spokes of a cart-wheel, for instance.   *Then you
leave him in the sun, without any water, and he takes his*

chance. An officer in the army of the Potomac told me that he had seen as many as a dozen men tied up in lines and undergoing this infernal torture. Pray remember that not a blow is struck. Here is no brandishing of the scourge, no sibilant whirr of knotted thongs. You only tie your man up and leave him. It is the simplest thing in the world. I think the Holy Inquisition, if that delightful tribunal be ever re-established again, might take a leaf out of the punishment-book of the Army of the Potomac. There is a fiendish nicety, and a devilish completeness about this "tying up," most edifying to contemplate. It beats keelhauling, picketing, and the strappado. It approaches the dignity of breaking on the wheel.

I do not know who can rightly claim the honour of having introduced torture into an army whose daily boast is that it is governed without corporal punishment. "Tying up" is said to have been brought from Mexico twenty years ago, at the time of the war, and to have been for centuries a favourite Aztec punishment. But Mexico is too cold for the infliction in all its refinement of broiling heat which cannot be alleviated, and thirst which cannot be slaked. Save in the sweltering region of the Tierra Caliente, "tying up" would lose half its horrors. Close to General Meade's head-quarters I saw, up to five o'clock in the afternoon, numbers of prisoners, men belonging to the Federal army, engaged in loathsome and degrading tasks. The clean and well-appointed chain gang at Havana, who leave the Presidio every morning to go through a little light work in street-sweeping, were infinitely better off than these wretches. I saw one miserable object,

dirty, haggard, and bloodshot-eyed—a week's mud, a fortnight's dirt, and a month's beard upon him ; his *kepi* tied
over his head with a foul clout, his feet swathed in bandages,
and his body robed in the usual blue-grey overcoat, but inconceivably ragged and stained—who was kept by two
soldiers with fixed bayonets, continually sweeping. There is
a little dry ground about the quarters of the General-in-Chief,
and a plank road has been laid over the mud from the
principal tents to the main guard-house. The man with the
clout round his head had been in the hands of the tormentors
—so a person who had been watching him told me—since
early that morning. The sentries had relieved each other
over and over again, but for him there had been no surcease.
First, they forced him to make from tangled brushwood his
own broom, bind the twigs together, and shape and fit a stick
to them ; and then they gently pricked him onwards with
their bayonets—sometimes, perhaps, not very gently—the
while he swept. The Abracadabra potency of the steel goad
was in them, and he, poor devil ! was bound to sweep. I see
him now, tattered and torn and foul, his back bent, his
knotted-veined hands clutching the besom, and ever and
anon turning his head, and with blear eyes, and the rheum
of exhaustion on his hairy muzzle, glaring at the tormentors,
as though to say, "Whither next, damn you ?" Besides the
sweeping, they had been putting him to all kinds of sorry
uses during the day, making him roll barrels full of ordure,
clean out stables worse than Augean, and the like. I
wondered, when I saw him glare over his shoulder at the
tormentors, that he did not pluck up heart of grace, and at

least essay to knock one of them over with his broomstick.
He could but have been bayoneted on the spot, or shot a few
hours afterwards by sentence of drumhead court-martial, and
that scrape would not have been much worse, I take it, than
the one he was in already.   I dare say he was a craven hound.
I don't know what he had done, but it was doubtless something very heinous and very mean.   A shabby rogue—one
of Sir John Falstaff's Coventry men, who had stolen linen off
a hedge—only here there were no hedges, and no linen to
take off them.   There was nothing but mud to steal, and
that is a commodity scarcely marketable.   There were some
signs of shame, however, about this most forlorn rascal.   The
English ladies who were of our party were young and comely,
and as the Amazons rode up the luckless gaol-bird made a
dash at the hood of his gaberdine, and strove to hide his head
within its folds.   But the tormentors were at him again, and
he had to go on sweeping—on, on, like the Wandering Jew.

Many more prisoners under sentence of court-martial, I
suppose, are so kept at convict labour in the Army of the
Potomac.   The whole of the night long there are gangs of
them employed to chop and bring in wood to feed the guard-
house fires.   Of course, something must needs be done to
preserve discipline.   If the American army were allowed,
that army would very speedily go to the deuce.   When
General M'Clellan was first put in command of the Potomac
host, he found that he was merely the chief of an armed
rabble.   There was scarcely any discipline, and in many
instances the officers were greater ruffians than the men.
M'Clellan worked wonders with his soldiers.   He taught

them to obey. He taught them to be respectable. Un-
happily, and owing to the basest of intrigues, he was forced
into retirement; but the seed he sowed has never ceased to
bear good fruit. Nearly everything that is commendable in
the internal organization of the Army of the Potomac is due
to the perhaps over-cautious, but decidedly upright and as
decidedly ill-used chieftain, George B. M'Clellan. A variety
of military offences, which in Europe would be deemed
worthy of serious if not condign chastisement, are, in the
strangely-constituted crowd which has been bribed or bullied
into taking service under the stars and stripes, accounted so
venial as to escape well-nigh without rebuke.

Those who have seen French troops on parade, and heard
the incessant cries of "*Numero trois, consigné pour huit
jours!*" "*Numero cinq, trois jours de salle de police!*"
—dire disciplinary inflictions for a button divorced from its
hole or a strap fitting awry; those who know what is the
daily work of the British colonel, adjutant, and sergeant-major
in the orderly-room; and those who are aware of how many
hundred blows of a stick are necessary to perfect an Austrian
or Russian soldier in his drill, would be surprised to mark
the free-and-easy manner in which misdeeds, which at home
would draw on the offender the gravest censure, are treated
in the armies of the Great Republic. The time of regimental
officers is not taken up with incessant and meticulous attention to details. Soldiers are expected to obey the word of
command, and they do seem not only to obey it with much
alacrity, but to understand it with considerable quickness of
appreciation. They are held to render obedience to the

general ordinances of the camp, and as a rule, to do as they are bidden by their officers; beyond this, they are very little troubled with rules or regulations. I don't know whether any code of sumptuary laws exists for the *bonne tenue* of the Army of the Potomac; but this I *do* know, that the private soldiers allow their hair, their moustaches, and their beard to grow to whatever length their fancy may lead them, and that they are allowed to wash as little as ever they like, which is generally not at all. It has been my fortune, in the course of a pretty active career, to see English, French, Russian, Prussian, Austrian, Turkish, Italian, and Spanish soldiers, without counting those of the minor States of Germany; I have seen some tolerably ragged and dirty warriors; but I will take my affidavit that I never, until I visited the Army of the Potomac, set eyes upon desperadoes who so nearly resemble the brigands that Salvator Rosa used to paint as do the Federal warriors. It is not, I apprehend, the business of the American sergeants and corporals to look after the personal appearance of their men. That appearance is absolutely horrible. The uniform itself—abating its coarse materials, repulsive colours, and slovenly cut—is not so very ugly; but the way in which it is pitch-forked on to the soldiers' bodies, their unkempt hair, their dirty faces, their grimy hands, their grimier nails, the filthy saddles, the ungroomed horses, the uncleaned boots and accoutrements— the general slouching, out-of-elbows, up-all-night-and-drunk-again-the-next-morning appearance of this surprising armament—is beyond my powers of description, and almost beyond the powers of imagination to conceive.

But if I have done these brave men one iota of injustice,
let me at once recant. I qualified their aspect as of a too-
late-to-bed and too-early-to-rise kind. That look—so far as
the privates, at least, are concerned—is not the result of
intemperance. The Army of the Potomac is, compulsorily,
the soberest in the world. Cromwell's Ironsides drank their
Nottingham and Burton ales, and occasionally took their sip
of distilled waters ; but the Ironsides of the American civil
war are debarred from these enjoyments. It has been found
wholy incompatible with the maintenance of commonly
decent discipline to permit the men to drink any kind of
fermented liquors. To as much tea and coffee as they can
swallow they are welcome ; but they are sternly forbidden the
use not only of spirits, but of the comparatively innocuous
cider and lager beer. For wine they have never, at any time,
cared. Their soul thirsts for whisky ; but whisky, luckily for
themselves in particular, and the army in general, they cannot
obtain. That the illicit conveyance of spirits into the camp
to some extent prevails, need scarcely be said. The soldiers
do now and again contrive to procure, at exorbitant rates,
some fiery poison, miscalled Bourbon, Old Rye, or Monon-
gahela ; but the contraband spirit trade is rigidly looked after
by the authorities, and cases of smuggling, when discovered,
as rigorously punished. Any sutler detected in selling whisky
to soldiers has his stock-in-trade confiscated, is compelled to
" clear out," and is not infrequently packed off to Washington,
and incarcerated in the old Capitol. The strictest of internal
custom-houses is established at Brandy Station—whose very
name seems chosen in grim mockery of the forbidden luxury

—and all boxes and packages containing necessaries or comforts for soldiers are scrupulously examined before they can be
forwarded to the owners. Of course the soldiers grumble at
this, and seize the opportunity of every mail to flood the
columns of the Washington newspapers with complaints. "It
isn't our whisky being seized that riles us," wrote one sufferer
from the spirit taboo, "but it's the seeing of it *staggering
about afterwards with shoulder-straps on.* That's what
makes us mad." And that is where, indeed, the shoe pinches.
The officers seem to be able to procure as much wine, as much
brandy, and as much whisky as ever they choose. They may
have to smuggle it, but they do manage to smuggle it somehow. There are teetotal officers, no doubt, and there are
hundreds of temperate ones; but there are, on the other
hand, numbers of wearers of shoulder-straps who are neither
teetotal nor temperate, and these are the topers who "rile"
the soldiers. As to allowing the latter even to purchase the
very mild form of swipes known as lager-beer, I was informed.
that it was simply impossible. So long as the demon of drink
could be kept from the men, the army was all right; but once
allow them so much as a dram of liquor, and violence,
anarchy, rapine, confusion, and ruin must be the result. I
feel, however, that I am on dangerous ground, and must halt.
This is coming to a case of looking the gift horse in the
mouth. I received far too much hospitality during my
stay with the Army of the Potomac to argue dispassionately
the question of thirsty privates *versus* convivial officers.
The memory of certain huge and well-filled demi-johns of
whisky visible to me in certain tents is still fresh in my

mind. I will be discreet, and say no more on this head at
least.

The men console themselves for their enforced abstinence
by sucking any quantity of lollipops, by smoking any number
of short pipes, by chewing any number of quids, and by
reading any number of newspapers. The consumption of
journalism in the Federal armies is tremendous, and the
perusal of newspapers appears to yield the men unceasing and
unfailing delight. I have heard that on the battle-field of
Antietam, in the intervals of the bloodiest charges, the rowdy
little newsboys would come scampering along the ensanguined
ranks, crying " extras " of the New York papers. It is
certain that you can scarcely pass a soldier's tent in this great
camp without finding one or more of the occupants intent on
the study of one of the flimsy, ill and almost illegibly printed
sheets which are vomited forth every morning by the New
York press. They will continue reading them for hours,
although what they can find long to enchain their interest in
those said sheets I never could understand. To an European
there does not seem to be as much reading in an American
daily newspaper as in a London playbill. The leading articles
seldom condescend to an elaborate argument, or even to a
succinct statement of a case. They are brief, careless, decla-
matory, and scurrilous. But soldiers and civilians seem alike
to gloat over them. I suppose they read all the shipping
intelligence and all the advertisements—the " Help Wanted,"
the " Personal," the " Sales at Auction "—not by auction—the
" Matrimonial," the " Astrological," and the " Medical." At
all events, they must derive intense enjoyment from news-

paper reading. The soldiers are also to be found in throngs round the sutlers' stores, spending their abundant greenbacks —for each private musketeer seems to have a hundredweight of greenbacks at the very least—in candy, in hardbake, in toffee, in barley-sugar, in cocoa-nut, in fig and gum drops, in cranberry pies, in dough nuts, in jam-puffs—huge triangular cocked hats of pastry, such as you might think were worn by the courtiers of the King of Alicampane—in chewing tobacco, in pens, ink, and paper, in cigars, in drawing-books, and in playing cards. Never did I see an army so plentifully provided with pocket-money, and who found it burn so fiercely in their pockets. They are always spending their greenbacks, but not without grumbling fiercely at the prices charged them for the articles the sutlers supply. I have heard of fifty cents being demanded for a five-cent bottle of ink, a dollar for a quire of writing-paper, and other articles in proportion. The sutlers, on their part, doubtless think that they have as much right as any one else to make fortunes out of the war, and do their best to make them accordingly.

The grand predisposing cause of military crime, and of all other crimes, perhaps, being taken away, it might, at the first blush, be inferred that the Army of the Potomac had been brought morally to a state of quite Arcadian innocence, and that some Transatlantic King Alfred might hang up his golden bracelets by the highway, without any risk of their being stolen. Such, unfortunately, is not the case. The Americans will not tolerate crowned heads on their continent save when they cannot help themselves, as in Brazil, Paraguay, Canada, and Mexico. Nor are there any highways in

Virginia : only mud. And the golden bracelets have given way to greenbacks. Not in any sense has the state of innocence been realised. A great many broils, outrages, assassinations, are certainly averted by the liquor law. Still, the predatory instincts in the scoundrel element of the great army are not so easily conjured away. Of course, theft is common, when so many of the bounty-bought men have been, prior to their enlistment, professional thieves. Horsestealing is one of the most prevalent and one of the most ingeniously-managed of the offences committed. The stables are necessarily constructed on the most *al fresco* principle ; the horses being, in most cases, merely tethered to trees, and sheltered from the sun by a scrap of canvas here and there, or more commonly, by a screen of green boughs. Vigilant as the watch may be, horses, valuable ones sometimes, disappear every night. They are seldom recovered. The charitable mind may put ˌdown their absence to the account of the guerillas, select gangs of whom, slyly permeating between the lines, are always lurking about the camp after nightfall. But the knowing ones are better informed. There is a cunning underground railway for the spiriting away of illicitly annexed horseflesh. There is an occult market for the sale of stolen cattle. There are always sutlers and inferior *employés* of the commissariat and transport departments able to procure permits for the conveyance to Washington of cast or disabled horses. Blithely up from Brandy, then, goes the stolen horse ; and within a week, perhaps, he is again purchased on Government account, and is comfortably feeding in the Government *corral*, with a view to his being once more despatched to Brandy for the service of the Army of the Potomac.

Have I anything more to say about the American soldier? Much; but I fear to weary you. Let me still parenthetically observe that although an unclean, untidy, and raffish appearance is the prevailing characteristic of the American private, smartness and dandyism are not altogether absent from this army. There are a few corps, both of infantry and cavalry, *d'élite*. There is one regiment, hailing, I believe, from Brooklyn, quite gorgeous in the bright scarlet of its vests and pants, and another corps, whose name I was not able to discover, but from whose laudably ostentatious display of snowy collar and wristbands I ventured to name on the spot "The Clean Shirt Regiment." The rest are a dirty lot. At Washington I was shown some dragoon officers flaunting about in cloaks lined with yellow, and, of course, showing as much of the said linings as they possibly could. They were beautiful to look upon, bearing a considerable resemblance to gigantic canary-birds; but I did not see any of them down at the Potomac. About the Zouaves I had, of course, heard an infinity of tall talk. I saw a vast number of them, but was sadly disappointed. The uniform is a pretty close copy of the picturesque Oriental garb, the donning of which has turned so many *gamins de Paris* into dashing soldiers; but the American Zouaves are miserably shabby. Were they genuine Turks, most appropriately might they be commanded by Seedy Pasha. Very likely in the beginning, when the Yankee Zouaves were young and hopeful, their gear was glossy and good-looking. But the climate, or hard work, or both, has taken it out of them, and they are fallen into the sere and yellow leaf. Grubby and clumsily twisted are their turbans ; faded their fez-caps ; torn the tassels which used to droop therefrom ; braidless the once brave jackets ; cleft in unseemly rents, or branded with disgraceful patches, the baggy breeches. The whilom bright yellow jackets have grown dirty brown, like a portmanteau too long in use ; and the once white gaiters have come to be of no colour at all. As they are too careless to shave the hair off the temples and forehead, as the French Zouaves do, *pour se donner un air crâne,* and as many of the Yankee Zouaves have very low brows, the ungraceful spectacle of a shock head of hair appearing beneath the folds of the turban is not at all un-common. On the whole, the Zouaves of the Potomac have, in outward mien, a decided affinity to the "supers" one sees on the stage. You know what a "super" soldier is like. The uniform never fits ; his accoutrements have an untanned look ; his hair is untrimmed ; his moustaches are plainly "crape hair" or burnt cork.

There are, or were, or have been, at some period or another of the war, a corps of so-called Scottish Highlanders, duly philibegged, plaided, bonneted, and sporanned in the Army of the Potomac. I say "so-called," for I will not believe that any true Scottish men, really entitled by birth or kindred, to wear the garb of old Gael, can have so far forgotten their glorious belongings as to take part in this sorrowful struggle. Their fathers wore the kilt at Culloden—they wore it at Alexandria in Egypt, not Alexandria in Virginia. In America, too, they wore it ; but it was at Quebec when they stormed the heights of Abraham, "and marched up rocks that were quite perpendicular." The slogan was heard and the Highlandmen marched shoulder to shoulder on those famous plains where WOLFE and MONTCALM met a common death, and inherited a common glory. The English and the French hero stand hand in hand, brothers-in-arms till time shall be no more; and if caryatides were needed for their temple, I would place on one side a Highlandman and on the other a Gaul of the Regiment of Royale Cravate. No, no; I cannot believe in the sham clansmen of the Federal army. A great deal may be swallowed; but a Braemar gathering in the Bowery is rather too much. The so-called Gaelic soldiers of the North must have been fellows to the impostors pilloried by Theodore Hook in his ballad on the presentation of the address to Queen Caroline :—

> " Two hundred Mile-enders,
>   Dressed up as Highlanders,
>   Shiv'ring in kilts."

I am glad to say that I did not see any of these tartan travesties.

I found, to my great astonishment, a considerable number of ladies in camp. At a gathering held on the evening of our arrival, and of which more anon, there were present at least fifty fair dames and damsels, belonging to the different corps. The fact of the army having gone into winter quarters may account for this pleasurable invasion of the gentler sex. Many of the officers had sent for their wives; and some of the officers' spouses had, I dare say, come down to the

camp without being sent for. It is a way they have in civil
as well as military life. Were you never "fetched"? It is
one of the peculiarities of the American nation to look upon
everything as a show. Life and Death are to them only
spectacles, and, as they are a gallant people, they always
reserve a place for the ladies. The ladies have had a great
deal too much to do with bringing about this woful quarrel
to be discarded from it, now that it is in full operation.
There are a hundred ways in which the women are mixed up
with the war, from getting up fancy fairs to intriguing for
contracts. Of their presence in camp, however, every one
has reason to be glad. Their influence softens and humanises
much that might otherwise be harsh and repulsive. In their
company, at least, officers who should be gentlemen do not
get drunk, and I wish there were more ladies down at the
Potomac.

You may see a few white washerwomen scattered among
the various corps, mostly brawny, vituperative-tongued
females, of the Irish persuasion. I was unable to ascertain
whether, when the army is on active service, these Moll
Flaggons are as unscrupulous in their treatment of the
wounded and the dead as those camp-followers with whom
the great Duke of Wellington was compelled to deal so
ungallantly in Spain. It is probable that they are neither
much better nor much worse than their predecessors. I
suppose that war is war—has been and will be war, all the
world over. Begin it with rose-water and caraway comfits
if you like—open your trenches with fiddles and send presents of fruit and ice to your foe as the besieged did to the

besiegers of Gibraltar; but to the complexion of plunder, devastation and murder, it must come at last. It is a bloody business. I dare say the American baggage-waggon woman is not more dishonest or more cruel than her sisters in the Peninsula, to whom, according to the Highland sergeant quoted in Scott's "Paris Revisited," the great Duke caused to be administered "sax and thretty lashes apiece on the bare doup;" and such as she was in Arthur Wellesley's time, the camp-follower was very probably in the time of John Churchill, and of Wallenstein, and of Genseric, and of Saul, the son of Kish, when he went forth to battle.

The Northern papers made at one time a doleful outcry about the practice common among the Confederates of stripping the Federal dead. *Harper's Weekly* had a horrifying whole-page engraving, representing the wicked, wicked rebels, after a battle, uncasing the Northern slain of their vests and pantaloons. Why should you not strip your enemy when you have despatched him? To the victors the spoils! The North intend to deprive the South of their estates after they have subjugated them, do they not? If you take a man's house, and his ox, and his ass, and his man-servant, and his maid-servant, why stop short at his nether garments? To appropriate his pantaloons completes the sum of "everything that is his." When you have killed a bear you take his skin; why not flay your fallen foe? As I was coming down in the train to Brandy, and with considerable pride was exhibiting those notable leathern encasements of mine to an officer of light dragoons, an interesting discussion arose between us as to how far it was morally justifiable to kill a man for the sake of his boots. Escobar or Don Sanchez should have been present. The celebrated controversy of the Jesuit casuists, *Occidere pro pomô*, was nothing to it. The light dragoon argued that to kill a man for his boots was the most natural thing in the world. " Suppose you haven't had a new pair for six months," he pleaded, "and sole and upper leather will scarcely hold together. Well, you meet a fellow with a bran new pair. What's the good of taking him prisoner ? To strip a live man who is in your power would be mean, shabby, ungentlemanly—worthy of a Riff pirate or a Mexican quaser. Kill your man, and there is an end of the matter. A dead man can't want boots, so you take them." He eyed my boots as he stated his case, with an evil eye. I am afraid he coveted them. On a lonely road, and without a six-shooter, I should mistrust meeting that light dragoon.

There was in attendance in the tent appropriated to the English ladies of our party, one of the most beautiful Quadroon women I ever saw. She was the lady's maid to an officer's wife who had gone up to Washington, and had kindly lent her for our ladies' convenience. She was about two-and-twenty, in complexion a clear olive, with large swimming eyes of purple black, wavy raven hair, a ripe cherry mouth, prettily-shaped hands and feet, most delicate ears, and a form that for suppleness and symmetry was perfectly exquisite. She had been a slave, and as a domestic servant, the ladies informed me, was utterly useless. She could pull the hair-brushes about, and smell the eau-de-cologne, and listen to the conversation with an occasional

giggle and a constant grin ; but that was all. When she
could get away to the tents at the back, among the negro
cooks and plate-washers, she seemed most in her element;
and there you heard her tongue clack faster and her laugh
ring louder than all the others—the sharp, shrill, chuckling
nigger laugh. She was Topsy yellow-washed, and with the
form of the Venus de Medicis. She was, to most intents
and purposes, as much a nigger as the coal-black wenches I
had seen at Alexandria, and civilisation and teaching could
do little more for her than for the darker-skinned daughters
of her unhappy race.

Before I quit for good and all the subject of *physique* of
the soldiers I saw, it behoves me to mention one curious fact.
Plentiful as are the mercenaries in the ranks, swarming as
are the Irish and the German, the American—the Yankee—
type in feature, mien, and gait is predominant and absorbent.
It is only when they speak that you can discover the soldier's
nationality ; and even then it is surprising in how short a
time the Saxon and the Celt acquire the nasal drawl and
twang of the " cunning men of Pyquag." For the rest, they
all look like Yankees. It is the climate, I think—that climate
which gives your pulse ten extra beats per minute, which
exhilarates and impels you to short, spasmodic bursts of
feverish energy, and then leaves you haggard, weary, care-
worn, and melancholy. Depend upon it, the trying temperature of this country has everything to do with making young
men old before their time, with withering and wrinkling
matrons that should be blooming, with drawing the life-blood
out of the checks of young girls, and making the very babes

and sucklings pallid and angular. The Americans are very
angry when they are told that they are sad ; but that outward melancholy has marked them for her own is palpable.
Columbia is the home of hypochondria. She is dyspeptic.
Hence her political distress. The old fantastic scholar has
proved as much. Hear him quote the learned Boterus : " As
in human bodies," he says, " there be divers alterations pro-
ceeding from humours, so there be many diseases in a commonwealth which do as diversely happen from several dis-
tempers, as you may easily perceive from their particular
symptoms. *For where you shall find the people civil,
obedient to God and princes, judicious, peaceable and quiet,
rich, fortunate, and flourish, to live in peace, in unity,.and
concord*, many fair built and populous cities *ubi incolæ nitent*,
that country is free from melancholy ; as it was in Italy in
the time of Augustus and the Antonines, and now in many
other flourishing kingdoms of Europe. *But whereas you
shall see many discontents, common grievances, complaints,
barbarism, beggary, plagues, wars, rebellions, seditions,
mutinies, contentions, riot, epicurism*, the land lie untilled,
waste, full of bogs, fens, deserts, cities decayed, *bare and poor
towns, villages depopulated, the people squalid, ugly, uncivil;*
that kingdom, that country must needs be discontent, melancholy, hath a sick body, and hath need to be reformed."

This mournfulness, I repeat, is chequered by occasional
bursts of merriment. There was one the very night I arrived
in the camp of the Great Army of the Potomac. I had been
warned to take down a dress suit and a white cravat for the
ball that was to come off at General Carr's head-quarters. It

x 2

came off in the very grandest style. We had been most
hospitably entertained at dinner, and duly provided with
coffee, *chasse*, and cigars, when we were told that it was time
to dress. Our ladies had been respectfully entreated to
" draw it mild " in the way of toilette, as many of the ladies
who were to be at the ball had not been to Washington for
a long time, and had been unable to procure full evening
dress. Our ladies faithfully promised to draw it as mild as
possible; but when they made their appearance in most
splendid array, I felt rather uncertain as to what the con-
sequences might have been if they had drawn it strong.
Dauntless equestrians as they were, they could scarcely be
expected to ride on horseback in white tulle over pink silk,
and a couple of spring ambulances, drawn by four horses
apiece, had consequently been provided to convey the ladies
and the civilians to the festival. The general's aides-de-camp
accompanied us on horseback, and the kind-hearted general
himself, who had probably seen quite enough of balls in his
time, bid us all good night, and went to bed. Then uprose
the moon, for whose advent, indeed, we had been waiting
before we could start at all, pitchy darkness being unfavourable to nocturnal locomotion, and away we jolted. There
was nothing to complain of on the score of dignity. The
ambulance was a brigadier-general's; and in the van and the
rear of the cortége rode a body of dragoons, pistols in their
holsters, and drawn swords in their hands. " Come," I said,
as we floundered through the mud, " this is not so bad after
all. I am not one of the governing classes, and was not born
to sit in high places; but this manner of procession is, to say

the least, genteel. I have been to a good many evening
parties, but never, until now, have I gone forth to the festival
in a four-horse waggon with an escort of cavalry. It is
quite royal."

Bump! "There's royalty for you!" I had soon to murmur ruefully. A sway, a heave, a lurch, a hitch, a stumble,
a succession of bone-dislocating jerks. What do you think
of your gentility now? Splash, splash! we are in the middle
of a morass. Thud! we are stuck in the clay. Bump!—
w-w-w-rah—bump! my opposite neighbour is thrown violently against me. I make a desperate clutch at a wreath
of camellia japonicas worn by the most amiable of her sex.
By Jove, we're snagged! There was no use in calling on
Jupiter to help us out of this worse than rut. Three dragoons had to dismount, and put their shoulders to the wheels.
The horses were backed; the ambulance performed a series
of agonising summersaults, and at last we were free. It is
no light matter to be "snagged" on a dark night in Virginia. A snag is the stump of a hewed-down tree, and when
a wheel happens to get locked in the cleft of a snag, there
is no way very often but to get out and walk. On the Mississippi, as you may have heard, there are both snags and
sawyers, and when a steamer strikes one of these her bottom
is often pierced, and her passengers, who have not been
blown up the day before, are drowned. After half-an-hour's
rumbling and bumping, we saw the lights of Brandy Station.
Then we got on to a "piece of corduroy;" and hideously
unpleasant the piece of corduroy was. Finally, the braying
of many brass bands came on our ears, and we found our-

selves in the midst of a rolling ocean of waggons and horsemen struggling to approach a house which was lit up from
top to bottom.

There had galloped furiously by us, backwards and forwards during our journey, a tall man, mounted on a taller
horse. Blue-eyed, fair-bearded, strapping and stalwart, full
of loud cheery laughs and comic songs, armed to the teeth,
jack-booted, gauntleted, slouch-hatted, yet clad in the shoot-
ing-jacket of a civilian, I had puzzled myself many times
during the afternoon and evening to know what manner of
man this might inwardly be. He didn't look like an American ; he was too well dressed to be a guerilla. I found
him out at last, and struck up an alliance with him. The
fair-bearded man was the "war-artist" of *Harper's Weekly*.
He had been with the Army of the Potomac, sketching, since
its first organisation, and doing for the principal pictorial
journal of the United States, that which Mr. Frank Vizetelly,
in the South, has done so admirably for the *Illustrated London News*. He had been in every advance, in every retreat,
in every battle, and almost in every reconnaissance. He probably knew more about the several campaigns, the rights
and wrongs of the several fights, the merits and demerits of
the commanders, than two out of three wearers of generals'
shoulder-straps. But he was a prudent man, who could keep
his own counsel, and went on sketching. Hence he had
become a universal favourite. Commanding officers were
glad to welcome in their tents the genial companion who
could sing and tell stories, and imitate all the trumpet and
bugle-calls—who could transmit to posterity, through wood-

cuts, their features and their exploits—but who was not charged with the invidious mission of commenting in print on their performances. He had been offered, time after time, a staff appointment in the Federal service ; and, indeed, as an aide-de-camp, or an assistant-quartermaster, his minute knowledge of the theatre of war would have been invaluable. Often he had ventured beyond the picket-lines, and been chased by the guerillas ; but the speed and mettle of his big brown steed had always enabled him to show these gentry a clean pair of heels. He was continually vaulting on this huge brown horse, and galloping off full split, like a Wild Horseman of the Prairie. The honours of the staff appointment he had civilly declined. The risk of being killed he did not seem to mind ; but he had no relish for a possible captivity in the Libby or Castle Thunder. He was, indeed, an Englishman—English to the backbone ; and kept his Foreign Office passport in a secure side-pocket, in case of urgent need. My travelling friend, cherish your British nationality as the apple of your eye. You may call it brag, boast, bunkum, if you like ; but that *"civis Romanus sum"* of my Lord Palmerston still holds good in the remotest regions. Foreigners may scowl, glower, affect to undervalue it ; but they acknowledge its potency at last. As a *Subdito Ingles* I should be quite content to land alone in Yucatan or at Tehuantepec. There is an old patois song—

> " Tiene el Ingles un cañon
> Que se llama bocca negra,
> Quando dice canonazo,
> Todo la Francia tiembla "—

and all the world trembles too. We may underrate our-

selves as much as we choose; but abroad, thank Heaven,
Queen Victoria's name is still a tower of strength.

General Carr had fixed his head-quarters at an ordinary
Virginia planter's house. These houses are pretty nearly the
same all over the State of Virginia, and, in fact, the South.
They are mostly "frame houses," the basement of brick or
stone, the superstructure of planks, the roof of shingles.
One storey, plenty of large cool rooms, and a staircase running up the centre, is the rule. All round the house runs a
verandah, supported by wooden pillars; and here in hot
weather the family mostly live. The house is painted white,
and in some very grand mansions there are Venetian blinds
to the windows. Behind is an orchard, perhaps a pleasure-
garden, certainly a kitchen one; and, at the back of all, the
negro quarters, which resemble pigstyes, neither more nor
less. It is quite patriarchal, but rather rough. The exigencies of General Carr's head-quarters had made short work
of the cabbages and fruit-trees. They had all disappeared.
The whole of the back garden had been canvased in, floored,
and converted into an immense ball-room. The decorations
were of the simplest, consisting mainly of fasces of regimental
colours and Federal flags; and over the gallery at the lower
end, which was simply the verandah of the house, a kind of
triumphal arch was arranged, made out of flags, branches of
fir, and three big coloured lamps, borrowed from the locomotives at Brandy Station. Any number of cressets full of
kerosene oil hung from iron hoops and illumined the gay
scene. The whole effect was pretty, but rather dim. When
the dancing commenced, the dust arose in clouds, and

asphyxia seemed imminent. The dust, however, had the desired effect of making the guests very thirsty, and there were oceans to drink.

We were handed out of our ambulance by a colonel with a pink rosette in his button-hole, who was one of the managing committee of the fête. Our ladies were conducted to a *cabinet de toilette*, where I heard they found plenty of eau-de-cologne, fresh bouquets, and negro girls to wait upon them. I was presented with a little gilt-edged programme of the dances to be gone through at the " Third Corps Assembly," and the colonel with the rosette whispered in my ear, " Come upstairs and have some rum-punches." With rum-punch as a unit I was tolerably familiar ; but the suggestion thereof in the plural number was novel to me, and I went upstairs. There was a committee-room, which, in accordance with established American custom, had been converted into a bar, and there the consumption of rum-punches was enormous. Nor would the scene have been thoroughly American without another apartment, full of combs and hair-brushes and pomatum and looking-glasses, where the gentlemen could re-part their hair, twist their moustaches, and generally " fix themselves up." Never lived there such a people for having their hair dressed as our curious cousins. Truefitt, you are wasting your sweetness on the desert air of the Burlington Arcade. Go out to America, and " fix up " the citizens, and they will make you a Minister of State.

I was introduced to a stout general, who was laboriously pulling off a pair of very muddy jackboots—for he had ridden to the ball—and replacing them with a pair of most dainty

patent leathers. As soon as he was "through" with the
task, he was good enough to ask me how my health was, and
to suggest that we should partake of a "whisky skin" hot.
Opining, however, that it might grow too hot, so far as I was
concerned, before supper-time, I compromised the invite for
negus, and then went down to see the show. There were,
perhaps, three hundred officers present, of every grade above
that of second lieutenant, and all in full uniform. There
were not any non-commissioned officers. With the exception
of our party and one solitary Virginian gentleman who owned
an estate close by, and had made his peace with the Government, there were no guests in mufti. The show of tunics
and shoulder-straps was immense. The ladies did not exceed
sixty in number, and they were of course devoured, metaphorically speaking, by the gentlemen. Every lady was soon
engaged five-and-twenty deep ; but, as there were a dozen
sets of quadrilles going on at one time, the gentlemen had
frequently to dance with one another. When Americans
dance—and they are always ready to dance—they *do* dance.
There is no lounging through the figures. The performance
is, in every respect, thorough.

I could not avoid a feeling of sadness as I looked on the
trappings of this strange scene. Yet, to behold them, a
native-born American would not have felt sad, but rather
proud and jubilant. On every side hung the American cognisance—floated the American Stars and Stripes. In every
other country of the globe, save perhaps China, you would
have found, on such an occasion, the flags of many nations
intermingled. There would have been the Union Jack, the

cross of St. George of Russia, the French tricolor—"blood-red to the fingers' ends"—the crimson and orange of Spain, the German, the Italian blazons. The Americans are at war with none but themselves; yet they acknowledge the exist-ence of no banner but their own. They have shut themselves out from the comity of nations. They have chosen to be Alone, and, in their tremendous loneliness, they are certainly presenting to the world a spectacle which must amaze, if it does not edify.

At one o'clock a grand military march was played, and the whole of the company, arm-in-arm, promenaded slowly at least half-a-dozen times round the ball-room. Then the ladies went into supper, taking in those gentlemen who had been fortunate enough to be their partners during the last dance. The supper, set out in an interminable series of mess-tents joined in one, was laid out on rough-hewn planks, supported on trestles. Underneath was the bare earth, and some narrow strips of board to walk upon. The supper was a stand-up one, and there was a good deal of scrambling; but I have seldom seen a more sumptuous repast. Abating the gold and silver plate, the Sèvres porcelain, and the damask napkins, it threw the famous suppers given at the Hotel de Ville, when Louis Napoleon was Prince President, into the shade. *Carte blanche* had evidently been given to some Washington Delmonico, and the result was gorgeous. There were mountains of ice creams, hecatombs of lobster salads, archipelagoes of stewed oysters, pyramids of quails, mallards, and canvas-backed ducks. Every kind of wine graced the board, but nobody seemed to care for anything but champagne, and of that festive vintage, Veuve Cliquot, the most expensive, was the only brand. Did you ever see Americans of the gentler sex at supper ? We will leave the rest, if you please, to the imagination. They sup, as they dance, thoroughly.

After supper all went "merry as a marriage bell." When I came downstairs again and looked at the revellers, I found myself unconsciously repeating the magnificent episode from "Childe Harold." Yes, here was the sound of revelry by night; the lamps shining o'er fair women and brave men; the thousand hearts beating, I hope, happily. I almost fancied that I was at the Duchess of Richmond's ball in Brussels, and half expected to see "Brunswick's fated chieftain" sitting within a niche of the high hall. But the night passed by without the cannon's opening roar, and the hurrying in hot haste, and the roll of the drum to arms. Something else had occurred to remind me that I was in the Old Dominion, and not in the Low Countries. There was a good-looking mulatto lad on the staircase peeping at the dancers, and I asked him to whom the house had belonged prior to its being utilised as the General's head-quarters. He mentioned the owner's name—the which is neither here nor there. "Where is he ?" I asked. "In Washington, Mas'r." "Oh, then, he's a Union man ?" I continued. "*No, Mas'r; he's in gaol,*" the mulatto replied quite coolly. The old, old story. To the victor the spoils ; and as for the vanquished, lock him up in gaol.

The ball was to be wound up by an odd, hurry-scurry dance called a Virginian reel. It somewhat resembles our Sir

Roger de Coverley, and is danced to an olla podrida of tunes. Among the sixty ladies who had accepted the hospitality of the Third Corps there were two tall, slender, pale young damsels, the daughters of the Virginian gentleman I mentioned who had made his peace with the Government, and so saved his estate. One of the young ladies was footing it in the Virginian reel. She danced to "Wait for the Waggon," "I wish I was in Dixie," "Buffalo Gals," and so forth ; when suddenly the strains of the band glided into "Yankee Doodle." The abhorred air was too much for the Virginian young lady. She broke away from her partner, and flung herself indignantly on a settee. I could not help thinking that, since the Virginian young lady's papa had made his peace with the Government, two courses only were open to her—either to dance to whatever tune the Yankees chose to pipe, or to stay away from the ball altogether.

We came home in the ambulances at five in the morning very tired, but infinitely pleased with our most hospitable entertainment. Sterner occupations, however, were now before us. I slept the sleep of the weary in a tent which a staff captain had courteously vacated for my convenience ; and, thanks to a good pile of ammunition blankets, rested very well. We had next morning the same mild, balmy, delightful June weather. The leaves rustled, and the birds sang on the branches of the few trees in the rear of our quarters which had not been cut down. It was the Indian summer, the officers in camp declared—the sweet respite from hybernal asperity which should properly have come in November, but had this year chosen to visit us in the

middle of January. Indian or American, it was a blessed
time, a delicious time—a time of peace and tranquillity—a
time to be lounging on lawns and reading novels and twisting cigarettes and sipping cool drinks—and not at all the
kind of time for killing people and laying a fair country
waste.

I wandered, after breakfast, round about the camp, as far
as the encircling sea of mud would let me. The plank-road
was only laid down in the immediate vicinity of head-
quarters, and elsewhere you had to take your chance, and
trust in the width of your stride and the length of your
boots. Is was, for instance, a very painful pilgrimage to the
tent of the chief barber of the army—a most important personage, I can assure you, and who charged officers no less
than twenty-five cents for "barbing" and "fixing them up."
A very filthy little marquee he occupied. For flooring there
was nothing but hardened mud; but there were the never-
failing displays of broken mirrors, sofa-like shaving-chairs
and leg rests, tonics, bay-rum, floral water, essences, hair-
dyes, infinite unguents, and nasty messes for making the
moustaches spiky. The chief barber was absent at Washington. State affairs, no doubt. Had been sent for by the
Government, perchance. His place was supplied by a dusky
professor in a cloudy-white jacket, who apologised very profusely for being without the "patent elliptical hollow-backed
Canton razor," and having nothing but a plain "Thermopylæ
wedge-blade" to shave with. The chief had taken all the
hollow-backed Cantons with him to Washington. For what
purpose? Surely not to cut his country's throat. The

Administration can manage *that* trifling task without the assistance of chief barbers. There seemed to be something else, too, that was gone to Washington, namely, the sub-barber's ability to shave. When he had cut me thrice and barked my skin in innumerable places, I insisted upon completing the operation myself. Hereupon he retired in dudgeon, but speedily solaced himself with a banjo, and made the air of the Indian summer hideous to the tune of "Come along, darkies."

I was permitted to peep in at the Chief Quartermaster's office where, almost since daybreak, the scribes in uniform had been employed. I was taken to the printing-tent, where a couple of compositors were busy setting up a general order. There is not, so far as I know, a newspaper published in camp; but, were a journal established, it would find plenty of subscribers. I asked whether theatrical entertainments had ever been thought of as a means of diverting the occasional monotony of winter quarters. I was told that the soldiers had no turn for getting up private theatricals themselves, and that the practicability of procuring a professional company from Washington was questionable. The American in fact, as I observed at Niagara, does not care about doing anything himself. He would rather some one else did it for him. He likes "bossing," or directing, scheming and superintending, but not working. Take away the Helots from the commonwealth—take away the Irish, the Germans, and the Negroes from the States, and the native Americans, I fancy, would not have had, during the past forty years, quite so much to boast about in the way

of railway mileage, docks, wharves, and town-lots covered
with giant stores and brown stone palaces with marble
fronts.

The soldiers are, however, as has been observed, passionately fond of reading, and almost as passionately addicted
to hearing orators "speak a piece," or men of letters deliver
a lecture.   Mr. Bayard Taylor would make a fortune at
head-quarters : but I don't think Mr. Wendell Phillips, or Mr.
George Thompson, would draw very large or very enthusiastic
audiences.   To judge from the way in which the nigger is
treated in camp—that nigger for whom they are fighting to
the death, and for whose sake these thirty months past so
much blood and treasure have like water been poured out—
I can scarcely persuade myself that the soldiers of General
Meade belong to the Black Abolitionist faction.

I was shown, in the course of the morning, a remarkably
practical and ingenious contrivance for carrying on the
business of the adjutant-general's department in the active
service of the campaign.   There stood, under a tent, a com-
pact-looking machine upon wheels, varnished black, and
picked out with a good deal of red, and looking remarkably
like a fire-engine.   It occupied very little space, and four
horses could easily take it over the roughest ground.   Still,
for all its lightness and compactness, it was a whole Horse
Guards in itself.   Directly the word was given to unlimber,
a complicated battery of flaps flew down ; compartments
started out ; writing-desks, hitherto invisible, rose into view ;
and there were disclosed whole nests of drawers and pigeon-
holes, containing every variety of printed form, and all kinds

of stationery. A dozen or more clerks could be at once set to work at this improvised bureau ; and the tent that sheltered them could, when it was requisite to move the office on wheels, be struck in a few moments and snugly furled on the top of the vehicle. This was but one of the thousand devices, from a mortar to a match-box, which this surprisingly dexterous people have hit upon with a view to economising space, and saving themselves unnecessary trouble. The diminution of friction is one of the primary canons of mechanics. The American has extended the principle, by analogy, to the human body, and is perpetually scheming out means for preventing his own joints from being too much frictionised by hard work.

The Chief Quartermaster was good enough this day to take me over the whole of his department, but in order to combine pleasure with business, and to afford amusement to our ladies, our tour of stores and workshops was to be wound up by a visit to the neighbouring town of Culpepper Court-House, and, if possible, by an ascent to the signal-station on Poney Mountain. It was at this period of time that my mind, hitherto placid and serene, began to misgive me. I was haunted by the dreadful phantom of a horse. The ghostly charger in Bürger's "Lenore" was not, to my imagination, a more fearsome steed. On the previous day I had been most courteously offered a mount from half-a-dozen different quarters. I had politely declined the honour. I urged that I didn't ride, and that I couldn't ride ; but nobody seemed able to realise the fact in its naked verity. The tallest captain of artillery I ever beheld informed me that he had heard literary men were generally "poor horsemen," but that he would bring over for me, in the morning, a pony that was "as quiet as a lamb." I grinned a ghastly smile of gratitude; but how devoutly did I wish that tall captain of artillery, and his pony to boot, at the bottom of the River Rappahannock! "Depend upon it," the fair-bearded "war-artist" told me, at the Third Corps Assembly, overnight, "you'll have to get across a horse to-morrow. The ladies are death on riding; and, besides, from Culpepper to the Mountain the ground is impassable for wheeled carriages. You don't know how to ride? Well, you can have an orderly to lead your horse; only take my advice. You know what the M'Clellan saddle is. *You* have a blanket put on the saddle, or you'll suffer." I remembered Mr. William Russell's advice to the senator at the battle of Bull Run, about whisky poured into melted tallow, and well rubbed in. I remembered it, and groaned.

The two civilians who were to accompany me in our tour of inspection with the Chief Quartermaster were no more riders than I was; and we so earnestly pleaded our non-equestrianism to the General, that he, kind-hearted man, who would have supplied us with gondolas, or balloons, or Hippopotami, had those means of conveyance been procurable, ordered the spring-waggon and the black team to be brought out, and so, with the usual cavalry escort, and the General's charger led by an orderly, away we went. But those vexatious ladies—I beg their dear hearts' pardon for so naming them—were to the fore, habited and hatted, and booted, and mounted; and arch glances of good-humoured sarcasm were darted at us, as they cantered past us in the spring-waggon.

We had scarcely got clear of the main-guard, when the tall captain of artillery came galloping up, reining in the pony that was as quiet as a lamb, the which, with many apologies for keeping me waiting, he tendered to me. The pony that was as quiet as a lamb, was a long, low-bodied, brown brute, very shaggy, and with stumpy legs, like an old-fashioned spinet that had been rubbed with macassar oil, and so grown hairy. Suddenly he began to rear, and to kick, and to show his teeth, and to assume generally the similitude of a roaring lion. I told the tall captain of artillery that I would have nothing to do with the lamb-like pony, and, thanking fortune for spring-waggons, we jogged away. Our road, or rather our faint track, lay by Brandy Station, and then some four or five miles southward to Culpepper Court-House. A hundred times in the course of the war you must have heard of these court-houses, Culpepper, Fairfax, Orange, Spottsylvania, Madison, and the like. They bore, when Virginia was in the Old Dominion, and in the King of England's peace, a close resemblance to English county towns. There met the landed gentry, the magistracy, and the quorum, and there sessions were held, rates stricken, and county business transacted generally. Thus, too, as in our assize towns, there was an assembly room, and after the rogues had been comfortably sentenced to the gallows and the whipping-post, the ladies and gentlemen of the country side danced gaily to the music of fifes and tabors. Ah! halcyon days, gone to return no more. Over the muddy

swamp, through which we were floundering, old Lord
Fairfax's fox-hounds used to bark cheerily. George Washington, in a scarlet frock and a gold laced hat, has ridden to
those hounds many a time. What has become of the
Fairfaxes now? He who is legally entitled to bear the name
is still living, they say, a lawyer in California, but he disdains
to claim the dormant peerage ; while, strange caprice of
Fortune, a member of the English branch of the family was
not long since an attaché in the British Legation at Washington. And Lord Bottetourt? and Lord Baltimore?
Whither has the Transatlantic aristocracy fled! There was
a "Virginia Herald" once, who looked after the pedigrees and
the cognisances of the Old Dominion. Fancy a Virginian
Libro d'oro. Strive to realise a Maryland *Sangre azul*.
The sovereign of our country was King of Great Britain,
Ireland, France, and Virginia. They say there are some old
families still left ; but what has all this to do with the Chief
Quartermaster and his spring-waggon ?

I was lost in a dream of old times, between the real and
the fabulous Virginians, and should not have been surprised
to see Madame Esmond ambling towards us, or young War-
rington come riding up with despatches from General Brad-
dock, when we halted at the great Transport Repairing
Works of the department. Carpenters' shops, wheelwrights'
shops, painters' and varnishers' shops, blacksmiths' forges :
hundreds of men were here as busy as bees. They were all
white, and all, I was told, civilians earning high wages. The
American mechanic is a stern, proud man, exacting the most
unscrupulous consideration from his "boss" or employer, and

suffering no black brother near his bench ; no, not to grind his tools, or blow his furnace bellows for him.   The B.B. may hew wood for the furnace, and draw water for the boiler, that is all.   From which I conjecture that there will be difficulties between the black and white brethren some time before the year three thousand and three.

Ambulances, tumbrils, and trunks are all that are ostensibly repaired in these works ; but the heads of departments and officers of a certain grade have the privilege of sending their vehicles hither to be "fixed up ;" and mending very often assumes, virtually, the proportions of making.   " Send them a spoke, and you get back a carriage," whispered one of the Quartermasters' staff to me.   The amount of legitimate repairing done is, however, prodigious.   The mind can scarcely imagine, the eye can scarcely realise, the tongue can scarcely find utterance for the extent of transport which is needed to convey the baggage, the food, and the forage of an army—even fifty thousand men.   Mr. Gardner, the photographer to the army, gave me a view of the waggon-train of one corps only.   It looked like a boundless ocean of caravans.   What do you think of fifty miles of waggons—fifty continuous miles ?   That sight has often been seen when the army has been on the move.   What do you think of a block-up of these fifty miles of waggons, and their being unable to stir an inch for hours, notwithstanding the exertions of lancers employed to prick the negro drivers onward ?   The entire direction, the organisation, the starting and halting of these colossal *impedimenta,* must be centred in one head.   Our kind-hearted general had to originate and to be responsible for it all,

We saw every kind of work during the morning—tent-makers labouring in droves, coopers bending staves and welding hoops, and hammering casks together. I could not help laughing the bitter laugh when I saw the barrels being trundled about and headed up. The last cooperage on a grand scale I inspected was at Burton-on-Trent, in England, and I remember following the casks till they were branded "full to the bung"—full of harmless pale ale. O blood and beer! what an odd world it is, and how the useful and the futile, production and destruction, dovetail into one another, to be sure! Always somebody being born, and always somebody dying ; always something being made, and always something being spoilt, for Ever and Ever. And you can destroy nothing, after all ; for the atom is eternal, and this Virginia, stamped under foot and rooted out and ground into powder as it is, will arise and have form, and grow into a living thing again, some day.

Commissariat stores—but I will not tire you out with dis-quisitions on beef and biscuit. Of the thousands of blankets and boots, too, I saw, I will be silent. At the chief sutler's tent, nevertheless, I may linger a moment. The chief sutler is a personage. He has made, perhaps, since the commence-ment of the war—and made them passing honestly, too—a hundred and fifty thousand dollars. He may look con-tractors and financeerers boldly in the face, for his gains have been acquired by a trade more legitimate than theirs. Three years ago he was not worth a cent. The Chief Quartermaster, who had been acquainted with him in Cali-fornia, knew him to be an honest man. He set him up with

a waggon and an old broken-down pony. From small be-
ginnings, the sutler rose to do an enormous business ; and he
is now, certainly, one of the most remarkable men in the
army, if not in the country.   It is no trifling matter to supply seventy thousand soldiers with sugar-candy.   But come,
as we did, behind the scenes of the chief sutler's store, and
you will see what else he has to sell besides lollipops.   Writing-paper, pens and ink, hymn-books and song-books—for
one section of the army is just as partial to devotional
psalmody of the "John Brown" order, as another is to
" When this cruel war is over," and " Who will care for
Mother now ?"   Valentines—for we are verging on February,
and every unmarried soldier has a sweetheart.   Cheap novels,
drawing materials, and *cartes-de-visite* of favourite generals,
blacking and scrubbing brushes ; gingerbread nuts, treacle-
puffs, apple-pasties, hundreds of huge trays of which delicacies are made fresh every day ; humming-tops, playing-
cards, cheese, crackers, sardines, potted meats, tooth-powder,
pomatum, antibilious pills, and indiarubber goloshes.   Let
bitters also not be forgotten.   Bitters of every kind, from
the famous " Drake's Plantation"—which with their mystic
legend, " S. T.—X., 1860," are to be found advertised all over
the American continent, from Point St. Charles to Patagonia,
from Cape Cod to the Rocky Mountains—down to Hoch-
stetters, which are reputed to cure every disease under the
sun, and of a great many of which, perhaps, old Sol is scarcely
cognisant.   Some of these preparations are taken in good
faith, to cure that scourge of the constitution of the United
States, to wit, dyspepsia, or to guard against ague and marsh

fever. The convivial properties of other bitters are notorious. They are merely tipsification in disguise. Nor for
the wants of those more exalted in the military scale is the
chief sutler unprovided. Outside his tent there is a whole
grove of canvas-back ducks, red-heads, squabs, quails, and
prairie-hens—all delicious eating, and all frightfully dear—
some of the game having been brought by "lightning express" from a distance of two thousand miles. "On the
quiet" too, perhaps, the chief sutler has champagne of the
very finest brands, and clarets of the very choicest vintages
to dispose of to discreet purchasers ; but of these, and of his
rare old cognacs, superior London Dock gins, and curious
whiskies, he makes no ostentatious display. Of tobacco
however, for chewing and smoking, he has hogsheads on
hand.

We might have made a hearty lunch at the sutler's expense ; for the Chief Quartermaster can say "*yo el Rey*," and
is lord paramount here ; but we forbear to dispoil him, and
take no toll beyond a few apples and gingerbread nuts from
the open casks. Then we rejoin our spring-waggon, and
follow the ladies, who are far ahead by this time, towards
Culpepper Court-House. We meet procession after procession
of baggage-waggons laden with provisions, string after string
of heavy drays piled up with forage, and dragged, somehow,
through the mud (which is almost boiling in the hot sun), by
teams of hardy mules. The negro drivers are riding pack-
saddles or sitting on the shafts, or bestriding the mules without any saddles at all, now whooping and yelling to their
beasts, now singing barbaric songs with words of bosh, now

—and this last is very frequently the case—fast asleep and snoring, sweltering in the sun and happy.

Here is a mild little bit of sensation. A Federal dragoon comes pricking towards us with a man on foot, who has hard work to keep up with him that is mounted. The man on foot is a prisoner—a "Confed," as the General tersely puts it. This is the first rebel I have seen. He is a tall, lank, bony young fellow with a sandy beard, but strong and wiry-looking. I am disappointed not to find him clad in the "butternut" coloured uniform of which I have heard so much. The "butternut" hue, I was informed, is a kind of warm grey—perhaps Lady Morgan's celebrated "dun-ducketty mud-colour." The "Confed" does not wear any uniform at all. He has on a sit-down-upon wideawake, a jacket and trousers of some indescribable tinge, both desperately tattered, and I think—but am not quite certain—a shirt. So bad are his shoes, that he would lose little by going barefoot. A very poor specimen of a rebel this. He has, perhaps, been drummed out of the Confederate army; very probably he is a spy; at all events, the dragoon has him safe, and backed by the irresistible argument of the flat of a sabre, will have little difficulty in trotting him to head-quarters. "He'll be right enough when he gets there," quoth the General. "He'll have plenty to eat and drink; and, round the camp fire, there's little difference between North and South."

Nor, curiously, is there much difference between the hostile pickets. It is difficult to get up individual animosities in war. Now and then, when some fresh picket line is established, some skirmishing takes place. Occasionally, on one side or the other, the pickets are driven in, and now and then a man is killed; but, as a rule, the outposts are on the most courteous, not to say friendly terms. It is, "Hallo, Yank!" and "Say, Confed!" from opposite sides of the river. Often the pickets "get up a trade." Tobacco is very dear on the Northern side, and very cheap on that of Secesh. The Confederates, too, had, at the time of which I speak, plenty of "red-eye" whisky—a coarse and fiery liquor, to which the Russian Vodka is, in strength, but as skimmed milk;—whereas the Federal soldiers cannot get any spirits for love or money. On the other hand, the Confederates are destitute of such little comforts as tea, sugar, and coffee; and these, with Northern newspapers, are the articles they chiefly covet. So, little rafts, on either side, are constructed and freighted with the commodities most in request, and floated down the stream to convenient landing-places; and thus the "trade," with much bandying of jocularities as to extortionate prices and adulteration of merchandise, is effected. All commercial transactions are conducted strictly and equitably on the principle of barter;—goods for goods, on delivery—and no trust; for the Confederates refuse to take greenbacks at a premium, while the Federals, with more financial reason on their side, decline to accept Confederate scrip at anything less than five hundred per cent. discount. Of course, all this trading is done under the rose—is strictly prohibited by the authorities; and, if too ostentatiously carried on, is gravely censured by them; but the pickets are wary, and whenever an officer makes his appearance, they immediately blaze away at him, for decency's sake. The commanding officers know perfectly well what is going on, and discreetly close their eyes to the "trade" system. When it is mentioned, they affect, officially, to reprehend it ; but I fancy that the General-in-Chief would be very much chagrined were two mornings to pass without his breakfast-table being supplied with copies of the *Richmond Whig* or the *Examiner*. As a rule, the pickets do not fire upon one another. Now and then there is a skirmish, and the outposts, on one side or the other, are driven in ; but in isolated instances, mutual slaughter is almost unknown. The thing can't be done. You can't develop a soldier to such a point of moral depravity that he will assassinate his brother opposite in cold blood, and feel no remorse for it. Occasionally, far away, in camp, some sharpshooter with a sure eye, a steady hand, and a hard heart, will lie on his stomach for hours behind an epaulement, with an opera-glass in one hand and a rifle in the other, and when he sees a chance, will " pot" a stray " rib ;" but such a proceeding is looked upon as sport, not war.

Let me mention, also, to the great honour of the officers as well as the soldiers of the Federal army, that they are accustomed to speak of their opponents with a commendable abstinence from bitterness or personal ill-feeling. If you wish your fill of invective, calumny, passionate spite, malignant disparagement, vapouring braggadocia poured forth, silly threats uttered, fiendish aspirations for the extermination of the South indulged in, the words " rebel" and " traitor" made use of at every breath, you must go to Washington, to New York, or to Boston, and listen to the philanthropists,

and the pietists, to the shoddy-contractors, and the Wall-
street brokers;—to the men of religion, or the men of Mam-
mon. Here, where the real work is going on, where the real
life-blood is being shed, the Northern soldiers are calm and
temperate in their allusions to the brave men arrayed against
them. They speak of them as "the enemy," and rarely as
" the rebels." They know them to be foemen worthy of their
steel ; and, as warriors should, have a stern joy in them. It
is not alone in the Union lines that Grant and Meade are
respected ; it is not alone in the Confederate camp that
" Uncle Robert" is loved and admired.

We used to read at school about that which Hannibal once
said to Scipio :—" It had been a blessed thing for you and us
if God had given that mind to our predecessors that you had
been content with Italy, we with Africa. For neither Sicily
nor Sardinia are worth such costs and pains, so many fleets
and armies, or so many famous captains' lives." I am willing
to believe that sentiments as noble as those expressed in the
preceding sentence are latent in the breasts of many of the
higher class of American commanders on both sides of the
Rapidan, and that it is the consciousness, from near and
hourly experience, of how horrible is this war, how fertile it is
in misery, and how barren of true glory, that induces the
Scipios of the North and the Hannibals of the South to look
upon one another with feelings widely different from that dull,
blind, bitter rage with which bureaucratic Washington looks
on Richmond, and stockjobbing New York on Charleston, and
fanatical New England on all. The very first day of my
landing in America I remember, in the train between Boston

and Stonington, sitting next to a sailor who had been on
board the Federal cruiser which had just captured the Ella
and Annie, a noted blockade runner. The Ella and Annie
showed fight, and having an iron-cased prow, ran right into
the midships of the first vessel that essayed to take her; but
a larger cruiser coming up she was boarded, and after a smart
hand-to-hand fight, surrendered. The crew of the Ella and
Annie were placed in irons; but, when they came to the
captain, who do you think he turned out to be ? Why, an old
schoolfellow of the Yankee officer commanding the cruiser;
and my informant found a brother of his in the boatswain.
The old, old story of civil war. Is there not that wondrous
scene in *Henry VI.*, crude and bizarre as it may read, and
yet a whole commentary on the bloody contest between the
White and Red Roses ? The same miserable tale of enmity
between brethren, the story of Cain and Abel.

But the soldiers are still, to my mind, the least blood-guilty.
They have a duty to perform, and they perform it. It is
their business to fight, and they fight. Where the cauldron
simmers and bubbles fiercest, where the hell-broth is concocted and the gruel is made thick and slab, and envy, malice,
and all uncharitableness rise like a waterspout, is in the pulpit
and the counting-house, on the brokers' exchange, and at the
intellectual tea-table. I sat once next a young lady, very
clever and very far North, who expressed her surprise that
" something was not done with those Rebel prisoners " at
Johnson's Island and elsewhere. " Why were they allowed
to live in idleness," she asked, " costing the Government ever
so much money ? Couldn't they be punished ? sent to work

on the roads, or to dig in the mines, or something?" I heard
so many strange theories propounded during my Northern
experience, that, my interlocutor being young and well-
favoured, I bore this with as much equanimity as though she
had favoured me with an opinion as to how sleeves should be
worn or paper flowers cut. Astonishment, however, asserted
its rights, and indignation came to help it out, a few days
later, when I found this self-same doctrine—a doctrine absurd
in the mouth of a blue stocking, but atrocious in that of a
reasoning being, and monstrous in that of a public journalist
—put forward in a newspaper of no less respectability than the
New York Times. And I have little doubt that the leading
article, in which the Lincoln Government was counselled to
treat and to employ as convicts the prisoners whom the
chances of war had thrown into their hands, was read with
approval by many thousands of loyal Northerners. Why,
indeed, should these wicked Secesh captives be suffered to
eat the bread of idleness? Didn't Napoleon shoot the
Spanish guerillas, and send Major Schill's free-lances, when
he had caught them, to the galleys of Toulon? Why should
these rebel rogues be more tenderly treated? Away with
them to dig and delve on the Pacific Railroad! Set them
to make the new line between Washington and New York.
Banish them to the yet undeveloped regions of Arizona and
Sonora. Force them to unload Federal transports, to drag
Federal waggons, to hew Federal wood, and to draw Federal
water. Manacles and thongs—a collar for the neck and
leather for the back—are good enough for such as they. This
is the orthodox loyal reasoning. I have not the least doubt

that the fanatics and the unscrupulous politicians of the North would put this theory into practice, and that they would willingly enslave, torture, nay, hang or shoot their prisoners, but for the fear of one little thing—reprisals. The dread of this it is which prevents them ; otherwise, they would slay and spare not, in cold as well as in hot blood. But the suggestion of reprisals daunts them. In the history of their own war of independence, they may remember the significant label pinned to the breast of a man who was hanged, "Up goes Huddy for Philip White." They had better take care of what they do with the Huddy of 1864. The Confederates have got Philip White safe in hold ; and, as sure as fate, they will string him up if anything happens to Huddy.*

These are the wretched, carking bickerings of the cities. In the camp a higher, better tone prevails. I was told recently of a Northern cavalry officer who for months was opposed to the renowned Confederate *sabreur*—the Murat of the South—Fitzhugh Lee. The two gallant foemen fought each other like a couple of wild cats ; but they were, out of the fight, always on the friendliest of terms. Both happened to be gentlemen, schoolfellows, classmates, West Point men, who had puzzled their heads over the same mathematical problem, and smoked the same prohibited tobacco. They could find time in the intervals of fighting to keep up a bantering correspondence. Thus the Confederate would write to the Federal, " Clear out ; you've no right in this part of

* They have hanged up Huddy to some extent, since these lines were penned.

the country, anyhow. *Send me a bag of coffee.*" To which
—having sent the coffee—the Federal would reply, a few
days later, " I played the deuce with you on Thursday, and
mean to finish you up next week. *Old Rye is scarce.* Could
you manage to let me have a few bottles ?" And the Old Rye,
or, in default thereof, Bourbon, was punctually sent. These
are the amenities of war. It chanced that one of the aides-
de-camp of a Federal officer was taken prisoner. He met at
first with some rough treatment in the Confederate lines, and,
being slightly wounded, would have fared but ill, when he
bethought himself of sending his card to General Fitzhugh
Lee. The Murat of the South was exceedingly kind to him.
He could not set him free—that was against the rules. He
had no wine, no fruit, no jellies, no delicacies, and but few
comforts, to offer him ; *but he sent him every day at noon a*
hot whisky-toddy. Whisky-and-water warm is, perhaps, not
the best of diet for a wounded man ; but you have little idea
of the strange things one gets accustomed to in war. My
belief is that the aide-de-camp throve on the whisky-toddy ;
but in any case the intention of Fitzhugh Lee was as kind,
and as tender, and as noble as that of the poor Highland
caterans, who when they might have sold Charles Edward's
head for 30,000*l.*, sheltered their fugitive prince in a cave, but
had no better fare to give him than a pennyworth of gingerbread.

We met a gentleman in black, with a most orthodox white
cravat, and a felt hat that was a kind of cross between the
shovel and the wide-awake. I cannot say we met him on the
road, there not being any road to meet him on ; but we passed

him toiling through the simmering mud. He was on foot,
but leading a most reluctant and ragged-coated Rosinante.
Perhaps he was a merciful man, and merciful to his beast.
Perhaps he was a bad rider—in the which case I sympathise
with him. The general told us that the gentleman in black
was a missionary. There is an organisation called the
" Christian Commission," which, in pious emulation, is running the Sanitary Commission very hard. Many tens of
thousands of greenbacks have been subscribed to purchase
Bibles and Testaments, and to print tracts for distribution
among the soldiers. It does not appear to strike any one—and
this is a matter that should come home to my own countrymen
as well as to the Americans—that war is a matter with which
religion can have clearly nothing to do, and that to strive to
introduce any element of piety or morality into warfare is
hypocrisy, and a mockery at which the devils of the pit must
grin. I admit war to be an institution of immense antiquity,
and of the most Conservative consistency. The naked savage
of New Zealand and the bearded tatterdemalion of the
Potomac, the Zouave and the Sepoy, the burnoused Kabyle
and the kilted Highlander, all own a common creed in killing.
There was never anything so Catholic as war ; and if, after
many thousands of years of civilisation, mankind are pretty
nearly unanimous as to there being no way of settling
national difficulties save by shooting or stabbing, I suppose
that war must be regarded as inevitable. But I cannot look
upon it as holy and apostolic. I would rather not see any
blessings invoked upon regimental colours. As well might
one pray Heaven to bless gunpowder and Greek fire. I

would rather not have any military chaplains. Their office seems to me a wicked anomaly. Much better would it be to have a war troubadour attached to each regiment, who should sing the song of " Roland" to the tune of "Yankee Doodle," and excite the warriors to fierceness in the strife, and tell them that if they are killed their reward shall be to dwell in a Walhalla of heroes, there to quaff Eternal Cocktail out of the skulls of their enemies. I know well enough what the answer will be to this : It is possible to carry on hostilities without resorting to acts of barbarism. Is it? Civilised nations carry on war in a civilised manner. Do they? Oh lie of lies ! oh, casuistry of casuistries ! Here, before me, is one of Mr. Gardner's photographs representing a dead soldier on the field of Antietam. A shell has caught him in the middle, ripped him up, and scattered his bowels about. There they are, most beautifully depicted. This is what your civilisation has come to. A free government, religious tolera- tion, universal education, wise laws, national wealth, camera obscuras, collodion, and a skilful photographic manipulator at forty dollars a week ; and the result of all these wonderful engines of amelioration is a poor devil with a hole in his stomach and his entrails protruding. His entrails, madam. In the photograph I can see a locket, hung by a riband round the dead boy's neck. He is but a boy. The locket contains, perchance, the portrait of a mother, sister, sweet- heart, or some rubbish of that kind. This is civilisation in warfare. I suppose that a shell is a more civilised implement of destruction than a dart, or a pike, or a tomahawk. Conical bullets are more humane, of course, than slugs ; and a Swamp

Angel is a mild and sugary article in comparison with a battering-ram. Still we go on prating about civilisation in war, while the same hideous gashes are made, while the same maggots fester in the same wounds, while it is the same Death that overtakes him who is slain by a Malay kreese and him who falls by a Colt's revolver. And yet I have heard Christian clergymen, on both sides the Atlantic, spouting vehement platitudes about the God of Battles. Pagans and cannibals, Brahmins and Bonzes, and Talapoins and Medicine-men, can spout as fluently and as vehemently the same plati-tudes in their several jargons. As though there ever was, or ever could be, a God of Battles, any more than there could be a God of Blood and Famine and Desolation.

We came when the sun was shining its strongest, and the blue of the vault was almost intolerably intense, to Cul-pepper. We passed the court-house, a squat brick building, of Queen Anne's time, I conjecture, but approached by a portentous flight of stone steps. Here of old time the Virginian country gentlemen used to sit once a month, and invested with a jurisdiction so wide that it covered almost the whole field of cognizance—civil, criminal, and equitable. Any one justice could hold a court with power to adjudicate on all causes of which the value did not exceed twenty dollars ; but four justices were needed for a session in banco. At the monthly or quarterly quorum deeds and wills might be proved, and Chancery suits and actions at common law heard and determined—with an appeal, however, to a superior court. These courts tried slaves for all offences, even to capital ones ; but free persons they could only examine prior to their trial by the Circuit Court. Free negroes and Indians were on the same footing with slaves. All this is quite an old wife's tale now. The court has gone to the dogs, and the court-house is turned into a barrack. There is no more law but that of drumhead court-martial. What has become of the lawyers is uncertain. I suppose they are fighting in the Confederate army. There, for certain, are nine-tenths of the male inhabitants of Culpepper. The actual population appeared to be composed of Yankee soldiers, old men, children, a few white women, and a whole horde of lolloping, lazy negroes, basking in idleness and in food they had not earned. In the main street there were a few shops, from whose signs you could read that the occupants had once been milliners, tailors, haberdashers, butchers, confectioners, and so forth; but nothing to eat, to drink, or to wear was exhibited for sale. Empty as Stonehenge were all the shops. Their shutters had been torn down and burnt up for fuel. Of the original pavement of the streets, a few flagstones here and there remained; the rest was mud. The hotel, a reputable-looking two-storied edifice, with a verandah, was occupied by troops. As for the churches and meeting-houses, I could not find them at all. They had probably been converted into stables or forage stores. In Virginia the places of worship that have been destroyed were poor one-horse affairs, but they were God's houses nevertheless. At head-quarters an officer pointed out to me with great glee a part of the mantelpiece over his fireplace, which had been made of the pulpit of a neighbouring church. The building itself had been thrown down, body and bones.

There was not a cock, nor a hen, nor a chicken, nor a pig, nor an egg, nor an onion, nor an apple—there was not so much as a cabbage-stump or a potato-peeling—there was nothing that lives and nothing that grows by Heaven's bounty for man's sustenance to be seen at Culpepper Court-House. The war had eaten it all up. There was nothing brought to market. There was no market to bring anything to, no crops, no kitchen gardens, no anything. For aught I can tell, the few hovels and fewer brick houses of Culpepper itself may by this time have been demolished. The Dragon of Wantley had been here, and there was no Moore of More Hall to vanquish that monster. The townspeople were preserved from abso- lute starvation by the humanity of the Federal Government. They were supported on Federal beef and Federal biscuit, and I hope they prayed for Abraham Lincoln every night. My hope is, however, but a faint one, and I am afraid that the natives of Culpepper are all Secessionists at heart.

As we jolted through the main street, I saw two ladies dressed in black standing under the porch of a house of the better class, and which had enjoyed apparently singular good fortune; for the windows had not been smashed, the green outside shutters had not been wrenched off, the iron railings in front had not been torn away, the few shrubs in the garden had not been rooted up. The master of that house must have been a very strong loyalist indeed. Who were these ladies, I wondered. His wife and daughter perhaps; for one was old and dignified, the other young and comely. Pater- familias was, doubtless, strenuously " sound on the goose ;" but, of a surety, I never saw Secession beam so strongly and so fiercely as it did from the countenances of the two ladies. They turned their heads to look upon us as we passed. They darted on us a glance of concentrated hate—of unutterable scorn and loathing; and then they gathered up their garments and swept within doors. Had they been at the first floor window instead of the basement, it would have surprised me little if one of them had flung a tile down on our heads, like that woman in old Judæa.

Halting by the office of the Adjutant-General of the Great Army of the Potomac, a gentleman in uniform, with spectacles on his nose, a cigar in his mouth, and a pen behind his ear, came running out to tell us that if we had any ladies with us we had better not attempt the ascent of Poney Mountain. " Why, there's a lady there already," remarked a bystander. "True, but she's the captain's wife, and on duty," returned the gentleman in uniform. The guerillas had been very troublesome during the last two or three days, he told us; and the jungle, with which the mountain sides were thickly covered, was reported full of them. However, if we were determined to go, we had better wait till two o'clock. By that time the pickets, which had been driven in over-night, would be re-established, and the ascent of the mountain comparatively safe.

Now, I need scarcely point out that, although I was as brimful of professional zeal as a newspaper correspondent could be, it was no part of my business to get killed. From conviction, and by temperament, I am a non-combatant. When the battle rages, " 'tis distance lends enchantment to the view," so far as I am concerned. I like to arrive on the scene the day *after* the battle, and speculate on what may have been going on. If a broken leg or a bullet through the thorax will gain you a regiment, a peerage, the cross of the Bath, or a good-service pension, be a fire-eater by all means—overflow with the rapture of the strife. But to fight, and be perchance killed, with no hope of a funeral in Westminster Abbey, or of the annual pecuniary remembrance of your widow by a grateful country, seems to me in the highest degree absurd. Let others rush unbidden into the next world, and vitiate their life policies; "Safety, the companion of prudence," shall be my motto. So I thought when the gentleman in uniform discoursed of the perils of Póney Mountain. Those pestilent guerillas are by no means particular as to whether the people they knock over are combatants or non-combatants. "If you air from Massachusetts, shoot right away," says the proverb; and the guerillas, albeit Secesh, are all, on the powder and lead question, of the Massachusetts way of thinking. They shoot first, and inquire afterwards. We were unarmed, we had two ladies with us, and but four troopers as an escort. Besides, if the guerillas don't kill you, they have a character-istic way, first of appropriating all your valuables, and next of stripping you to the buff. "Git out of that hoss. Git out of that hat. Git out of them pants." This is the guerillesque formula. You will agree with me that this course of pro-ceeding is at once immoral, degrading, and embarrassing. It is true that when they have made you "all face," as the Indians say, the Virginian Rapparees will occasionally lend you a coat or a pair of pantaloons of their own, to cover your nakedness. The claims of decency may be satisfied; but the attire of the Secesh partisans is, as a rule, horribly ragged, and is infested, moreover, by an insect sportively termed a "greyback," which in Shakspeare's time went by another name, and was held to be a little animal familiar to man, and signifying love.

All these things considered, I would very willingly have given the guerillas the slip, and gone back, in peace and contentment, to head-quarters. But the ladies wouldn't hear of such a thing. What heroines they were, bless them! Guerillas! they cried—pickets driven in!—danger!—delightful! On to Poney Mountain! The kind-hearted General told us there was really not much danger, so we agreed to go on. An officer of the Corps of Guides was to accompany us; and he, having sent a little black boy for his sabre and pistols, vaulted on horseback and led the way.

At the base of Poney Mountain—the precise altitude of which above the sea I do not know, but which seemed to me to be about three times higher than Snowdon—we found a select stud of saddle-horses awaiting us. Our ladies were already mounted. Our own turn was now to come. They brought me an awful red horse—a "bright bay" may have been his correctly technical description, but to my eyes he was flaming scarlet—of a hue that made itself heard like the blast of a clarion. His neck was thatched with a long and dishevelled mane; but his tail was a switch or greyhound one, which gave him a weird and ghastly appearance. He was like the horse of the Commandatore in *Don Giovanni*, only with sun instead of moonlight shining upon him. I don't think I ever saw so high a horse. He was as tall—

well, as a flight of steps, or a Corinthian column, or a lamp-post. Gazing in dumb horror upon his prodigious head, his preposterous flanks, and his never-ending legs, like "unto the masts of some tall ammiral," I called to mind a story which had been told me in New York by a Southerner. This Southerner, who had not the slightest desire to offer any active opposition to the Lincoln Government, was unfortunate enough to own a large silver mine in the territory of Arizona. On this silver mine a certain Federal general in command in those parts had cast longing eyes. As a preparatory measure to getting possession of the ingots, and having, besides, an old personal grudge against the Southerner, he caused him to be arrested and clapped up in prison as a disloyalist. The capture was accompanied by many aggravating circumstances, and the captive was forced to ride away to durance on a wretched donkey. But, as he started, he turned and shook his fist at the triumphant Yankee. "I wait for retributive justice," he cried, in accents solemn and minatory; "you've sent me away on a jackass, but by —— *I'll come back on a horse sixteen feet high.*" The Federals kept my poor Southern friend in hold for many months; but let that pass. This brute at the base of Poney Mountain was evidently the threatened horse that was sixteen feet high. Why wasn't he an agent of retributive justice in the territory of Arizona? Why was he in Culpepper, county Virginia, and I doomed to ride him?

Laugh not at my lamentable plight—it may be thine to-morrow. I think I have seen, in one of the admirable cartoons by John Leech, a picture of a sporting gent,

bestriding a livery-stable screw, toiling up the steep downs of
Sussex after the Brighton harriers. I should like to see a
portrait of that gent mounted on a horse trained nobody
knows how long—if at all—and nobody knows where, by
nobody knows whom, trying to reach the top of Poney
Mountain. Sometimes the monster seemed to be standing
on his head; anon he would rear erect on his hinder legs,
and hop, like a kangaroo, or an industrious flea seen under
a microscope. I had been warned that he was a horse
with a tremendously hard mouth—a combination of gutta-
percha and adamant—and that I might pull at him as much
as ever I pleased. Most of the pulling was on his side,
however, and he nearly pulled my arms out of the sockets.
He had an ugly trick, too, of turning his head, and snapping
his jaws, as though he wanted to bite me; but that may
have been only his fun. I wonder if that horse had a
name. Had I the naming of him, I would have called him
Beelzebub.

We got at last to the top. The track through which we
forced our painful way was, where there were no holes,
strewn with monstrous jagged stones and huge boulders. Sir
Charles Lyell might have gone into ecstacies at some new
geological revelation here: for my part, I did not seem to
care about it. Above, the jungly underwood sometimes
developed into trees, with interlacing boughs, the ends of
which, protruding at uncomfortable angles, now smote you
across the countenance—now forced sharp spikes of ligneous
matter down your throat—now progued you, as conscience
progues, in the ears and on the nape of the neck. Ere we

reached the summit of this abominable mountain, my face was scored in parallel gashes, like a loin of pork for the bakehouse.

And at the top ? On the plateau had been erected a scaffold of rough timbers, some thirty feet high ; and on a few loose boards laid on the crest of this, approachable only by a rope-ladder, were two powerful telescopes. This was the Look-out Station. I was bound to see the show to the end, now that I had come so far, and I went cheerfully through the minor torture of the rope-ladder. I was amply rewarded for my trouble. I saw a sight which I can never hope to see again. Adjusting the lens of the telescope, I obtained at last the proper focus, and, plainly, clearly, sharply, distinctly, I saw, far to the South—far beyond the river—far beyond a tract of green, which seemed to be some kind of cultivated land, the first I had seen for days—height after height, crested with long rows of white bell-tents. I could see the sentries pacing to and fro. I could see men on horseback galloping up and down. I could not make out faces, but I could discern uniforms, and I had before me plainly, and almost palpably, the Rebel soldiers and the Rebel camp—or, if you would rather have it so, the army of the Confederate States of America, commanded by General Robert Lee.

I drew my eye back, and the scene was withdrawn in a closing prism like a summer afternoon's day-dream. I had peeped into the distant land. I had seen Secessia, and that was all. And then I stood up, and turned to the North, and the East, and the West, and saw even a stranger sight.

There were the Federal head-quarters; there the tents of the various corps; there the white tilts of the myriad waggons; there Brandy Station; there Culpepper; there the Rappahannock—the Rapidan was behind me; there the planter's house where the ball had taken place. What else was there to be seen in that astonishing panorama? Literally nothing. A vast dusky desert loomed beneath me. You might have taken it for a colossal ploughed field; but it was only mud. Culpepper, without suburbs, without a straggling environment of cottages even, without a road or so much as a by-lane leading to it, just looked like a big lump of sugar inadvertently dropped into the midst of a mass of dark mould. There were no trees, hedgerows, gardens visible. All was incult and horrid—without form and void.

This, then, was the State of Virginia—this howling wilderness, that looked as though it were "smitten with the botch of Egypt, and with emerods that cannot be healed." This was the State of Virginia, whose peaceful and prosperous population paid taxes, twenty years since, on 331,918 horses, 9962 coaches, 87 stages, 2625 carryalls, 5290 gigs, 27,000 gold and silver watches, 50,000 clocks, and 2876 pianofortes —that paid 15,000 dollars a year taxes for interest on stocks, and 7000 on incomes above 400 dollars. Aye, truly so; but twenty years since duty was also paid on 252,176 slaves belonging to this State alone. The curse has departed, and so have the blessings. The slaves are gone, and so is the land, and the fatness thereof.

On the table-land, and in front of a little breastwork, two

soldiers were frantically waving flags of different hues and
sizes, bearing various mystical devices. There being nothing
politically pressing on hand, they were signalling our safe
arrival at Poney Mountain ; and anon came an answer from
head-quarters to say that dinner would be ready at six
o'clock. Under the look-out scaffold there was a little
sheeting run up, occupied by the signal officer and his young
and pretty wife. Poor little woman ! There she sat and did
her sewing, and read novels. She must have loved her
husband very dearly, for she had turned a deaf ear to all
persuasions to live at Culpepper, and persisted in coming to
dwell in this hole. I was permitted to take a peep at their
modest housekeeping, and saw just by the bed a great
grinning fragment of rock, which had lain there perhaps for
ages. A nice thing for a lady's little foot to light upon the
first thing on a frosty morning ! It is not always Indian
summer at the top of Poney Mountain.

The General kindly lent me his docile and sure-footed
charger to come down the mountain, and the descent of
Avernus was facile. We drove back through Culpepper to
head-quarters and dinner.

CHAPTER XIII.

THE GLORIOUS FOURTH OF JULY.

"I SHOULD advise you to go out of town on the Fourth of July," said friend A. to me. I asked him if it were customary to hang Britishers, or to parade their heads on pikes, *à la Lamballe*, through the streets on that glorious anniversary. "It isn't exactly that," he replied, "but New York is not a very pleasant place of residence on the Fourth ; and even Americans of the quieter sort are glad to clear out till the hubbub is over." Friend B., friend C., and friend D., and many others, only echoed the counsel of A. "Go to Saratoga," said one ; "Fly to Niagara," advised another ; "Delaware Gap is a nice, quiet place," hints a third ; "If I were you, I should run down to Long Branch," quoth a fourth ; "Were you ever in the White Mountains ?" asked a fifth ; and so on almost *ad infinitum.* It is best, under certain circumstances, not to listen to the advice of any one ; and, for good and sufficient reasons, I decided to remain in New York. I was confirmed, moreover, in my determination by the sagest of my acquaintances, whom I will christen Z. "Unless you run across to Canada," said he—"and, with gold at two hundred and fifty, I fancy you will hardly care about sacrificing your greenbacks to change them into sovereigns—

you might as well remain in New York as anywhere else.
They are not keeping the Fourth of July South, it is true ;
but then you can't get into Secessia without forcing the lines,
and running the risk of being caught and locked up indefi-
nitely in the Old Capitol or Fort Lafayette. I should, if I
were you, remain in New York; for, throughout the length
and breadth of the Federal States, you will find it impossible
to escape from the Fourth of July. From the remotest
village down East to the latest cleared station out West,
you will have to endure about the same sort of thing.
You had better try to live through it in West Fourteenth
Street. If you are troubled with nerves, you can stuff
your ears with cotton, or take a dose of laudanum or chlo-
roform, or shut yourself up in a back-room until the thing is
over."

But why should quiet people fear the Fourth of July?
Why should its imminence fill the minds of the most patriotic,
if they are fond of peace as well as patriotism, with a shivering kind of terror, mingled with præcordial anxiety ? Why,
on the evening of the second, which fell on a Saturday, was
there a general stampede of well-to-do merchants and store-
keepers into the country ? Why flocked the families on
board the ferryboats ?—why swarmed they on the steamers,
so as to nearly swamp them ? What induced them to brave
the heat, the dust, and the dangers of outgoing railway trains ?
Why on Fifth Avenue were so many princely mansions
barred and bolted up, with so unmistakably an out-of-town
look ? Why was the Central Park almost deserted on the
eve of the great day ? How came it about that on Sunday,

the third of July, you found the waiters at the Brevoort with
nothing to do, and could procure a table at Delmonico's
without having to wait thirty-five minutes for it ? Why, at
6·30 a.m. on the very Fourth itself did I, fanning myself at
the window after a heat-oppressed and sleepless night, see an
old gentleman, fresh-shaven, straw-hatted, linen-coated, his
travelling bag and umbrella in hand, cautiously emerge from
his front door, rapidly descend his " high stoop," and scuttle
away as quick as his legs could carry him in the direction of
Twenty-seventh Street, where there is a railway terminus?
It was a case of very close shaving—of sailing very near to
the wind. He had had important business perchance to
transact overnight—letters to write, accounts to make up—
before his Hegira ; but now he was free, and he was clearly
going out of town. The early bird picks up the worm ; and
he was safe, he thought, from the Fourth of July. Deluded
old gentleman ! He forgot the converse of the proverb. The
early worm gets picked up by the bird, and is but a fool for
his pains in early rising. A rowdy little boy, lying *perdu*
behind an acanthus on the side walk, espied this old gentleman. By his garb, the insubordinate child may have been
a member of one of the first families in Uppercrustdom ; but
on the Fourth of July all little New York boys are rowdies.
He started in pursuit of the intending traveller, and, in a
succession of lightning leaps, combining the velocity of the
springbok with the muscular agility of the cat-a-mountain, he
speedily was at his heels. Little knew the old gentleman
whose fearsome trail it was upon the war-path, and how soon
his venerable kibes were to be galled. Fly, ancient man !

Run for thy life! for the Mohawk is upon thee. Too late! too late! The arm of the youthful rowdy was raised on high. The missile flew from his paw. *A monstrous cracker hit the old gentleman just between the coat-tails*, and, rebounding, exploded on the pavement with dreadful noise and sickening stench. He, with hideous howl, fled, knowing the foe was upon him ; but the signal was responded to. From round innumerable corners darted cohorts of little rowdy fiends, and bang! bang! whiz! whiz! the Eumenides in the shape of crackers pursued the venerable man right up the Avenue and into Madison Square, where he must have either bolted into the bar of the Fifth Avenue Hotel, or paid a hack-driver five dollars and a half to convey him to Twenty-seventh Street.

There you have the Fourth of July in a nut-shell. It has come to mean this : simply crackers. You may throw in as many skyrockets, Catherine-wheels, torpedoes, squibs, catamarans, *frictions brandels*, and Roman candles as you like ; but the Fourth is best generically typified by the cracker. How many millions of these combustibles are sold every year about this time I have not the slightest notion, but the consumption must be tremendous. The tons of gunpowder which are wasted would be much better employed, one might fancy—if gunpowder, that real " devil's dust," can ever be well employed—in blowing the Confederates to atoms ; but, as the Northerners prefer to blow themselves up instead, there is no more, I suppose, to be said on the question. It is held as an axiom in this country that you have no right to assume yourself to be in danger from a house in your neighbourhood being on fire until the wall of your room is so hot as to scorch your hand. By a parity of reasoning, you have no call to complain of the crackers until one frightens your horse so that he shies and throws you, or until another puts your eye out. What right have you to grumble? In some of the non-fashionable wards of the city a cheerful practice prevails of placing at the street corner a barrel full of squibs, crackers, loose cartridges, and broken bottles. A train is then laid, and fired at a convenient distance. The whole mass flies up into the air, and the fragments of broken glass go whirring about in all directions. If anybody is hurt, so much the worse for him. This is a land of liberty. Then, again, when gunpowder is scarce, the rowdies collect heaps of shavings and waste timber on the edge of the pavement, and set fire to the mass. In England we kindle our bonfires at night, and in deserted places, and that even very rarely. The Americans prefer to illumine their joyful pyres at broad noon-day, and in crowded thoroughfares. On the Saturday preceding this Fourth of July, a charming little girl coming home from school, where she had just won a prize, and had been promised promotion into a higher class, incautiously approached one of these bonfires. Her light clothing caught fire; she was soon a mass of flames; and she died next day from the frightful injuries she received. We manage these things differently in England. What a pother we make when a ballet girl is burnt to death! How the nation bewails another victim to crinoline! How eloquently we talk about the fiery Moloch of Vanity! How sternly the putting down of the 5th of November ruffians at Guildford was insisted upon! How sharply the police magistrates punish the boys who are bold enough to let off fireworks on Guy Fawkes night! These restrictions, I shall be told, would never do in the United States. In other countries the discharge of fire-arms—sometimes loaded, in order that they may make a greater noise—is a grave offence. Here, on the doorsteps of fashionable mansions, you see boys, lads, and young men, standing from sunrise to sunset, and long after that, blazing away with pistols, fowling-pieces, and even small cannon; while Paterfamilias and Materfamilias, and all the young ladies, look from the parlour window and grin approvingly. Often the head of the house is good enough to come to the door and help to prime and load the artillery. I have heard of a gentleman residing at Staten Island who took home last Saturday night a hundred dollars' worth of squibs and crackers to his olive-branches. I have heard (although the *Philadelphia Press* may deny the fact, and dub me a malignant Munchausen for repeating the rumour) of an old gentleman at Washington who spends the entire Fourth of July on his doorstep. He sits on a rocking-chair, between two brass cannons, which he continually discharges in honour of the day, his negro boy bringing him ammunition and helping him to load. Between every three or four rounds or so he refreshes himself with a cocktail; and this merry pastime goes on until the cannons become red-hot, or the old gentleman gets " tight," when he is carried to bed and the guns are dragged to the stable.

And why not? This is a free country, is it not? None but the slaves of effete oligarchies are bound to submit to nonsensical municipal ordinances. Precisely so; only the question resolves itself into this. Is it worth while to mar the peace and quietude of a city containing one million of inhabitants—to render it for twenty-four, and often forty-eight, hours in every year, uninhabitable by and intolerable to decent people—to kindle dozens of conflagrations, and sacrifice scores of human lives, merely for the sake of making a noise and a stench? · In recounting the success of the first volume of the "Cornhill Magazine," the editor, quoting from a hand-book of Roman Antiquities, told his readers that it was customary with conquerors, on the day of their triumph, to paint themselves a bright scarlet, and sacrifice certain human victims to the gods; but he added that on the present occasion he proposed to dispense with both these ceremonies. Is it absolutely necessary for the anniversary of American independence to be celebrated by burning down houses and mutilating and slaying human beings? Is there no other way of expressing one's patriotic feelings? Why not send up · five hundred balloons, duly decorated with the stars and stripes? Why not illuminate the city at night? Gas is plentiful enough; iron is to be had; petroleum is cheap; coloured glass is abundant; "fifty thousand additional lamps" might be easily procured; but from one end to the other of Broadway not a gas star or a wreath—not so much as "our banner" even made out in gas-jets—is to be seen on the evening of the Fourth. The only real illuminations, as we understand them, I have hitherto seen in New York are at a certain Museum—not Barnum's, which is amusing and inno-cent—where the filthiest anatomical models are exhibited by

a gang of impudent quacks for the worst of purposes. This
bestial hole blazes every night with gas devices.

The partiality of the American people for noisy pyro-
technics—a partiality, by the way, which they share with the
Chinese—may be traced to two causes : *the lingering presence
of barbarism in the land, and the inherent childishness of
the people.* They are doing exactly in 1864 that which we
used to do in 1664. Mr. Pepys's Diary is full of accounts of
bonfires at the street corners, of " powder noises " and " brim-
stone pastimes." In Old England, as we all know, the amusements of the people were marked, two hundred years since,
by a great deal of roughness and brutality. Remnants of
brutal roughness are yet to be found in our sports ; but they
are confined to the very lowest of the mob, and we don't let
off crackers in Regent-street on Christmas-day, nor light
bonfires in Piccadilly on Easter Monday. Now, we will take
the last of our two predisposing causes first. With regard to
the childishness of the people—a childishness that would be
droll were it not frequently painful—it reaches an extent
absolutely incredible to those who have never visited the
United States. They play at law, religion, government, education, physic, and science. The children are the most precocious
in the world ; but the grown men and women, with all their un-
deniable smartness and cleverness, are in many respects the
biggest babies I ever saw or knew. I would scorn to instance
the fondness of the ladies for sugar-candy, and the *penchant*
of the gentlemen for whittling, as proofs of their puerility.
These are trifles. I am alluding to the childishness of their
minds. The better class, the cultivated class, the travelled

class of Americans themselves, tacitly admit this when they say, with a smile and a shrug, on some particularly outrageous piece of absurdity becoming the popular rage, "Oh, this kind of thing tickles our folks." But my complaint against the cultivated and travelled men of America is that they never strive to laugh, or to frown, or to scold their "folks" out of the silly ways that tickle them so; and that, instead, they stoop to pander to and to pamper their foibles and their caprices. Whence this childishness springs it is not easy to say. Certainly not from want of intelligence; a keener, brighter, more ingenious people than this never lived. As certainly not from want of education, for here the very meanest are educated after a fashion; the newsboy knows quite as much about the leading articles in the paper he is selling as does the purchaser when he has read them; and the hack-driver, waiting for a fare, squats down on the step of his vehicle, and buries himself in the perusal of the *Police Gazette* or the *New York Ledger*. And yet, with all this, they are the veriest children alive. Not a lying rumour floats but they catch at it; not a bogus tale is told them but they credit it; not a slavering compliment is paid to them but they swallow it. Not a stricture, however good-natured, is passed on their naughtiness, but they strive to bite, to kick, or to rend their censor. They are children in their vapours and tempers; in their sudden rages and as sudden reconciliations; in their addictedness to over-eating themselves and being sick the next morning; in their tendency to petty boasting and their proneness to telling fibs; in their absence of shame and shortness of memory; *in their many generous*

*impulses, their genuine warmth of heart, their frank and
engaging simplicity, their open-handed liberality, their utter
incapacity for logical reasoning, their gratitude to those who
have been kind to them, and their incorrigible perversity.*
This may seem a bundle of paradoxes, but it is the American
character. The indifference to life which prevails among
them, their recklessness, their laughing disregard of certain
danger and possible destruction—what are all these but
childish traits, beautiful and admirable in infancy, but
disastrous and deplorable in a people who have won their
manhood's spurs on a hundred famous battlefields, and have
done in their time deeds of the truest nobility and worth?

In this Fourth of July morning's issue of the *New York
Tribune,* that red-hot organ of ultra philanthropy,—which is
nevertheless to be respected for the sincerity of its principles
and the personal character of its conductor,—you may see a
vilely executed woodcut, purporting to represent " the late
pirate 'Alabama.'" It is just such a kind of engraving as
Seven Dials will furnish at two hours' notice, and at half-a-
crown outlay, to head a broadside of the last dying speech
and confession of a murderer, or the narrative of " the
lamentable affair between a lady of fashion in Brompton
Square and a distinguished member of the H—e of L—ds."
In England, servant-maids and costermongers buy these
catchpennies as they are howled round the streets at night
by the " death and fire hunters." Here the *New York
Tribune* goes into the most pious and moral families. What
is this but mere barbarous childishness? What would be
thought of a grave London newspaper if it came out some

morning with a view of Copenhagen or a portrait of Field-Marshal Wrangel on the front page? New York cannot plead in such an issue that this woodchopper's caricature is the best it can give. There are numbers of first-rate engravers in the States, and in New York city alone there are not less than four special illustrated papers, which all seem to sell and to pay well.

But Barbarism! I see the American fist clenched; I see its eye flash; I hear its teeth gnashing, as I dare to utter the word. "The insolent hound!" the "depraved villain," the "ungrateful cuss," I seem to hear Columbia yell. The word was Barbarism. I repeat it. *Barbarism, in a thousand details of daily life, may be found in this country side by side with the most elaborate and luxurious civilisation in the world.* You know it, dweller in the Fifth Avenue, with your trotting horses, your gallery of Frères, and Meissonniers, and Courbets, your villa on the Hudson, your tapestried dining-room, your yacht at Islip, your library of Elzevirs and Plantins, your egg-shell and *bleu du roi* porcelain, your engravings after Mark Antonio and Raphael Morghen, your box at the Academy, your drawers full of coins of the Twelve Cæsars, your eighteen-hundred dollar pianoforte, and your Danish dog trotting behind your carriage. You know it in your heart of hearts, although you curse a foreigner for telling you the truth. The cause is obvious. The civilisation has been sudden—imported in a hurry, unpacked, duty paid upon it, and carted away up town. Nothing has grown—nothing has gone through gradation of development. Europe has been to America as that which Jove's head was in the case of Minerva; and from the teeming brain of the old

world civilisation has started up, armed at all points, and
swooped down on the States. But it has not entirely jostled
barbarism out of the way. In Russia you see two civilisations
side by side—the old Oriental and the new Parisian ; the
Arabian Nights rub shoulders with the Rue de Rivoli. But
here all that is polished is new, and what is old is simply
savage. A marble palace, seven stories high, and beside it a
livery stable, and next to that a log cabin ; a lodging-house,
with grand pianofortes and Venice mirrors in every room,
and an Irish " help " who, when you put your boots out to be
blacked, smears them with lard ; all is abrupt and violent
transition. Your landlady wears diamond rings, laces herself
tightly, and carries a parasol with a gold handle, and spends
four months out of the twelve between Newport and Saratoga;
but the washing is done at home, and the rose-bushes in the
garden are covered with chemises and pantalettes. Go out
of town, and you step at once from the Sybaritic luxury of
Delmonico's and the Maison Dorée to a horribly coarse mess
of pork and beans, with a two-pronged fork to aid you in
devouring them; you leave your hotel bed-room, with its
bath and hot and cold water laid on, for some hovel in the
wilderness, where you are bidden to sleep with a drunken
" shyster " who goes to bed in his boots, or to make one of a
" camp " of travellers who pig in one room together, twenty
strong.* But the civilisation is all here, nevertheless. You

---

* A Western gentleman told me not long since a story amusingly illus-
trative of the pleasures of double-beddedness. A very dirty and greasy
foreigner, with a beard that Julian the Apostate might have envied, so long
and lively-looking was it, arrived at an hotel at Detroit, entered his name on
the books as Ivan Somethingoff, hailing from St. Petersburg, and demanded

have only to go to the great cities for it. The walls and ceilings of private houses are painted in fresco by the best German and Italian artists, in a manner which only the proprietors of palaces could afford in Europe; but the marble corridors of the hotels are the veriest Augean stables of tobacco juice. In the ladies' drawing-room of one of the handsomest hotels in New York I marked the other day *a porcelain spittoon,* royal purple, picked out with gold. I think it would be difficult to find a more striking instance of extremes meeting—of a brass knocker on a pigsty door.

The truth would seem to be that, although the pushing Yankee has gradually ground the aboriginal Red Man to the wall, or crowded him out of his confines—although to find the " noble savage" you must explore the fringes of the Far Western prairies, or grope among the scarps of the Rocky Mountains—the Savage Spirit, unseen but not unfelt, haunts the Aladdin's palaces of the New World. There he is, that " Salvage Man," squatting on his haunches at the door of his shadowy wigwam. There he is, with his moccasins and his tomahawk, his war-paint and his wampum belt, puffing at his calumet, and watching the white man's devices. At the two " Dead Rabbits" striving to gouge each

---

sleeping accommodation. The hotel was full, and the Muscovite looked so very uncleanly and wore a sheepskin pelisse of so very loud an odour, that the guests unanimously and indignantly refused to have him billeted upon them. The hotel clerk, not wishing to lose a customer, was in despair, when a tall, bony Western man stepped forward, dashed his fist on the counter, and exclaimed: " H——! it's risky, I know, but I'll try him. *I never did ' room' with a Rooshian before, and I'd like to know them stript.*" A remarkable instance this of the pursuit of knowledge under difficulties, and the American characteristic of " wanting to know."

other at a grog-shop bar—at the United States' Senator
starting up at an hotel *table d'hôte* and striving to brain his
fellow-legislator with the water-jug—at the "Medicine Man,"
the priest of Religion, who joins in the war-dance, and yelps
to be allowed to seethe his hands in the bowels of his foes, if
he could—at the General who gets "whipped" by the hostile
tribe, because at the moment of the assault he was over-
taken in "fire-water"—at all these things the Savage Spirit
must look on thoughtfully, if not admiringly.

Meanwhile, the Fourth of July is waiting for me. I have
before remarked on the American habit of early rising. They
seem, these restless kinsmen of ours, to be abroad, and the
stores are in "full blast," almost so soon as it is daylight ; and
as American gentlemen of a convivial turn are much given
to singing "John Brown's bones are mouldering in the
grave," or "We'll hang Jeff. Davis on a sour-apple tree,"
until five in the morning, I have often wondered whether the
New Yorkers ever go to bed at all. While I was dressing,
and before it had struck seven, I heard the *fanfares* of martial music, and hastened to the window of the front room
giving on West Fourteenth-street, which crosses Fifth-avenue
at right angles. I was just in time to see the Eighth Regiment of New York State Infantry go by. These, I apprehend, were militia. The men were exceedingly clean, and
well set up—qualities which the "blue-bellies," or volunteers
on active service, and enlisted men, have not the time to
acquire ; but they do not fight the worse for being dirty and
dishevelled. The flags, too, looked quite bright and genteel ;
and the officers, some of whom were tremendous swells,

mounted on well-groomed horses, suggestive of up-town livery stables, and two dollars and a half an hour, wore, instead of shoulder-straps, the loose bullion epaulettes of cauliflower size in which the American civilian-soldiers were wont, previous to the war and the rise in the price of gold lace, to delight. Swords too, of somewhat theatrical pattern and excessive ornamentation, glanced in the sunshine; but against the thoroughly soldier-like appearance of the rank and file there was not one word to be urged. By-and-by came another regiment, and then another, and then several squadrons of cavalry. There was to be a dress parade of the First Division of New York Militia, this morning, and infantry and cavalry presently formed in line in Fourteenth-street —one wing resting on Delmonico's, and the other I am sure I don't know where, unless on the Fire Tower in Sixth-avenue. I went down into the street, and had a look at the dragoons. There was a "Lumber troop" air about them not to be disguised. There was the short fat trooper, and the long lean trooper—the trooper who bestrided his horse like a pair of compasses or a miller's sack, and the trooper who was perched on his saddle with his knees reaching to his chin, like a monkey in a circus; there was the trooper who *would* wear spectacles; the careless trooper, who had come to parade in a wide-awake hat instead of a busby; and the epicurean trooper, whose holsters were stuffed with the good things of this life. And all these bold dragoons cut their hair and trimmed their beards, or *didn't* cut or trim either, precisely as they "dam pleased." Probably not a strap, nor a buckle, nor a hook, nor a button, in the whole of this mounted array, was in its proper place; but the men were athletic fellows, mounted on stout and serviceable nags, and looked as though they had plenty of fight in them. It is possible, I need scarcely hint, to carry military dandyism to too great an extent. I remember the landlady of a house in London, where a party of soldiers who had been sent up to town to attend the funeral of the great Duke of Wellington in 1852 were billeted, telling me that her guests had borrowed a pair of scissors of her in the morning *to clip and trim the down on the tufts which surmounted their shakoes;* and among the brave grenadiers we sent out to America in '76, to fight the rebels, but who failed in beating them, there must have been many who couldn't shut their eyes owing to their pig-tails being so tightly tied, and who suffered from chronic rheumatism from the continual presence of damp pipeclay on their small-clothes.

Behind and in front of these civic warriors, who, standing or sitting at ease, were smoking or taking "a suck at the monkey" (otherwise the whisky flask), there marched another "dress parade." It is one you never fail to see at celebrations of the slightest claims to publicity in this country. By fifties and hundreds came the young ladies in hoop skirts, lace shawls, bright-coloured dresses, with parasols, and streaming "cataract curls," or preposterously-bulging back hair; and their beaux, the young gentlemen in light suits, straw hats, eye-glasses, and turn-down collars. The beaux and the belles don't walk arm and arm unless they are engaged; and this state of semi-companionship gives the parading couples an odd and almost melancholy appearance. They always remind

me of the phantoms pacing to and fro in the Hall of Eblis in
" Vathek." They don't talk much. Now and then you hear
a " Yes, indeed," or an " Oh, mayeigh ! " or a " I tell yeou," or
a " That's so "—but *not* a "do tell," or a "quit now, Mr.
Jones ;" those are Trollopisms—and, if they ever existed, have
for a long time been " played out." But as the ladies are in
general somewhat too much given to biting their pretty lips
—they have very pretty lips, but not pretty teeth ; they
spoil them with candy and hot-bread eating and iced-water
drinking—and as the gentlemen have often " that within that
passeth show," to wit, a " chaw " of tobacco : all this is not
very conducive to volubility in conversation. Wherever you
go you see these dress parades. At strawberry festivals and
sanitary fairs,—I went to a fancy fair, in aid of the funds of a
Baptist church last winter, where no " grab-bags" or lotteries
were allowed, but where there was a hot turkey supper and
oyster soup enough to wake up the late Mr. Dando from his
tomb,—on steamboats, and on fashionable promenades, the
procession of taciturn phantoms in showy dresses haunts you.
When the dress parade takes place indoors, say at the
" exercises " of a college, or the exhibition of a school of design, the ladies take off their bonnets and display low corsages
and redundant chemisettes, after the manner of the female
choristers in the opera of the " Sonnambula," and then there
is sure to be a brass band somewhere in the distance bleating
out the waltz from " Faust." To a citizen of the world who
has been used to mark the jovial, rollicking, downwright
working exercise of the cliff at Brighton, the cheerful strolling
of Kensington Gardens or the Serpentine banks, the frolic-

some promenading of Regent Street, the airy giggling and
flirtation of the Boulevards and the Tuileries gardens, the fan-
play and Manilla-gymnastics of the Spanish alamedas and
paseos, and the languorous but delightful dilly-dallying of the
Italian corsos, these solemn dress parades of our cousins
appear slightly monotonous, slightly wearisome. Did you
ever have the blues for twelve months together? I have.
The dress parades make me melancholy, because the people
all seem to be under constraint, and to be glancing furtively
towards some, to me, invisible master of the ceremonies, who
is crying "Deportment! Deportment! Attitude! Attitude!
Shoulders, dear ladies, pray attend to your shoulders! The
eyes of Europe, the malignant, envious, oligarchical eyes of
Europe are upon you." Well-dressed society in the United
States always gives me the notion of a gigantic conversazione
—a place where people go to stare, and look embarrassed
and pompous, and do everything but converse. There is a
refreshment buffet for the ladies, and a bar for the gentlemen; and it is but just to admit that when the latter
are "tight" they are very good company and capital
fellows.

They tell me there was a "difficulty" with some of the
regimental brass bands this morning. The drums and fifes
were staunch enough—I can conceive the possibility of a man
playing the drum for nothing; it produces such a thundering
uproar, and, with a very slight stretch of imagination, you
may fancy that you are drubbing an enemy—but the trom-
bones and trumpeters, being mostly Germans, were mercenary,
and refused to blow "ary toot" before they were paid. The

public organisations of New York are continually having money "difficulties" with their employés. Now it is the Park labourers who can't get their wages, and now the Municipality refuse to pay the street-sweepers. The refractory musicians, however, consented to a compromise on the payment of their bills being guaranteed by the commanding officers; and, matters being thus arranged, the waltz from "Faust," interspersed with "Yankee Doodle" and "Hail Columbia," went on in grand style, with a *staccato* accompaniment of squibs and crackers from the door-steps.

After breakfasting to the sound of squibs, and reading the newspapers to an accompaniment of crackers, I went down with an esteemed American friend to witness the Grand Democratic Fourth of July "Pow Wow" at Tammany Hall.

To give you some faint idea of what the society of St. Tammany is, or rather was, endeavour to combine a notion of the Reform Club, the Union Debating Society at Cambridge, Lodge number anything of the Manchester Union of Odd Fellows, and the Ancient Society of Cogers. Tammany Hall used to be a place not only for speechifying, for spread-eagleism, and for baiting the British Lion—not only the Hall of Debate for a numerous and powerful political party— but also a place where the most elaborate organisations were developed, and the meshes of the most complicated intrigues perfected. At Tammany Hall, Presidents, Ministers, Congressmen, foreign ambassadors, consuls, tax-collectors, and postmasters have been made and unmade. Tammany has, in its time, been a tyrant; Tammany has, in its time, revelled in the "unclean drippings" of patronage; and in Tammany

Hall and the adjacent Astor House there probably has been
fostered and carried out as monstrous a system of venality
and corruption as ever was known in this wicked world—
venality at which Robert Walpole would have rubbed his
hands; corruption that would have rejoiced the souls of
Sidmouth and Castlereagh, and the rest of the borough-
mongers.

"Tammany" is an Indian name. The officers of the
society are called "Sachems," and wear mystic badges; and
almost every man of eminence in the Democratic party has
at one period or another of his career been affiliated to Tammany Hall. It is an old organisation, dating from the very
early days of the Republic, and was first established to
counteract the influence of the Federalist or Old Whig party,
who wished to centralise power in the Government at Washington, in contradistinction to the Democrats, or followers of
Tom Jefferson, who were staunch advocates for the several
and separate sovereignty of the States. Fifty years ago the
Democrats were sympathisers with the French Revolution,
and almost Jacobins; whereas the Federalists were decidedly
Conservative and pro-Anglican in their tendencies. Do you
know that on two occasions New England—the fanatically
loyal and Unionist New England—*threatened secession from
the Union and the formation of a separate confederacy?*
Do you know that the last occasion of her thus threatening
to secede was at the famous Hartford Convention, held during
the war of 1812-14, to which war New England was violently
opposed? And will you be good enough to contradict me,
and brand me as a sayer of the thing which is not, O ye

consistent New Englanders, who, in 1864, maintain that to
meditate even withdrawal from the Union is treason, and
deserving of a traitor's doom? Now, if I can make anything
out of the astounding jumble of American politics, the Conservative Federalists have become red-and-black Republicans,
anxious to abolish State rights, to strengthen the hands of
the despotism at Washington, and clamouring for war with
England; and whilom Democrats have become Conservatives,
calling for the maintenance of the constitution, and the
inviolability of the laws, and bitterly opposing the high-
handed measures of Messrs. Lincoln, Seward, and Co.

Tammany has not passed unscathed through the ordeal of
this universally upheaving war. There have been splits in
the platform and traitors in the camp. There have been
those who have refused to swallow the Tammany shibboleth
whole, and others who have pretended to swallow it, but
have rolled it as a morsel under the tongue, and then withdrawn privately and spit it out. Mozart Hall was a kind of
schism from Tammany. Then came the war, and the great
split into Peace Democrats and War Democrats. Tammany
is against arbitrary arrests, press-gagging, foreigner-kidnap-
ping, contract-jobbing, and shoddy generally; but still Tammany is all for war against the South. Perish Abraham
Lincoln, but perish Jeff Davis too, is the Sachem's creed;
and if both these aspirations are to be fulfilled, one can hardly
discover how much is expected to survive, except, perhaps,
Tammany. The brave old Wigwam still keeps its head
above water, however. Its periodical "pow-wows" are still
held, its "free lunches" still given, and it continues to be

called to order by its Grand Sachem Elijah Purdy, an old
gentleman of venerable aspect but of most valorous soul, who
has been in many a difficulty in his youth, and is popularly
known as the " War Horse of Tammany."

We rode down town two and a-half miles to the City Hall.
There were scarcely any passengers in the " stages," as the
small and very inconvenient omnibuses on Broadway are
called; but the proprietors insist on running them, and their
drivers, with the Jehus of the horse railway cars and the
hackney coaches, with the police and the bar-keepers, must
be very nearly the only New Yorkers who don't get a holiday
on the Fourth of July. The unequalled thoroughfare of
Broadway was hung from end to end with flags—the American
banner, always, but in an endless variety of sizes. Already
you have been informed that our cousins, as a rule, elect to
be alone, and make no display of the standards of other
nations. The American flag, however, when waving, or
drooping in voluminous folds, is one of the most beautiful of
insignia. Small and stiff it is exceedingly ugly, and looks
like a square piece cut out of the pantaloons of a Southern
negro.* I was astonished to see so few people in the streets.

* You will be good enough to pardon the apparent irreverence of associa-
ting American flags with the nether habiliments of mankind; but it is to a
Federal source that I am indebted for the simile. When the Federals first
occupied Baltimore, and the fair dames of Maryland used to signify their
abhorrence for their invaders by spitting on the pavement, or gathering up
their skirts, or "making a face," when they passed a Federal officer in the
street, the Yankee soldiers, unreprehended by their officers, hit upon an
ingenious, but not very delicate, device for retaliating on the Secesh ladies.
*They used to sew a small Confederate flag in the hinder part of their pan-
taloons*, and when a lady passed them they would contrive that this ensign
should be discovered after the manner of that famous patch on Mr. Buck-

Not at any point—not even at Canal Street or at the Astor House, which on ordinary week-days is well-nigh impassable —was there anything approaching a crowd in density. All the shops' shutters were shut, and in none, save the bars and the tobacconists', was there any business transacted ; but at many stores the iron door curtains were half-drawn up, disclosing the proprietor and his assistants engaged in the pursuit of happiness, by sitting in their shirt-sleeves and "taking tobacco." I have been seeking felicity for a good many years, and I am not at all certain at this date whether to take off one's coat, put up one's legs, ruminate, and spit, is not about as near an approach to happiness as can be enjoyed in this distracted orb.

Tammany Hall occupies the first-floor of the Tammany Hotel, which might have been a first-class establishment about the time when Brillat Savarin was playing the fiddle at the only New York theatre, and Irving and Paulding were gathering their first crude materials for " Salmagundi." The hotel is in a street branching off Broadway, close to the City Hall, and not far from Barnum's Museum. The bar was thronged, but not inconveniently, with those who love cocktails, and after awhile my friend, who was a Sachem, not of Tammany, but of the New York press, managed to gain the ear of one of the officials of the society, to whom I was introduced, and with whom, of course, I shook hands, and who courteously admitted us into the hall a good three-quarters of

stone's trousers in *Box and Cox*, accompanying the *exposé* by a manual gesture of derision. For the authenticity of which merry little tale, read the life of the Federal General Benjamin Franklin Butler, by the Federal gazetteer James Parton.

an hour before the public were allowed to enter. The Sachems were busily engaged in their inner wigwam initiating a novice, or burying the hatchet, or digging it up again, or scalping a traitor, I presume; and for a long time we had Tammany all to ourselves. Architecturally, there is little to be said about it. It is a wide room with a low roof, and would hold, I should say, when crammed, from 800 to 1000 people. The spectators sit on large high-backed benches, seemingly of Teutonic origin—precisely the kind of benches I remember, ever so many years since, during a run through Schleswig-Holstein, in use in the porches of the old wooden houses at Rendsburg, whither come the elders of the town at sunset to smoke their pipes and gossip. There was some attempt at Fourth of July decoration in Tammany. Over the platform you read, flamboyant on a large scroll, "THE UNION MUST AND SHALL BE PRESERVED." On the wall opposite the range of windows was a rudely-executed portrait of General Dix, with the legend, "Whoever attempts to haul down the American flag shoot him on the spot!" This famous saying or telegram of General John A. Dix has made him, next to General M'Clellan, the most popular man in New York. It is quite useless to tell an American that the locution is mere clap-trap—that every patriotic man is bound to resent, even to the death, any insult offered to the flag of his country, and that, too, without being told or tele-grammed to shoot anybody; and that, for any rational purpose, such a command as, "Whoever stutters when he reads the Declaration of Independence cut his head off," would be just as useful. But our cousins are devotedly fond of these catch-phrases, and some very brilliant reputations have been made by uttering them.

In lieu of window blinds, there floated and flapped opposite General Dix's effigy a number of rough transparencies and banners with portraits of Grant, Meade, Hancock, Wright, M'Clellan, and other noted Federal commanders, which had doubtless seen good service in out-door processions. They were the sort of banners that Odd Fellows, Druids, and Foresters display at their annual gatherings—in intention admirable; in execution, wretched. Each portrait had from four to six lines of doggerel beneath it, implying that each particular general was about the biggest hero on record, and that the rebels were by this time pretty well " played out." In the corner of each banner I noticed that the Dick Tinto, who had produced the work, had, discreetly, and with an eye to business, inscribed his name and address at full length. Dick Tinto, forsooth ! The sign and banner painters at New York are business firms, and form a powerful corporation. A " boss sign-painter " is " some punkins." As for putting the name on the banners, don't the undertakers put their names and addresses on the coffins they make, and the manufacturers of artificial limbs on their cork legs and willow arms ?

I was glad to see that Tammany had deviated a little from that egotistical rule about flags which I noticed down in Broadway and elsewhere, and that here some international feeling was absolutely displayed in the shape of the French tricolor, and, yes, the British Union Jack, blended with the stars and stripes. Bravo, Tammany !

I looked from the open window on to the Old Park, which must have been at one time a pretty place enough, but which is now half built over with rows of whitewashed wooden barracks for soldiers, and disfigured by enlistment huts and rendezvous tents for the army and navy. The grass is cut up and trampled down, but the entire area is not out of keeping with the edifice in its front, the City Hall, one of the meanest edifices for its place and its purpose to be found on the American continent. The façade is of inferior marble, and the body of the building of brown stone. Altogether it is not a tithe so handsome as the State House at Boston, which is admirably situated, and which, were its yellow-daubed dome only gilt, à la Russe, would be a very imposing structure. But I am not about to lay the faults of the New York City Hall at the doors of the Yankees. Those faults are chargeable to George the Fourth's pet architect, Nash; he did not build it, but the period over which he exercised so maleficent an influence did. The example of that tasteless man's most false, most vicious, and most paltry style is palpable in the bandy-legged columns, the top-heavy capitals, the splay-footed pedestals, the overloaded architraves, the squinny-eyed windows of the Manhattan Hotel de Ville. Surely, if there be an architectural Rhadamanthus in Tartarus, Nash must long since have been doomed to build perpetual stucco houses, which as soon as finished tumble down and crush him. The New York City Hall is bad Waterloo Place, than which one can scarcely imagine there could be anything worse. To be just, it must be stated that the New Yorkers have long been heartily ashamed of their Town Hall, and that they are building another, and a really sumptuous one, in its rear. For a wonder, however, on the Fourth of July the City Hall looked beautiful. It was hung from end to end with flags and streamers, and on the roof floated, side by side, the great American banner, and the standard of the State of New York—on a field argent, the two "salvage men" of Manhattan and other heraldic devices azure. The wonderfully clear blue sky, and these trophies fluttering and glittering in a delicious breeze, were enough to put the sourest critic in good temper. Again I was surprised to see no great crowd in the area. There were scattered groups; loafing, or waiting for the horse-cars to go up town, but not anywhere was there a throng. Few things struck me more forcibly than the paucity of those Bohemian industrials, those small hucksters, marchands forains, saltimbanques, and buffoons, who in Europe are afoot on every holiday. You sought in vain here for bawling costermongers and cake vendors, for tumblers and thimbleriggers, for gipsies and nigger minstrels, for girls with vesuvians, and boys to turn cart-wheels. Those impudent but diverting vagabonds are not to be found in the States. The few organ-grinders come in, as I told you, with the measuring worms, and go out with them. Both—let us thank Heaven for all things—have now disappeared. The measurers have turned to dusty millers, and the organists have migrated to Saratoga and Niagara. I trust that when Mr. Bass and Sir Robert Peel—whose jokes in the British Parliament concerning the Hundredth Psalm cannot be too highly appreciated—have succeeded in putting down organ-grinding in England, Mr. Babbage will be satisfied, and my countrymen be made good and virtuous and beautiful for ever. But I doubt it. I see before me a people destitute of outdoor amusements, ignoring the harmless tom-fool tricks and petty industries which God Almighty has suffered to be exercised on this earth thousands of years before the Babbageites called for blunderbusses to kill butter-flies withal ; I see a huge metropolis bereft of the " city's busy hum," but fraught instead with the screech of railway whistles, the jarring of car-wheels upon rails, and the yells of the stockjobbers in Wall Street. And I cannot see that they have advanced much in civilisation, in sobriety, in brotherly love, or in Christian charity, by dispensing with outdoor minstrelsy, peep-shows, dancing Highlanders, itine-rant conjurors, and learned dogs. I can scarcely hope that rowdy London will cease to get drunk, beat the police, and abuse its wife, because there are no organ-grinders left to frighten the pony of the little Belgravian lady in Mr. Leech's picture. I wonder what that pony would have felt under the influence of the Fourth of July crackers.

A few stands for the sale of effervescing sarsaparilla, sliced pine-apple, iced lemonade, and "root beer"—a beverage apparently composed of equal parts of a weak infusion of quassia and mangold wurzel—a few women offering ginger-cakes, apple-candies, fig and gum drops, and whortleberry tarts for sale, and many more boys with baskets full of cartridges and other combustibles : these were all the small industries to be seen in the park in front of the city Hall. No songs, no laughter, no lively "chaff" arose from the holiday-makers. The silence was only broken by the periodical explosion of crackers. I would have given something for a "Catch-'em-alive-O" to have come roaring down, or for an acrobat on the summit of his *perche* to have looked in at the second floor window of Tammany.

Aha! Here is something startling at last. Loafer in a red shirt, striped pants, "mudsill" boots, and slouched felt hat. Other loafer in a yellow-brown "duster" reaching to his heels, broad-brimmed straw hat, and no vest. Both heavily moustached; both very drunk. Round the first: Loafer number one heavily grassed; Loafer number two kneeling on his chest, and essaying to crack his head against the kerb-stone as though it were a cocoa-nut. Round the second: Loafer number two is up again, and has his fingers firmly twisted in Loafer number one's hair. The straw hat has been picked up by a "scallywag" boy of dishonest proclivities, who makes off with it in the direction of Chatham Street. Interregnum. Time called; but both antagonists absorbed in the contemplation of a dog-fight. Round the fourth: the combatants rolling and tumbling, clawing and biting in the dust. Divertissement: a child run over by a Fourth Avenue car. At this moment the City Hall bell begins to toll the alarm. There is a fire somewhere; the familiar "Hi-yi," and the roll of the truck hose, hand and steam engines, are heard. Loafer number two knocks down strange and innocent boy, whom he wrongfully suspects of stealing his straw hat. Strange dog comes up and bites the winning dog of the previous combat on the nose. Other fight. Foreman of the Fire Company hustles Loafer number one into the gutter for treading on the engine leather. "Git

out of them hose." Two apple-stands capsized ; apples, pea-
nuts, candy, &c., scattered about, and scrambled for by gaunt
little children ; shrieks and objurgations of infuriated Irish-
women, proprietors of the apple-stands in question. Other
drunken man appears on the scene, hitting out wildly, and
crying "Hooroar for H—, and who's afraid of fire?"
Symptoms of a free fight. Straw-hatted, linen-trousered,
and athletic policeman appears on the scene. Crowd knows
that, although he only carries a little switch in his hand, he
has a locust-club in one pocket and a revolver in the other.
Les esprits sont calmés. General reconciliation. Loafers
one and two dive down the steps of a cellar where "oysters
in every style," and "clam chowder" are advertised, there
doubtless to sign preliminaries of peace over rum. The brass
band in the balcony at Tammany strikes up the waltz from
Faust. Tableau.

I was wrong you see, and there is some holiday-life to be
seen down town on the Fourth of July. The gentleman—not
my esteemed friend, but a stranger—who sat beside me in the
balcony with his legs comfortably on the railing, was at first
much interested in the fight, and seemed disposed to back
the Loafer in the red shirt ; but, disgusted with the manifest
inebriety of that gladiator, he muttered, " Psha ! he's as tight
as a peep," and replunged into the perusal of the *World.* To
be as tight as a peep is to be very tipsy indeed.*

---

* A "Peep" is a very abject and idiotic little bird found in New England.
He is to the feathered what the "Scallywag" is to the finny creation.
Occasionally when he is caught the housewives will condescend to put him
into pies, but in general he is contemned, and "left out in the cold." He is
weak on the wing, and weaker on his legs ; and when the miserable little

The waltz, followed by a march from the *Puritani*, and some native patriotic airs, was the signal for the commencement of the "pow-wow." The doors were flung open, and a thousand people came pouring into the hall. Where they came from I do not know; but they were decidedly "on hand." There were some ladies in the throng, not young and not fashionable in appearance—comfortable, serious, Nonconformist-looking dames the rather, who looked upon a public meeting as a kind of preaching, and the proper thing to patronise when there was nothing theological in the way—but room was at once respectfully made for them; and men who had taken their seats cheerfully resigned them to the ladies. The male part of the audience seemed mainly to

---

object alights on earth, he is given to staggering about in an imbecile and helpless manner, suggesting the idea of extreme intoxication. The sharp New England mind, ever on the look-out for similes, has long since indorsed the locution "as tight as a peep," to express an utter state of tipsification. One of the best Yankee stories I ever heard is told, "in this connection," of Mr. Macready the actor. Once when the great tragedian was starring at Boston, at the Howard Athenæum I think, there happened to be in the stalls a gentleman who, like Roger the Monk, had got "excessively drunk." His behaviour at last became so scandalous that he was forcibly expelled the theatre, not, however, before he had completely spoiled the effect of the "dagger" soliloquy in *Macbeth*. Mr. Macready was furious; and, the moment the act drop had descended, indignantly demanded who was the wretched man who had thus marred the performance. "Don't distress yourself, Mr. Macready." explained the manager, "it is but an untoward accident. A little too much wine, and that sort of thing. The fact is, the gentlemen was ' as tight as a-peep.' " " Titus A. Peep !" scornfully echoed the tragedian. " I'll tell you what it is, sir. *If Mr. Titus A. Peep had misconducted himself in this gross manner in any English theatre, he would have passed the night in the station-house.*" Mr. Macready's error was excusable. He had been introduced to so many gentlemen with strings of initials to their names, that he had taken the bird meant by the management to be the name of a human being; and it must be confessed that " Titus A. Peep " *sounds* very human and very American.

be composed of decent mechanics. There were very few ferocious beards, straggling goaters, or long-haired heads visible. Shaven lips and side whiskers, such as we English wore prior to the beard mania, were prevalent. There was not one "dandy" in the entire assemblage ; nor even on the platform could you see a dozen persons whose garb denoted that they belonged to the upper classes. This was in fact and purely a people's meeting ; but almost every man I saw had a good broadcloth coat on his back and a gold watch chain at his vest. The nearest approach you could find in England to the outward aspect of this would be perhaps at a meeting of working engineers, than whom there are not to be found a body of working men more respectable or more intelligent in the whole world. From what I was told, however, the Tammany audience by no means exclusively belonged to the superior class of mechanics. They were bricklayers, tailors, shoemakers, wheelwrights, butchers— anything you like to mention ; but in this country corduroy is almost unknown, and a day labourer wears often much better clothes than a master tradesman does in England.

There were three or four policemen present, clad in the cool and sensible attire which the police commissioners of New York city have fixed upon for summer wear. A constable, I take it, is not the less efficient for the reason that in the dog-days he wears a tunic of thinner texture than his winter coat—and wears it unbuttoned, too—no waistcoat, a ribbon round his neck, linen trousers, and a broad brimmed straw hat, instead of being choked in a tight tail coat, garotted with a leathern stock, and extinguished with a heavy stove-pipe hat. Did there ever come over the ineffable mind of Scotland Yard, I wonder, anything like. a reflection that even in chilly England the thermometer sometimes stands at eighty-six in the shade. In New York within the last fortnight, it has been at ninety-nine; and numbers of persons have died in the street from apoplexy and sunstroke.

The audience was a very patient one; for although the "Exercises" were advertised to commence at one, p.m., it was twenty minutes to two ere the committee made their appearance on the platform. At length, after some mild expressions of fatigue at the delay in the shape of hand-clapping, an imposing procession swept up the middle aisle of the hall : Members of the committee, with parti-coloured ribbons and badges at their button-holes; Sachems; Grand Sachem Elijah F. Purdy, with the "cap of liberty" in red silk, and looking remarkably like the "grab bag" in a raffle, borne on a pole before him.

This was the "Order of Exercises" at the Tammany celebration : First, overture and national airs—those we had had; the Waltz, from *Faust, passim.* Next, an opening address, by the Grand Sachem Elijah F. Purdy. Subsequently a chorus, "My country, 'tis of thee," by twenty-four scholars of the public schools, led by Professor Colburn, with piano accompaniment by another professor; after which the Declaration of Independence, to be read by a brother of the society. To be followed by another chorus, "The Voice of '76." After which the oration of the day, to be spoken by Hon. A. Oakey Hall. To conclude—so far as the large hall

was concerned—with the "Star-spangled Banner," sung by
the twenty-four pupils, accompanied by the band of the
Seventh Regiment, the audience rising, and joining in the
chorus. Does it not strike you, calling a little philosophy
and a few historical reminiscences to your aid, that this
"Order of Exercises" very intimately resembles the order of
orisons in a Puritan meeting-house in the time of Oliver
Cromwell? The overture by the band, that is a voluntary.
The opening address, that is the extempore prayer from the
minister. The chorus, "My country, 'tis of thee," that is the
first hymn. The Declaration of Independence, that is the
Confession of Faith. The second chorus stands for the second hymn. Mr. Oakey Hall's oration answers for the sermon; and the "Star-spangled Banner" for the doxology.
The analogy is curiously striking. Hugh Peters or Praise-
God-Barebones could not have arranged a more orthodox
programme, and there are scores of Presbyterian churches in
this city where every Sabbath you may find the same formula applied to religious exercises as is here applied to
secular ones. The truth is, that the Americans have never
shaken off the early discipline of the Pilgrim Fathers. The
outward form still remains in nearly all their observances,
although the substance has long since departed. I went to
hear a mad spiritualist medium, one Mrs. Cora Hatch, rant
at Boston last winter. The proceedings began with a hymn;
then she pretended to pray; then there was another hymn;
and then she had a long-sustained rant. At the recent
Spiritualist Convention at New York, the "Order of Exercises" was the same. At nearly every public meeting the

speeches are interspersed with those songs, glees, and cho-
ruses, which we only indulge in at public dinners, and
which could be well spared from them. This is not convi-
viality, but a dull, dim sense of bygone ecclesiastical usance.
The platform becomes a pulpit. But then, on the other
hand, the pulpit has become a platform. I have ever had
the greatest difficulty in persuading myself that the coarse,
violent, vulgar, bearded man who occupies the rostrum in
American Dissenting churches—now spouting like an auctioneer, now like a strolling player, now lolling in an arm-
chair while the hymn is being sung—was a priest of any
creed. This, of course, arises from prejudice, and from
having been brought up in the Church of England. To prejudiced persons, the Service of the Church should be to a
certain extent a mystery, and elevated far beyond the petty
environments of daily life. Prejudiced persons look upon
the priest as a man set apart. When their priest is a funny
priest, or an abusive priest, they are apt—in their prejudices
—to look upon him not with admiration but with horror.
There is nothing mysterious about the religion of the masses
here. The "Episcopal Methodists" have "hot turkey supper
celebrations;" and the "Church of the Holy Trinity" adver-
tises a "clam-cake feast and strawberry ice cream festival."
The pulpits are draped in party flags, the preacher reeks
from last night's stump oratory, and the printer's devil is
waiting with the proof of his last political sermon to be inserted in next week's *Independent*. Everybody is familiar
with the Scriptures, and Scriptural jokes, of the most abominably blasphemous·kind, are the choicest pearls in the

garland of American humour. In fact, the money-changers
have got into the temple, and there are no means of driving
them out; but then the Priests and Levites have in their
turn gone down town, and are great in Wall-street and at
Tammany. It is the most desperate of muddles. In lay
American life there are, I dare say, numbers of men as pure
and holy as the hermits of old, and who shudder at the
derogation and degradation of the Northern American clergy,
but those whose vocation it is to be pure and holy, don't see
it. Religion becomes a trade to men who are too ignorant
to teach school, or who have not enough impudence to succeed at the bar. "Pharaoh cures wounds, and Miriam is
sold for balsam." Barnum, or Drake the bitters-man, does
not advertise more ingeniously and more enterprisingly than
the rival churches and chapels. Aaron, the patriarch, is
speculating in Harlem, and Zadok, the priest, does a good
thing in New York Central.

Grand Sachem Elijah F. Purdy's opening address was
not, oratorically speaking, a success. The good old war-horse
was wheezy, and all but inaudible. He had written out his
harangue, but the MS. had somehow become disarranged, and,
after vainly endeavouring to find the right page, he stopped
short in the midst of a most flowery sentence. I remember
once being present at dinner-time at a large lunatic asylum
in England. One of the unhappy inmates rose, not to *say*,
but to *read* grace, the form of thanksgiving being printed on
a board for that purpose. He got very well through the first
line, when, by some accident, he dropped the second and went
on with the third. A malevolent idiot who sat next him

and who knew the grace by heart, broke into a grin. In the woolgathering head of the poor fellow who was reading there was evidently a dim perception that something had gone wrong. He tried back; but he did not succeed in restoring coherence to the grace. Then his scant wits clean vanished, he lost his temper, flung the board at the head of the male-volent idiot, and, with a howl, closed with him in mortal clutch. Then the keepers dragged him away to a padded room. Now, Grand Sachem Elijah F. Purdy was in precisely the same dilemma as that luckless maniac I spoke of. It was certain that he could not find the proper place in his speech; but this wary old war-horse had all his wits about him. Blinking over his spectacles like a highly astute owl, he piped forth, "Three cheers for George B. M'Clellan!" The audience gave the three cheers and three more—the last in "tigers"—with a will. The welkin—wherever that may have been—rung; the banners shook; the transparencies tumbled; several crackers exploded, in unconscious response underneath the window, and a few doors off some lively young pianiste, who had not gone out of town for the Fourth, struck up the waltz from *Faust*. I heard that waltz whistled the other day by a juvenile criminal at the reformatory on Blackwell's Island. The weird melody seems to be the *chant du depart* of the Republic.

Then, a chorus being sung, Brother Somebody read the Declaration of Independence—a composition which, perhaps, next to Junius's letter to the King, and Johnson's letter to Chesterfield, must be regarded as the noblest in the English language. As the lecturer, in that sounding prose—prose some of the sentences in which part themselves into pure blank verse—as he rehearsed the turpitudes of the British Government, and recited the manifold misdeeds of poor dead-and-gone George the Third, I began to feel slightly uncomfortable. Had I any part, I asked myself, in taxing the American colonies without granting them representation —in sending them shiploads of tea which they did not want —in stamping their leases, dragooning them with Hessians, letting loose wild Indians upon them, burning up their apple-trees, and tearing down their fences? Did anybody in the room besides my esteemed friend know that I was a Britisher? But while these thoughts occupied my mind, another train of reflection was engrossing the audience. You know all the counts of that tremendous indictment preferred by the American people against the mad English King and his wicked advisers. As the speaker went through them, reciting how corrupt judges had been put on the bench ; how the administration of civil justice had been crushed by military tyranny ; how fraud and peculation and oppression had run riot ; how smiling provinces had been devastated and peace-able citizens despoiled ; how the public speech had been gagged and public newspapers suppressed ; how robbers and mercenaries, and savages had been sent to outrage and to slay unarmed and defenceless women and children—a broad grin broke over the countenance of the assemblage. I saw it spread and spread. The parallel was too close. The deduc-tion was no longer to be resisted. Poor old George the Third faded away into nothingness ; and a great shout arose of " Abraham the First! Abraham the First ! " The cry was

followed by others of " How are you, Shoddy ? "   " Where's
Chase ? " and " How about Welles ? "   I never saw a more
amusing example of the bolt hitting the mark that was little
meant.   Only take up the Declaration, and read it with a file
of American newspapers as a gloss, and you will find that
very nearly every arbitrary act of *malfeasance* ascribed by
the patriots of '76 to Queen Victoria's grandfather can be
charged to Our Uncle at Washington.

Another chorus—" The Voice of '76 "—which appeared to
me " slightly mixed."   For instance, one verse read :—

> Heed the boon your heroes claim ;
> Will ye dim their well-earned fame ?
> They have met the sons of shame
>   On the land and sea ?
> Let the spangled colours fly ;
> Fill with shouts the golden sky ;
> Join the nation's glorious cry,
>   Union, Victory !

Now, these are right, sound, Republican, Loyal League sentiments.   The next verse, however, seems to have been put in
by " another hand " :—·

> In the freest spot of earth
> Will ye see the freeman's hearth
> With its plenty turned to dearth ?
> " No !" cries Tammany:
> Hear the Constitution's cry ;
> Law shall reign beneath the sky;
> E'en the gentle breezes sigh,
>   " Banish Tyranny."

In another stanza the descendants of Washington were ex-
horted to " keep their press e'er free."   I don't think that the
" sons of shame "—the Southerners—have had any active

hand in gagging the press, suspending the habeas corpus, pooh-poohing the judges, proclaiming martial law, and kidnapping foreigners in the Free States of the North. The upholders of the " star-spangled banner " have done all these shameful things, and more. The poetic inconsistency of this ditty might lead to the inference that Tammany is not very certain about its policy; and, indeed, the Republicans go so far as to say that Tammany, or the War Democracy, hasn't got any policy at all.

Mr. A. Oakey Hall's oration, which I have neither space to transcribe nor to criticise in detail, was really a very powerful discourse. Mr. Hall is the District Attorney of the State of New York, a barrister of eminence, and a tried Democrat. He quoted Locke, Bacon, Algernon Sidney, Edmund Burke, and Bolingbroke—and quoted them all well. He had the courage—which to me, an Englishman assisting at an American mass meeting, was astounding—to say, that in the crown of foul weeds which posterity had placed on the brow of George III., there was at least this laurel : that he did not, when his colonies were in revolt, avail himself of the opportunity to vex and oppress his own people. This remark elicited a storm of applause and fresh cheers for General M'Clellan, groans for the President, renewed denunciations of " Shoddy," and three rousing huzzas for Lieutenant-Colonel Bowman, late military superintendent at West Point, who has recently been arbitrarily dismissed from his situation by Mr. Stanton, simply because the hated M'Clellan was permitted to deliver an oration at West Point on the erection of a monument to the officers of the regular army.

Mr. Hall said a great many bold things, too, about the
Confederates and about peace ; but he hinted that he could
say a great many more were not the fear of Fort Lafayette
before his eyes. Fort Lafayette ! An American citizen—a
denizen of the "freest spot on earth"—had to make this
confession in Tammany Hall.

I was felicitating myself when the star-spangled glorifica-
tion had been sung—and very well sung, too—that the
celebration had been brought to a close without any reference to Great Britain as she is—without the British lion
being trotted out to have his tail twisted and his whiskers
pulled. But just as the audience were departing, up jumped
Hiram Wallbridge, and began to scream. Hiram is old, and
evidently well broken to the stump. Nobody wanted to hear
him ; but he wanted to hear himself, and in his vehemence
he made others hear him. He moved a series of resolutions,
of a nature, I dare say, similar to many others that are daily
and nightly moved and carried *nem. con.*, in the Bloomingdale
Lunatic Asylum. Any interference with the domestic dissen-
sions of the Americans on the part of Great Britain was to be
immediately met by a declaration of *War*, WAR, WAR ! I
must follow Mr. Charles Reade's typographical eccentricities
in endeavouring to give you an idea of Hiram's manner. In
the next resolution, England was assured, àpropos of Mr.
Gladstone's reform speech, that the American people deeply
sympathised with them in their endeavour to free themselves
from tyranny, and gain their long withheld rights ; although
Hiram might have remembered that, if what is sauce for the
goose is sauce for the gander, America, which so bitterly

deprecates any interference with her domestic concerns on
our part, should, in common decency, refrain from interfering
in ours. But enough of Hiram Wallbridge. I left him
pumping out a quantity of vitriol about the Alabama, it
being wisely decreed that, at that moment, Hiram should
not have the slightest inkling that the Alabama had been
satisfactorily knocked to pieces by the Kearsage ten days
before ; and declining the courteous offer from a member of
the committee of a " free lunch," made the best of my way
up town again.

But, ere I bid hospitable Tammany farewell, let me say
this : A better-tempered and better-conducted audience I
never saw at any public meeting anywhere. What the
Republicans may be in a *sederunt* I cannot tell ; but the
Democrats decidedly know how to behave themselves. There
was one gentleman at the back of the hall who, suffering
from whisky in the hair, thus causing his hand to be heavier
than his hat, called incoherently for " John Brown," proposed
the health of Andrew Jackson, with other irrelevant matter ;
but he was promptly made to sit down, and was, I believe, sat
upon. Beyond this there was not the slightest rowdyism.
The services of the police were only in requisition to dis-
tribute the programmes of the " Order of Exercises " among
the audience, and they had time to listen to the speeches, in
which trustworthy municipals appeared to take a keen
delight. And, finally, I have dwelt on this meeting thus, in
perhaps wearisome detail, not only because I wished my
readers to understand something of the organisation and pro-
cedure of political parties in New York, but because on this

day the powerful and dominant Republican party made not
the slightest utterance ; and the meeting at Tammany was
the only oratorical demonstration in honour of the eighty-
eighth anniversary of American Independence in the capital
city of the commonwealth.

CHAPTER XIV.

HOW THEY FIGHT.

Is there any other country in the world but America where whole armies, tens of thousands strong, with arms, artillery, and baggage, melt away like snow in summer, like the froth from an *omelette soufflée*, or the mirage in the Gulf of Finland? The Indians discovered by Peter Wilkins flitted from China to Peru by means of "graundees;" one would think that the Transatlantic hosts were composed of nought but flying Indians. And these perpetual flank movements, this system of burning up towns as though they were wasps' nests, laying whole tracts of country waste by means of raids, and fighting at a hundred and fifty miles from one's base of supplies? Was there ever a war in which great battles were followed, as in this, by no tangible results—in which the victors are unable to pursue their routed foe, and the defeated party turns up, a fortnight afterwards, as invaders of the most aggressive order? Mr. Carlyle sometimes loses his temper with his authorities, and rates the "Prussian Dry-asdust" in unmeasured terms, because he cannot at once understand the intricacies of the Seven Years' War; but is it possible to conceive a more hopeless hash than even a contemporary Jomini, or Brialmont, or De Segur, resident in

Europe, would make of the technicalities of this struggle, or the desperate strait to which future historians will be reduced in order to give form and coherence to a narrative made up of telegrams, surmises, hopes, lies, partisan leading-articles, and events of which even those who have participated in them are impotent to give a rational and consistent account ? When Napoleon the First was urged to write his memoirs "for the sake of Posterity," he replied very coolly that what he had done he had done, and that Posterity might put what construction she chose on it, and get out of the scrape as she could. In after ages, when the history of the American War becomes a labour urgently called for by another, and, let us trust, a more pacific generation, the Federals and Confederate writers of futurity will have to agree on some common theory, purely mythical, on which they may assume facts both pro and con. And this is the way, I fancy, in which most histories have been written.

I observe that Colonel Charras, the able historian of the . campaign of 1815, has gone out to America, and visited the seat of war. If he have any intention of writing a narrative of the American War of 1860-4, I most sincerely pity him. The best thing he could do would be to buy Mr. Frank Moore's "Rebellion Record," Mr. Greely's "History of the Rebellion," and Appleton's "American Cyclopedia," and going home, trust to a lively imagination for the rest. He might not, in the end, produce a work much more apocryphal than Victor Hugo's Waterloo episode in "Les Misérables," or Sir Walter Scott's "Life of Napoleon." There is certainly something to be learnt from M'Clellan's "Report;" but that scho-

larly performance must be held as of the same family as Dr.
Newman's "Apologia ;" and is less a history than a laudably
laborious endeavour to vindicate the fame of George Buriton
M'Clellan. As to procuring any definite information from
officers in either army, the task is hopeless. You may get a
horse-shoe, but all four shoes will not give you a very tangible idea of the appearance of the horse. If even the taciturn General Grant could be induced to unbosom himself, I
don't think his communications would amount to much more
than what the Great Duke told the lady who pestered him
for an account of the battle of Waterloo : " Well, ma'am,
they pommelled us and we pommelled them." There was a
" tag," however, to this well-known reply, which the American General, perchance, might be chary of using. Another
remark of the Duke's, related in " Rogers's Table Talk,"
struck me very forcibly when I was camping down at Brandy
Station. " When at our head-quarters in Spain," once related
the Iron Duke, " —— wished to see an army, and I gave
directions that he should be conducted through ours. When
he returned, he said, ' I have seen nothing—nothing but
here and there little clusters of men in confusion—some
cooking, some washing, and some sleeping.' ' Then you have
seen an army,' I said." It took me a dozen columns to explain what the Duke of Wellington managed to make per
fectly clear in half a dozen lines. His apophthegm, however,
applies to all armies ; it would have been as true of Hannibal's as of his own ; but it would puzzle a Tacitus to give a
true description of the manner of fighting adopted by Americans. When you look into that glass case at the United

Service Institution in Whitehall-yard, and scan Captain Siborne's wonderful model of the field of Waterloo, the view, with the assistance of a handbook, and perhaps the counsel of an intelligent non-commissioned officer, will give you a tolerable idea of what a battle is really like. There is the vast champaign, there the two heights, the dale between; there Hougomont; there the Belle Alliance; there Braine-la-Leude; there the Forest of Soignies. Thence Blucher debouched; there Michaud's cuirassiers rode up to the English squares; there Picton fell. But no American officer with whom I have ever conversed could give me a succinct word-picture, much less a chart or plan, of the Battles of the Wilderness. It is all a haze, a tangle, a labyrinth, a muddle. It is like the misty chase of the characters after each other in the *Midsummer Night's Dream*, the mischievous genius of Puck setting all at cross purposes. One general has a notion that his adversary has massed large bodies of troops in a certain direction. His big guns thunder for a while in that direction, and then he hurls huge masses of his own troops against where the enemy is supposed to be.

They advance till they find the fire from the opposite but invisible side too hot for them. Then they retreat, slowly or quickly, in good or in bad order, as their pluck and stamina may be strong or feeble. As the sound of their firing grows fainter, the opposite and still invisible foe advance. The next day you read in the newspapers that the Federals drove the Confederates, or *vice versá*, three miles. "Being driven" implies the idea of one man running away as fast as his legs can carry him from the hot pursuit of another man; for

example, Horace Vernet's woodcut of Napoleon scampering
away at Toulon from an English sailor, who at last gives up
the pursuit, but bestows on him a parting lunge with his
bayonet, which wounds him in the thigh, conveys a substantial idea of "driving." But could any man, even with
half a dozen pairs of air-pumps and as many pairs of bag-
pipes for lungs, be "driven" three miles? A centipede
couldn't do it: Deerfoot would be winded at it; the steam
leg would break down at it. So is it with the colloquialism,
"The enemy were whipped handsomely." The pugilistic
gentlemen who keep the ring at prize fights manage to get
a pretty good purchase with their gutta-percha whips, and a
Cossack can reach far over the heads of a crowd with his
sinuous lash; but it is difficult to realise the possibility of
"whipping" an enemy whom you don't see, and who is but
just within rifle range. It would be quite safe to say that,
save in isolated skirmishes, the Federals and Confederates
have not crossed bayonets, nor the officers used their swords,
half a dozen times within the last four years. Indeed, the
belligerents very seldom see each other, much less look "at
the whites of their eyes." I asked an officer who had been
all through the Potomac campaigns what the Confeds were
like. "Well," he says, "I've seen plenty of them dead; but
alive and in masses, all I can say is that they have a kind of
warm dust colour." A more painful account of what civilians
imagine to be a scene of bustle, cheering, drumming, and
trumpeting, "fights for the standard" after the style of Mr.
Ansdell's picture, and hand-to-hand combats à la Coburg
melodrama, I heard from an officer who was actively engaged

in the dreadful fight of Spottsylvania Court House. All day
long the corps to which he belonged was posted on the skirts
of a wood. From hour to hour whole regiments were sent
into this wood. Reinforcement succeeded reinforcement. A
dull booming sound of cannonading never ceased ; and as the
doomed men went in fatigue parties continued to come out,
bearing shattered and mutilated forms on stretchers. Was
not this going into the jaws of Death and the mouth of Hell ?
There was no excitement, no sensational melodrama. When
your time came you went in to be killed. "And the dead in
that wood," added my informant, "have never been buried."
To have stood firm through that awful day, "waiting for
death," and calmly obeying the grim summons when it came,
argues the possession, I think, of a higher grade of personal
bravery than is displayed in rushing, amidst the applause of
one's comrades, into the embrasure of a fort, or even heading
a forlorn hope. The truth is that, since the introduction of
arms of precision and artillery of long range, fighting under
cover has become the almost invariable rule in America, as it
must become when—God avert the evil day !—war breaks out
in Europe. The slaughter, even in ambush, is frightful
enough ; but in the open—as after the explosion of the mine
at Petersburg—it would be aggravated to a perfect *battue.*
And here let it be sorrowfully noted that an illusion long
entertained by the fanatics for Peace—of whom the subscriber hopes that he is one; the humblest, but not the least
earnest—has been dispelled. It was long represented that
the perfection of offensive weapons—of Miniés, and Arm-
strongs, and Whitworths—must have a tendency gradually

but surely to discourage war; and, at last, by increasing the chances of mutual destruction in a ratio too frightful for contemplation, render war impossible, and abrogate it altogether. When each side could do no more in devising means of annihilation—when the irresistible force met the immovable body —the result was to be inertia. But the Devil is not to be so easily outflanked. His resources are infinite. In proportion as weapons are becoming more formidable, defences against them are becoming stronger. Whole fleets and armies go into panoply of proof. The loss of human life is much greater than of yore, but it is not in excess of proportion to the means of destruction brought to bear. An average army in the last generation, which, fighting a hundred miles from its base, had lost ten thousand men, was virtually ruined; but now, within a dozen hours, a dozen railway trains can reinforce it to twice the amount of its casualties. Like a witches' prayer—a saintly orison read backwards—the phenomena of modern warfare present a horrible parody of the doctrine of compensation. More men can be killed than in the old time; but more men can be procured to be killed, and they can hold out much longer before they *are* killed. Soldiers are fain to become earth-clads, as, on the ocean, sailors trust in iron-clads. Analogically, the difference is very slight between plating the sides of your ship and burrowing in the earth like a mole. Almost the first proceeding of an advancing corps is to throw up earthworks, and these, the tools being carried with them, are constructed with wonderful speed. The opposing force has done the same, and then both parties "blaze away." If one side can't stand the fire, they retire, and entrench themselves somewhere else; the other side feel their way into the abandoned pits; this is called "carrying the earthworks in gallant style." The movements of the cavalry are as mysterious as those of the infantry. The real use of the American dragoons is for the marauding expeditions known as raids. For burning houses, cutting railroads, gutting stores, and destroying crops, they are invaluable; but very little employment can be found for them in a pitched battle, and nothing is more common than to dismount them, leaving their horses picketed in charge of a few of their number, and send them into ambuscade to "blaze away." The sabre they are scarcely ever called upon to use.

I have now done my best to describe what, at the risk of paradox, I may term the indescribability of Transatlantic warfare, in which the opposing elements are not only angry and resolute men, but Dahlgrens and Parrotts, Sharp's rifles, and mounds of earth. And these elements, I apprehend, conspire to make scientific warfare more venomous and more persistent than the old hand-to-hand fighting. No little David can come out to the Philistine front to challenge Goliath of Gath to the duello. The "gentlemen of the guard" fire first, and whenever they have an opportunity, without waiting for an invitation. The slaughter of human beings has come to be a mere matter of settled calculation and mute volition. The Engineers of Murder are only called upon to make the working drawings, and draw out the specifications of bloodshed. Tinkle a bell, touch a wire, and our enemy is dead. Jean Jacques Rousseau's dream of killing the mandarin at Pekin by a simple effort of mental will is fast approaching realisation. In primitive ages the member of a community who had offended was taken without the camp, and stoned to death by his brethren. As civilisation advanced, executioners were appointed to fulfil the behests of human justice; and society saw a Sanson with his inclined plane on rollers, and Calcraft with his pinioning straps. It may be that, in the end, soldiers likewise will grow weary of performing the hangman's office, and about the time when the gallows and guillotines shall be worked by steam there may be perfected processes for destroying whole brigades by noxious gases, or razing fortresses by hydraulic pressure. Still, scientific warfare can scarcely fail to render mankind more unrelenting. Dahlgrens and Parrotts have no more conscience than corporations. They have no souls to be saved. The artillerist who pitches a shell towards where he supposes the foe to be stationed feels no personal responsibility, and may jocularly exclaim, as the dread messenger wings its way, "How are you, Secesh?" He does not see, he cannot form any notion of, the mischief he is doing. They christened one of the guns down at the Appomattox the "Petersburg Express." But a man, unless he happens to be a devil incarnate, *very soon gets tired of killing those whom he can see.* Even the surgeon who is dissecting a corpse covers up the face of his subject. Those orbs have sunk their fires into the abysm of death, but they are still human eyes. To mark the death-gaze of the slaughtered, the poor fellow who never did us any harm—to feel our feet slippery in his blood—to have his blood spurt on to our hands and his hot brains brash into our face—this kind of business very soon sickens and revolts the bravest soldier. When you have seen a few men slashed or shot to death, my Christian friend —my melodious poet, with your sing-song about the "tented field" and the "embattled strife"—my mellifluous pastor, with your eloquence about the "God of battles"—you will think as I do, and mayhap you may come to acknowledge how comparatively tender and merciful are the men in shoulder-straps whose trade it is to kill, and how often the gorge of their soul rises at their dreadful calling. Turn to the Book of Maccabees, and read that one tremendous pregnant passage—that one line : "And Nicanor lay dead in his harness." When you have seen him thus, lying stark and stiff, his brave clothes all dabbled in gore, his mouth wide open, grinning awful, the bloody foam on his lips dried into a purple crust, and the camp-follower—the Thénard of the army—creeping up to rifle his pockets, and draw off his boots, and cut off his ring-finger, and smash his jaw for the sake of the gold setting to his false teeth, you may form some ideas about the "Romance of War" very different from those you have previously entertained.

Let me not be lightly accused of irreverence if I thus from time to time quote adventures and remarks of a nature to call up a shudder in the well-regulated mind. Amidst the abuse to which, of course, as a foreigner and a journalist, I was daily and hourly subjected by the Yankee press, I once noticed lately a charge in a Philadelphia paper, that I related anecdotes which were not true. "What is truth ?" asked jesting Pilate, and would not stay for an answer. It is, indeed, a crucial task to define the scope and meaning of truth in America. I can only plead that I set down what I hear, and that I have never vouched for the authenticity of anything unless it has occurred within my own knowledge. I was quite long enough in America to be aware that perhaps the safest side to take is to believe nothing that you hear, and only half of what you see. Let me point these remarks by an illustration quoted from a verbatim report of the proceedings at the Cleveland Convention. It is clearly not my business, but that of the Americans themselves, to determine whether the reporter whom I quote told the truth or a lie, or whether there was ever any Cleveland Convention at all. Here is the story : " Some of the Fremont leaders had settled on John Cochrane as their candidate for Vice-President, with a view to aiding in their movement at Chicago. But the question was, how they should get the Germans to vote for him, who composed a large majority of the convention, but were all in favour of B. Gratz Brown, of Missouri. A few, however, of the leaders were worked for Cochrane, but they made but little head-way among the large body of the Germans. But a *providential circumstance* [*sic*] soon settled the point. The committee on resolutions brought up their report of platform ; and it was decided that the vote on each resolution should be taken separately. The first read as follows : ' Resolved—That, with God's blessing, the Federal Union must and shall be preserved.' This caused quite a sensation among the Germans, *many of whom are infidels ;* but Mr. Cochrane promptly put the question, ' All those in favour of amending the resolution *by the omission of God's blessing* say "Aye ; " all those opposed, " No." ' There was a storm of ' Ayes.' ' *God's blessing is lost,*' said Mr. Cochrane. The suddenness with which it was put, and several circumstances connected, caused quite a sensation. The moment order was restored the Germans could be heard whispering to each other, 'Dat ish de man—dat ish de man. Vat's dat he shays 'bout Gott's blessing ? Dat ish de man.' From that moment it was impossible to get the Germans to think of any other person for Vice-President than General Cochrane ; and when his name was proposed they rushed it through with a will, all owing to one trifling circumstance, *which shows how a little thing determines a man's fate in political campaigns.*" I repeat that, if this report be false, I am not responsible for the falsehood. You will remember that this was no hole-and-corner meeting, but a solemn national convention held to nominate a candidate for the chief magistracy of the republic. Is Christianity, or any other kind of religion, in a very hopeful way, I wonder, in a . country where such things as these can pass by without comment ? Assuredly William Cobbett lost his labour when he brought the bones of Tom Paine from America to England. The spirit of the atheistical staymaker still lingers here, or has been regenerated by the Germans, "many of whom are infidels."

In the placid, equable flow of English society, firmly established, equally balanced, unemotional, devout, thoroughly domestic as it is, there rarely occur those wild and almost frantic eccentricities of which every traveller, even for a few weeks resident in these States, must be perforce a spectator.

We go in England to the church of our choice, fear God, and honour the Queen, and in our innocence imagine that our cousins across the Atlantic, substituting the Union for her Majesty, are as sober and regular as we are. So they may be in isolated instances, far away from the jar and turmoil of the great cities; away from the contaminating influences of a too-suddenly developed and unhealthily redundant civilisation; away from Vanity Fair, where politics and religion are but one trade, and the mountebank puffs his quack pills with texts from the Bible. In quiet New Hampshire villages, in sequestered New Jersey hamlets, in the prim towns of Connecticut, on the snug farms of Pennsylvania, there may be households—nay, whole communities—living quiet, decent, and virtuous lives, as unconscious of the shipwreck of morals which is going on in the great sea of American life as a cottager of the Forest of Dean might be of a storm off the Goodwins. We in England hear now and then of Mormons, but their neighbourhood is so remote, their record so vague, that we regard them as mere excrescences and monstrosities of civilisation. There are Chinese opium-smoking houses in Blue Anchor Fields and Tiger Bay, are there not? but what influence have these dens on the general tenour of society? In America, unfortunately, the excrescences are manifest at your every footstep; the monstrosities surround you continually. There is a Spiritualist Convention next door; there is a Bloomer meeting over the way; your neighbour at dinner may be a Mormon; you are invited to a tea-party of Free Lovers. The shocking contempt for sacred things which an ill-regulated familiarity with the Scriptures has begotten

is visible and palpable at almost every conjuncture in
American daily life. I have striven to draw attention to
this fact in that which I wrote concerning the "exercises" at
Tammany Hall, and in a dozen places besides ; and I have
done so deliberately, not through want of reverence, *but with
a design to show that the practice of the Christian religion
on the North American continent has degenerated and dete-
riorated through the unworthiness of the ministers of that
religion—that its vital spirit has been gradually waning
during the last generation—that a nation once renowned
as confessors and almost as martyrs, and who elected to
endure exile and privation that they might keep their faith
intact, have as a body either sunk into scepticism, or
retained of religion only its worst features, its forms and
simulacra—and that active and earnest Christianity has
become practically a failure among twenty-two millions of
people who contemn its charitable and merciful doctrines,
and have for four years abandoned themselves, with scarcely*
*a dissenting voice,—meeting remonstrance with curses, and
with no stronger apology than that political dominion is
superior to the Gospel,—to an unbridled lust for rapine
and slaughter.* I may offend hundreds on both sides of the
Atlantic by what I have written ; but a time is surely approaching when plain things must be stated in a plain
manner. Dozens of the steeples of the churches in New
York are surmounted by a flagstaff whence, when victory
crowns the arms of the republic, the Stars and Stripes flaunt
forth. In that you may behold the question I have raised
brought to its narrowest issue. The Stars and Stripes are

above the Cross. The Americans claim to be a religious people; but they plead that patriotism is a sacred duty. May I ask, calmly and dispassionately, whether patriotism, according to the American acceptation of the term, is not a potent, arrogant, insatiate desire that the United States of North America should be a republic so vast in her territory, so powerful by her population, her wealth, and her industry, as to command the respect and fear of the rest of the world; and whether patriotism of this kind is not, after all, only so much collective selfishness and corporate vanity? Religion is all very well in times of peace, but when patriotism is concerned religion must go to the wall. Hypocrisy, however, or a wish to "keep up appearances," is not deemed incompatible with patriotism, else patriots would have the honesty, as the revolutionists of '90 had, to shut up the churches and abolish religion altogether. But do not lose sight of this reservation: patriotism, in its modern sense, may have very little to do with love of country. The men of '76 were really pure and disinterested patriots, attached to the soil on which they were born, fighting for their actual hearths and homes against that which they conceived to be the unjustifiable tyranny of George III. But there can be very little sentimental attachment to the soil in the patriotism of '64. If there be any " sacred soil " in dispute, it must be that for which the South are grimly fighting; for they were born and bred on it, and it belonged to their great-great-grandfathers. Of the patriots who are fighting on the side of the North many thousands are not Americans at all; they are aliens who have sold themselves for certain sums of money. Of the great body of the public who support the war, not only thousands, but millions, are born Irishmen and Germans. New York is, in population, the fourth German city in the world. The swarms of republican aliens settled here, and who are more furious against the South than the native Americans, may be patriots, but they are surely not "lovers of their country." They have only become citizens of this once free republic since the day before yesterday, and they have abandoned their own countries to take care of themselves. Converts are always more bigoted than those to the manner born of a creed, and to the Irish and German patriots their adopted country may have greater charms than those which they have deserted; the honest and naked truth being, however, that Irish and German patriotism means simply so much satisfaction at being in a land where work is plentiful, wages good, and provisions abundant, and where the very lowest of the population has a chance of rising to political power and place—mingled with a rankling spite against their old homes in Europe, and a subdued desire to bully and overawe the Government under which they were hardly worked, poorly paid, and shut out, through the existence of a long established aristocratic or governing class, from political advancement. You may hear a good deal of nonsense talked from time to time about the Fenian brotherhood; and, let me tell you, *that* nonsense is, like most nonsense when properly read, as full of instruction as a sermon, or as a paper read at the Meeting of the British Association at Bath. There was a fancy fair held by that chivalrous order at Chicago in the summer of '64. The catalogue of articles donated by enthusiastic Fenian sym-

pathisers was one of the funniest I ever read. Item, there
were two photographs of the Venerable Archbishop M'Hale;
a moiré antique gent's vest; a piece of Lord Edward Fitz-
gerald's coffin; an Irish MS.; a few numbers of "Punch;"
several Ninety-eight pikes and shillelaghs; a bog-oak
négligé; a jar of whisky that had never paid duty—by
cock and pye, it would have to pay duty, and a swingeing
excise too, to the U.S. Government!—the stone on which
Sarsfield signed the violated treaty; a doll dressed to represent a Tipperary man's "dark-eyed Mary;" a sod from the
grave of Theobald Wolfe Tone; a pair of lady's boots
worked with a '98 pike; a portrait of Emmett, "in one
of his pensive moods;" a Scottish claymore, taken at
Wexford; a watch-pocket, "worked by a lady who hopes
it will be worn next to a manly heart;" "A Bird's-eye view
of the Protestant Reformation;" a pair of pink cork-soled
slippers; a gross of pins, manufactured expressly for the fair;
a portrait of St. Patrick; a crowbar, used by the Crowbar
Brigade in '46-7; and a "curious bone, discovered on the
island of Inchidonig." Next to the "cook's drawer" of
Thomas Hood, the Fenian collection must have been about
the queerest *omnium gatherum* ever brought together. Now,
I don't think these Fenians will do much harm to the Saxon
domination, or that the majority of the Celts who come to
this country trouble themselves much more about the emancipation of the Green Isle from British rule, than the great
body of the Teutons trouble themselves about German unity
or the creation of a Federal fleet. Patriotism and love of
country are—if the whole truth must out—only questions of

nomenclature. The supremely governing power in the human mind is selfishness, and nine hundred and ninety-nine patriots out of a thousand love that country the best where they can make the most money, and do the most harm to those whom they hate.

CHAPTER XV.

I HAVE somewhere seen it remarked that Ireland would be a very nice country if they would only sweep it out, and make the beds about once a fortnight. So, likewise, would New York be one of the most magnificent cities in the world, if the authorities would only take the trouble to put its streets in some kind of decent order. It may without exaggeration be said that, with the exception of Broadway and Fifth Avenue—and they even are not wholly immaculate—there is no single thoroughfare in New York which does not most strongly and offensively remind the foreigner equally of Seven Dials, London, the Coomb in Dublin, and the Judegasse in Frankfort-on-the-Maine. This is surely not a political question. I may bring forward the expediency of drainage and the unsightliness of openly-displayed offal without becoming amenable to the charge of libelling the Americans and wilfully misrepresenting their institutions. My strictures are addressed simply to "whom they may concern," for I am not aware at whose door precisely the responsibility of the Empire City's sanitary shortcomings may lie. I merely argue on what my own eyes and nose have taught me at every hour of the day and night. There is, I suppose, some kind of "Ædility" here. There is a mayor; I have been introduced to him, and a very worthy soul he seemed to be. There is also, I presume, a board of aldermen, to assist Mr. Godfrey Gunther in his municipal duties. There is, I know, a board of councilmen. There are also, I should imagine, paving and lighting boards, district surveyors under Building Acts, and commissioners of police, nuisances, markets, and health. It is singular, if this city of over a million souls be indeed provided with all these "Ædiles," that the streets should be in so very disgraceful a state. They cannot, it is true, be termed dirty in the active or moist signification of the term. Dirty is not precisely the word—they are more and less than dirty. In summer time there is scarcely any mud in New York, for the reason that the streets are rarely if ever watered, that it seldom rains, and that the power of the sun is so tremendous that any deposit of liquid formed on the roadway is almost instantaneously dried up to an impalpable powder, and in the form of dust careers from north to south, and from east to west, in wild simooms, or wafts itself down your throat, and settles on your lungs, and chokes up the pores of your skin. Mr. Mechi would not do much with his liquid-manure process on the island of Manhattan. The sun would so fry and dry him up as speedily to drive him to desperation. But dry dirt may become as intolerable as wet. The uncleanliness of New York is best expressed by a word inelegant in itself, but suggestive to all observant housewives of a very pregnant meaning—that of "Muck." The inhabitants of every street, with the two exceptions I have named, seem to revel in a perpetual licence to shoot rubbish wherever they like. Muck, garbage, offal meet the eye at every turn. In front of the nicest houses you see barrels full of kag-mag sweltering in the sun. If an Irish "help" has a pail of slops which weighs heavy on her mind, she comes to the brink of the kerb and empties the pail into the gutter. The best streets wear an aspect of incurable untidiness. Nearly all the washing seems to be done at home, and groves of under-linen compete with the Stars and Stripes of the National Banner for the honour of fluttering in the breeze. In con-sideration of the sultriness of the weather, the natives are much given to sitting on their doorsteps ; whilst the attire of the industrial class of the female population is, to use the mildest term, slatternly ; and their children are, as a rule, destitute of shoes and stockings. The cotton "uglies" worn by these barefooted young patriots to shield them from the sun, give them an indescribably savage and Bosjesman-like aspect ; nor are the pastimes in which they indulge of a nature to awaken confidence in the mind of the passing stranger. At him they hurl, by way of salute, the pretty but spiky clam-shell. For him they lay the artfully-devised pit-fall, made of brickbats and faggots of kindling-wood, and, should he chance to tumble over it, yell with derisive delight ; or round him they slowly circle, while, to measured tread and guttural strain, they intone a hideous *lied*, in bastard German, beginning "*Johnny Schmoker, Johnny Schmoker, Ich kann spielen: Mein toodlesack, mein bimbom,*" and so forth ; the whole winding up with an unearthly whoop, supposed to represent the *fanfare* of

musical instruments. "They have the Pyrrhic dance as yet
—where is the Pyrrhic phalanx gone?" Oh! behold it
coming! A serried band of infantile desperadoes march
screeching along the side-walk, with sticks and staves to
represent firearms, and to the foremost bâton, of course, a
ragged parti-coloured clout is tied to do duty for the Stars
and Stripes. Happy the country which so early indoctrinates
its children with the glorious idea of national defence! In a
dozen years these young Gracchi will be members of the
M'Clellan Minute Guards, or running "wid der masheen" of
Hose Company Number Seven.

Meanwhile, I wish the authorities, whoever they may be,
would smarten up the bye-streets a little. Their state is
absolutely scandalous. The good folks of Liverpool will
remember the praiseworthy efforts made some years since to
get rid of those abominable cellar-tenements, the haunt of
poverty, of disease, and of vice, which then disgraced the
Queen city of the Mersey. Those efforts were successful, and
Liverpool is now all but entirely free from those yawning
caverns of filth and debauchery. We have one street in
London which still swarms with them, but one alone—the
monstrous Dudley, whilom Monmouth Street—and this blot
must soon be erased by metropolitan improvement. But
these noisome cellar-dwellings are to be found by scores in
dozens of streets in New York. Broadway, too, is full of
them, although there they are generally converted to the
purposes of tavern-bars, oyster-saloons, eating-houses, and
concert-rooms. In other parts of the city, the cellars are
used for shops and dwellings. Many feet below the level of

the pavement, whole families live—wallow rather—eat, sleep, fight, wash their linen, cook nasty messes, ply their trades, smoke, play cards, get drunk, are born and nursed, and sicken and die.   I don't know if there be any Building Act against these nuisances; but I do know that I have seen these cellar tenements attached to houses which to all outward appearance were not six months old.

That the windows, in a country where the summer is unbearably hot, should be habitually open, is reasonable.   That men in their shirt-sleeves, and smoking short pipes, and frequently in a state of intoxication, should lean from those windows, are facts not peculiar to New York.   I have seen similar sights at many English casements.   That back yards should re-echo to the howling of spanked children, and to the fiercely contending tongues of Irish beldames, is a fact easily ascribable to a redundant juvenile population, and a more redundant immigration from the shores of the Green Isle. But I cannot see the necessity for throwing so many things into the street.   If the boots of the inhabitants offend them, they pluck them off and cast them into the gutter.   If a kettle or a saucepan shows symptoms of leakiness, it is ruthlessly flung into the kennel.   If a chair be crippled, or a pitcher cracked, or a hat crushed, out with it into the street. All kinds of marine stores strew the roadway.   Few seem to think it worth their while to pick them up.   They have played their part; they are no longer of any account; they have "gi'n out."   Away with them ! let them moulder and rot, like the horse that is old, and the bowel that is broken, and the President that has served his turn.   This is no land for invalids.

And yet in all this shameful untidiness there is much less evidence of poverty and squalor than of careless prosperity and heedless waste. The shoeless and stockingless children go barefoot because they like it, not because they lack the means of being shod ; and they are otherwise clad in garments which, on European children, would be, comparatively speaking, purple and fine linen. The tipsy, unshorn men, smoking the short pipes, wear almost invariably thick rings of precious metal on their unwashed fingers. Stuck in the dirtiest shirt there is often a costly pin; and from the whisky-stained vest-pocket a showy watch-chain is often pendant. Finally, note this, fellow Englishmen at home, the pawnbrokers' shops are few and far between, and seem almost exclusively patronised by newly-arrived emigrants and "cleaned-out" sailors ; while in the dirtiest and apparently most poverty-stricken districts the savings' banks abound, and their portals are thronged all day by depositors in their shirt-sleeves, or in frocks seemingly put on with a pitchfork. "Did I enjoy the right," said an American friend to me, " to stop and search six of the first dirty little boys I met in the Bowery or East Houston-street, I would wager that five of them would have about them a little wallet containing one or more dollar bills, or at least a wad of fractional currency, and, in all probability, a savings' bank book." The propensity to waste seems, nevertheless, appalling. The odds and ends which lie scattered about unheeded might be sold for dollars and cents, and given to the poor. The poor, where are they ? They are just the people who waste. They waste their food, as they waste their chattels. The quantity of

food which is every day cast on the waters, not to be found
after many days, in New York, must be immense. With all
the famine prices demanded for articles of the first necessity,
with all the alleged insufficiency of wages, the embarrass-
ments of the humbler classes are but relative. The quantity
of animal food, of fruit and vegetables, consumed by the very
poorest day-labourers, is enormous. The stores, slatternly as
they are, overflow with coarse but substantial food. The
butcher's meat is skinny and ill bred, but there is plenty of
it. The American mutton, even in the most expensive restaurants, is detestable. Attenuated, scraggy little cutlets,
seem the only substitutes for those glorious mutton chops
with curly tails which we order "hot and hot to follow," at
the "Cock," or the "Cheshire Cheese." Now and then, in
private houses, and as a great delicacy, you are regaled with
a haunch or a saddle of English mutton, imported by Cunard
steamers ; but the American cooks do not understand the art
of roasting joints—the outside is generally burnt up, and the
inside sickeningly raw. Every joint is deluged with sham
gravy—hot water and fat. Carving, too, is an art which the
young ladies disdain to learn, and which the old folks—save
in the rural districts, where carving, cleanliness, piety, simplicity, and other virtues, really do flourish—have forgotten,
owing to the hybrid French and German kickshaw *cuisine*
which has of late years become fashionable. The gobbet,
semi-crude, hacked and hewed, of flesh which is brought to
you at an hotel, and called roast lamb, is enough to give you
nausea for a fortnight. The veal is exceedingly good, as in
France ; but the pork brought to table is but so-so, and I can
conscientiously aver that I have never eaten, during nine

months' sojourn in the States, a decent slice of breakfast bacon. It is the rustiest, fustiest, most salt, mahogany-looking, integuminous meat possible to imagine; and that it should be so, is all the more puzzling, considering what an important part is played by pork in American commerce; what mighty pigsties are Cincinnati and Chicago, and how many tens of thousands of barrels of slaughtered hog are annually exported to Europe. The defect, I apprehend, lies not in the meat, but in the mode of curing; still, I was bitterly disappointed, after hearing so many stories about the American pigs being fed on peaches, to find the pork worse than indifferent. The ham, to an English palate at least, is not much better. There is one kind, however, called Phipps's ham, which is usually served with champagne sauce, and is very appetising. The American beef, in its roasted form, is distressingly tough, and the butchers in cutting it seem to have been taking lessons from the live-collop hunkers of Abyssinia; but in the guise of steaks and *filets* beef occupies a proud position in the United States. I undertook, many years since, a course of Travels in Search of Beef; but when I came to America I felt inclined to cry "Eureka!" The "tenderloin," the "porterhouse" steak of America, are infinitely superior to our much-vaunted rump steak, and can even vie with the Chateaubriands and *entre-côtes* of the Trois Frères. Prejudiced Britons, however, have been heard to declare that the Yankee steak is so called under false pretences, and is cut from the body of the beef in the most illegitimate manner. On the whole, I think our cousins do not shine in butcher's meat; but in their fish, their poultry, and their game, they may challenge the rivalry of the whole world. The fish makes you half sick when you look upon it raw, but the supply is well-nigh inexhaustible, and the flavour delicious. Shops that look nastier than the hucksters' stalls in the Brill of Somers Town, are full of venison, and grouse, and squabs, and partridge. Turtle and terrapin are to be found in holes and corners where, in Paris, they would be selling their centime's worth of garlic sausage, or two sous' worth of fried potatoes. Huge pumpkins and water-melons, squashes and tomatoes by the hecatomb, enormous cabbages, beets and radishes, peaches by the cartful, and apples by the waggonload, are displayed in tumble-down shanties to which the meanest coal and potato shed in London would be a palace; while, to complete the incongruity, there will very probably be next door to the shanty a four-storied brown stone house, with a florid Renaissance façade, and a high stoop, with three young ladies in moiré antique skirts and helmet hats, sitting on the topmost step, if it be evening, surveying the passers-by. There are dozens of streets in New York which begin like Pall-mall and end like Petticoat-lane; or sometimes they start with a row of palaces, fade away into a double line of hovels, pursue the uneven tenour of their way as factories and churches, then have more hovels, and more palaces, subsiding at last into a half-formed bridle-path, strewn with fragments of naked rock and considerably grass-grown, and with a bone-boiling establishment on one side and a row of pigsties on the other to finish up with. But in every one of these streets you will find so many groggeries, so many lager-beer saloons, so many ice-cream ditto; and of this, finally, you may rest assured, that from so many open windows you will hear the strains of the waltz from *Faust*

elicited from tortured pianos, and that on every vacant spot
of wall, hoarding, post, and rail, you will find advertisements
of Kimball's Amboline, Van Buskirk's Sozodont, and Drake's
Plantation Bitters.

But streets, you may urge, displaying such characteristics,
are not necessarily dirty or untidy. Wait a minute. You
will bear into mind the rubbish shot into the roadway and
the barrels of kag-mag by the kerb. What do you think of
flocks of geese parading the public thoroughfares? They
waddle about in the most impudent and aggressive manner,
as though there were no such things in the world as sage and
onions. I suppose they think that, as their ancestors saved
the Capitol so many hundred years ago, they are safe from
molestation in a democratic country. Now a goose is all
very well at Michaelmas; and his liver, entombed in a
Strasburg pie, or embalmed with truffles, is at all times
a most toothsome dainty. But I object to the goose
multitudinous, to the goose urbane, to the goose with
dirty plumage flapping his preposterous wings, and strad-
dling wide between the legs on the pavement of a splendid
metropolis.

Add to the annoyance of the geese any number of coarse-
haired goats, cocks, hens, and chickens, and wind up with an
occasional ancient and misanthropic ram, his horns blunted
in innumerable "free fights," and his fleece foul and matted
like a flock-bed ripped up at the end of twenty years' service.
These creatures—beautiful and admirable in their proper
places, insufferable in the busy haunts of men—wander up
and down precisely as their own sweet will directs them. I
suppose they belong to somebody, and live somewhere; but

during the day they claim free warren in any avenue or
street they may choose to patronise, and pick up such pas-
turage as they can, from half-eaten apples, decayed peaches,
corn-shucks, small coal, pumpkin and melon peelings, brickbats, cabbage-stalks, and "muck" generally. Goodness
knows, there is enough of it lying about. To conclude the
catalogue, there is the pig. I must do the New Yorkers the
justice to admit that of late years they have shown some
activity in banishing the wandering porker from their thres-
holds. He formerly roamed over the whole of New York,
from the Battery to High Bridge; but I hasten to confess
that I have never yet met a pig, save under the guardianship
of a drover, in Broadway or Fifth Avenue. From the larger
parallel thoroughfares he is likewise lacking. The horse-
railways have been too much for him. But in the eastern
districts of the city the pig still goes to and fro, unmolested
and unconfined. Does he sleep in the cellars at night, I
wonder? Did he come over with the Irish emigrants in the
steerage of the packet-ship? He is a very ugly pig—a cross
between the Irish "greyhound" and the Yankee "rooter"—
a pig that might properly wear a goatee, and chew pig-tail,
and liquor up. He is the same pig, or that pig's great-
grandson, that Mr. Dickens saw when he was here; only a
pig that has fallen on evil days—a pig that has been exiled
from decent society—a pig that has gone to the dogs. He
shambles about in a disconsolate manner, trailing a stalk of
Indian corn in his gash of a mouth. The street children
have twisted his tail to the last bristle of the stump, long ago.
He looks as though a little Kimball's Amboline, or a dash of
Van Buskirk's Sozodont, or a nip of Drake's Plantation

Bitters would freshen him up. He is a most woebegone pig, dissolute in mien, uncertain in gait, shameless in manners, not fit to live, and, to the most sanguine, offering but a remote prospect of making tolerable pork when he dies. He lost an eye in a Dead Rabbit riot, and left his right ear in a "difficulty" down at Mackerelville. His father was a professed gambler, and his brother is in the States Prison for bounty-jumping. So he wanders about, and grunts, and picks up things that don't belong to him, till he is run over by a fire-engine, or, straying too near a factory, is caught up and made into glue, or sausages, or blacking brushes, incontinent.

I could bear with some other types of errant animals in the New York streets, but the particular creatures I mean are rarely to be found. The bow-wows are very scarce. The dog is, somehow, at a discount in New York. I am afraid the fierce young Bohemians of the back-streets have " run him out." Even the fashionables don't seem to patronise him much in the pug, or poodle, or toy-terrier shape. Shoddy sometimes sports a Danish dog behind his carriage, but his appearance in that capacity is infrequent. He is not much cared about as a lap-dog. The shrewd Yankee works him sometimes as a beast of draught, and the heavily-laden dog-barrows of the costermongers are, to those who love dogs and their honest ways, among the most painful sights of New York. You fail, however, to meet the dog at large, the dog who has business down town, and drops in on his way to make friendly calls on other dogs ; the dog who stops to see a fight or to ask a stranger—a dog, of course—what time it is. You miss the dog who runs at the side of the Hansom cab, or surmounts the pile of merchandise in the spring-van, barking furiously but harmlessly at society in general. You miss the dog on the doorstep, lazily basking in the sun, or running after his own tail; or blinking into immensity, in doggish abstraction inscrutable to us, or lunching frugally on the flies he, by artful snaps, can catch; or playing with the children, suffering himself by turns to be made a baby, a saddle-horse, a shuttlecock, and a railway locomotive; or with gruffly joyous bark welcoming home the working-man as he returns to dinner; or demurely trotting by the house-mother's side on her way to market, now taking a flying bite at the nose of the greengrocer's dog, an ill-conditioned brute with whom he has a standing grudge on a disputed question of paunch,—though blighted love had, perchance, something to do with the feud—now sitting in the butcher's shop, too honest to snatch at the pendent ox-tail, too wise to risk a clutch at the swinging leg of mutton, but inhaling the glorious aroma of the meaty Eden; now nervously sniffing as the saw goes through the bone of beef and the odour of marrow is wafted on the breeze; now pensively wagging his tail as the juicy liver plumps into the scale; now licking those chaps of his as the rich suet is pared from the edges of the steak. I don't see this dog in New York. The Yankee dog, when I find him, seems a gaunt, discontented, wolfish mongrel, loafing about bars, or shinning round gambling dens.

And the little birds. Alas! I have sought in vain for them in New York, I have not found so much as a peep. Underneath the eaves no brooding swallows sing, to show us their sunny backs or twit us with the spring. The swallows and the sparrows too, I am told, were wont to be very plentiful in New York city. People who can remember when the site of the Astor House was in the open country, and when barges sailed up Canal Street, will tell that once upon a time the island of Manhattan was merry with the songs of those little feathered creatures who never, so far as I could make out, did any harm to anybody—unless, indeed, the good gentlemen who have put down barrel-organs in London should deem it their duty to bring in a bill for the abolition of swallows and sparrows, on the ground that their twittering is of a nature to disturb the Basses and the Babbages at their labours. Through another kind of persecution have the small birds disappeared from New York and from most other large American cities. They have fallen victims to the spirit of destructiveness inherent to the American youth. A Yankee boy is always wanting to shoot something; and he has not been long out of long clothes before he possesses something to shoot with. Cheap pistols, easily-obtained powder and ball, and the absence of parental authority prohibiting the use of fire-arms to children of tender age, have been the ruin of the sparrows. They have been frightened away from New York; but the city is, I am afraid, not much the better for their Hegira. Long will it be, I hope, ere the sparrows disappear from *our* housetops, the storks from Amsterdam, the pigeons from the Russian towns. Even the Perotes pined when their abominably mangy curs were banished, by the Sultan's firman, to the Island of Princes.

There is one nuisance in New York streets to which I have not as yet drawn attention. The pavement is execrably bad. The normal rudeness of the roadways is aggravated by the rails laid down for the horse-cars, which render anything like skilful driving impossible, and would bring Hansom cabs, were they tried in New York, to speedy grief; but the foot pavement is very little better. Even in the oft-quoted Broadway and Fifth Avenue, the best paved streets in the city, bad is emphatically the best; the remainder are simply abominable. Huge blocks of ill-cut and ill-levelled stone alternate with shards and pebbles and shapeless fragments—with gaps and fissures and interregna of no pavement at all. Immense sums of money are periodically spent in keeping up the side walks, just as sums as immense are lavished on contractors who undertake to sweep and cleanse the streets; but the supremacy of " muck " is generally vindicated. It turns out, somehow, that somebody has stolen the money allocated for municipal improvements. The street-sweepers can't get their wages, and revolt. The contractors who have got the funds stick to them. Others, disappointed in their hopes of plunder, bring actions against the Corporation, recover damages, obtain judgment, and cause the historical portraits in the Mayor's Parlour, at the City Hall, to be taken in execution by the Sheriff. This has been done in two or three years—within the present year. Just imagine the sheriff's officer putting the brokers into the Mansion House, and seizing the loving-cup and the Swordbearer's fur porringer.

I hope I am not impertinent in descanting upon these little matters. I trust that I am not showing any envenomed and malignant hatred to self-government in general, and the United States of America in particular, by pointing to the fact that a metropolis whose wealth is enormous, whose revenue is prodigious, and within whose limits many if not

most of the elements of comfort, taste, and splendour are to
be found, is, for the want of a little management and a little
honesty among its governors, a slovenly, untidy, ill-kept
Augean stable. The New Yorkers have begun to find this
out, and are ventilating their discovery in a perfect whirlwind
of popular indignation. The long domination of " Muck " is
threatened, and Dirt begins to totter on its throne. There
was established when I left New York a Citizens' Municipal
Reform Association ; and the language used by members of
this society at a meeting held one night in August was far
more vigorous and far more trenchant in its censure than any
I should venture, of my own motion, to indulge in. Here is
one of the resolutions unanimously adopted by the meeting :
" That we make no vague and general charge of unfaithful-
ness and corruption on the part of our city authorities, but we
bring the specific and abundantly-sustained allegation, that
these officials deny to the people the convenience and pecuniary advantages of public markets in proper localities, where
the producer and consumer may meet and buy cheap and
fresh food. We charge on these officials ten thousand pre-
ventible deaths every year, and an amount of sickness and
suffering beyond computation, growing out of filthy streets,
choked sewers, and over-crowded tenements. We charge that
the waste and fraud of these men have entailed a tax equal
to seventy-five dollars a year upon every working man with
a wife and three children ; and we charge that, for all this
burden of taxation, neglect, and injury, we receive no other
return than the prospect of renewed and aggravated abuses."

This is strongish language ; but the speakers who followed
the mover of the resolutions spoke in even stronger terms.

" After more music"—our cousins can never get on, even at indignation meetings, without a brass band—Mr. Robert M. Poer made some remarks. I can but cull a very few flowers from his garland of rhetoric. " The slimy machinations of the pollywog politicians have usurped the government of our city," said Poer, " and there is no hope save in the organised effort of the working men. . . . . This organisation must harmonise capital with labour until there is not a politician left to sell to Barnum. (Applause.) He (the speaker) sometimes shook hands with some of the politicians from Tammany Hall, or the Republican head-quarters, and he confessed he felt as if he had got hold of the hand of a dead shad. Look at our markets ; Washington Market. The Japanese thought they were led into the Dismal Swamp when they went through it. (Renewed laughter.) It is as rotten as the catacombs of Egypt. With fifteen millions of dollars fleeced from the pockets of the mechanics of that city, it is an eternal disgrace to American civilisation. But the politicians are dancing on an earthquake. Let any one look into the Board of Aldermen, and see that conclave of calves' heads sent there to cry crocodiles' tears into the big pot of public opinion ; and if he does not come out and say they are the biggest set of boobies ever put together, he was no judge of modern sanity. The people are going to elect shirt-sleeve aldermen that work all day. They will turn these political paupers out to grass ; and if they have forgotten how to earn an honest living, it will be cheaper to support them in the almshouse than where they are." (Laughter and applause.) The speaker continued to criticise in similar terms the doings of the politicians and the Board of Education, and closed by

exhorting the workmen to organise citizens' associations in
the various wards.

In this harangue, coarse and violent and ignorant as it may
be, there is much calling for deep and sad reflection. Should
we consider the truth of such allegations as evidence of an
inveterate tendency on the part of Americans to venality and
corruption ? Heaven forbid ! Should we hold it as conclu-
sive of the failure of the principle of self-government?
Heaven forbid again. But the sincerest patriot, the most
ardent lover of human liberty, might justly lay the malprac-
tices charged against the "political" municipality of New
York at the door of absolute and unbridled democracy. The
very *argot* or dialect of their public life illustrates its spirit ;
and, pending the compilation of a new political dictionary, it
may be expedient to note down the definitions of a few terms
with which, in commenting on public matters in America, it
is well-nigh impossible to dispense, so incessant is the recurrence of the ideas which they represent. " Log-rolling "
means the mutual rendering of service. The expression is
said to have originated among the backwoodsmen, who, in
felling trees to build their cabins, used to say to one another,
" You help me to roll my log, and I'll help you to roll yours."
Thus, if A. wants to get a place in the Customs House of
which B. has the promise, and, knowing that B. desiderates
a post-mastership, is acquainted with C., who is in a position
to obtain the coveted berth from D., A. gets his place and B.
his through some quietly-arranged log-rolling ; or, to adduce
an illustration nearer home, if Pawkins has a friend up for
election at the Senior Coleoptera Club, he may go to Jawkins,
who has two men up for the election next following, and

quietly hint to him that if his (Pawkins's) man don't get it, his (Jawkins's) men are sure to be blackballed. " Pipe-laying " means simply the secret management, by intrigue and chicane, of a certain affair. It is all but synonymous with " engineering," although, for a transaction to be satisfactorily " engineered through," a certain amount of greenbacks should properly change hands, whereas pipe-laying may go no further than clever diplomacy. Pipe-laying is stated to have been invented by a well-known political auctioneer and Loyal Leaguer of New York, who many years since, wishing to carry a municipal measure for which two thousand additional votes were needed, imported a couple of thousand labourers from Philadelphia for the purpose of laying water-pipes, which only existed in his own fervid imagination. " Axe-grinding " is a term borrowed from one of the most charming stories told by the great apologist of shrewd common-sense, Benjamin Franklin. The story should be as well known to you as that of paying too dearly for one's whistle; but, at the risk of being held a bore, I may remind you that it bears on a little boy going to school, who is accosted by a man carrying an axe. The man calls the boy all kinds of pretty and endearing names, and induces him to enter a yard where there is a grindstone. " Now, my pretty little fellow," says he with the axe, " only turn that handle, and you'll see something very pretty." The boy turns and turns, and the man holds the axe to the stone and pours water over it, until the axe is ground. Straightway he turns, with strident voice and fierce gesture, on the boy : " You abandoned little miscreant," he cries, " what do you mean by playing truant from school ? You deserve a good thrashing. Get you gone, sirrah, this instant." " And after this," adds Franklin, " when anybody flattered me, I always thought he had an axe to grind." For example, when a newspaper speaks of Mr. Lincoln as the " Saviour of the Republic," and assures the public that on his " broad Atlantean shoulders " the happiness of the nation reposes, it may be reasonably surmised that the newspaper in question has " an axe to grind." " Wire-pulling " is applied to politicians behind the scenes, who make no speeches and write no letters, but, to bring about certain conjunctures in which they are interested, privately cajole, influence, and direct other politicians, who are their puppets to be used on the public stage. Thus Mr. Thurlow Weed has been any time these twenty years the great wire-puller of American politics. " Lobbying " is a word cognate with wire-pulling. A " lobbyer " is an intriguer who can serve his purposes and those of his party much better by hanging about corridors and committee-rooms than by being a member of the Legislature. He button-holes the Congress-men as they go in and out ; and a bill must be generally lobbied through before it is submitted to the arbitrament of the vote. To conclude, " financiering " does not apply exclusively to politics ; it means anything " smart," base, and fraudulent, from jobbing beef and blanket contracts to making money out of hospital lint or charitable donations. Thus the *New York Herald* declares that at least one-fifth of the five millions of dollars accruing from the Sanitary Fairs which have been held all over the country has been " financiered " away to private uses by the managers of the said fairs. There are two slang equivalents in English for " financiering," viz., " besting " and " chizzling," but at the police courts it is usually known as embezzlement. The " pollywog politicians " are an offspring as direct of universal suffrage and election to short terms of office as maggots are of putrid meat. The venal aldermen and corrupt councilmen against whom the working men of New York protest are of the working men's own making. If they were nominated by a clique, that clique has attained dominion by means of universal suffrage. They have no vested monopoly, no chartered rights, no hereditary hold on office. They are the nominees of the Sovereign People, of the Great Unwashed, of the Mob, of Tom, Dick, and Harry ; and now Tom, Dick, and Harry are infuriate against the monster they have themselves created. They denounce " professional politicians ;" but what scheme of government so inevitably conduces to making politics a profession as does a pure democracy ? In what other country but America would you read in a newspaper a narrative beginning with such a heading as this ? " A member of the City Inspector's department drugged in a public-house saloon, and robbed by the reigning queen of several hundred dollars.—Prominent politicians on a spree.—Gay and lively aldermen treat Cyprians with munificent patronage ; they lavish their hard-earned greenbacks on their favourite nymphs with gallant idolatry.—The lady turns the tables on a conspicuous customer, and relieves him of over six hundred dollars.— Spicy developments.—The city fathers behold the magic operation with dumb amazement.—The lady is brought before Justice Quackenbosh.—She is committed for grand larceny.— Side scenes and episodes.—Richer developments in prospect." I quote this from a cheap, vulgar, widely-circulated paper. Here we have no case of the down-trodden plebeian venting

his virtuous indignation against the vices of a depraved aristocracy, but the pure democracy gloating over the scandalous
exposure of its own nominees. The sons of toil elect the city
fathers. The aldermen are very frequently chosen from such
classes as publicans, livery-stable keepers, and corner-grocery
dealers ; the councilmen too often belong to the comprehensive genus " scallywag." They have intrigued and speechified,
and stumped their ward, and the mob have fashioned them
out of the mud ; and in process of time, I suppose, they
become " pollywog politicians "—whatever a " pollywog " may
be. Put how long does it take to transform the zealous
denouncer of abuses into the office-holding "pollywog"? Not
long, I am afraid.

END OF VOL. 1.

BRADBURY AND EVANS, PRINTERS, WHITEFRIARS.

MESSRS. TINSLEY BROTHERS' NEW WORKS.

GEORGE GEITH OF FEN COURT : a Novel, by

F. G. TRAFFORD, Author of "City and Suburb," "Too Much Alone," &c., is ready this day at all the Libraries, in 3 vols.

"This fine story, so rich in pathos, is not poor in humour. Its sadness does not tend to monotone, but is diversified by sketches of 'fine City ladies,' and notable of City sociabilities, which are keenly witty and genuinely entertaining. It is a rare pleasure to read such a novel as 'George Geith of Fen Court'—a pleasure for whose recurrence it is vain to look, except towards its author."—*Morning Post*, Dec. 30.

NEW WORK OF FICTION, by the AUTHOR of "PAVED WITH GOLD," &c.
This day is published, in 3 Vols.,

FACES FOR FORTUNES. By AUGUSTUS MAYHEW,

Author of "How to Marry and Whom to Marry," "The Greatest Plague in Life," "The Finest Girl in Bloomsbury," &c.

MR. SALA'S DIARY IN AMERICA.
This day is published, in 2 Vols. 8vo,

MY DIARY IN AMERICA IN THE MIDST OF

WAR. By GEORGE AUGUSTUS SALA.

TODLEBEN'S DEFENCE OF SEBASTOPOL :

being a Review of General Todleben's Narrative, 1854-5. By WILLIAM HOWARD RUSSELL, LL.D., Special Correspondent of the "Times" during the Crimean War. In One handsome volume of nearly 350 pages, uniform with Captain Burton's "Mission to Dahomey."

*** A portion of this Work appeared in the "Times ; " it has since been greatly enlarged, and may be said to be an abridgment of General Todleben's great work. [*Ready this day.*

LIFE OF MASANIELLO.
This day is published in 1 Vol.,

MASANIELLO OF NAPLES. By Mrs. HORACE ST.

JOHN.

NEW NOVEL.
This day is published, in 2 Vols.,

AVILA HOPE : a Novel.

In the press, in 2 Vols.,

SHOOTING AND FISHING IN NORTH AME-

RICA ; being a Sporting Tour through the United States in 1862-3. By HENRY REVOIL.

A VOLUME OF POEMS, by the AUTHOR OF "BARBARA'S HISTORY."
This day is published, in 1 Vol.,

BALLADS. By Miss AMELIA B. EDWARDS, Author of

" Barbara's History."

THE MARRIED LIFE OF ANNE OF AUSTRIA,

Queen of France, Mother of Louis XIV. ; and the HISTORY of DON SEBASTIAN, King of Portugal. Historical Studies. From numerous Unpublished Sources. By MARTHA WALKER FREER. In 2 vols. 8vo.. with Portrait.

"The married life of Anne of Austria as the Queen of Louis XIII., and her subsequent life as his widow and Regent of France, constitute one of the most important phases in French history, and certainly one of the best topics that a writer, up in the curious revelations of the French memoirs relating thereto, could select to make an amusing and even fascinating book. We have here a book entertaining in a high degree, and authentic as far as it goes ; discriminative even in special transactions—full of choice materials well combined."—*Times*, Oct. 25.   [*Second Edition this day.*

AN ARTIST'S PROOF : a Novel. By ALFRED

AUSTIN, Author of "The Season : a Satire," &c. In 3 vols. [*This day.*

MORNINGS OF THE RECESS IN 1861-4 : being

a Series of Literary and Biographical Papers, reprinted and revised from the "Times," by permission, by the Author. In 2 vols., uniform with Captain Burton's "Mission to Dahomey."   [*This day.*

THE NILE BASIN. By Captain R. F. BURTON,

Author of "A Mission to Dahomey." In 1 vol., with Three Maps. price 7s. 6d.

*** A part of this Work was read by Captain Burton before the Royal Geographical Society on Nov. 14th.   [*This day.*

A MISSION TO DAHOMEY : being a Three Months'

Residence at the Court of Dahomey. In which are described the Manners and Customs of the Country, including the Human Sacrifice, &c. By Captain R. F. BURTON, late H.M. Commissioner to Dahomey, and the Author of "A Pilgrimage to El Medinah and Meccah." In 2 vols., with Illustrations.

"He witnessed the grand Customs and the yearly Customs of that grotesquely cere-monious people, including the evolutions of their army of 'Amazons' and the traces of their cruel human sacrifices, of which he himself, with proper taste, declined to be an actual spectator, and he brought away impressions of the Dahoman proclivities which are really very curious and instructive, though they were not very satisfactory to himself nor to be commended to the imitation of the gentle philanthropists who patronise the Dahomans or their congeners under the fallacious impression that they can ever be elevated up to the same level of being as themselves."—*Times*, Oct. 5.
[*Second Edition revised, this day.*

ABBOT'S CLEVE ; or, CAN IT BE PROVED ? A

Novel. In 3 vols.

"The reader is really very sorry for Florence, but one could scarcely be expected to have much sympathy with a masculine school-girl who married an ostler. Aurora Floyd carefully conceals from her supposed husband that his new trainer is her rightful lord, while the heroine of 'Abbot's Cleve' has no guilt to conceal. The writer has displayed a delicacy, and introduced a certain amount of pathos, which contrast strongly with the former treatment of a slightly similar situation. . . . The writer possesses a very excep-tional amount of genuine dramatic power."—*Saturday Review.* [*Second Edition, this day.*

MAURICE DERING ; a Novel. By the Author of

"Guy Livingstone." Price 6s.   [*This day.*

EVERY-DAY PAPERS. From "All the Year

Round." By ANDREW HALLIDAY. In 2 vols.   [*This day.*

TINSLEY BROTHERS, 18, CATHERINE STREET, STRAND.

www.ingramcontent.com/pod-product-compliance
Lightning Source LLC
Chambersburg PA
CBHW030956110726
47900CB00004B/1295